REVIVAL

VOLUME ONE: YOU'RE AMONG FRIENDS

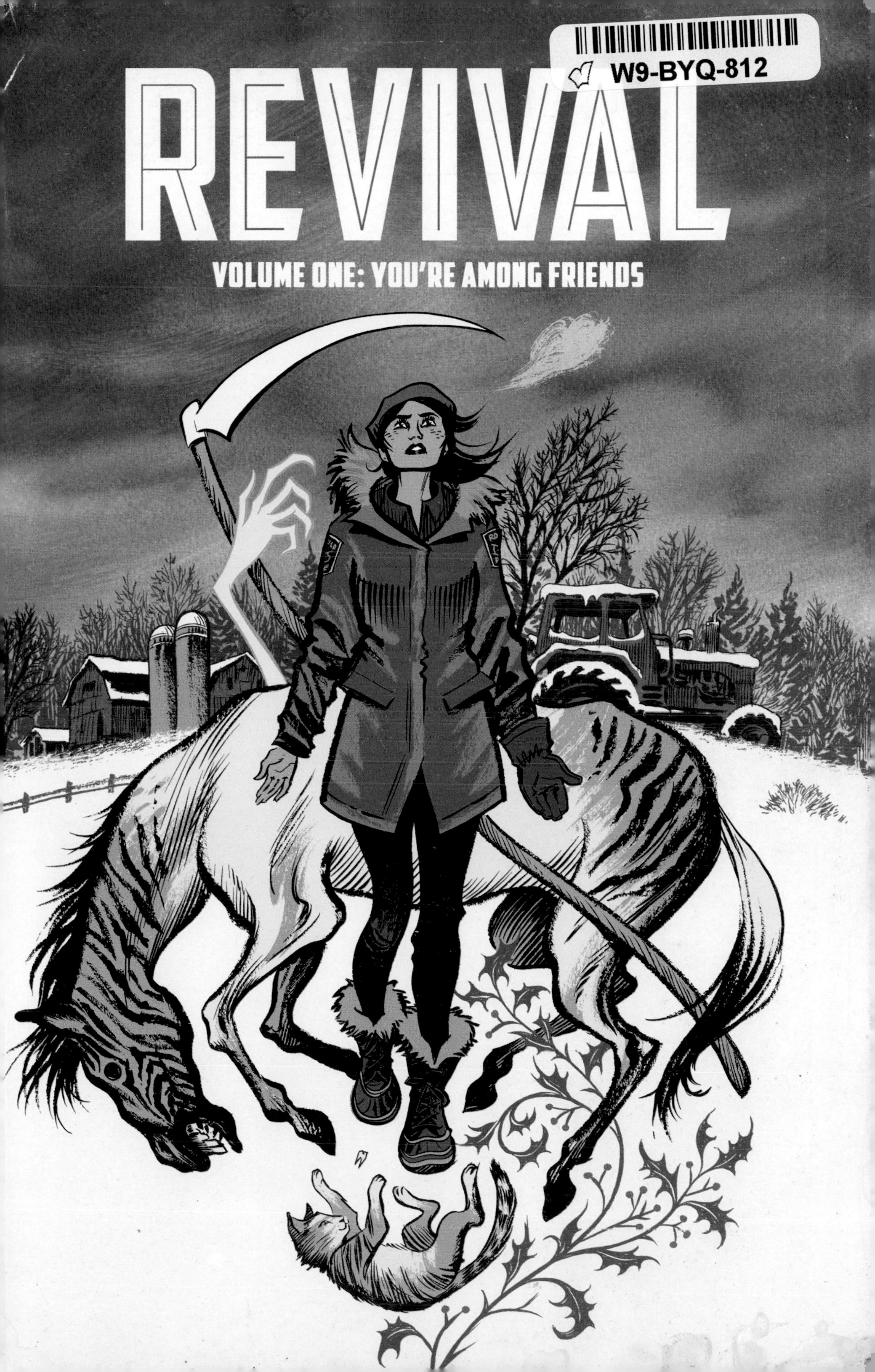

STORY BY
TIM SEELEY

ART BY
MIKE NORTON

COLORS BY
MARK ENGLERT

LETTERS BY
CRANK!

CHAPTER ART BY
JENNY FRISON

EDITED BY
4 STAR STUDIOS

DESIGN BY
SEAN DOVE

END PAGE ILLUSTRATIONS BY
CRAIG THOMPSON & FRANCESCO GASTON

FOR MORE INFO CHECK OUT
WWW.REVIVALCOMIC.COM

ALSO CHECK OUT THE SOUNDTRACK BY
SONO MORTI AT SONOMORTI.BANDCAMP.COM

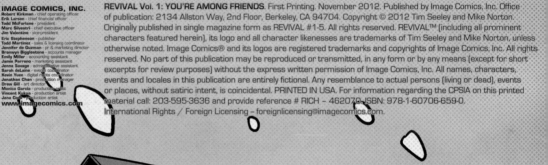

IMAGE COMICS, INC.
Robert Kirkman - chief operating officer
Erik Larsen - chief financial officer
Todd McFarlane - president
Marc Silvestri - chief executive officer
Jim Valentino - vice-president
Eric Stephenson - publisher
Todd Martinez - sales & licensing coordinator
Jennifer de Guzman - pr & marketing director
Branwyn Bigglestone - accounts manager
Emily Miller - accounting assistant
Jamie Parreno - marketing assistant
Jenna Savage - administrative assistant
Sarah deLaine - events coordinator
Kevin Yuen - digital rights coordinator
Jonathan Chan - production manager
Drew Gill - art director
Monica Garcia - production artist
Vincent Kukua - production artist
Jana Cook - production artist
www.imagecomics.com

REVIVAL Vol. 1: YOU'RE AMONG FRIENDS. First Printing. November 2012. Published by Image Comics, Inc. Office of publication: 2134 Allston Way, 2nd Floor, Berkeley, CA 94704. Copyright © 2012 Tim Seeley and Mike Norton. Originally published in single magazine form as REVIVAL #1-5. All rights reserved. REVIVAL™ (including all prominent characters featured herein), its logo and all character likenesses are trademarks of Tim Seeley and Mike Norton, unless otherwise noted. Image Comics® and its logos are registered trademarks and copyrights of Image Comics, Inc. All rights reserved. No part of this publication may be reproduced or transmitted, in any form or by any means (except for short excerpts for review purposes) without the express written permission of Image Comics, Inc. All names, characters, events and locales in this publication are entirely fictional. Any resemblance to actual persons (living or dead), events or places, without satiric intent, is coincidental. PRINTED IN USA. For information regarding the CPSIA on this printed material call: 203-595-3636 and provide reference # RICH – 462070. ISBN: 978-1-60706-659-0. International Rights / Foreign Licensing – foreignlicensing@imagecomics.com.

FOREWORD

Death seemed to have played an unnaturally large part in my childhood. I grew up in small farming community in Canada, which could easily have doubled for the setting of the incredible comic book you are about to read. And maybe it was just me, but death seemed to be everywhere when I was a kid. I can't tell you how often I was stuck going to some funeral for another great aunt or second cousin that I hardly knew. Maybe it was because in a small town everyone seems to know everyone else. Or maybe it was because my Mother had a large Catholic family and stayed close to all her cousins and distant relations. I'm not sure, but either way, it always seemed like someone was dying.

Now, I understand that my attitude towards death may seem a bit cold and callous, but that's not actually the case. The memories I was recounting above were for the dozens of funerals I had to attend for people I barely knew. But there were others. Too many others. I watched three of my grandparents die as a kid. My Dad's sister drowned in our swimming pool when I was five, as I stood on the deck watching him try to resuscitate her. And my cousin, only two years younger than me, was killed in a terrible car accident about ten years ago. Those were the deaths that mattered. Those were the deaths that leave a mark on a kid and stay with him forever.

Revival, the amazing new comic book series by uber-talented creators Tim Seeley and Mike Norton leaves a mark too. It's about small towns and it's about family and it's about death. All things I continue to go back to time and time again in my own work. But Revival adds a beautifully simple genre spin on it all by asking the question; what if the ones we love came back?

What's so brilliant about Revival isn't that Seeley and Norton explore the concept of the dead returning to walk the earth. We all know that's been done to death (sorry) in countless comics, films etc. No, what's brilliant about Seeley's approach is that these loved-ones return not as flesh eating zombies, or mummified B-movie ghouls, but rather just as we remember them. And that's when things really get interesting. Tim lets us watch as his beautifully flawed and compelling cast of small town characters struggles to cope with what comes next. How do we find a place in our lives again for someone we have already grieved for and whose loss we had already struggled to accept? It's equally chilling and fascinating stuff and Tim's scripts are pitch perfect, his characters beautifully flawed and compelling.

And of course it doesn't hurt that Revival is beautifully illustrated by Mike Norton. Mike, a mainstay on superhero comics from the "big two" over the last decade, really shines here. It's as if the freedom from spandex and fisticuffs has set him free, because as great a Tim's writing is, It's Mike's wonderful cartooning that brings these people to life (ahem...again, I'm sorry).

Frankly I'm jealous, because this is exactly the kind of book I'd like to do someday, a real rural noir full of heart and energy and ideas. Revival is great comics. Plain and simple and if I were to say any more about it I'd only spoil it for you. So sit back and enjoy. You can only discover your favorite new comic once, so savor it. I know I did.

– JEFF LEMIRE

Jeff Lemire is a Canadian comics artist and writer.
He is the author of the Essex County Trilogy, Sweet Tooth *and DC's* Animal Man.

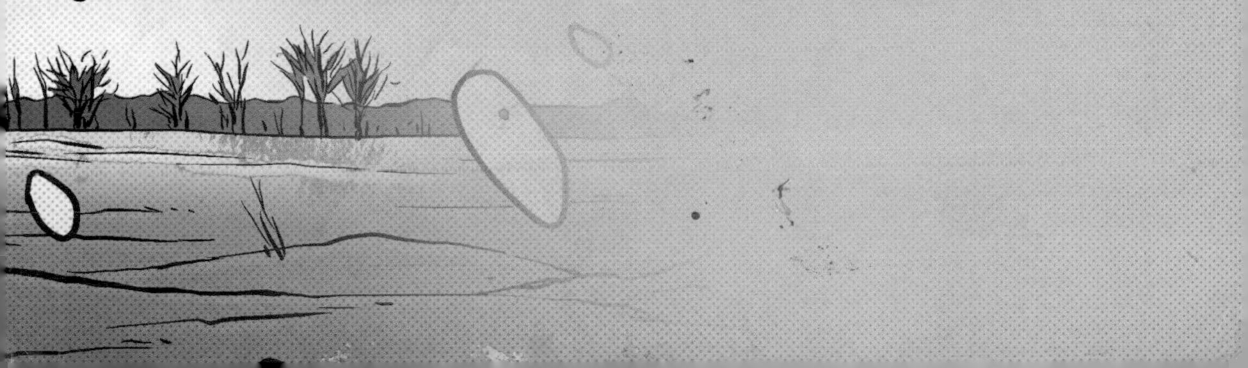

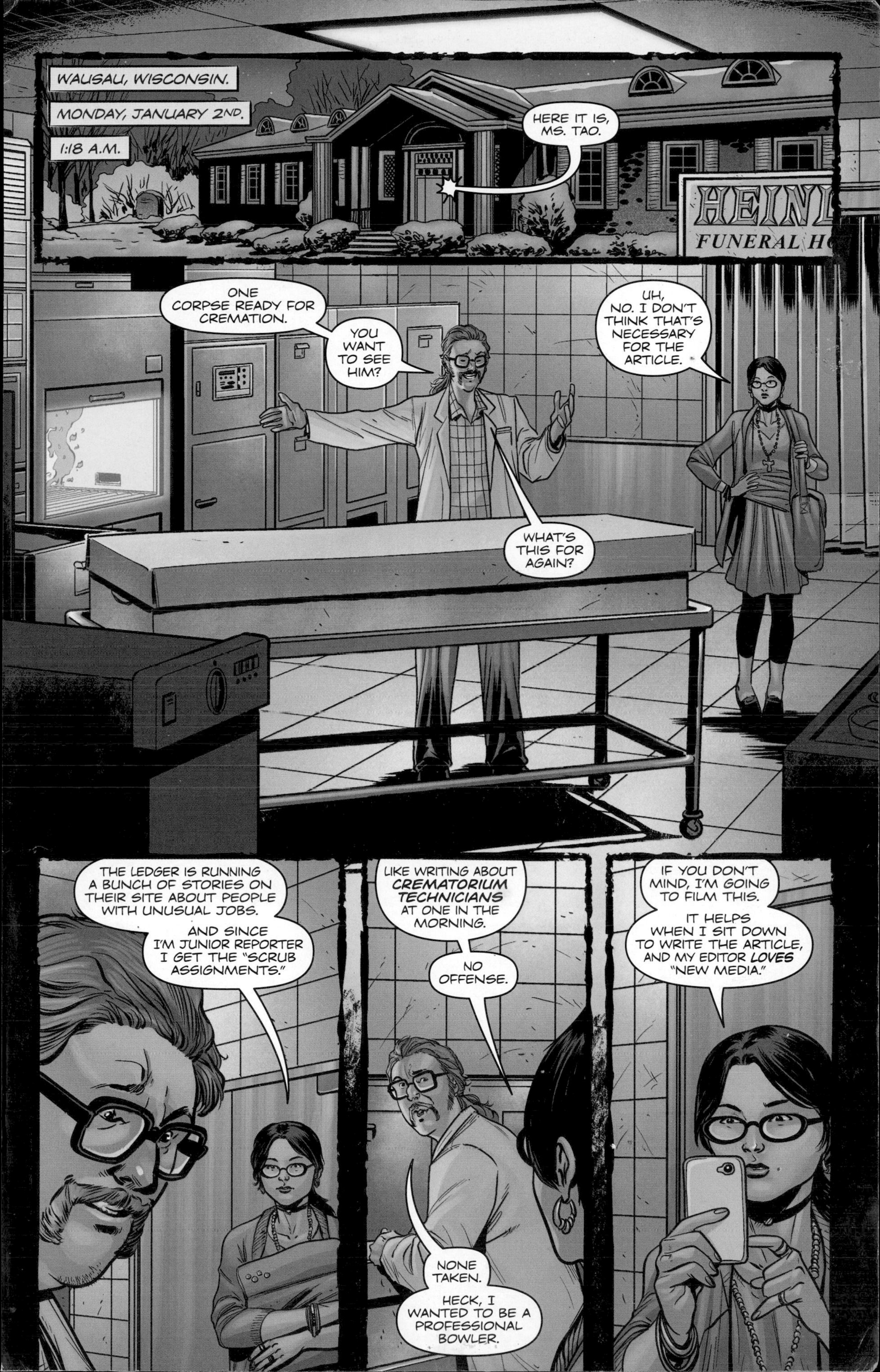
WAUSAU, WISCONSIN.
MONDAY, JANUARY 2ND.
1:18 A.M.
HERE IT IS, MS. TAO.
HEINL
FUNERAL HO
ONE CORPSE READY FOR CREMATION.
YOU WANT TO SEE HIM?
UH, NO. I DON'T THINK THAT'S NECESSARY FOR THE ARTICLE.
WHAT'S THIS FOR AGAIN?
THE LEDGER IS RUNNING A BUNCH OF STORIES ON THEIR SITE ABOUT PEOPLE WITH UNUSUAL JOBS.
AND SINCE I'M JUNIOR REPORTER I GET THE "SCRUB ASSIGNMENTS."
LIKE WRITING ABOUT *CREMATORIUM TECHNICIANS* AT ONE IN THE MORNING.
NO OFFENSE.
NONE TAKEN.
HECK, I WANTED TO BE A PROFESSIONAL BOWLER.
IF YOU DON'T MIND, I'M GOING TO FILM THIS.
IT HELPS WHEN I SIT DOWN TO WRITE THE ARTICLE, AND MY EDITOR *LOVES* "NEW MEDIA."

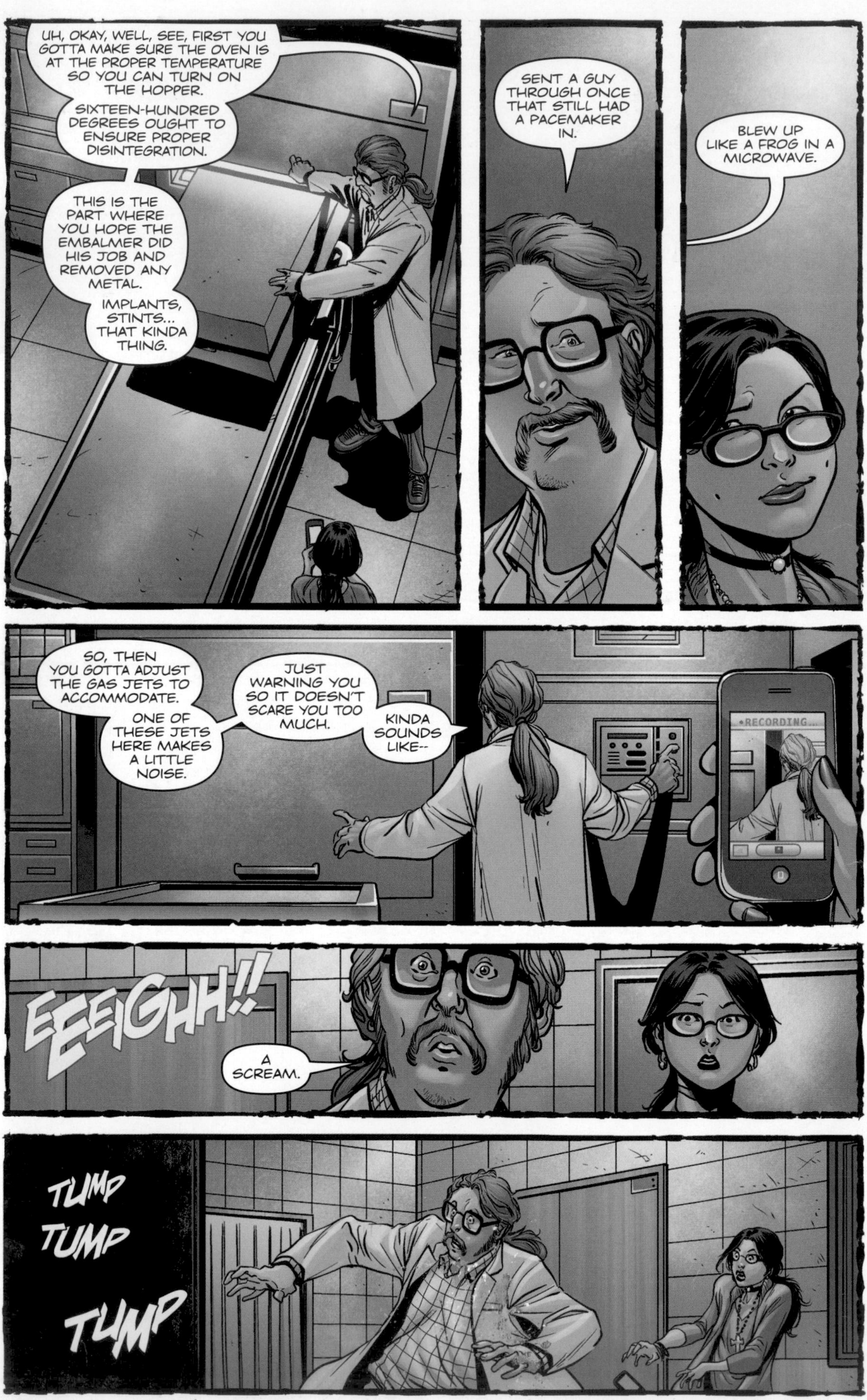
UH, OKAY, WELL, SEE, FIRST YOU GOTTA MAKE SURE THE OVEN IS AT THE PROPER TEMPERATURE SO YOU CAN TURN ON THE HOPPER.
SIXTEEN-HUNDRED DEGREES OUGHT TO ENSURE PROPER DISINTEGRATION.
THIS IS THE PART WHERE YOU HOPE THE EMBALMER DID HIS JOB AND REMOVED ANY METAL.
IMPLANTS, STINTS... THAT KINDA THING.
SENT A GUY THROUGH ONCE THAT STILL HAD A PACEMAKER IN.
BLEW UP LIKE A FROG IN A MICROWAVE.
SO, THEN YOU GOTTA ADJUST THE GAS JETS TO ACCOMMODATE.
ONE OF THESE JETS HERE MAKES A LITTLE NOISE.
JUST WARNING YOU SO IT DOESN'T SCARE YOU TOO MUCH.
KINDA SOUNDS LIKE--
RECORDING..
EEEIGHH!!
A SCREAM.
TUMP
TUMP
TUMP

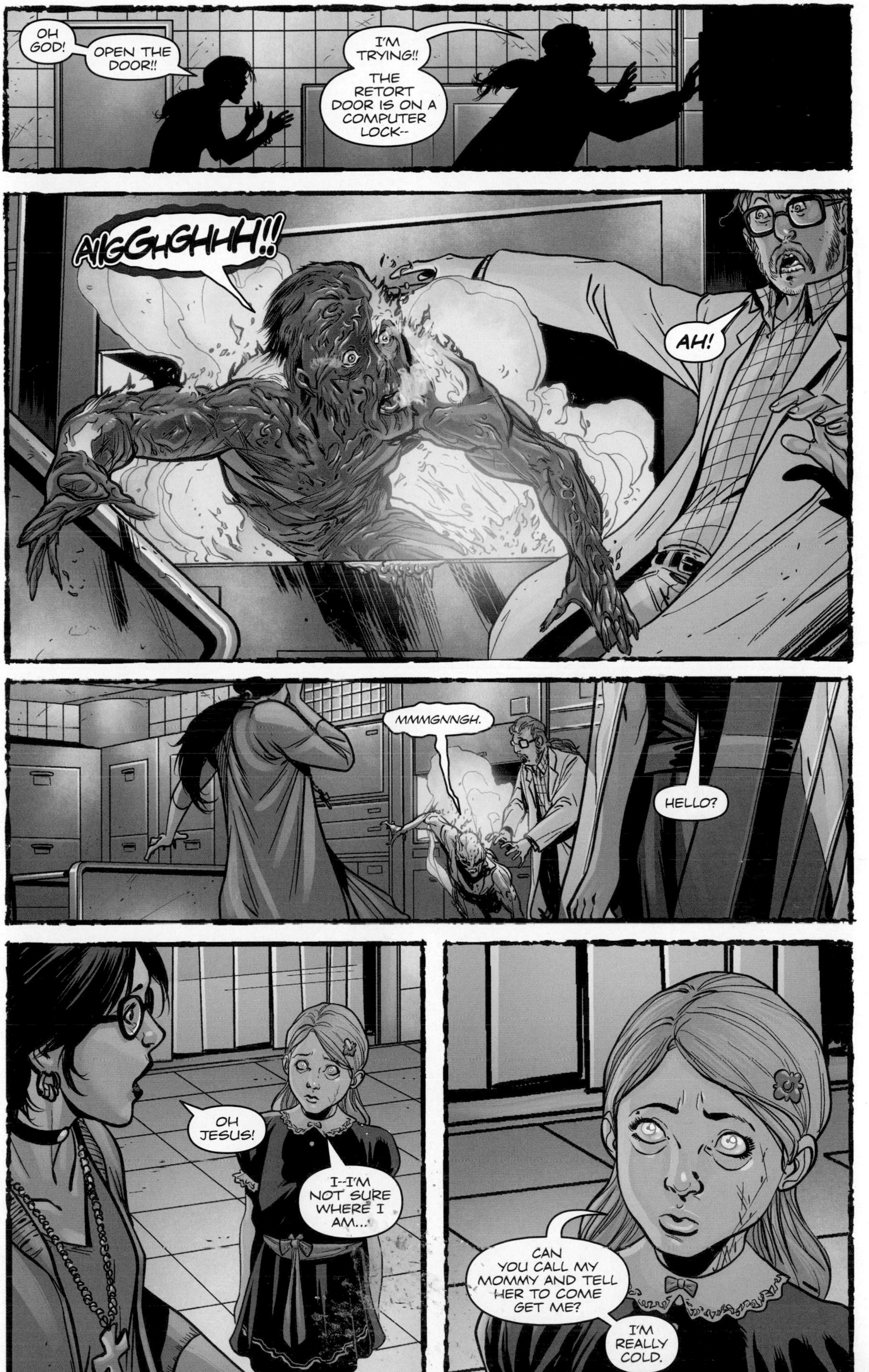
OH GOD!
OPEN THE DOOR!!
I'M TRYING!!
THE RETORT DOOR IS ON A COMPUTER LOCK--
AIGGHGHHH!!
AH!
MMMGNNGH.
HELLO?
OH JESUS!
I--I'M NOT SURE WHERE I AM...
CAN YOU CALL MY MOMMY AND TELL HER TO COME GET ME?
I'M REALLY COLD.

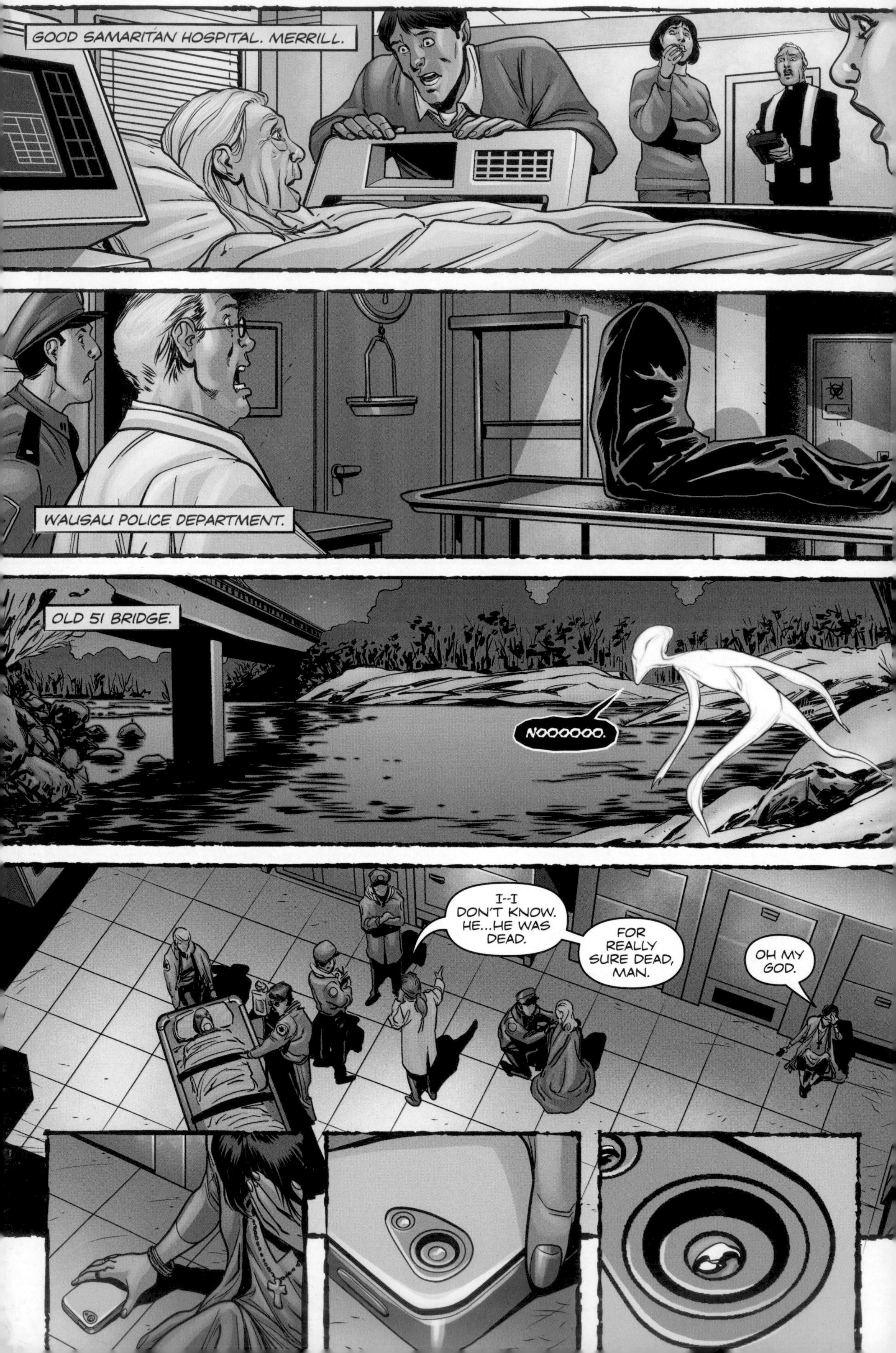
GOOD SAMARITAN HOSPITAL. MERRILL.
WAUSAU POLICE DEPARTMENT.
OLD 51 BRIDGE.
NOOOOOO.
I--I DON'T KNOW. HE...HE WAS DEAD.
FOR REALLY SURE DEAD, MAN.
OH MY GOD.

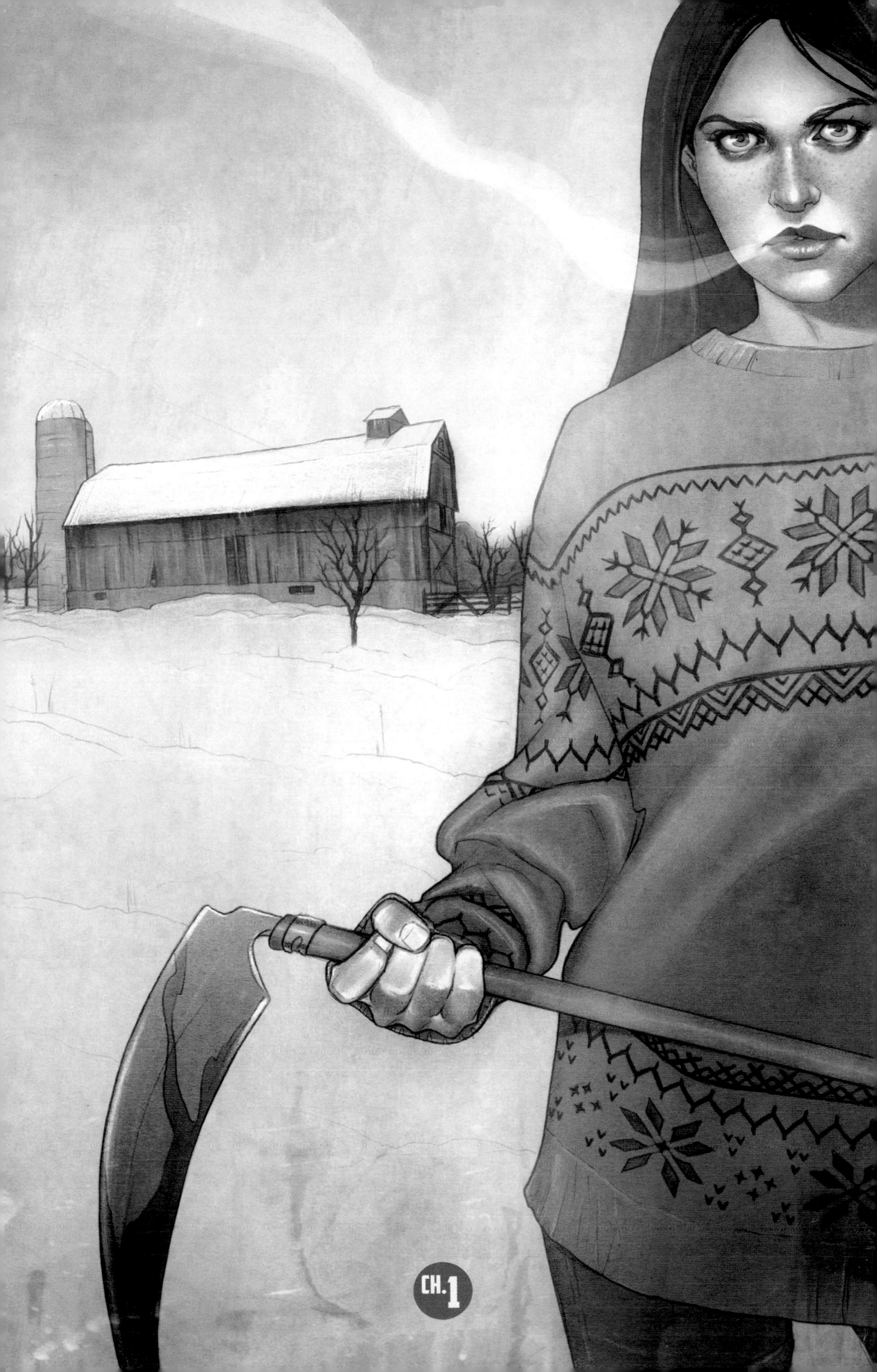
CH. 1

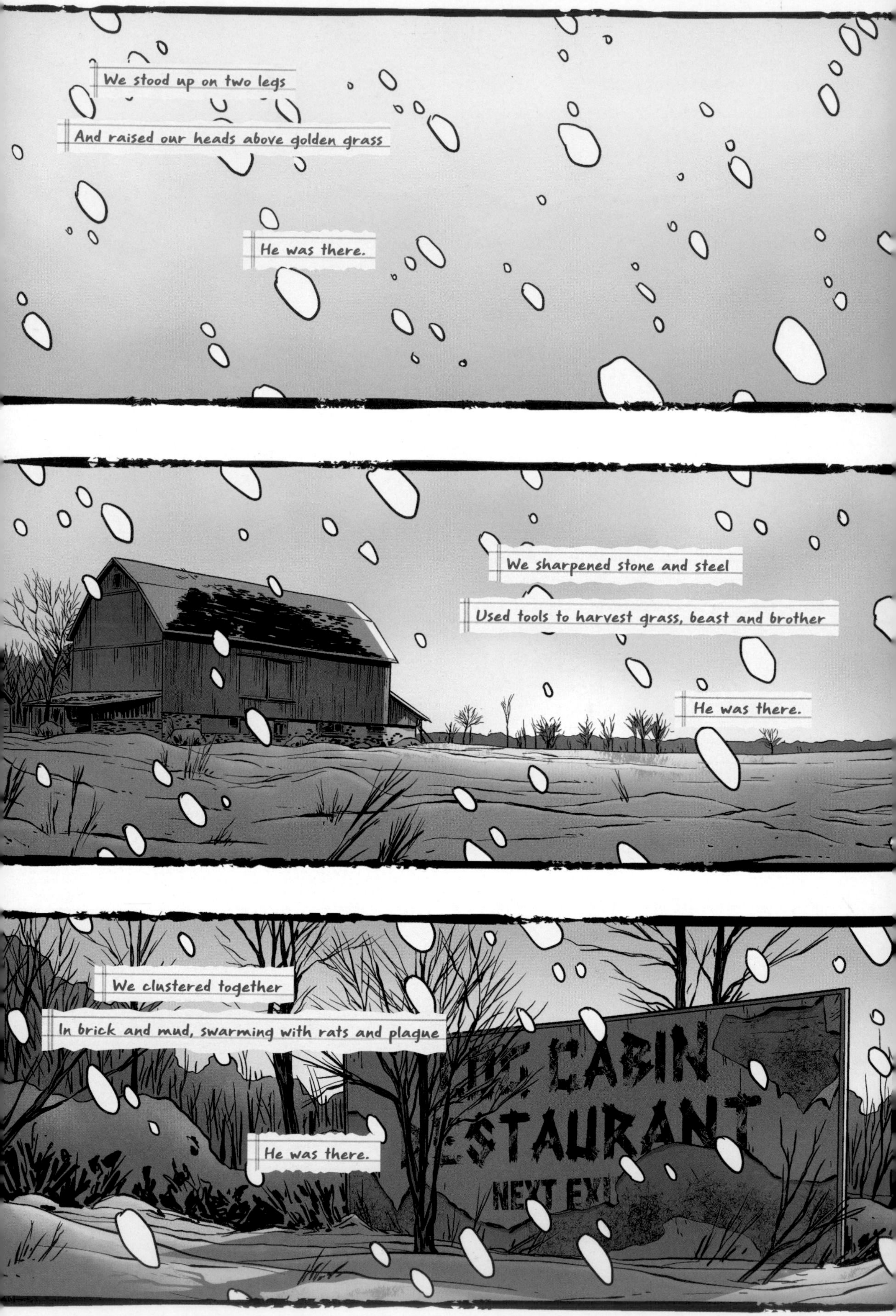
We stood up on two legs
And raised our heads above golden grass
He was there.
We sharpened stone and steel
Used tools to harvest grass, beast and brother
He was there.
We clustered together
In brick and mud, swarming with rats and plague
He was there.
CABIN
STAURANT
NEXT EX

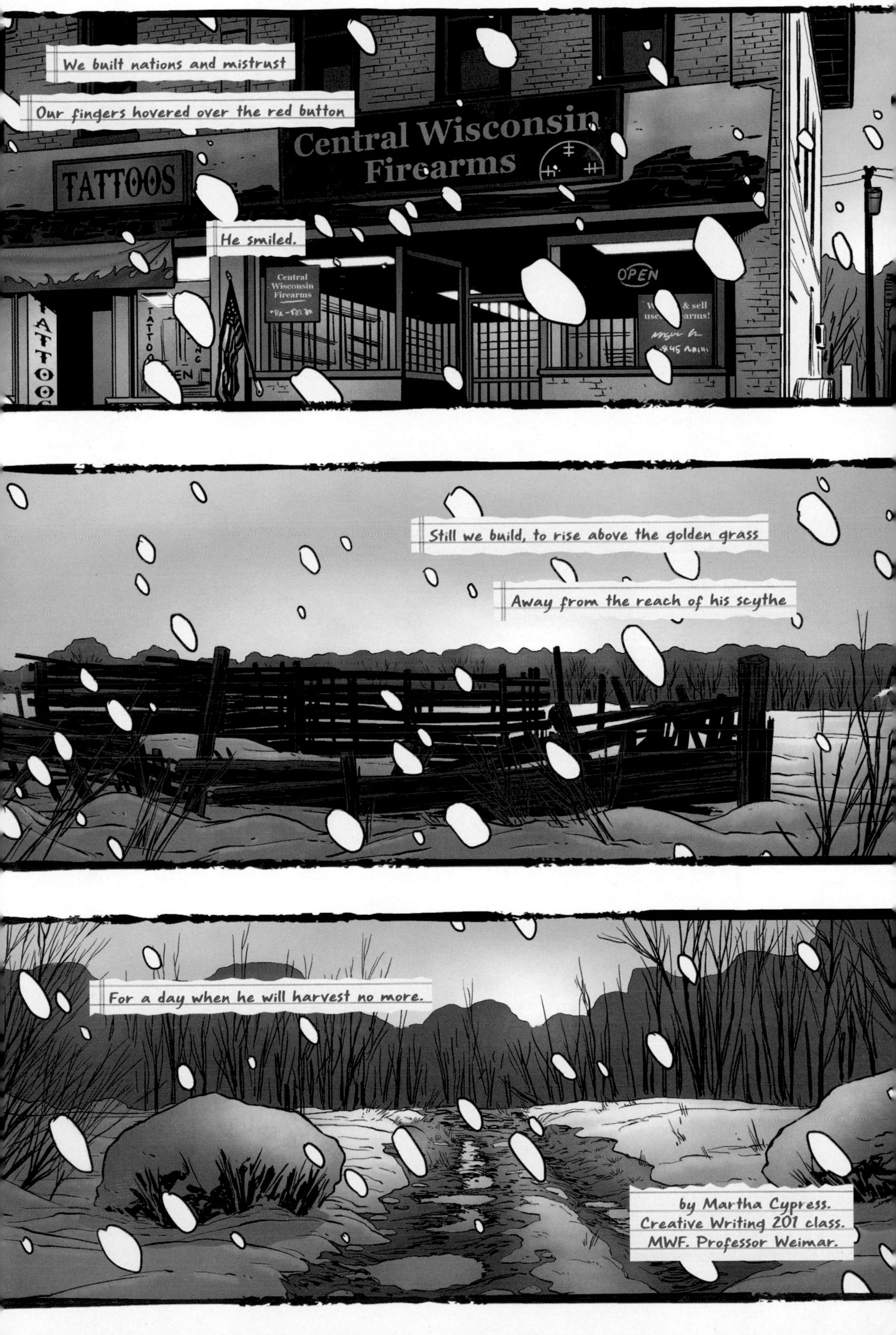
We built nations and mistrust
Our fingers hovered over the red button
Central Wisconsin Firearms
TATTOOS
He smiled.
Central Wisconsin Firearms
OPEN
TATTOOS
Still we build, to rise above the golden grass
Away from the reach of his scythe
For a day when he will harvest no more.
by Martha Cypress.
Creative Writing 201 class.
MWF. Professor Weimar.

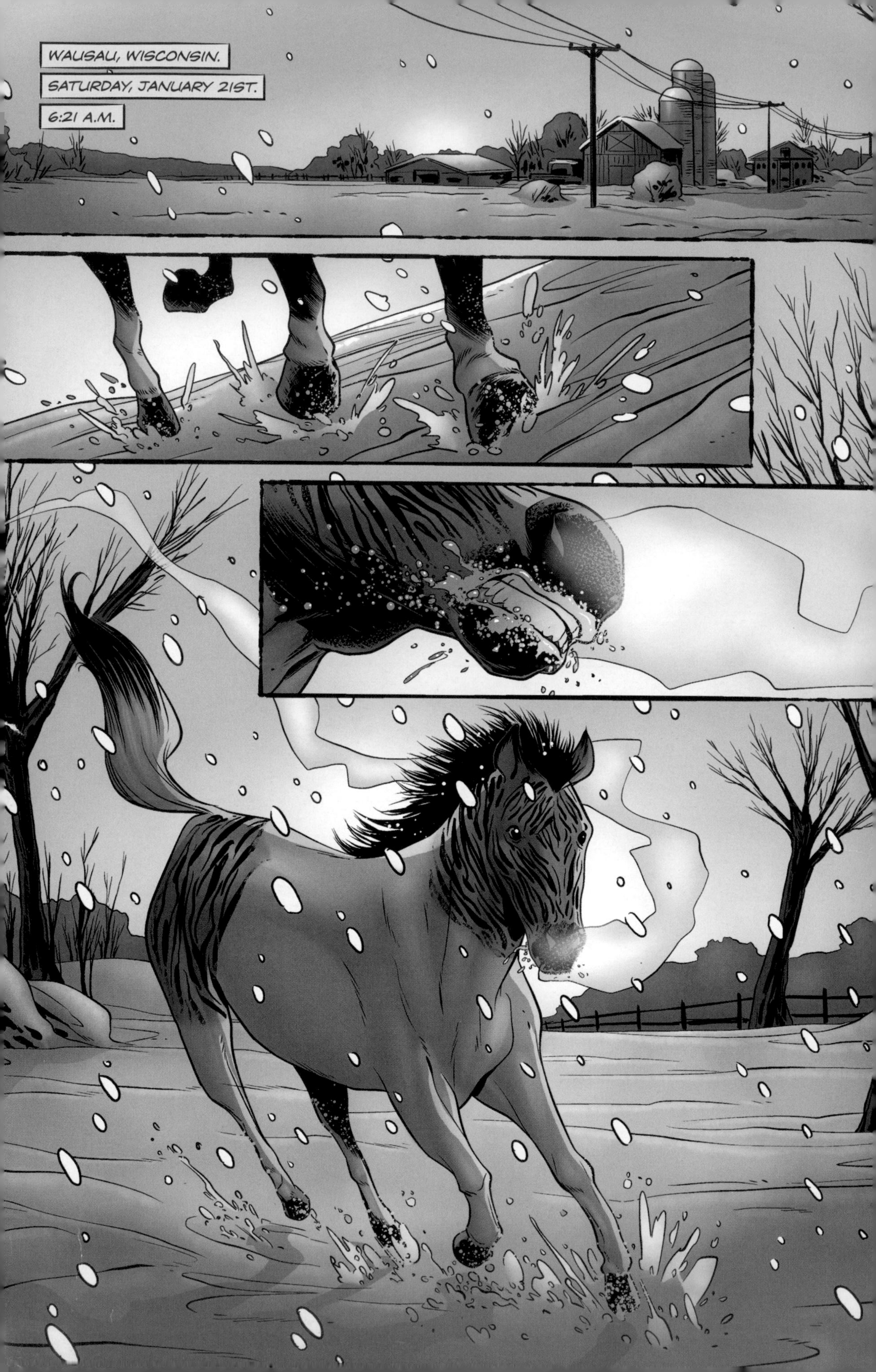
WAUSAU, WISCONSIN.
SATURDAY, JANUARY 21ST.
6:21 A.M.

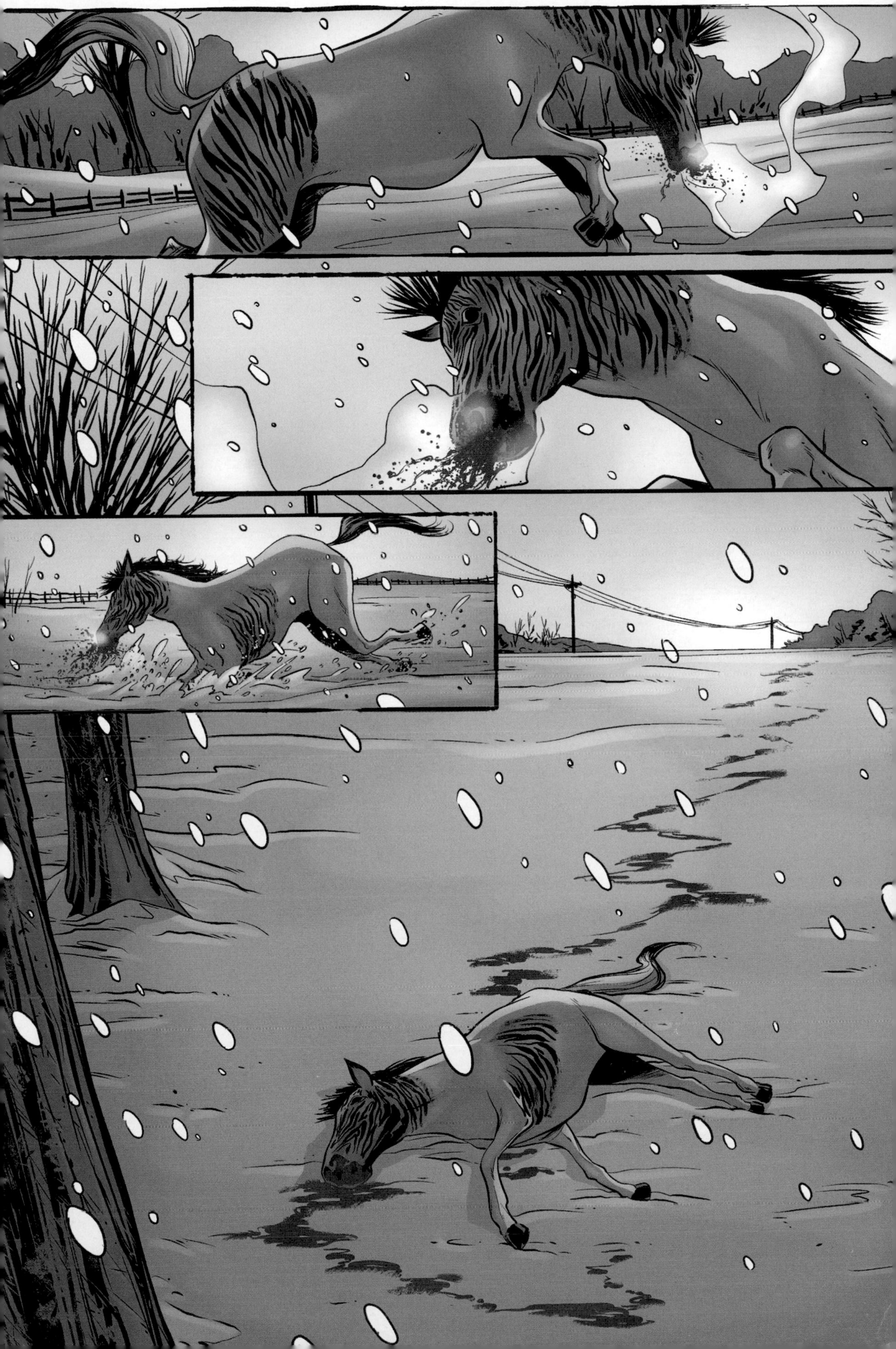

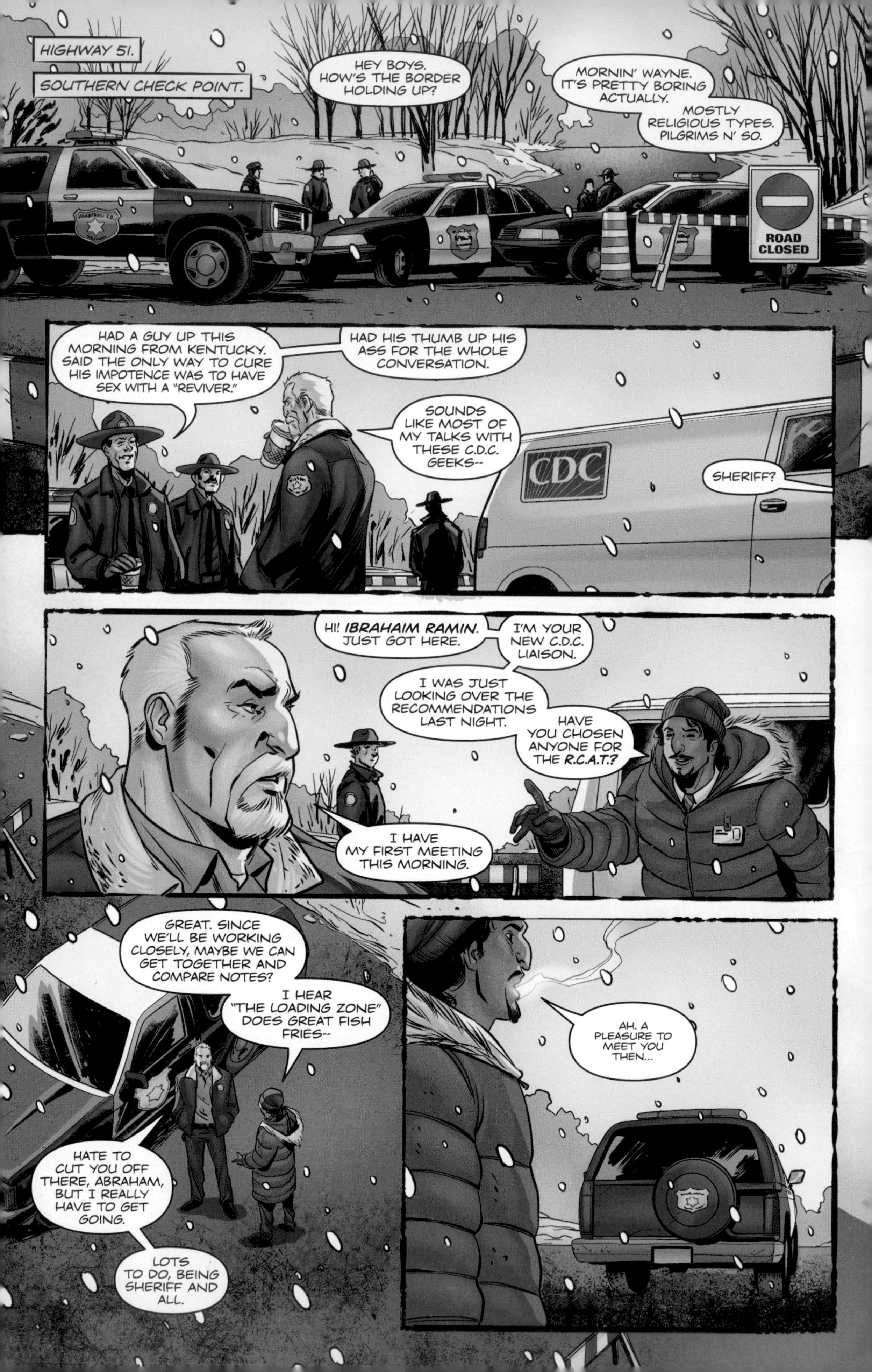
HIGHWAY 51.
SOUTHERN CHECK POINT.
HEY BOYS. HOW'S THE BORDER HOLDING UP?
MORNIN' WAYNE. IT'S PRETTY BORING ACTUALLY.
MOSTLY RELIGIOUS TYPES. PILGRIMS N' SO.
ROAD CLOSED
HAD A GUY UP THIS MORNING FROM KENTUCKY. SAID THE ONLY WAY TO CURE HIS IMPOTENCE WAS TO HAVE SEX WITH A "REVIVER."
HAD HIS THUMB UP HIS ASS FOR THE WHOLE CONVERSATION.
SOUNDS LIKE MOST OF MY TALKS WITH THESE C.D.C. GEEKS--
CDC
SHERIFF?
HI! IBRAHAIM RAMIN. JUST GOT HERE.
I'M YOUR NEW C.D.C. LIAISON.
I WAS JUST LOOKING OVER THE RECOMMENDATIONS LAST NIGHT.
HAVE YOU CHOSEN ANYONE FOR THE R.C.A.T.?
I HAVE MY FIRST MEETING THIS MORNING.
GREAT. SINCE WE'LL BE WORKING CLOSELY, MAYBE WE CAN GET TOGETHER AND COMPARE NOTES?
I HEAR "THE LOADING ZONE" DOES GREAT FISH FRIES--
HATE TO CUT YOU OFF THERE, ABRAHAM, BUT I REALLY HAVE TO GET GOING.
LOTS TO DO, BEING SHERIFF AND ALL.
AH. A PLEASURE TO MEET YOU THEN...

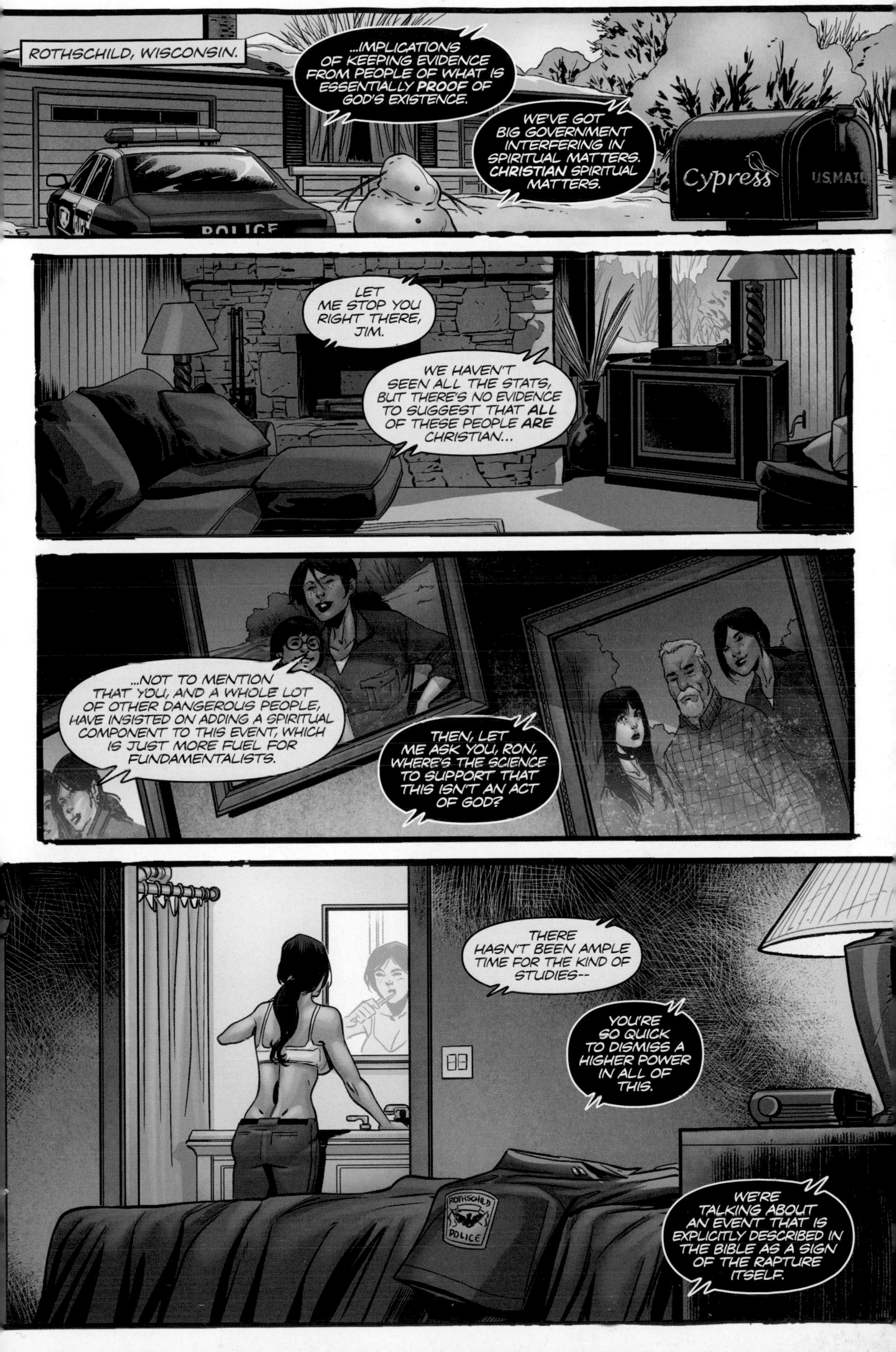
ROTHSCHILD, WISCONSIN.
...IMPLICATIONS OF KEEPING EVIDENCE FROM PEOPLE OF WHAT IS ESSENTIALLY PROOF OF GOD'S EXISTENCE.
WE'VE GOT BIG GOVERNMENT INTERFERING IN SPIRITUAL MATTERS. CHRISTIAN SPIRITUAL MATTERS.
Cypress
U.S.MAIL
POLICE
LET ME STOP YOU RIGHT THERE, JIM.
WE HAVEN'T SEEN ALL THE STATS, BUT THERE'S NO EVIDENCE TO SUGGEST THAT ALL OF THESE PEOPLE ARE CHRISTIAN...
...NOT TO MENTION THAT YOU, AND A WHOLE LOT OF OTHER DANGEROUS PEOPLE, HAVE INSISTED ON ADDING A SPIRITUAL COMPONENT TO THIS EVENT, WHICH IS JUST MORE FUEL FOR FUNDAMENTALISTS.
THEN, LET ME ASK YOU, RON, WHERE'S THE SCIENCE TO SUPPORT THAT THIS ISN'T AN ACT OF GOD?
THERE HASN'T BEEN AMPLE TIME FOR THE KIND OF STUDIES--
YOU'RE SO QUICK TO DISMISS A HIGHER POWER IN ALL OF THIS.
ROTHSCHILD POLICE
WE'RE TALKING ABOUT AN EVENT THAT IS EXPLICITLY DESCRIBED IN THE BIBLE AS A SIGN OF THE RAPTURE ITSELF.

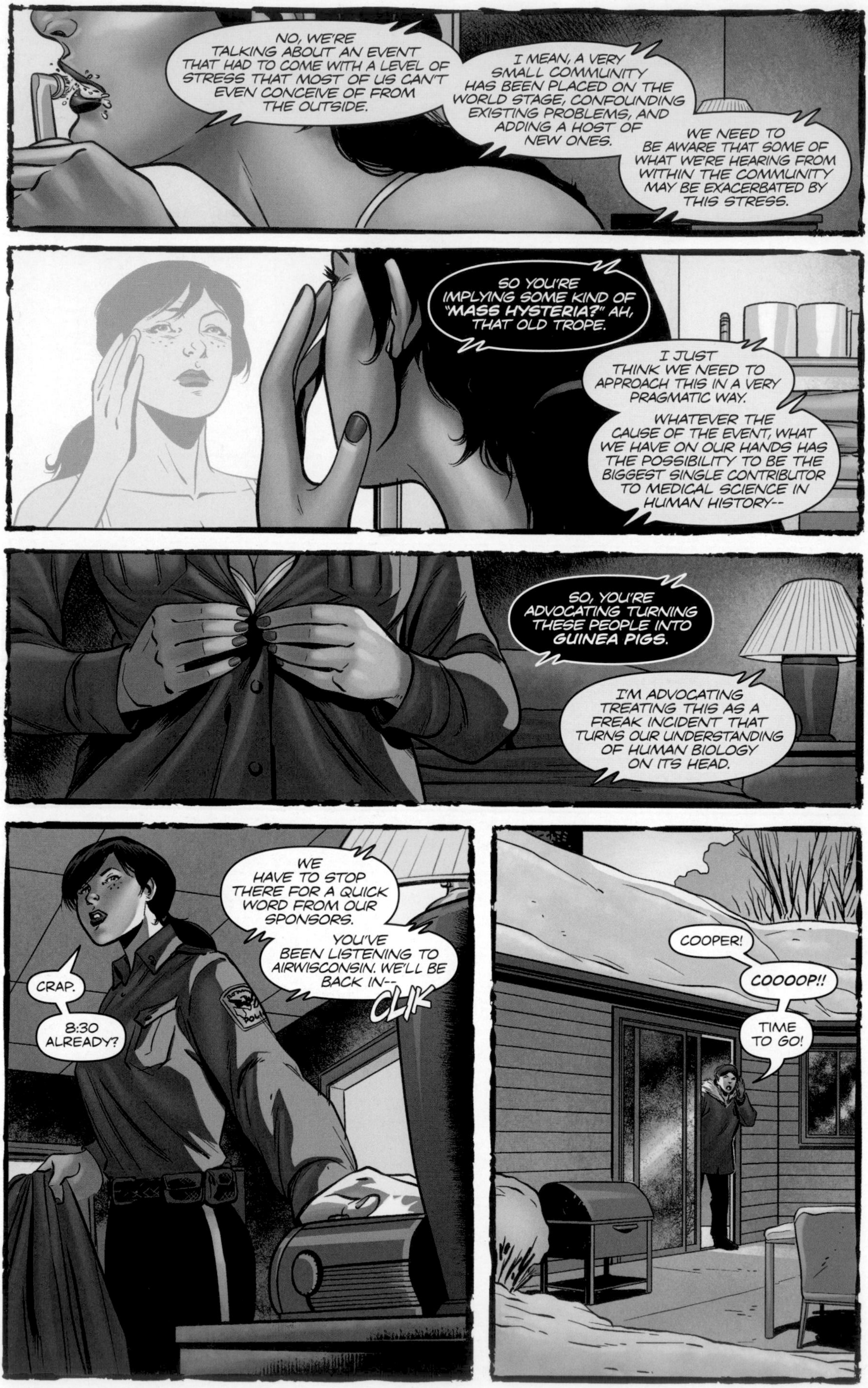
NO, WE'RE TALKING ABOUT AN EVENT THAT HAD TO COME WITH A LEVEL OF STRESS THAT MOST OF US CAN'T EVEN CONCEIVE OF FROM THE OUTSIDE.
I MEAN, A VERY SMALL COMMUNITY HAS BEEN PLACED ON THE WORLD STAGE, CONFOUNDING EXISTING PROBLEMS, AND ADDING A HOST OF NEW ONES.
WE NEED TO BE AWARE THAT SOME OF WHAT WE'RE HEARING FROM WITHIN THE COMMUNITY MAY BE EXACERBATED BY THIS STRESS.
SO YOU'RE IMPLYING SOME KIND OF "MASS HYSTERIA?" AH, THAT OLD TROPE.
I JUST THINK WE NEED TO APPROACH THIS IN A VERY PRAGMATIC WAY.
WHATEVER THE CAUSE OF THE EVENT, WHAT WE HAVE ON OUR HANDS HAS THE POSSIBILITY TO BE THE BIGGEST SINGLE CONTRIBUTOR TO MEDICAL SCIENCE IN HUMAN HISTORY--
SO, YOU'RE ADVOCATING TURNING THESE PEOPLE INTO GUINEA PIGS.
I'M ADVOCATING TREATING THIS AS A FREAK INCIDENT THAT TURNS OUR UNDERSTANDING OF HUMAN BIOLOGY ON ITS HEAD.
WE HAVE TO STOP THERE FOR A QUICK WORD FROM OUR SPONSORS.
YOU'VE BEEN LISTENING TO AIRWISCONSIN. WE'LL BE BACK IN--
CLIK
CRAP.
8:30 ALREADY?
COOPER!
COOOOP!!
TIME TO GO!

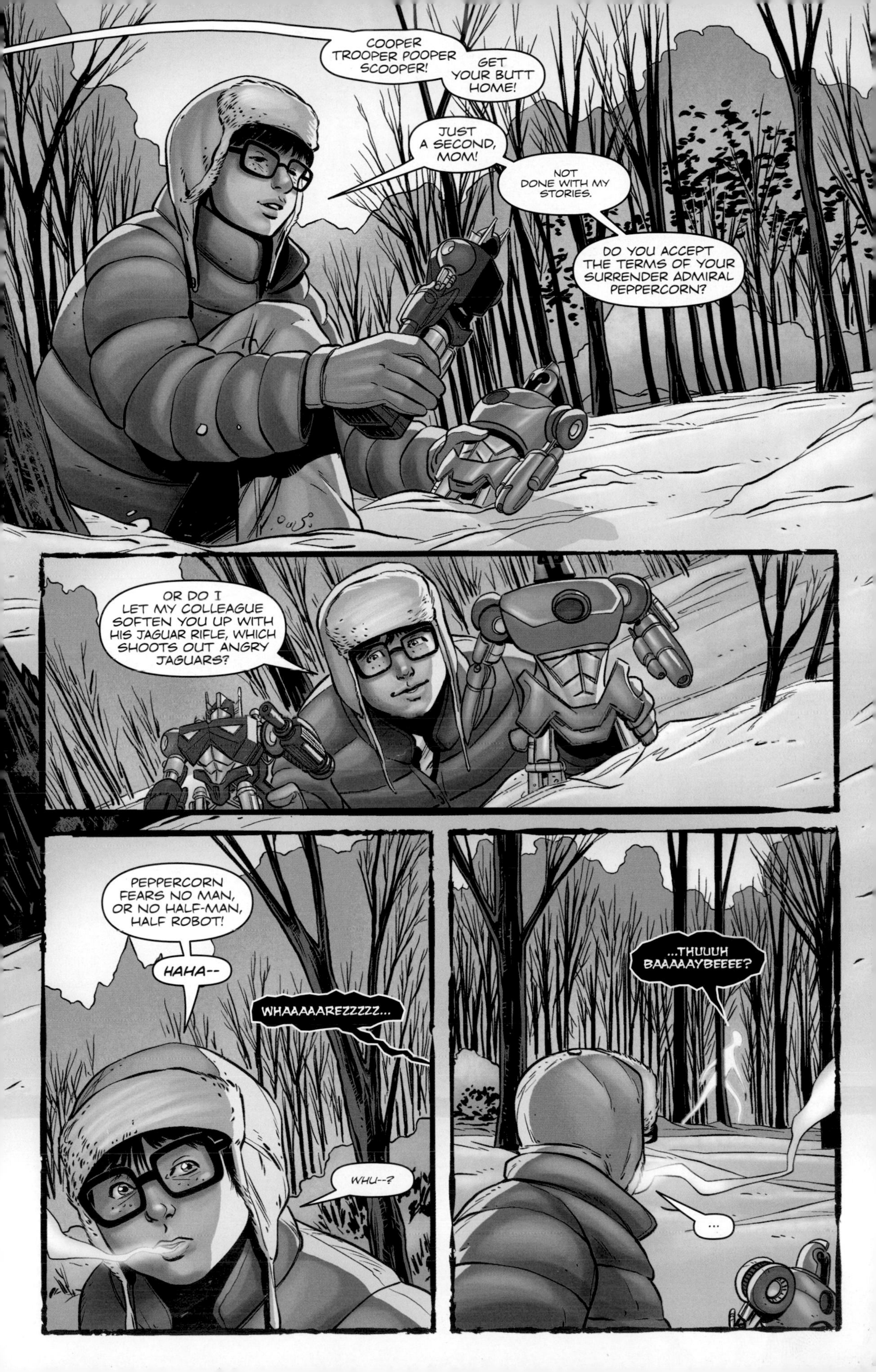
COOPER TROOPER POOPER SCOOPER!
GET YOUR BUTT HOME!
JUST A SECOND, MOM!
NOT DONE WITH MY STORIES.
DO YOU ACCEPT THE TERMS OF YOUR SURRENDER ADMIRAL PEPPERCORN?
OR DO I LET MY COLLEAGUE SOFTEN YOU UP WITH HIS JAGUAR RIFLE, WHICH SHOOTS OUT ANGRY JAGUARS?
PEPPERCORN FEARS NO MAN, OR NO HALF-MAN, HALF ROBOT!
HAHA--
WHAAAAAREZZZZZ...
WHU--?
...THUUUH BAAAAAYBEEEE?
...

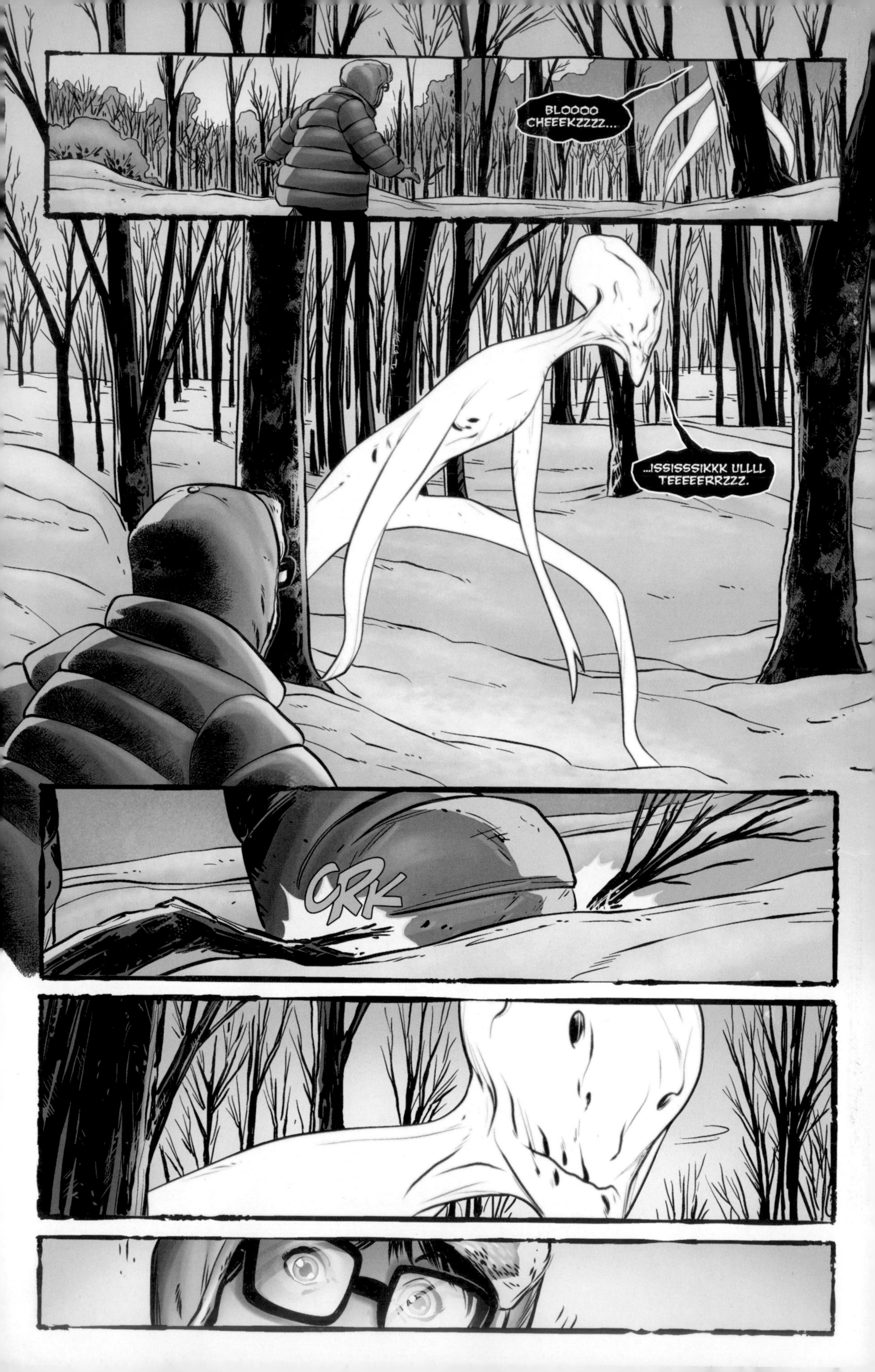
BLOOOO CHEEEKZZZZ...
...ISSISSSIKKK ULLLL TEEEEERRZZZ.
CRK

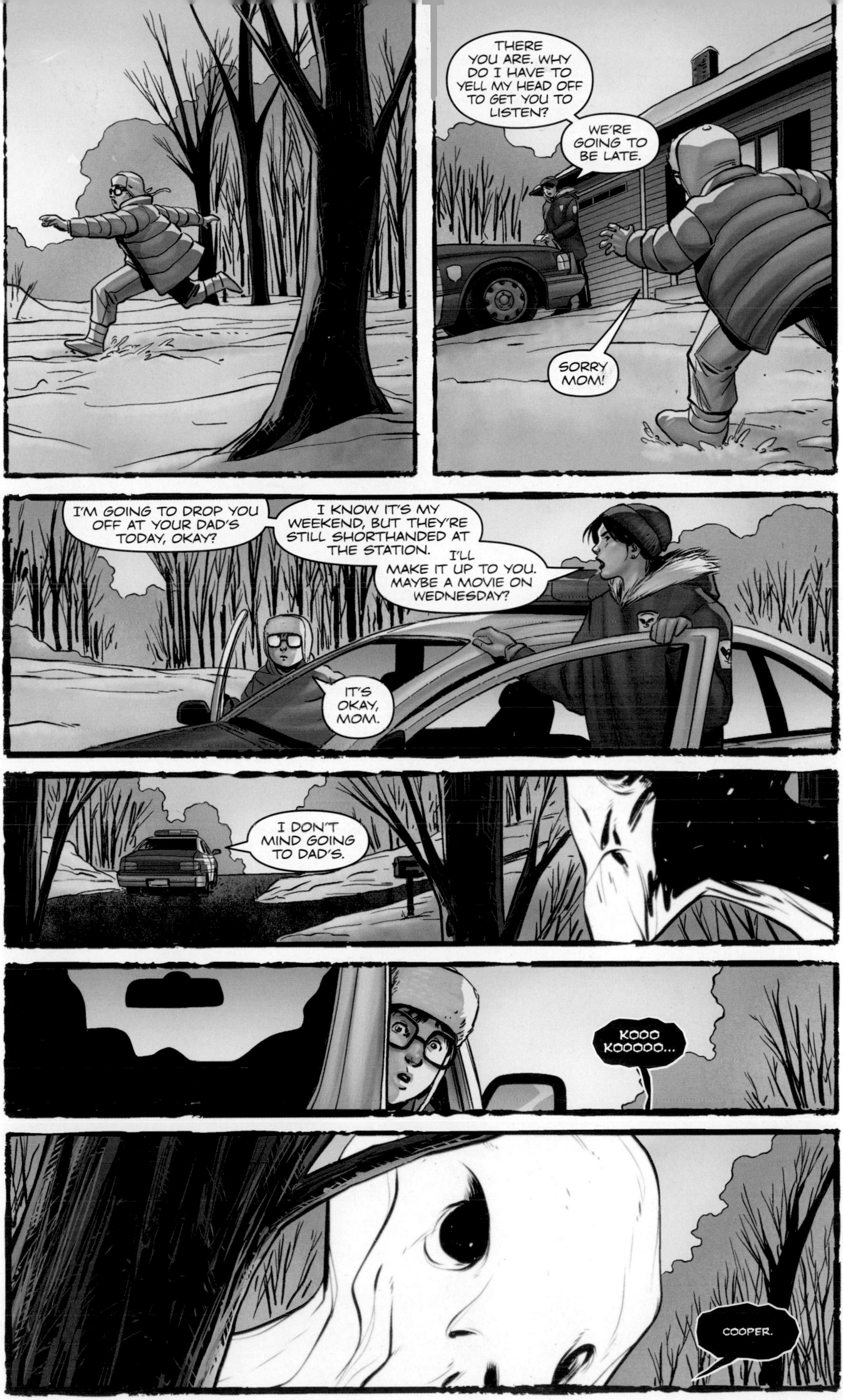
THERE YOU ARE. WHY DO I HAVE TO YELL MY HEAD OFF TO GET YOU TO LISTEN?
WE'RE GOING TO BE LATE.
SORRY MOM!
I'M GOING TO DROP YOU OFF AT YOUR DAD'S TODAY, OKAY?
I KNOW IT'S MY WEEKEND, BUT THEY'RE STILL SHORTHANDED AT THE STATION.
I'LL MAKE IT UP TO YOU. MAYBE A MOVIE ON WEDNESDAY?
IT'S OKAY, MOM.
I DON'T MIND GOING TO DAD'S.
KOOO KOOOOO...
COOPER.

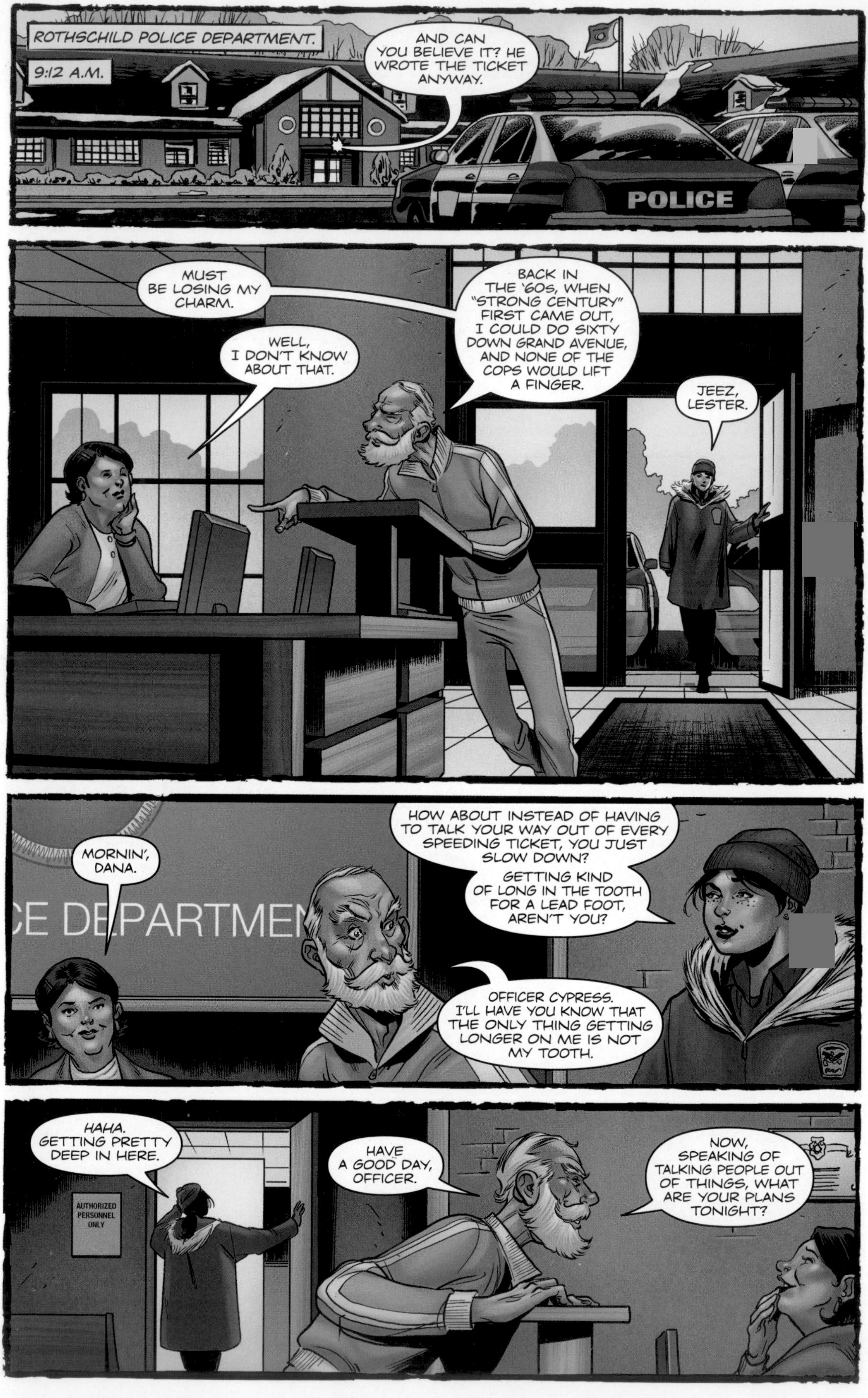
ROTHSCHILD POLICE DEPARTMENT.
9:12 A.M.
AND CAN YOU BELIEVE IT? HE WROTE THE TICKET ANYWAY.
POLICE
MUST BE LOSING MY CHARM.
BACK IN THE '60s, WHEN "STRONG CENTURY" FIRST CAME OUT, I COULD DO SIXTY DOWN GRAND AVENUE, AND NONE OF THE COPS WOULD LIFT A FINGER.
WELL, I DON'T KNOW ABOUT THAT.
JEEZ, LESTER.
MORNIN', DANA.
CE DEPARTMEN
HOW ABOUT INSTEAD OF HAVING TO TALK YOUR WAY OUT OF EVERY SPEEDING TICKET, YOU JUST SLOW DOWN?
GETTING KIND OF LONG IN THE TOOTH FOR A LEAD FOOT, AREN'T YOU?
OFFICER CYPRESS. I'LL HAVE YOU KNOW THAT THE ONLY THING GETTING LONGER ON ME IS NOT MY TOOTH.
HAHA. GETTING PRETTY DEEP IN HERE.
AUTHORIZED PERSONNEL ONLY
HAVE A GOOD DAY, OFFICER.
NOW, SPEAKING OF TALKING PEOPLE OUT OF THINGS, WHAT ARE YOUR PLANS TONIGHT?

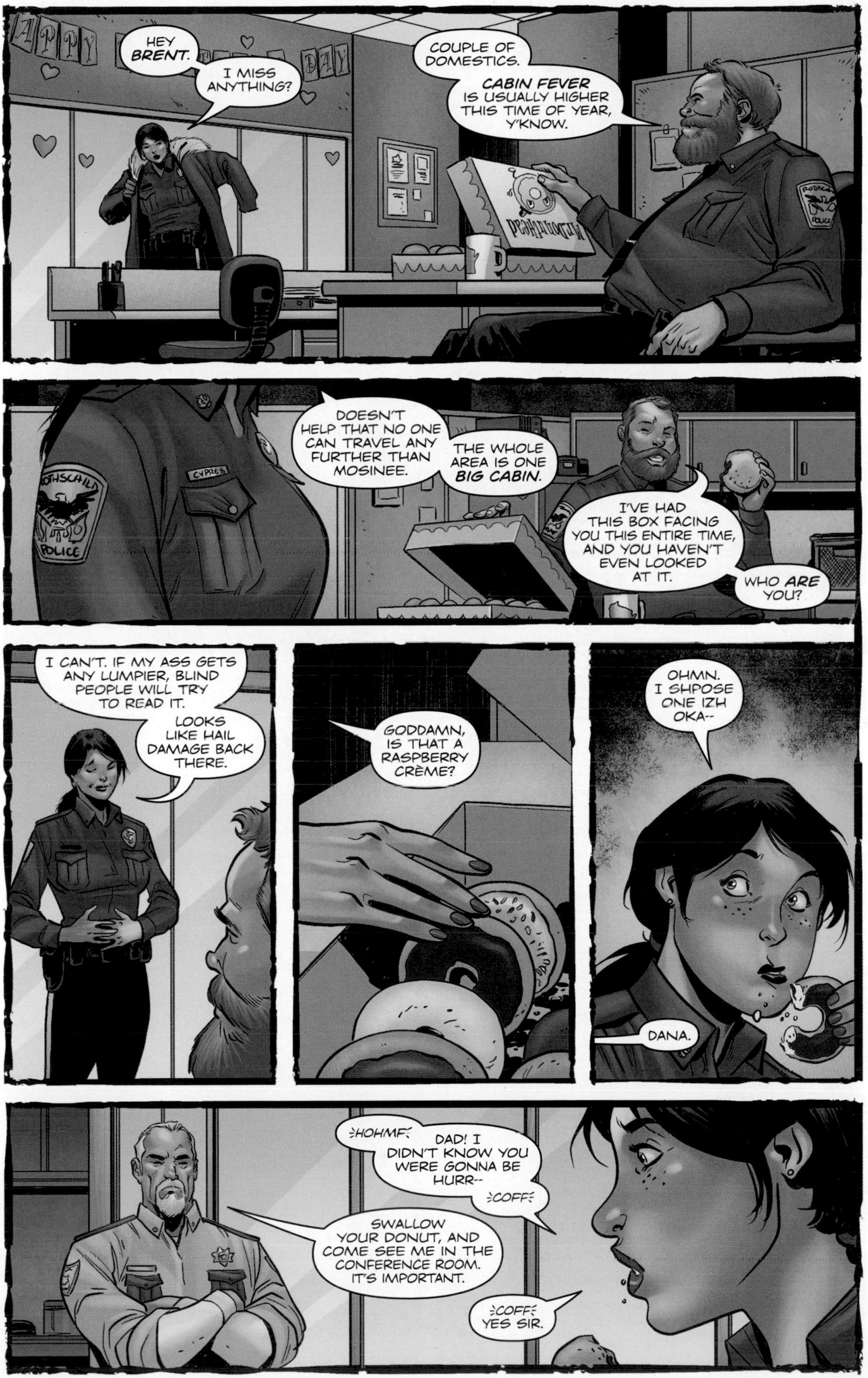
HEY BRENT.
I MISS ANYTHING?
COUPLE OF DOMESTICS.
CABIN FEVER IS USUALLY HIGHER THIS TIME OF YEAR, Y'KNOW.
DOESN'T HELP THAT NO ONE CAN TRAVEL ANY FURTHER THAN MOSINEE.
THE WHOLE AREA IS ONE BIG CABIN.
I'VE HAD THIS BOX FACING YOU THIS ENTIRE TIME, AND YOU HAVEN'T EVEN LOOKED AT IT.
WHO ARE YOU?
I CAN'T. IF MY ASS GETS ANY LUMPIER, BLIND PEOPLE WILL TRY TO READ IT.
LOOKS LIKE HAIL DAMAGE BACK THERE.
GODDAMN, IS THAT A RASPBERRY CRÈME?
OHMN. I SHPOSE ONE IZH OKA--
DANA.
HOHMF
DAD! I DIDN'T KNOW YOU WERE GONNA BE HURR--
COFF
SWALLOW YOUR DONUT, AND COME SEE ME IN THE CONFERENCE ROOM. IT'S IMPORTANT.
COFF
YES SIR.

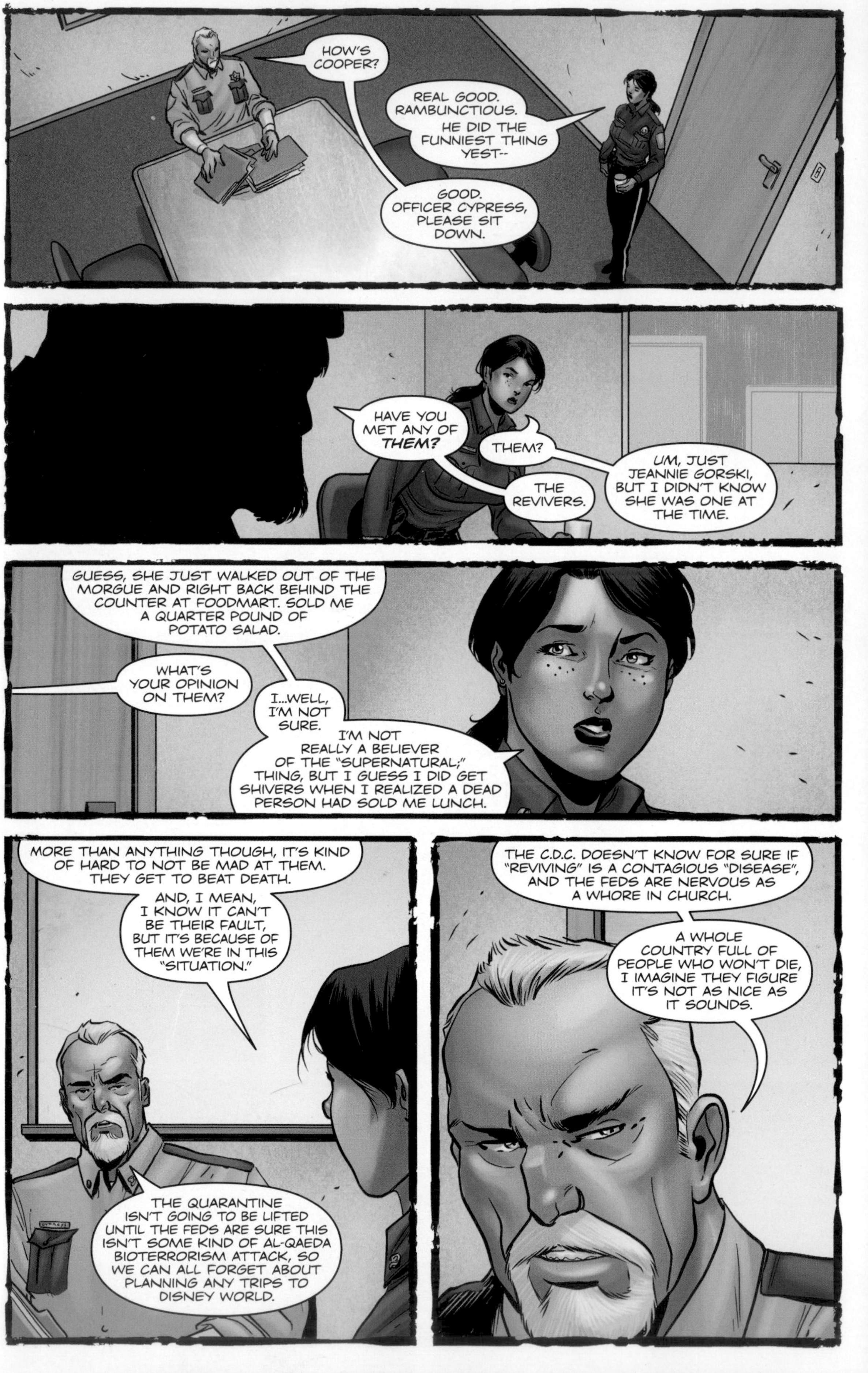
HOW'S COOPER?
REAL GOOD. RAMBUNCTIOUS.
HE DID THE FUNNIEST THING YEST--
GOOD. OFFICER CYPRESS, PLEASE SIT DOWN.
HAVE YOU MET ANY OF *THEM?*
THEM?
THE REVIVERS.
UM, JUST JEANNIE GORSKI, BUT I DIDN'T KNOW SHE WAS ONE AT THE TIME.
GUESS, SHE JUST WALKED OUT OF THE MORGUE AND RIGHT BACK BEHIND THE COUNTER AT FOODMART. SOLD ME A QUARTER POUND OF POTATO SALAD.
WHAT'S YOUR OPINION ON THEM?
I...WELL, I'M NOT SURE.
I'M NOT REALLY A BELIEVER OF THE "SUPERNATURAL;" THING, BUT I GUESS I DID GET SHIVERS WHEN I REALIZED A DEAD PERSON HAD SOLD ME LUNCH.
MORE THAN ANYTHING THOUGH, IT'S KIND OF HARD TO NOT BE MAD AT THEM. THEY GET TO BEAT DEATH.
AND, I MEAN, I KNOW IT CAN'T BE THEIR FAULT, BUT IT'S BECAUSE OF THEM WE'RE IN THIS "SITUATION."
THE QUARANTINE ISN'T GOING TO BE LIFTED UNTIL THE FEDS ARE SURE THIS ISN'T SOME KIND OF AL-QAEDA BIOTERRORISM ATTACK, SO WE CAN ALL FORGET ABOUT PLANNING ANY TRIPS TO DISNEY WORLD.
THE C.D.C. DOESN'T KNOW FOR SURE IF "REVIVING" IS A CONTAGIOUS "DISEASE", AND THE FEDS ARE NERVOUS AS A WHORE IN CHURCH.
A WHOLE COUNTRY FULL OF PEOPLE WHO WON'T DIE, I IMAGINE THEY FIGURE IT'S NOT AS NICE AS IT SOUNDS.

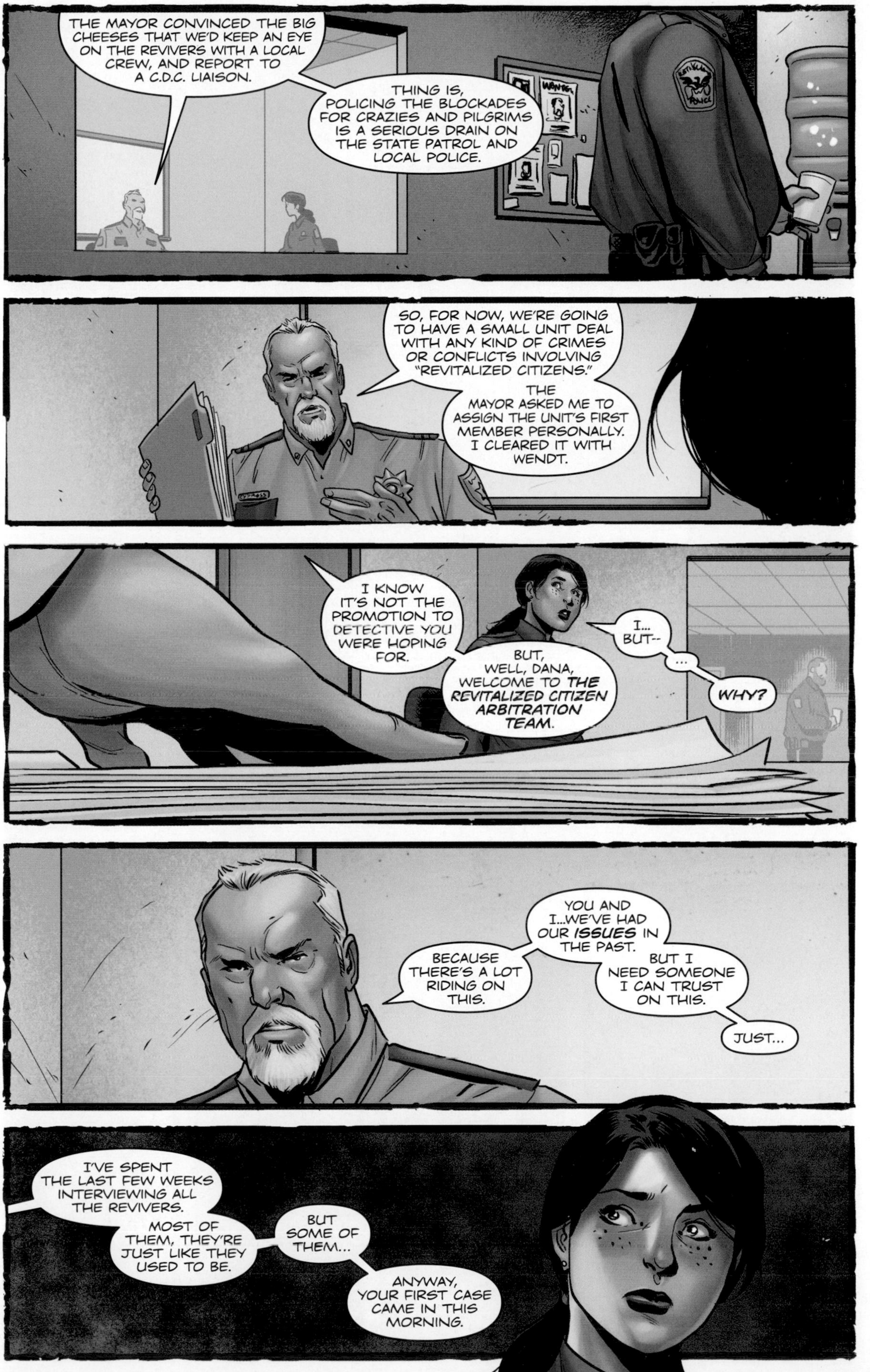
THE MAYOR CONVINCED THE BIG CHEESES THAT WE'D KEEP AN EYE ON THE REVIVERS WITH A LOCAL CREW, AND REPORT TO A C.D.C. LIAISON.
THING IS, POLICING THE BLOCKADES FOR CRAZIES AND PILGRIMS IS A SERIOUS DRAIN ON THE STATE PATROL AND LOCAL POLICE.
SO, FOR NOW, WE'RE GOING TO HAVE A SMALL UNIT DEAL WITH ANY KIND OF CRIMES OR CONFLICTS INVOLVING "REVITALIZED CITIZENS."
THE MAYOR ASKED ME TO ASSIGN THE UNIT'S FIRST MEMBER PERSONALLY. I CLEARED IT WITH WENDT.
I KNOW IT'S NOT THE PROMOTION TO DETECTIVE YOU WERE HOPING FOR.
BUT, WELL, DANA, WELCOME TO ***THE REVITALIZED CITIZEN ARBITRATION TEAM***.
I... BUT--
...
WHY?
BECAUSE THERE'S A LOT RIDING ON THIS.
YOU AND I...WE'VE HAD OUR ***ISSUES*** IN THE PAST.
BUT I NEED SOMEONE I CAN TRUST ON THIS.
JUST...
I'VE SPENT THE LAST FEW WEEKS INTERVIEWING ALL THE REVIVERS.
MOST OF THEM, THEY'RE JUST LIKE THEY USED TO BE.
BUT SOME OF THEM...
ANYWAY, YOUR FIRST CASE CAME IN THIS MORNING.

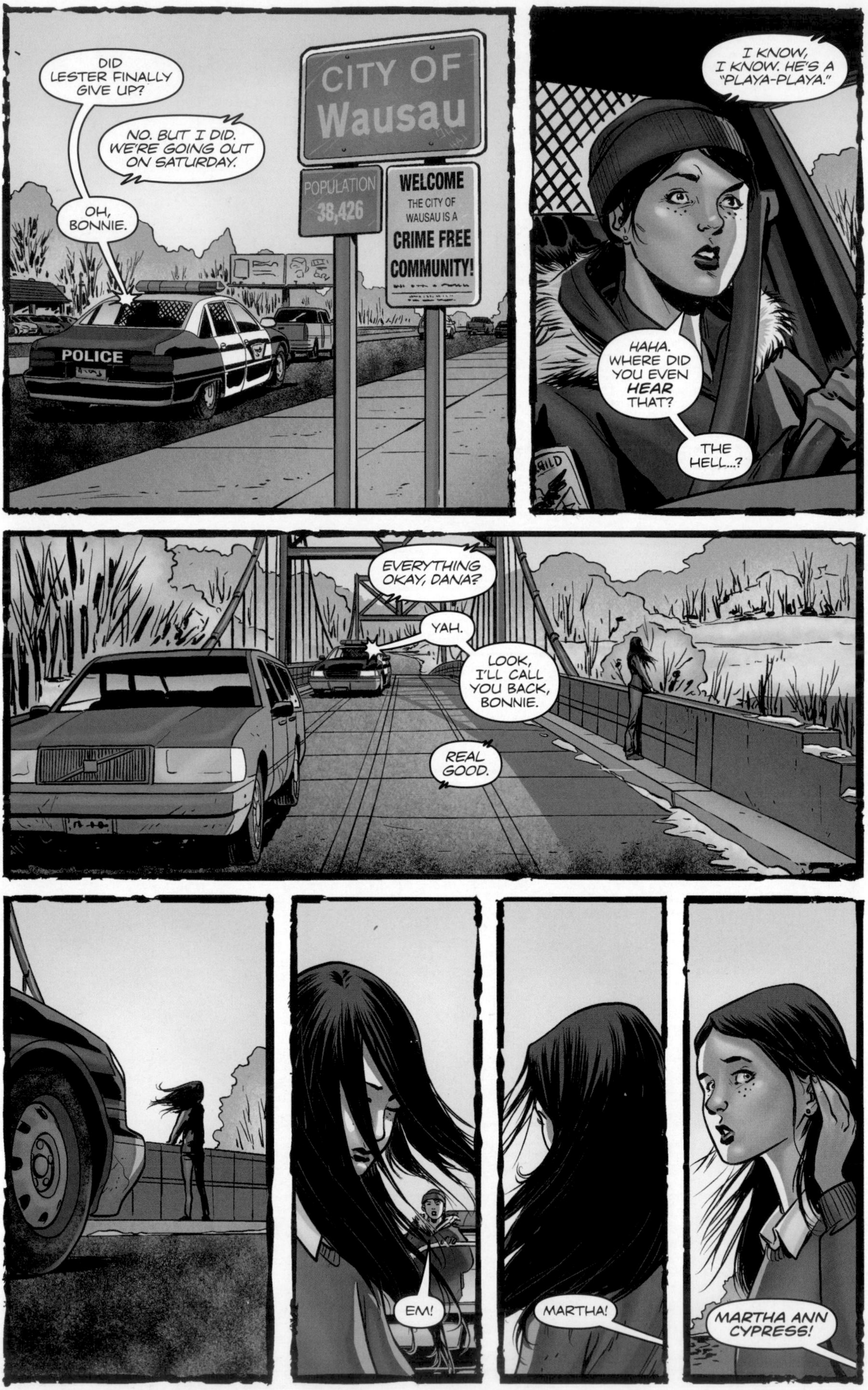
DID LESTER FINALLY GIVE UP?
NO. BUT I DID. WE'RE GOING OUT ON SATURDAY.
OH, BONNIE.
CITY OF Wausau
POPULATION 38,426
WELCOME THE CITY OF WAUSAU IS A CRIME FREE COMMUNITY!
POLICE
I KNOW, I KNOW. HE'S A "PLAYA-PLAYA."
HAHA. WHERE DID YOU EVEN HEAR THAT?
THE HELL...?
EVERYTHING OKAY, DANA?
YAH.
LOOK, I'LL CALL YOU BACK, BONNIE.
REAL GOOD.
EM!
MARTHA!
MARTHA ANN CYPRESS!

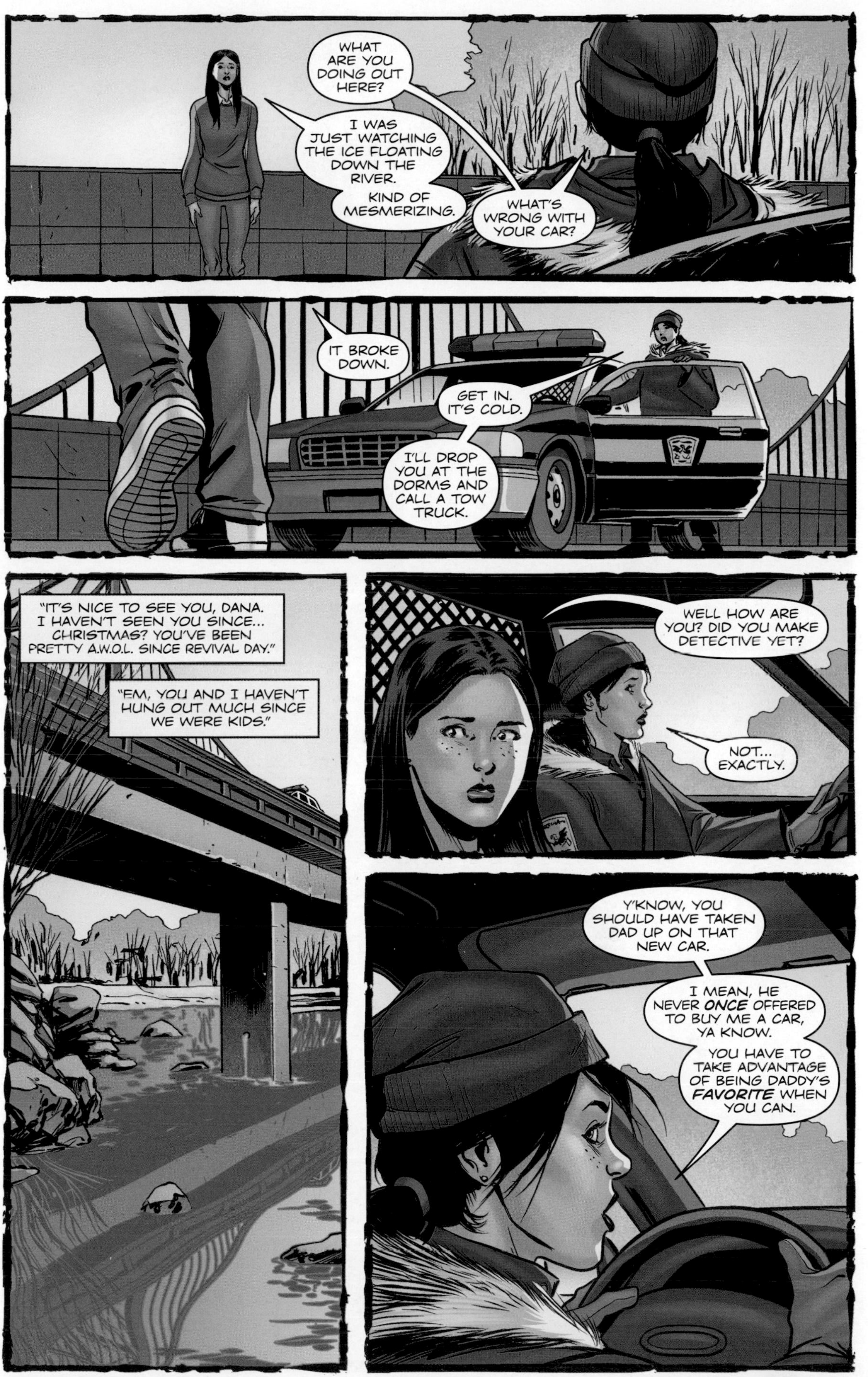
WHAT ARE YOU DOING OUT HERE?
I WAS JUST WATCHING THE ICE FLOATING DOWN THE RIVER.
KIND OF MESMERIZING.
WHAT'S WRONG WITH YOUR CAR?
IT BROKE DOWN.
GET IN. IT'S COLD.
I'LL DROP YOU AT THE DORMS AND CALL A TOW TRUCK.
"IT'S NICE TO SEE YOU, DANA. I HAVEN'T SEEN YOU SINCE... CHRISTMAS? YOU'VE BEEN PRETTY A.W.O.L. SINCE REVIVAL DAY."
"EM, YOU AND I HAVEN'T HUNG OUT MUCH SINCE WE WERE KIDS."
WELL HOW ARE YOU? DID YOU MAKE DETECTIVE YET?
NOT... EXACTLY.
Y'KNOW, YOU SHOULD HAVE TAKEN DAD UP ON THAT NEW CAR.
I MEAN, HE NEVER ONCE OFFERED TO BUY ME A CAR, YA KNOW.
YOU HAVE TO TAKE ADVANTAGE OF BEING DADDY'S FAVORITE WHEN YOU CAN.

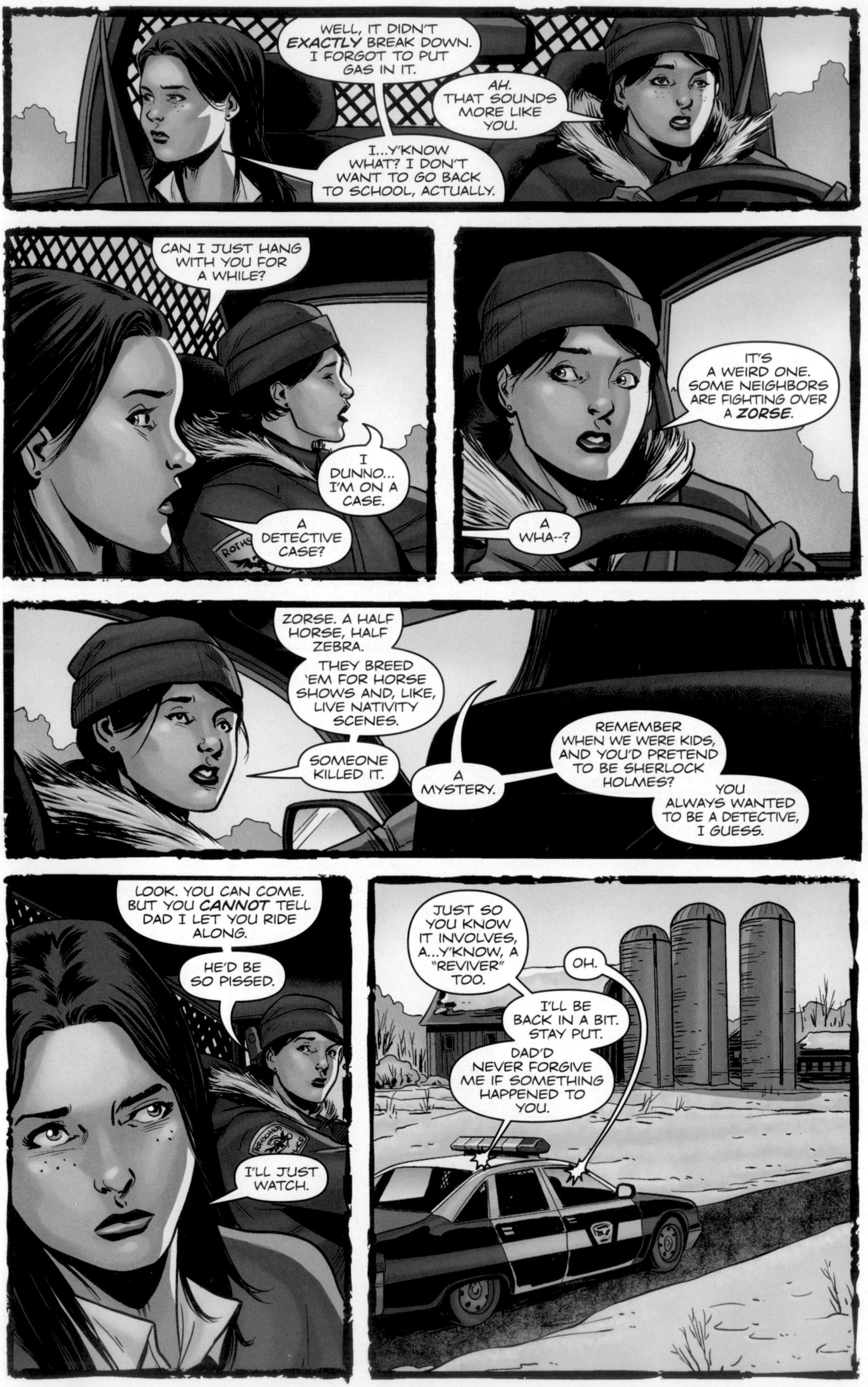
WELL, IT DIDN'T EXACTLY BREAK DOWN. I FORGOT TO PUT GAS IN IT.
AH. THAT SOUNDS MORE LIKE YOU.
I...Y'KNOW WHAT? I DON'T WANT TO GO BACK TO SCHOOL, ACTUALLY.
CAN I JUST HANG WITH YOU FOR A WHILE?
I DUNNO... I'M ON A CASE.
A DETECTIVE CASE?
IT'S A WEIRD ONE. SOME NEIGHBORS ARE FIGHTING OVER A ZORSE.
A WHA--?
ZORSE. A HALF HORSE, HALF ZEBRA.
THEY BREED 'EM FOR HORSE SHOWS AND, LIKE, LIVE NATIVITY SCENES.
SOMEONE KILLED IT.
A MYSTERY.
REMEMBER WHEN WE WERE KIDS, AND YOU'D PRETEND TO BE SHERLOCK HOLMES?
YOU ALWAYS WANTED TO BE A DETECTIVE, I GUESS.
LOOK. YOU CAN COME. BUT YOU CANNOT TELL DAD I LET YOU RIDE ALONG.
HE'D BE SO PISSED.
I'LL JUST WATCH.
JUST SO YOU KNOW IT INVOLVES, A...Y'KNOW, A "REVIVER" TOO.
OH.
I'LL BE BACK IN A BIT. STAY PUT.
DAD'D NEVER FORGIVE ME IF SOMETHING HAPPENED TO YOU.

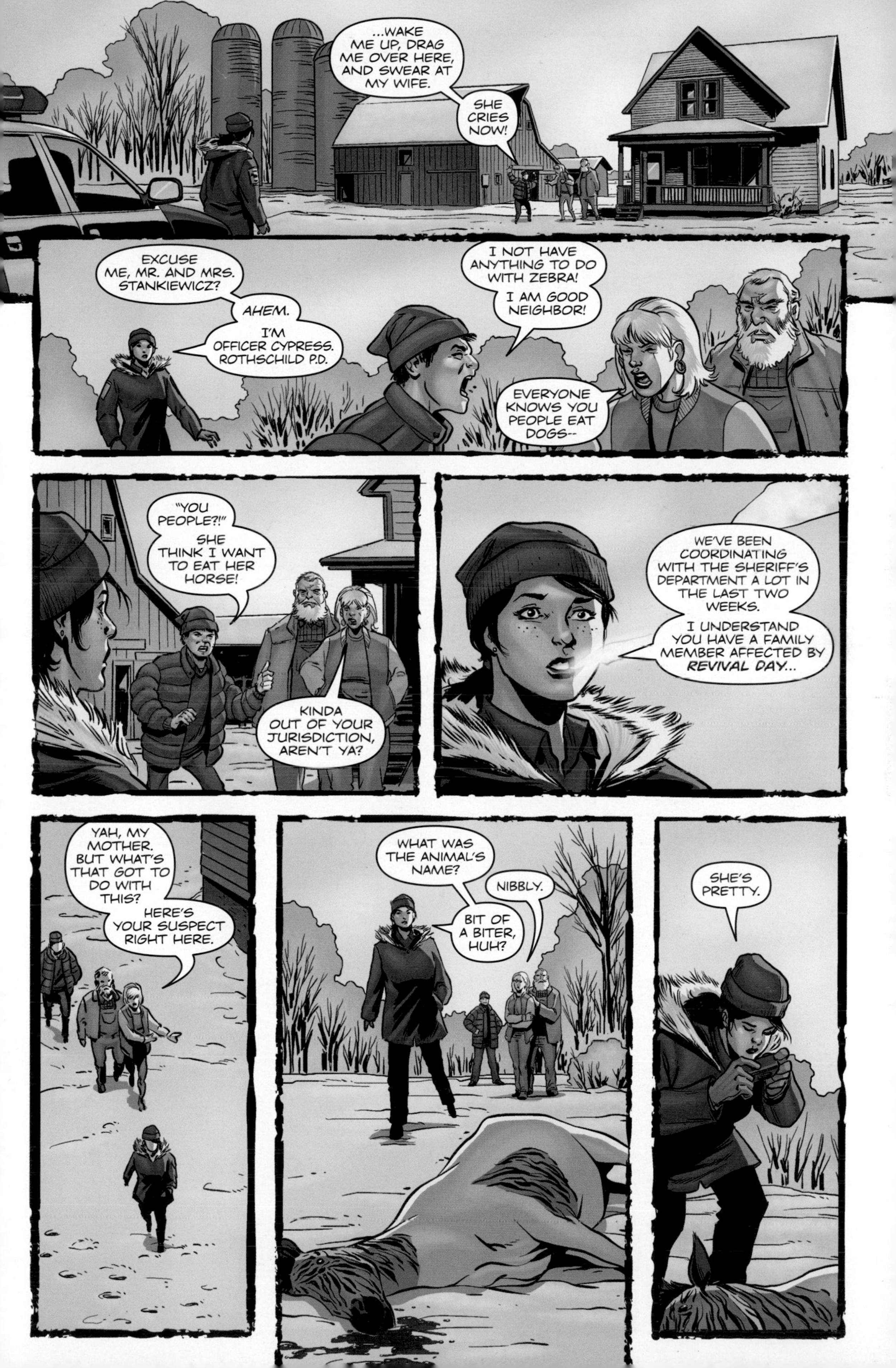
...WAKE ME UP, DRAG ME OVER HERE, AND SWEAR AT MY WIFE.
SHE CRIES NOW!
EXCUSE ME, MR. AND MRS. STANKIEWICZ?
AHEM.
I'M OFFICER CYPRESS. ROTHSCHILD P.D.
I NOT HAVE ANYTHING TO DO WITH ZEBRA!
I AM GOOD NEIGHBOR!
EVERYONE KNOWS YOU PEOPLE EAT DOGS--
"YOU PEOPLE?!"
SHE THINK I WANT TO EAT HER HORSE!
KINDA OUT OF YOUR JURISDICTION, AREN'T YA?
WE'VE BEEN COORDINATING WITH THE SHERIFF'S DEPARTMENT A LOT IN THE LAST TWO WEEKS.
I UNDERSTAND YOU HAVE A FAMILY MEMBER AFFECTED BY *REVIVAL DAY*...
YAH, MY MOTHER. BUT WHAT'S THAT GOT TO DO WITH THIS?
HERE'S YOUR SUSPECT RIGHT HERE.
WHAT WAS THE ANIMAL'S NAME?
NIBBLY.
BIT OF A BITER, HUH?
SHE'S PRETTY.

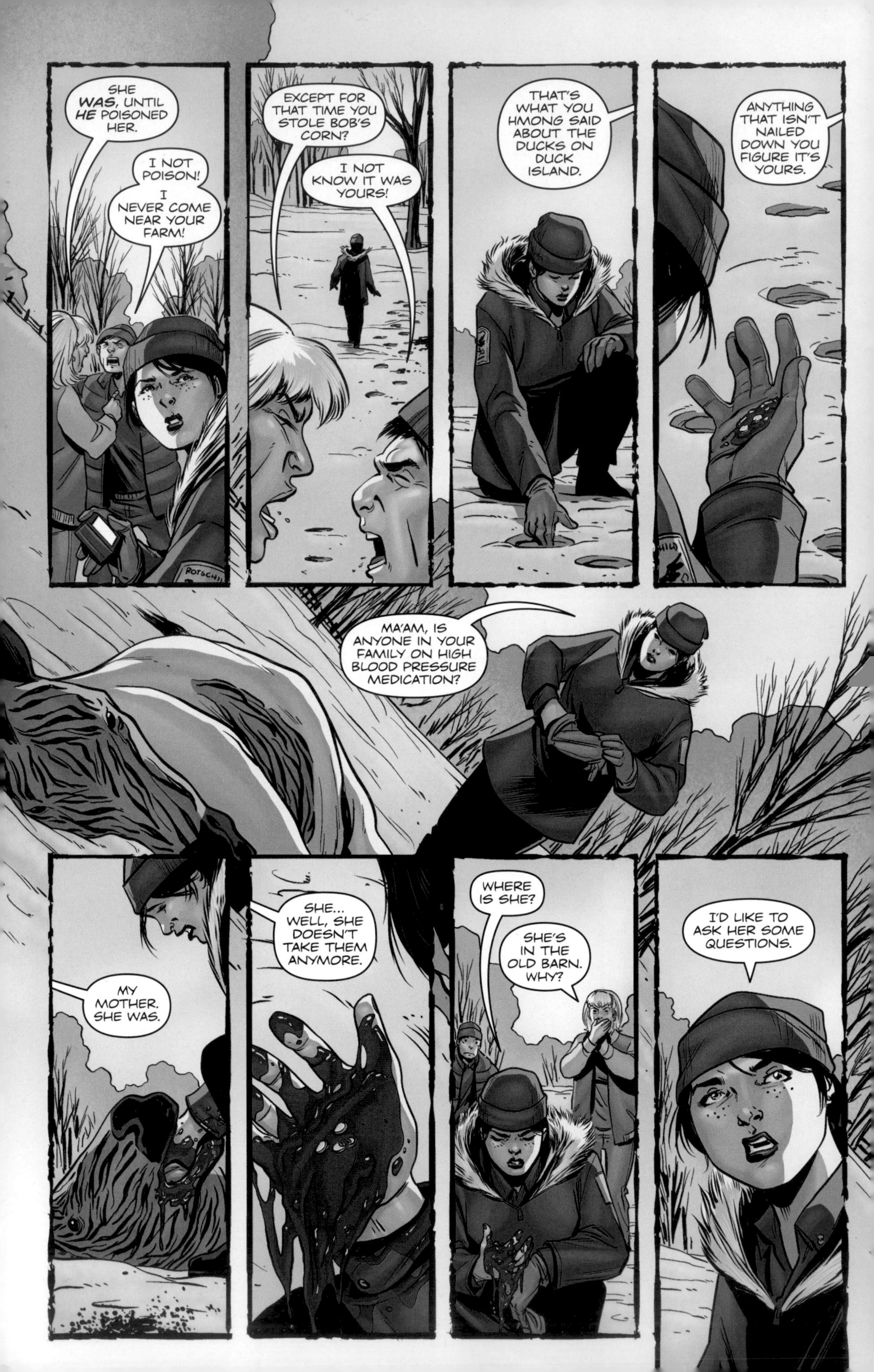
SHE WAS, UNTIL HE POISONED HER.
I NOT POISON!
I NEVER COME NEAR YOUR FARM!
EXCEPT FOR THAT TIME YOU STOLE BOB'S CORN?
I NOT KNOW IT WAS YOURS!
THAT'S WHAT YOU HMONG SAID ABOUT THE DUCKS ON DUCK ISLAND.
ANYTHING THAT ISN'T NAILED DOWN YOU FIGURE IT'S YOURS.
MA'AM, IS ANYONE IN YOUR FAMILY ON HIGH BLOOD PRESSURE MEDICATION?
MY MOTHER. SHE WAS.
SHE... WELL, SHE DOESN'T TAKE THEM ANYMORE.
WHERE IS SHE?
SHE'S IN THE OLD BARN. WHY?
I'D LIKE TO ASK HER SOME QUESTIONS.

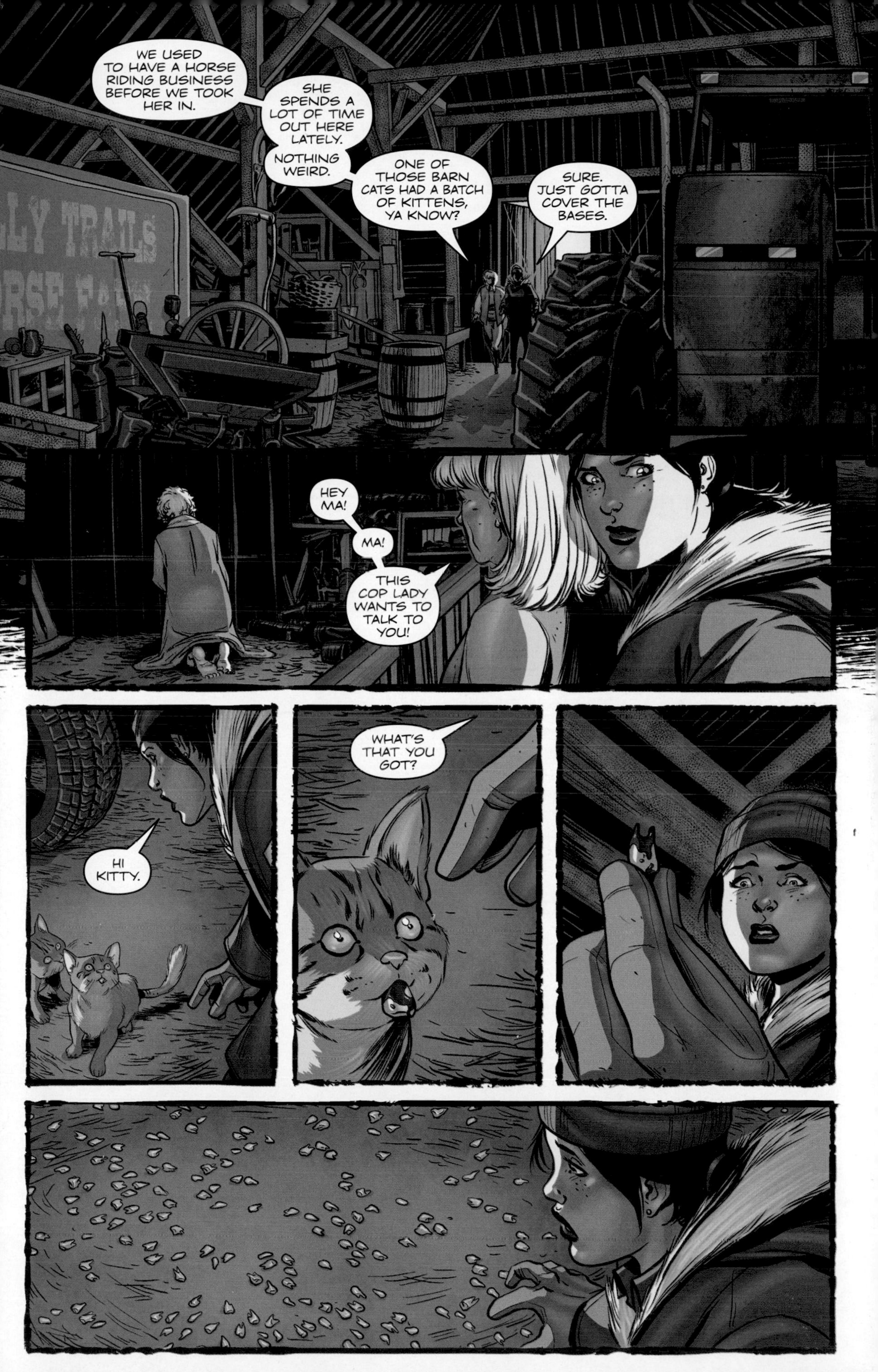
WE USED TO HAVE A HORSE RIDING BUSINESS BEFORE WE TOOK HER IN.
SHE SPENDS A LOT OF TIME OUT HERE LATELY.
NOTHING WEIRD.
ONE OF THOSE BARN CATS HAD A BATCH OF KITTENS, YA KNOW?
SURE. JUST GOTTA COVER THE BASES.
HEY MA!
MA!
THIS COP LADY WANTS TO TALK TO YOU!
HI KITTY.
WHAT'S THAT YOU GOT?

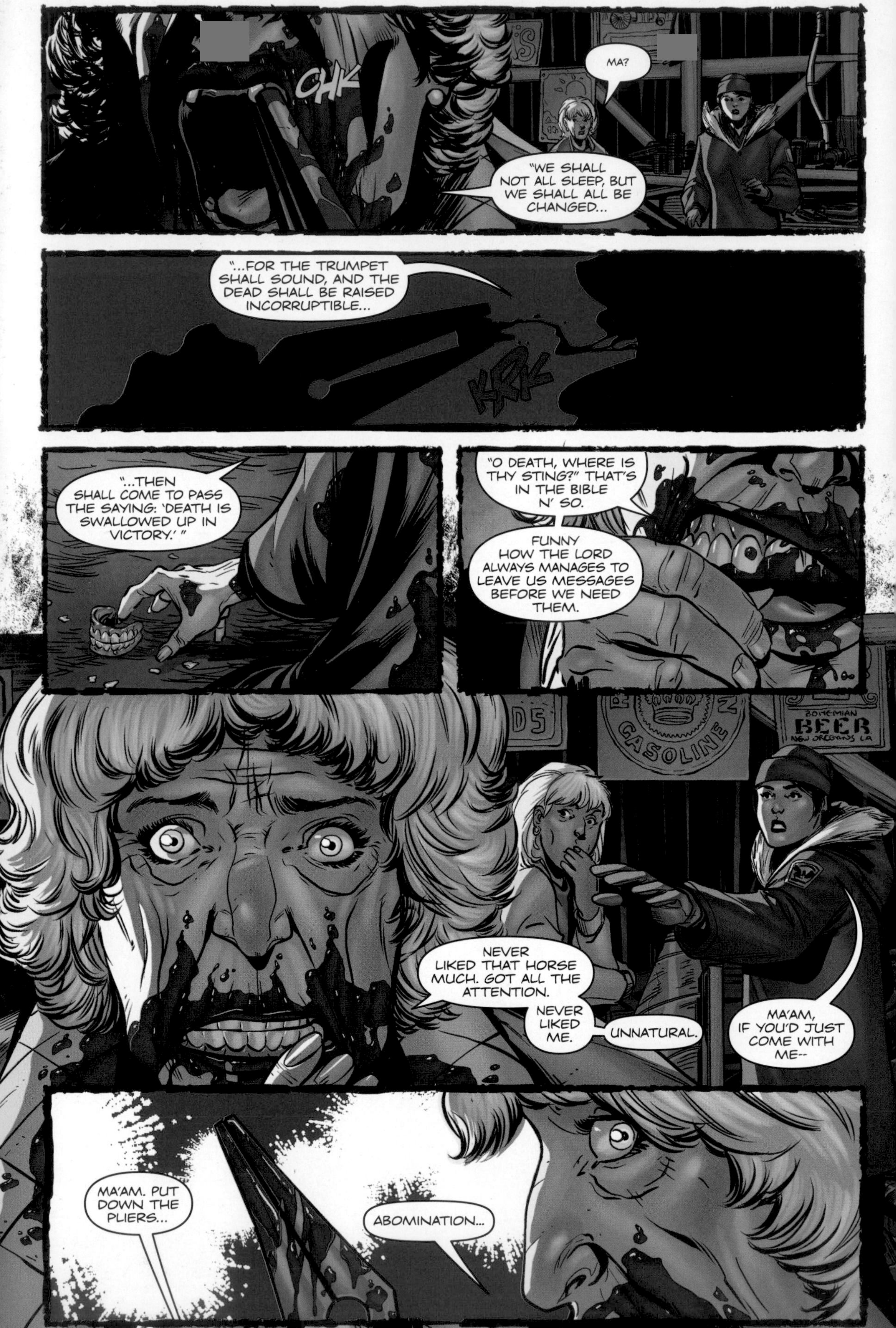
CHK
MA?
"WE SHALL NOT ALL SLEEP, BUT WE SHALL ALL BE CHANGED...
"...FOR THE TRUMPET SHALL SOUND, AND THE DEAD SHALL BE RAISED INCORRUPTIBLE...
KRK
"...THEN SHALL COME TO PASS THE SAYING: 'DEATH IS SWALLOWED UP IN VICTORY.' "
"O DEATH, WHERE IS THY STING?" THAT'S IN THE BIBLE N' SO.
FUNNY HOW THE LORD ALWAYS MANAGES TO LEAVE US MESSAGES BEFORE WE NEED THEM.
D5
GASOLINE
BOHEMIAN
BEER
NEW ORLEANS LA
NEVER LIKED THAT HORSE MUCH. GOT ALL THE ATTENTION.
NEVER LIKED ME.
UNNATURAL.
MA'AM, IF YOU'D JUST COME WITH ME--
MA'AM. PUT DOWN THE PLIERS...
ABOMINATION...

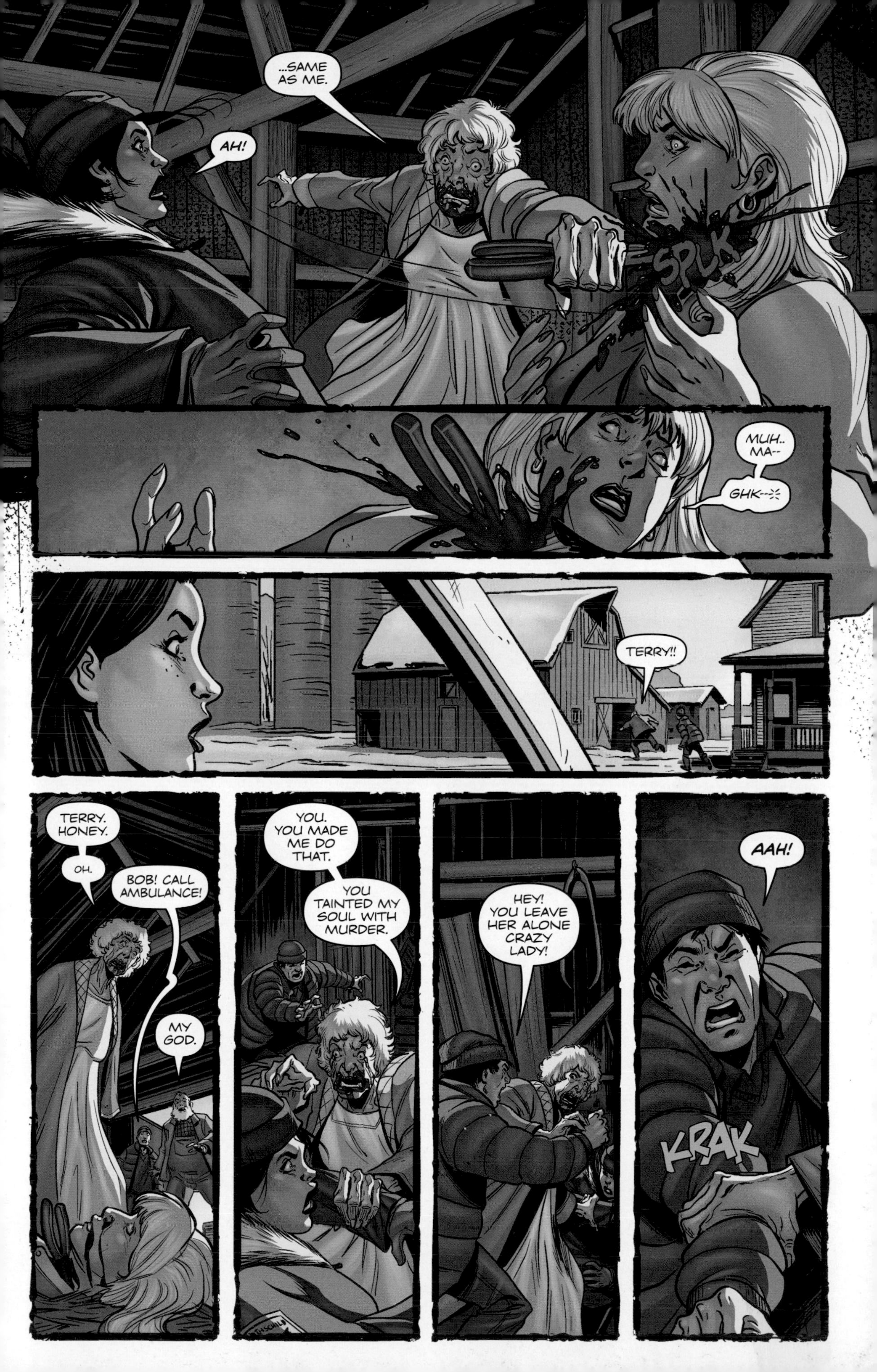
...SAME AS ME.
AH!
SPLK
MUH.. MA--
GHK--
TERRY!!
TERRY. HONEY.
OH.
BOB! CALL AMBULANCE!
MY GOD.
YOU. YOU MADE ME DO THAT.
YOU TAINTED MY SOUL WITH MURDER.
HEY! YOU LEAVE HER ALONE CRAZY LADY!
AAH!
KRAK

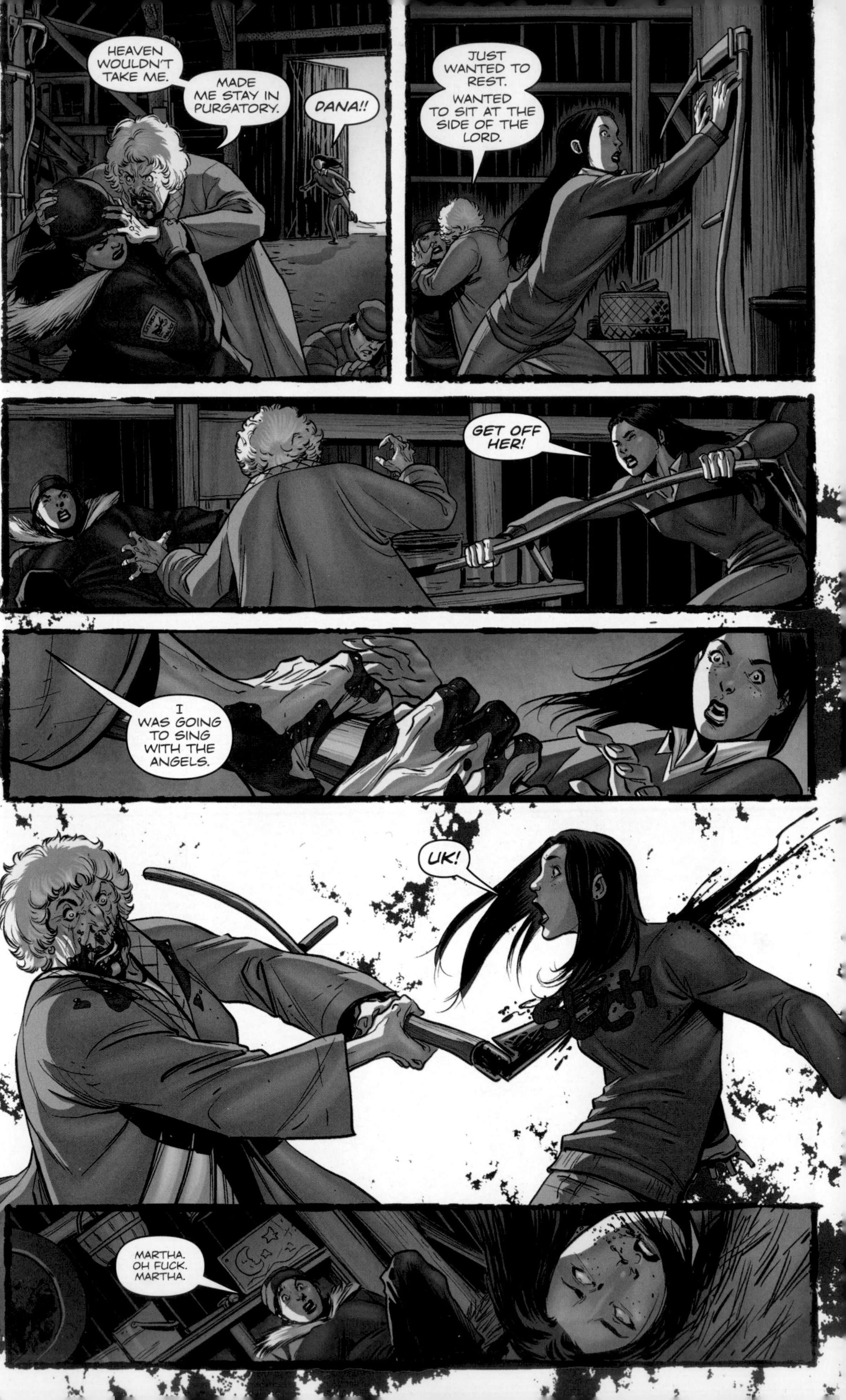
HEAVEN WOULDN'T TAKE ME.
MADE ME STAY IN PURGATORY.
DANA!!
JUST WANTED TO REST.
WANTED TO SIT AT THE SIDE OF THE LORD.
GET OFF HER!
I WAS GOING TO SING WITH THE ANGELS.
UK!
SSCH
MARTHA. OH FUCK. MARTHA.

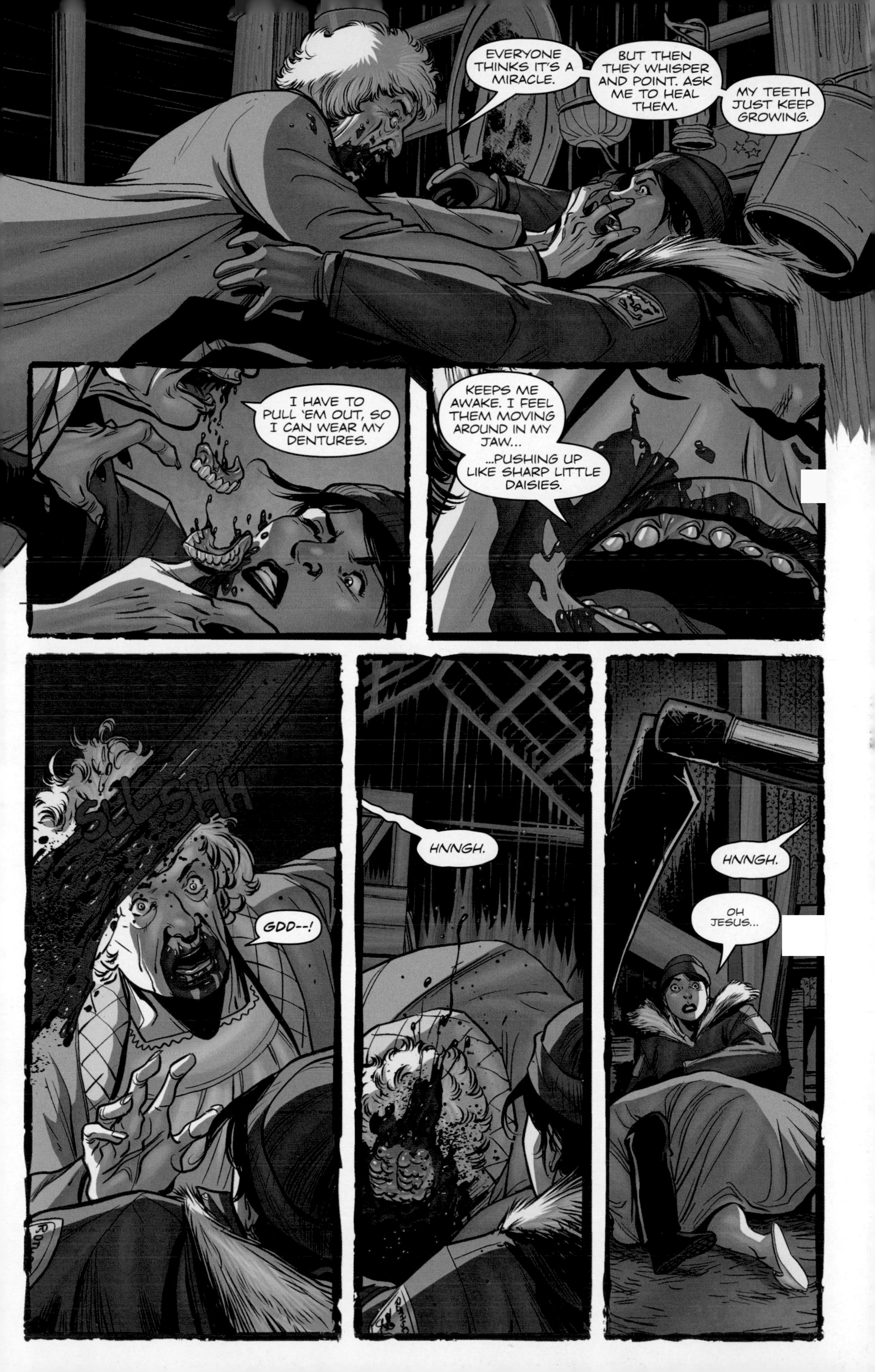
EVERYONE THINKS IT'S A MIRACLE.
BUT THEN THEY WHISPER AND POINT. ASK ME TO HEAL THEM.
MY TEETH JUST KEEP GROWING.
I HAVE TO PULL 'EM OUT, SO I CAN WEAR MY DENTURES.
KEEPS ME AWAKE. I FEEL THEM MOVING AROUND IN MY JAW...
...PUSHING UP LIKE SHARP LITTLE DAISIES.
SHLSHH
GDD--!
HNNGH.
HNNGH.
OH JESUS...

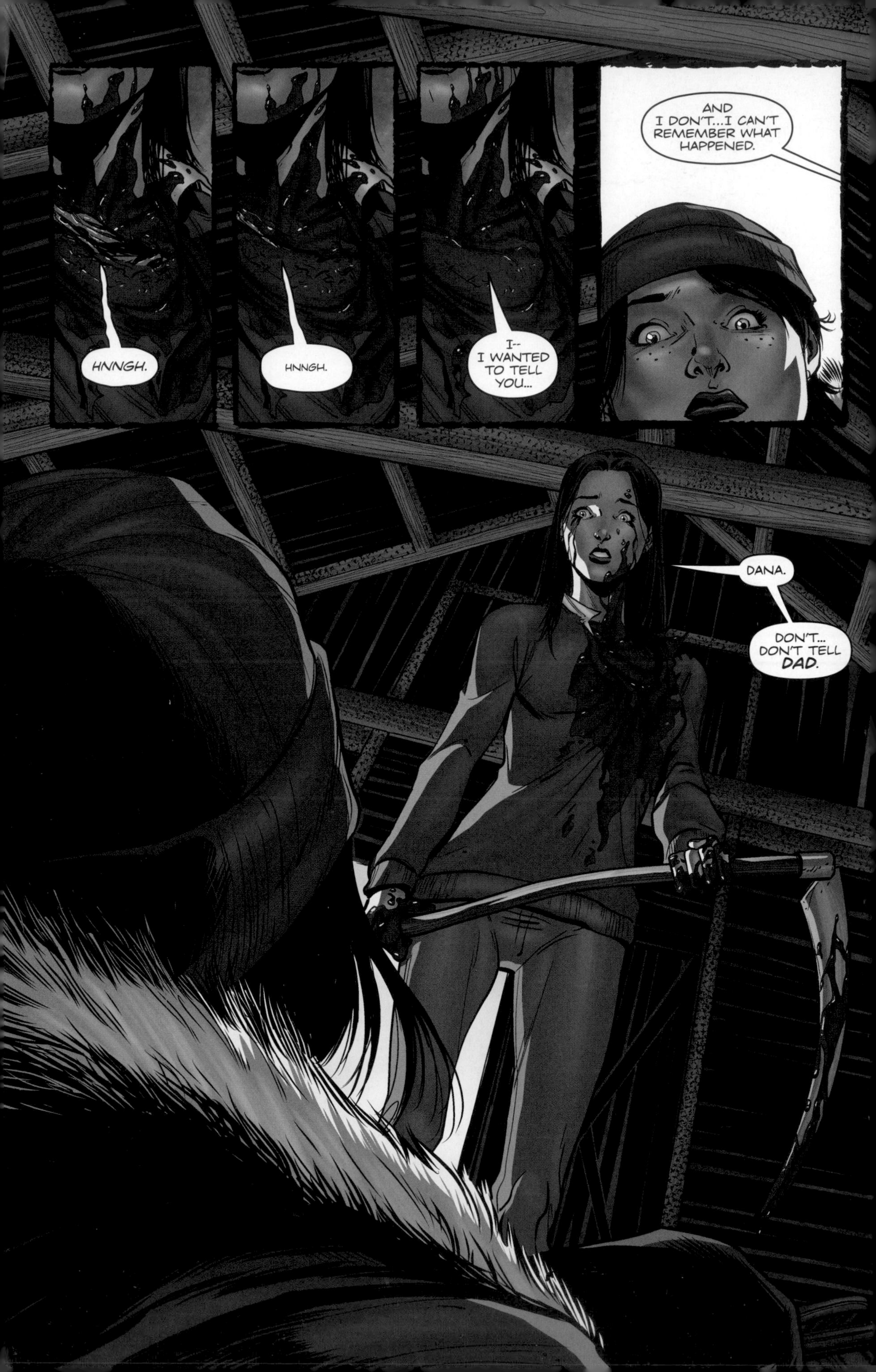
HNNGH.
HNNGH.
I-- I WANTED TO TELL YOU...
AND I DON'T...I CAN'T REMEMBER WHAT HAPPENED.
DANA.
DON'T... DON'T TELL **DAD**.

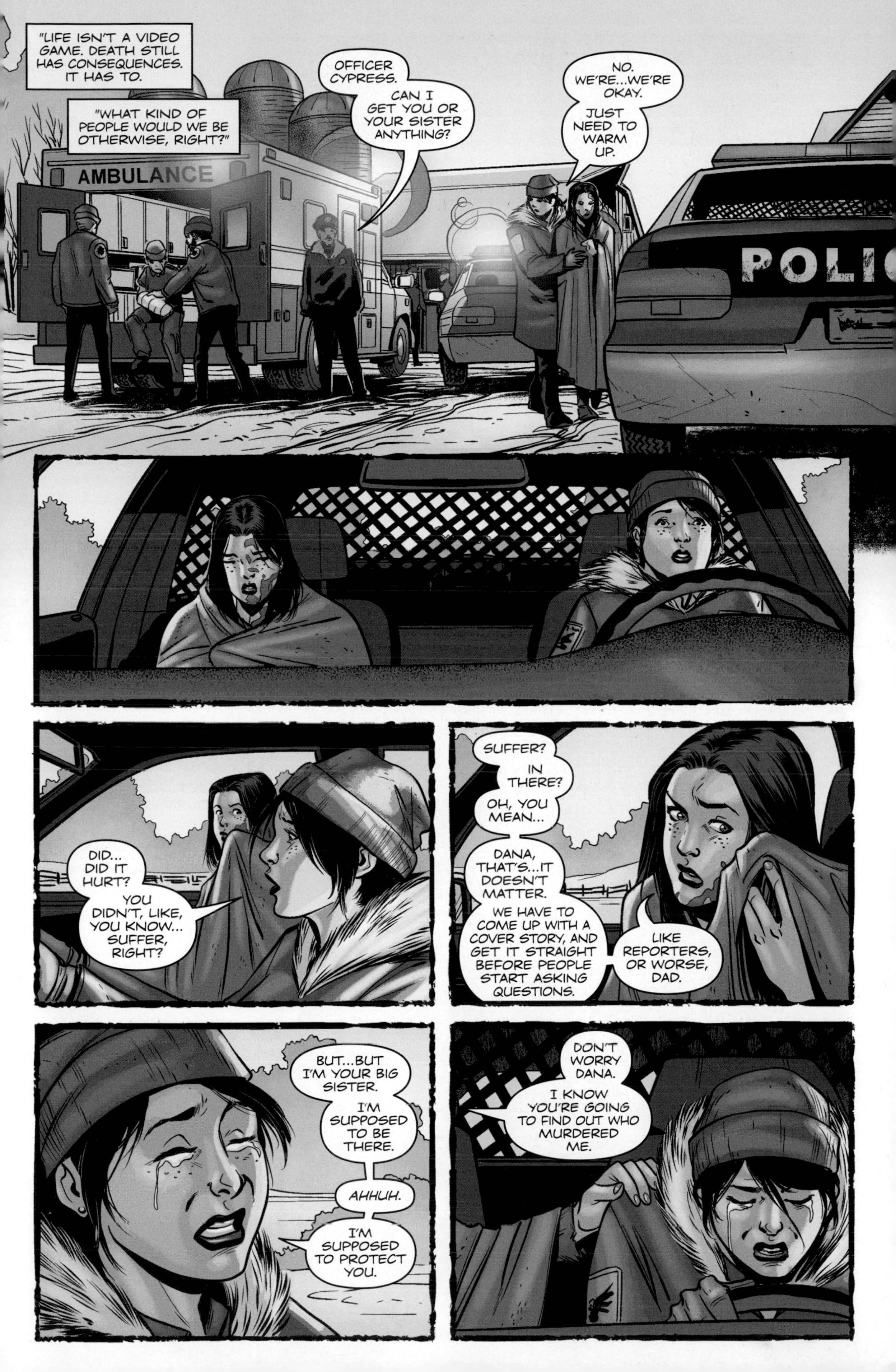
"LIFE ISN'T A VIDEO GAME. DEATH STILL HAS CONSEQUENCES. IT HAS TO.
"WHAT KIND OF PEOPLE WOULD WE BE OTHERWISE, RIGHT?"
AMBULANCE
OFFICER CYPRESS.
CAN I GET YOU OR YOUR SISTER ANYTHING?
NO. WE'RE...WE'RE OKAY.
JUST NEED TO WARM UP.
POLIC
DID... DID IT HURT?
YOU DIDN'T, LIKE, YOU KNOW... SUFFER, RIGHT?
SUFFER?
IN THERE?
OH, YOU MEAN...
DANA, THAT'S...IT DOESN'T MATTER.
WE HAVE TO COME UP WITH A COVER STORY, AND GET IT STRAIGHT BEFORE PEOPLE START ASKING QUESTIONS.
LIKE REPORTERS, OR WORSE, DAD.
BUT...BUT I'M YOUR BIG SISTER.
I'M SUPPOSED TO BE THERE.
AHHUH.
I'M SUPPOSED TO PROTECT YOU.
DON'T WORRY DANA.
I KNOW YOU'RE GOING TO FIND OUT WHO MURDERED ME.

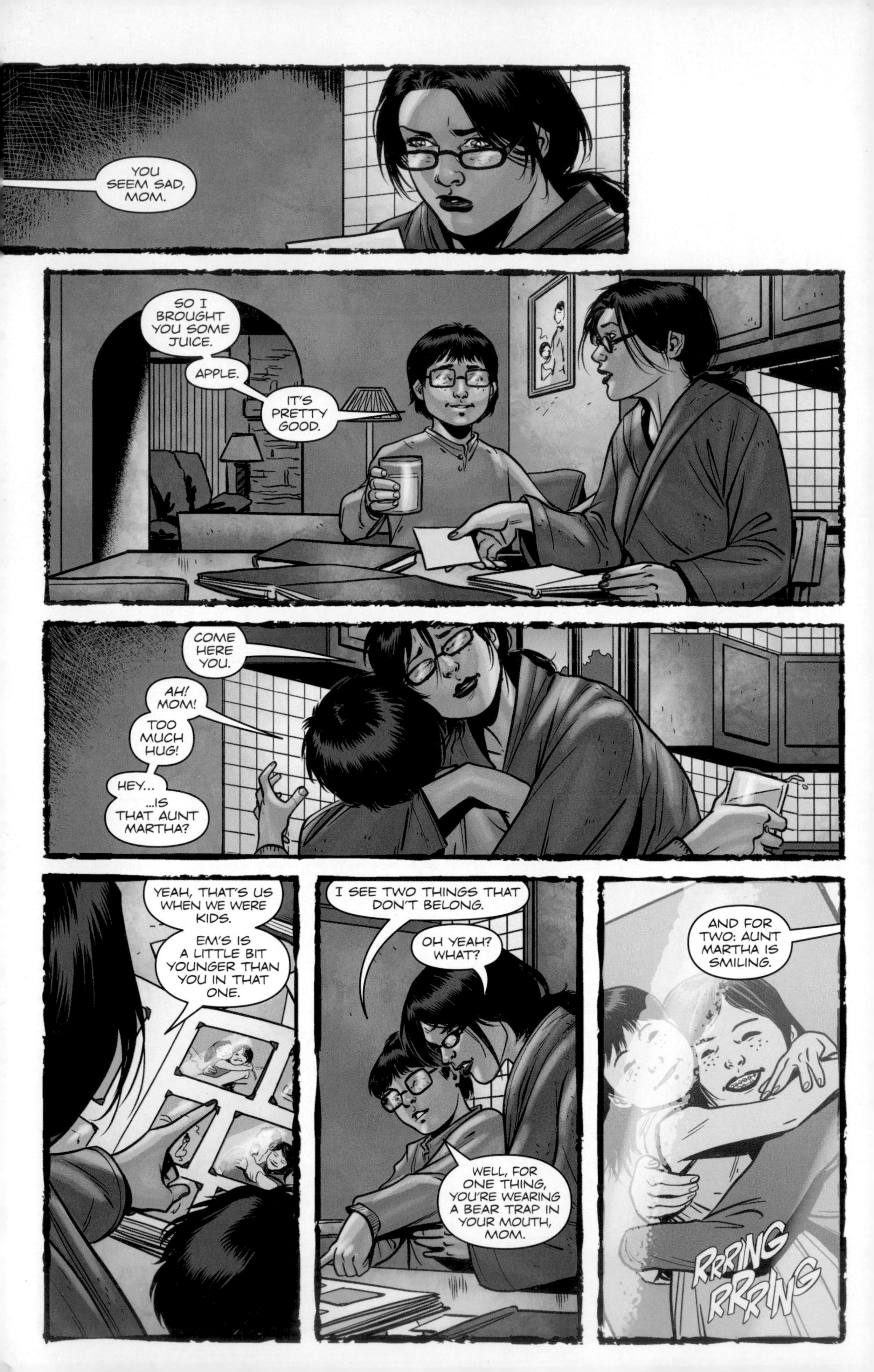
YOU SEEM SAD, MOM.
SO I BROUGHT YOU SOME JUICE.
APPLE.
IT'S PRETTY GOOD.
COME HERE YOU.
AH! MOM!
TOO MUCH HUG!
HEY...
...IS THAT AUNT MARTHA?
YEAH, THAT'S US WHEN WE WERE KIDS.
EM'S IS A LITTLE BIT YOUNGER THAN YOU IN THAT ONE.
I SEE TWO THINGS THAT DON'T BELONG.
OH YEAH? WHAT?
WELL, FOR ONE THING, YOU'RE WEARING A BEAR TRAP IN YOUR MOUTH, MOM.
AND FOR TWO: AUNT MARTHA IS SMILING.
RRRING
RRRING

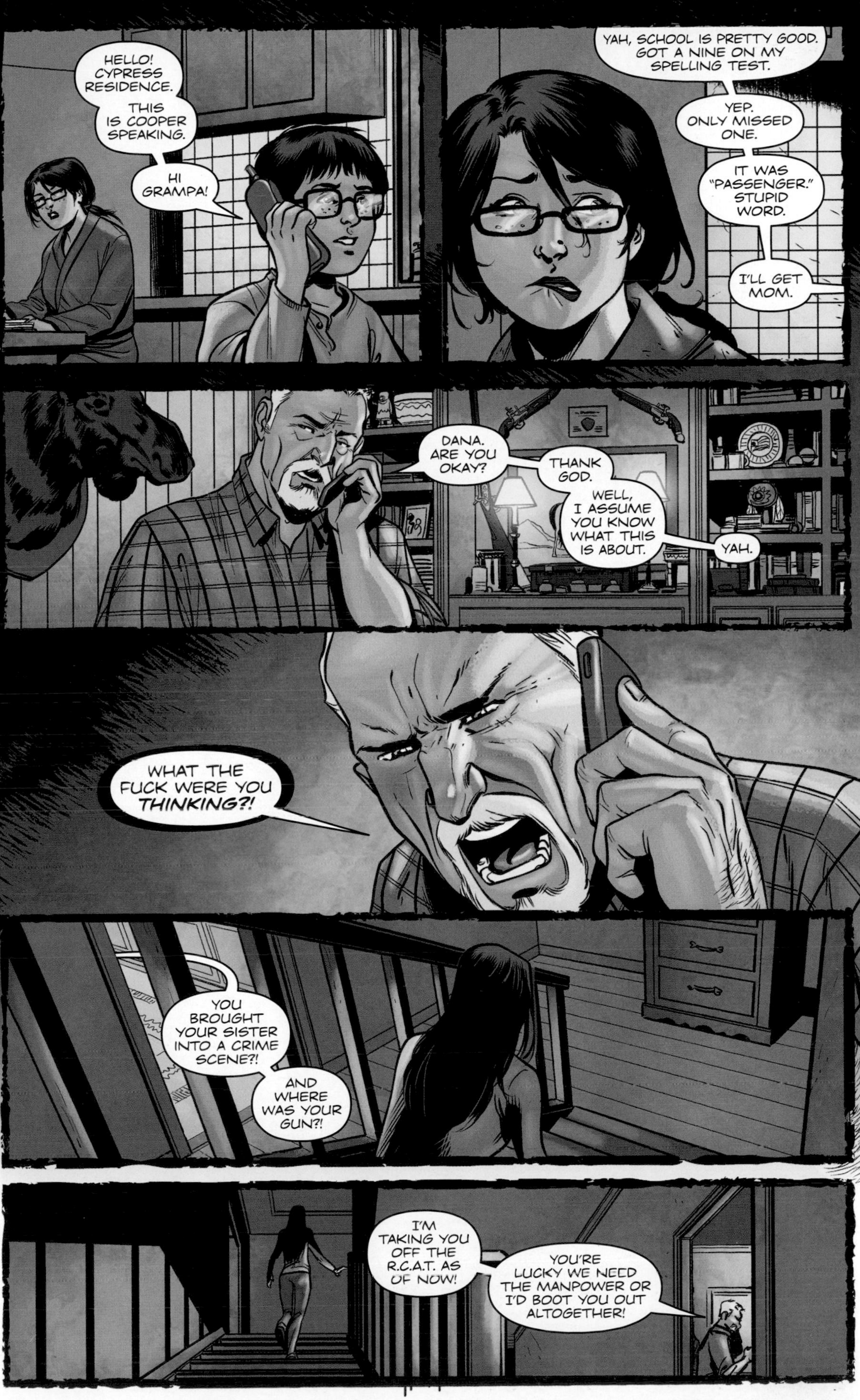
HELLO! CYPRESS RESIDENCE.
THIS IS COOPER SPEAKING.
HI GRAMPA!
YAH, SCHOOL IS PRETTY GOOD. GOT A NINE ON MY SPELLING TEST.
YEP. ONLY MISSED ONE.
IT WAS "PASSENGER." STUPID WORD.
I'LL GET MOM.
DANA. ARE YOU OKAY?
THANK GOD.
WELL, I ASSUME YOU KNOW WHAT THIS IS ABOUT.
YAH.
WHAT THE FUCK WERE YOU THINKING?!
YOU BROUGHT YOUR SISTER INTO A CRIME SCENE?!
AND WHERE WAS YOUR GUN?!
I'M TAKING YOU OFF THE R.C.A.T. AS OF NOW!
YOU'RE LUCKY WE NEED THE MANPOWER OR I'D BOOT YOU OUT ALTOGETHER!

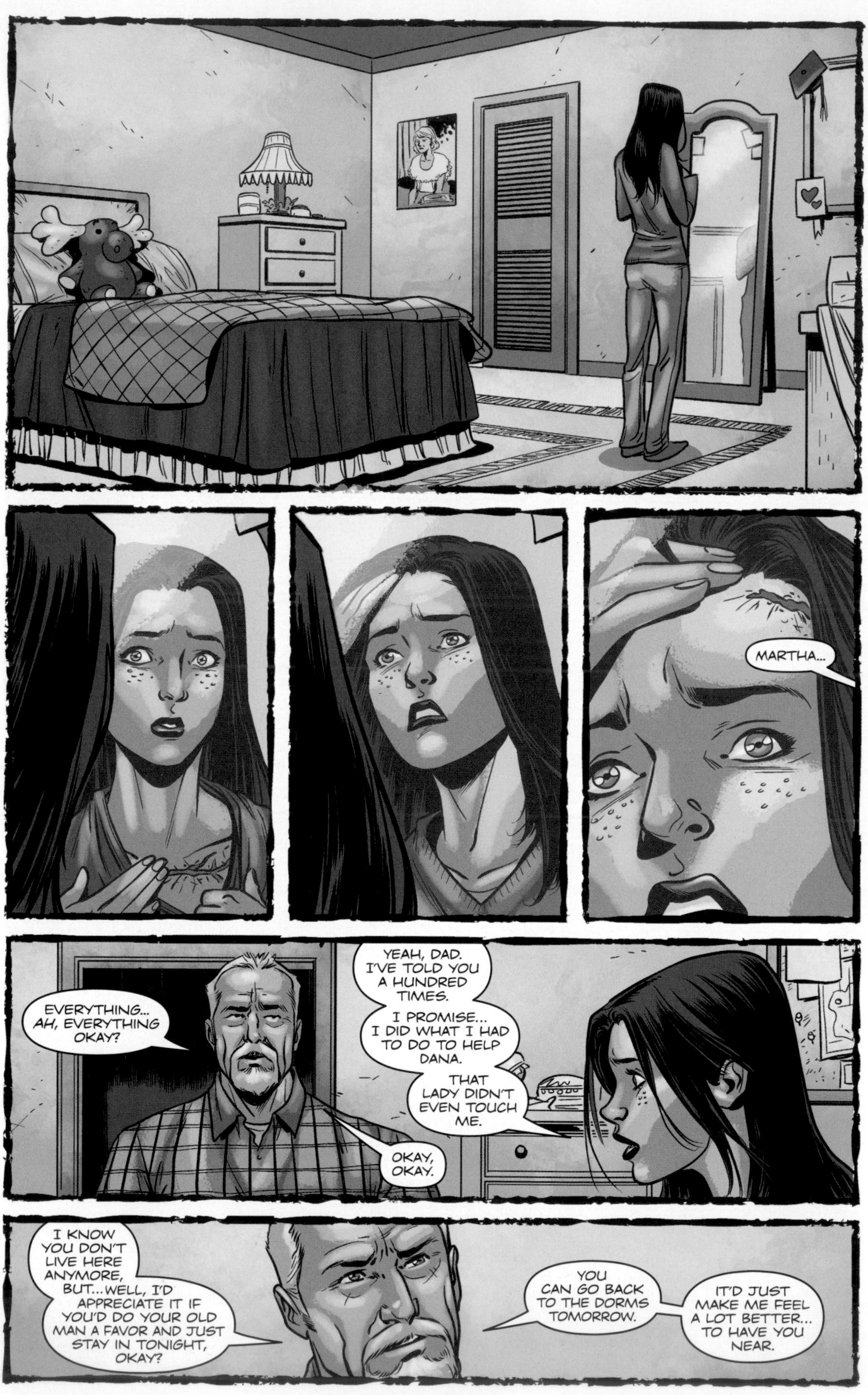
MARTHA...
EVERYTHING... AH, EVERYTHING OKAY?
YEAH, DAD. I'VE TOLD YOU A HUNDRED TIMES.
I PROMISE... I DID WHAT I HAD TO DO TO HELP DANA.
THAT LADY DIDN'T EVEN TOUCH ME.
OKAY, OKAY.
I KNOW YOU DON'T LIVE HERE ANYMORE, BUT...WELL, I'D APPRECIATE IT IF YOU'D DO YOUR OLD MAN A FAVOR AND JUST STAY IN TONIGHT, OKAY?
YOU CAN GO BACK TO THE DORMS TOMORROW.
IT'D JUST MAKE ME FEEL A LOT BETTER... TO HAVE YOU NEAR.

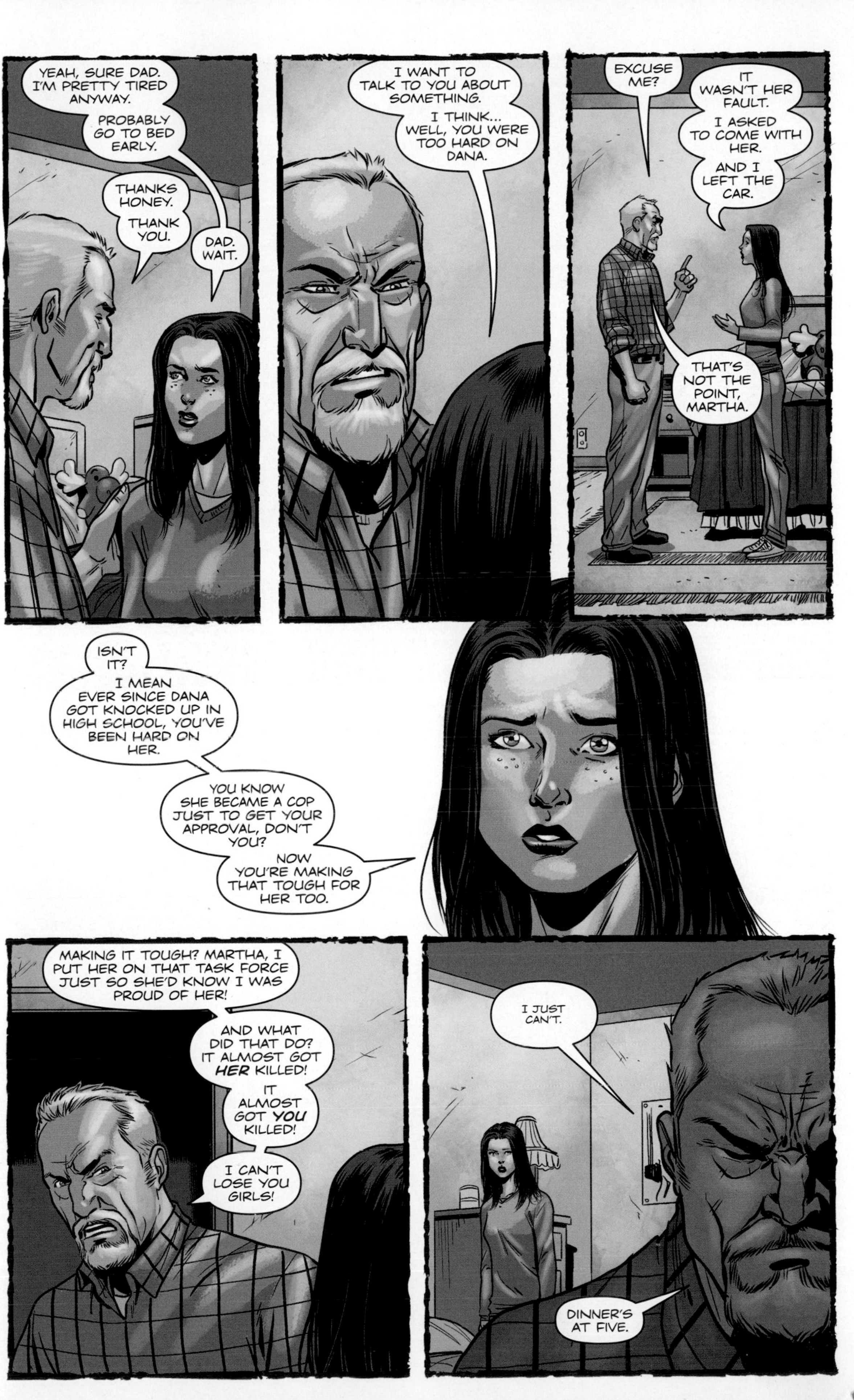
YEAH, SURE DAD. I'M PRETTY TIRED ANYWAY.
PROBABLY GO TO BED EARLY.
THANKS HONEY.
THANK YOU.
DAD. WAIT.
I WANT TO TALK TO YOU ABOUT SOMETHING.
I THINK... WELL, YOU WERE TOO HARD ON DANA.
EXCUSE ME?
IT WASN'T HER FAULT.
I ASKED TO COME WITH HER.
AND I LEFT THE CAR.
THAT'S NOT THE POINT, MARTHA.
ISN'T IT?
I MEAN EVER SINCE DANA GOT KNOCKED UP IN HIGH SCHOOL, YOU'VE BEEN HARD ON HER.
YOU KNOW SHE BECAME A COP JUST TO GET YOUR APPROVAL, DON'T YOU?
NOW YOU'RE MAKING THAT TOUGH FOR HER TOO.
MAKING IT TOUGH? MARTHA, I PUT HER ON THAT TASK FORCE JUST SO SHE'D KNOW I WAS PROUD OF HER!
AND WHAT DID THAT DO? IT ALMOST GOT **HER** KILLED!
IT ALMOST GOT **YOU** KILLED!
I CAN'T LOSE YOU GIRLS!
I JUST CAN'T.
DINNER'S AT FIVE.

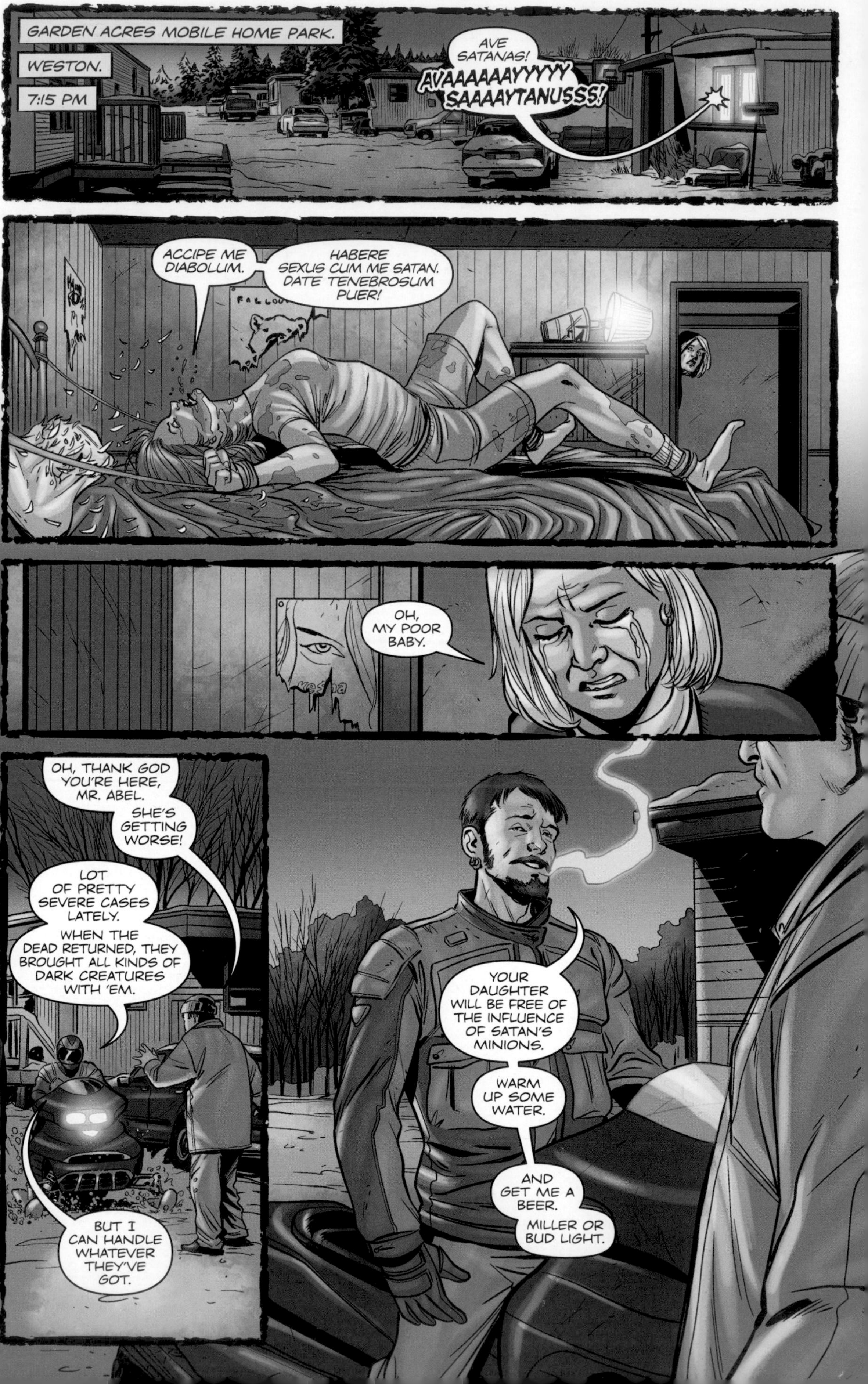
GARDEN ACRES MOBILE HOME PARK.
WESTON.
7:15 PM
AVE SATANAS!
AVAAAAAAYYYYY SAAAAYTANUSSS!
ACCIPE ME DIABOLUM.
HABERE SEXUS CUM ME SATAN. DATE TENEBROSUM PUER!
OH, MY POOR BABY.
OH, THANK GOD YOU'RE HERE, MR. ABEL.
SHE'S GETTING WORSE!
LOT OF PRETTY SEVERE CASES LATELY.
WHEN THE DEAD RETURNED, THEY BROUGHT ALL KINDS OF DARK CREATURES WITH 'EM.
BUT I CAN HANDLE WHATEVER THEY'VE GOT.
YOUR DAUGHTER WILL BE FREE OF THE INFLUENCE OF SATAN'S MINIONS.
WARM UP SOME WATER.
AND GET ME A BEER.
MILLER OR BUD LIGHT.

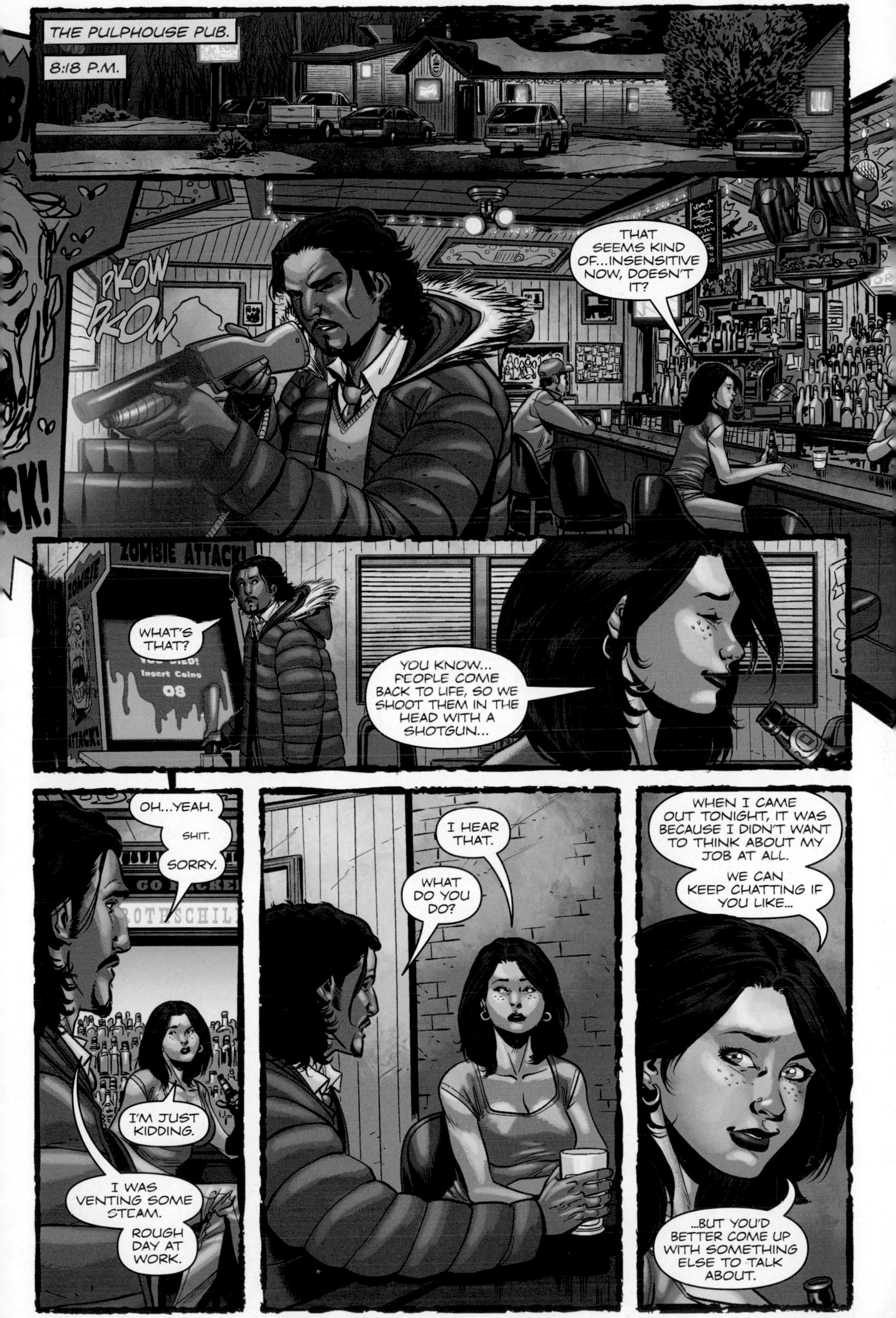
THE PULPHOUSE PUB.
8:18 P.M.
PKOW PKOW
THAT SEEMS KIND OF...INSENSITIVE NOW, DOESN'T IT?
ZOMBIE ATTACK!
WHAT'S THAT?
Insert Coins
08
YOU KNOW... PEOPLE COME BACK TO LIFE, SO WE SHOOT THEM IN THE HEAD WITH A SHOTGUN...
OH...YEAH.
SHIT.
SORRY.
I'M JUST KIDDING.
I WAS VENTING SOME STEAM.
ROUGH DAY AT WORK.
I HEAR THAT.
WHAT DO YOU DO?
WHEN I CAME OUT TONIGHT, IT WAS BECAUSE I DIDN'T WANT TO THINK ABOUT MY JOB AT ALL.
WE CAN KEEP CHATTING IF YOU LIKE...
...BUT YOU'D BETTER COME UP WITH SOMETHING ELSE TO TALK ABOUT.

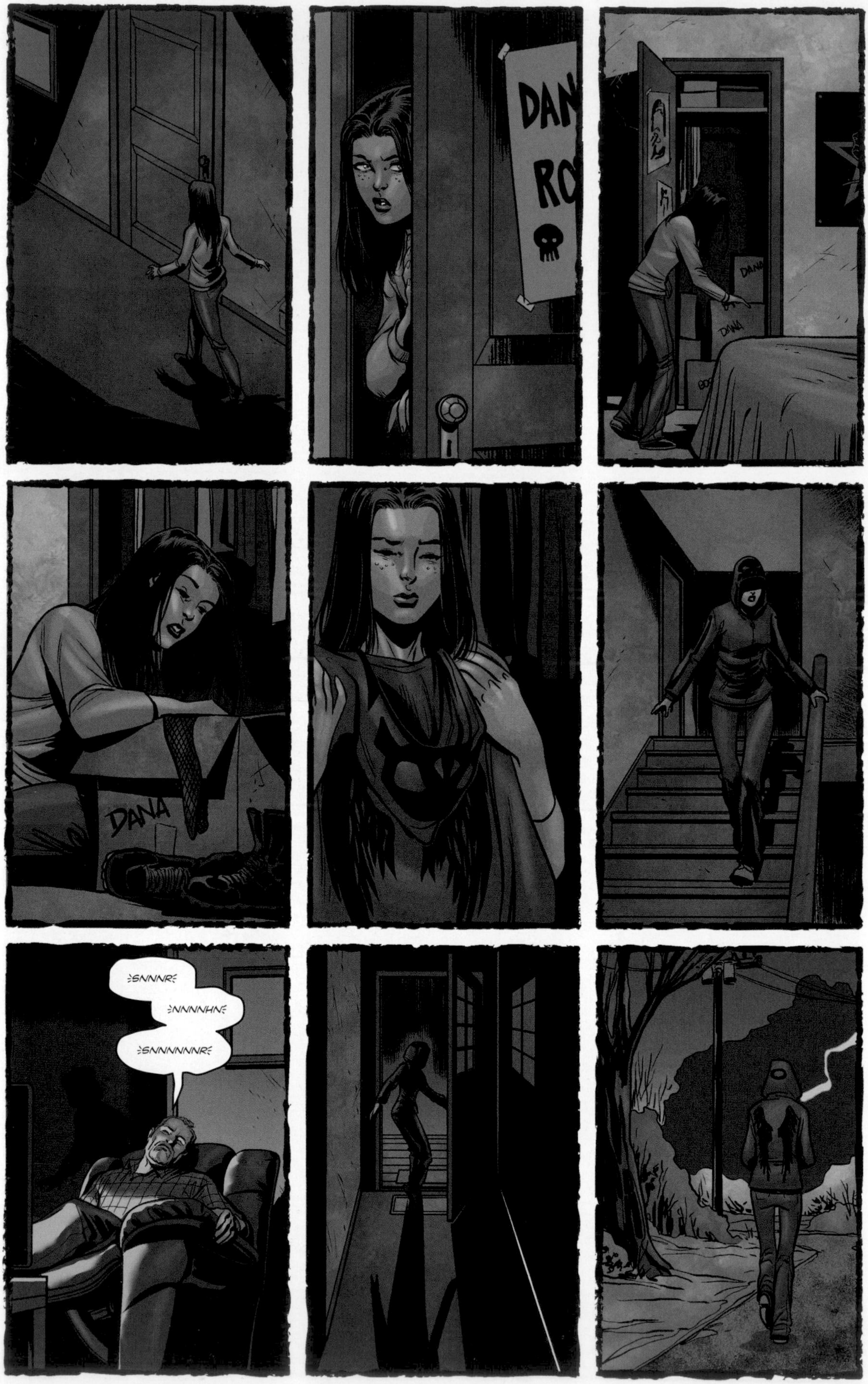
DAN
RO
DANA
DANA
DANA
SNNNR
NNNNHN
SNNNNNNR

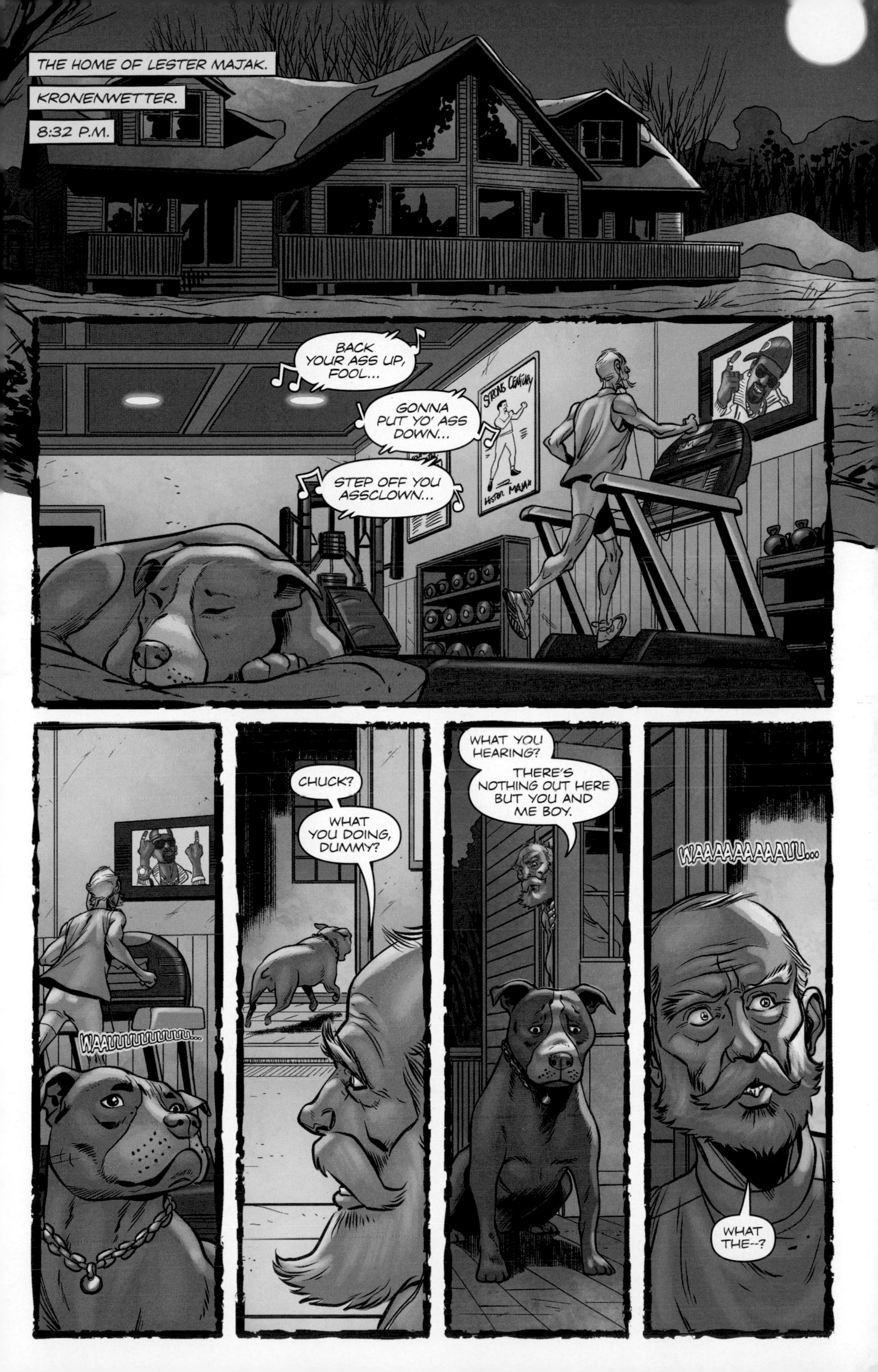
THE HOME OF LESTER MAJAK.
KRONENWETTER.
8:32 P.M.
BACK YOUR ASS UP, FOOL...
GONNA PUT YO' ASS DOWN...
STEP OFF YOU ASSCLOWN...
STRONG CENTURY
LESTER MAJAK
WAAUUUUUUUUUU...
CHUCK?
WHAT YOU DOING, DUMMY?
WHAT YOU HEARING?
THERE'S NOTHING OUT HERE BUT YOU AND ME BOY.
WAAAAAAAAAUU...
WHAT THE--?

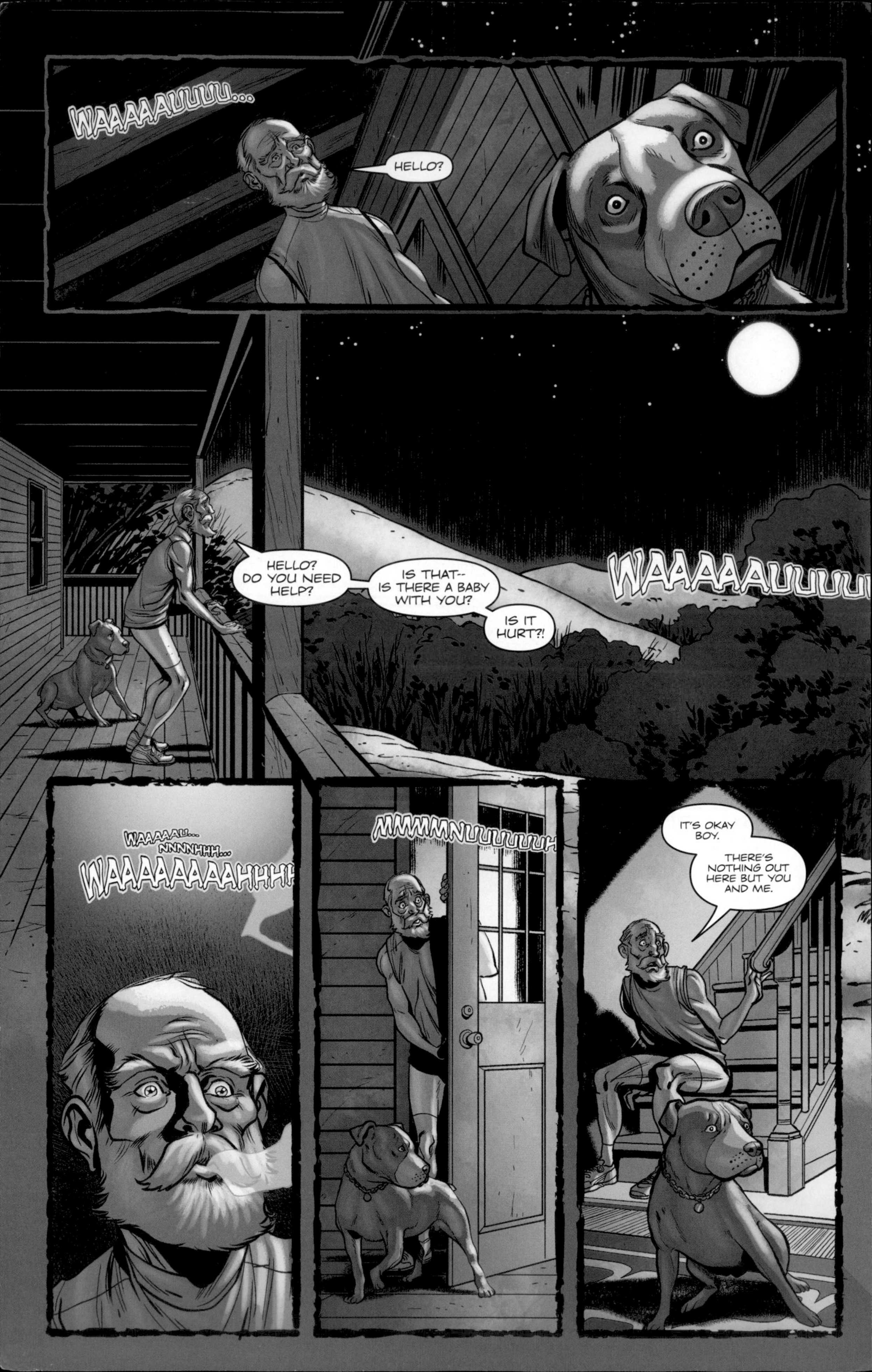
WAAAAUUUU...
HELLO?
HELLO? DO YOU NEED HELP?
IS THAT-- IS THERE A BABY WITH YOU?
IS IT HURT?!
WAAAAAUUUU
WAAAAAU... NNNNHHH...
WAAAAAAAAHHHH
MMMMNUUUUUUH
IT'S OKAY BOY.
THERE'S NOTHING OUT HERE BUT YOU AND ME.

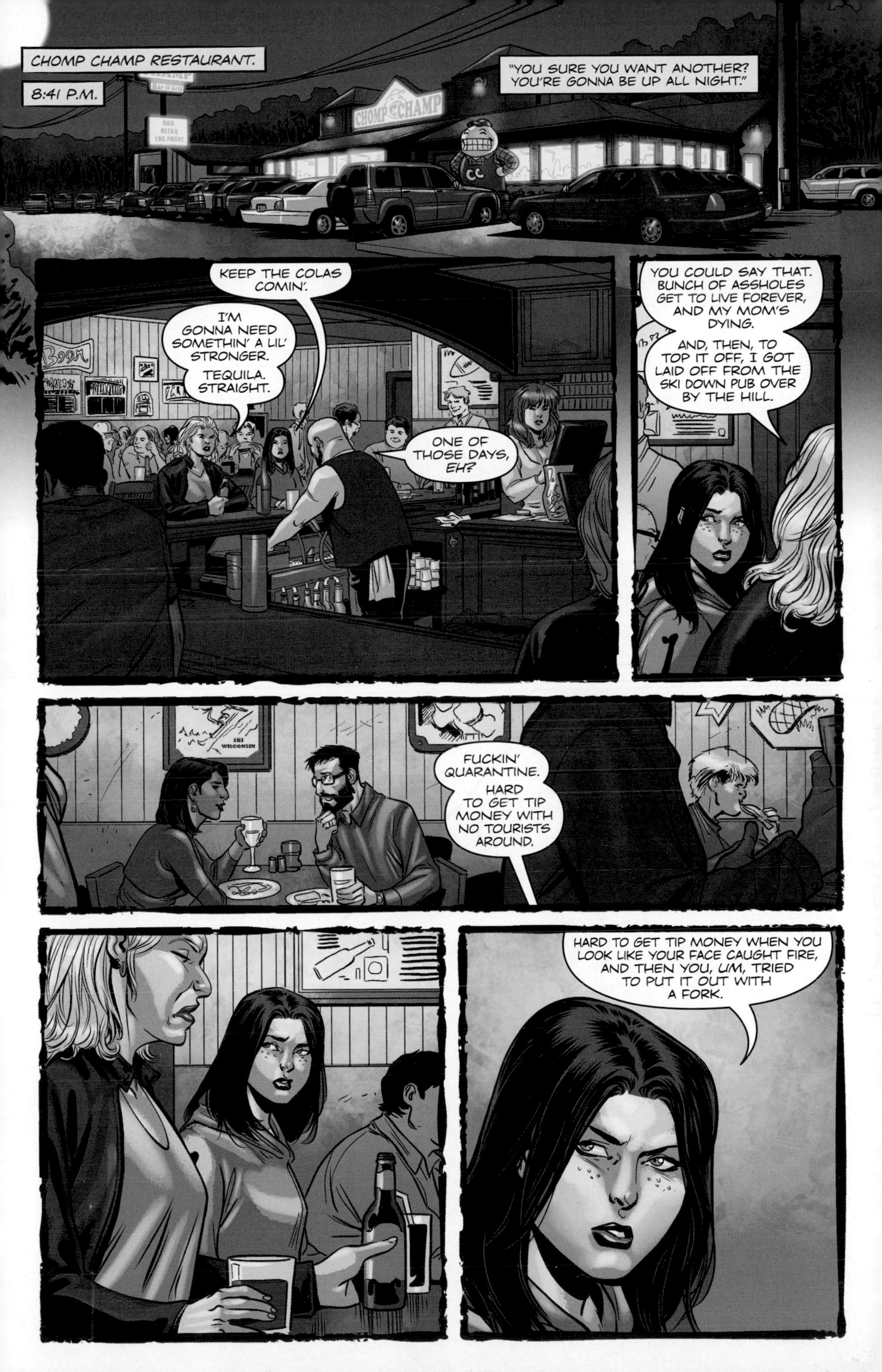

CHOMP CHAMP RESTAURANT.
8:41 P.M.
"YOU SURE YOU WANT ANOTHER? YOU'RE GONNA BE UP ALL NIGHT."
CHOMP CHAMP
GOD BLESS THE PACK!
KEEP THE COLAS COMIN'.
I'M GONNA NEED SOMETHIN' A LIL' STRONGER.
TEQUILA. STRAIGHT.
ONE OF THOSE DAYS, EH?
YOU COULD SAY THAT. BUNCH OF ASSHOLES GET TO LIVE FOREVER, AND MY MOM'S DYING.
AND, THEN, TO TOP IT OFF, I GOT LAID OFF FROM THE SKI DOWN PUB OVER BY THE HILL.
SKI WISCONSIN
FUCKIN' QUARANTINE.
HARD TO GET TIP MONEY WITH NO TOURISTS AROUND.
HARD TO GET TIP MONEY WHEN YOU LOOK LIKE YOUR FACE CAUGHT FIRE, AND THEN YOU, UM, TRIED TO PUT IT OUT WITH A FORK.

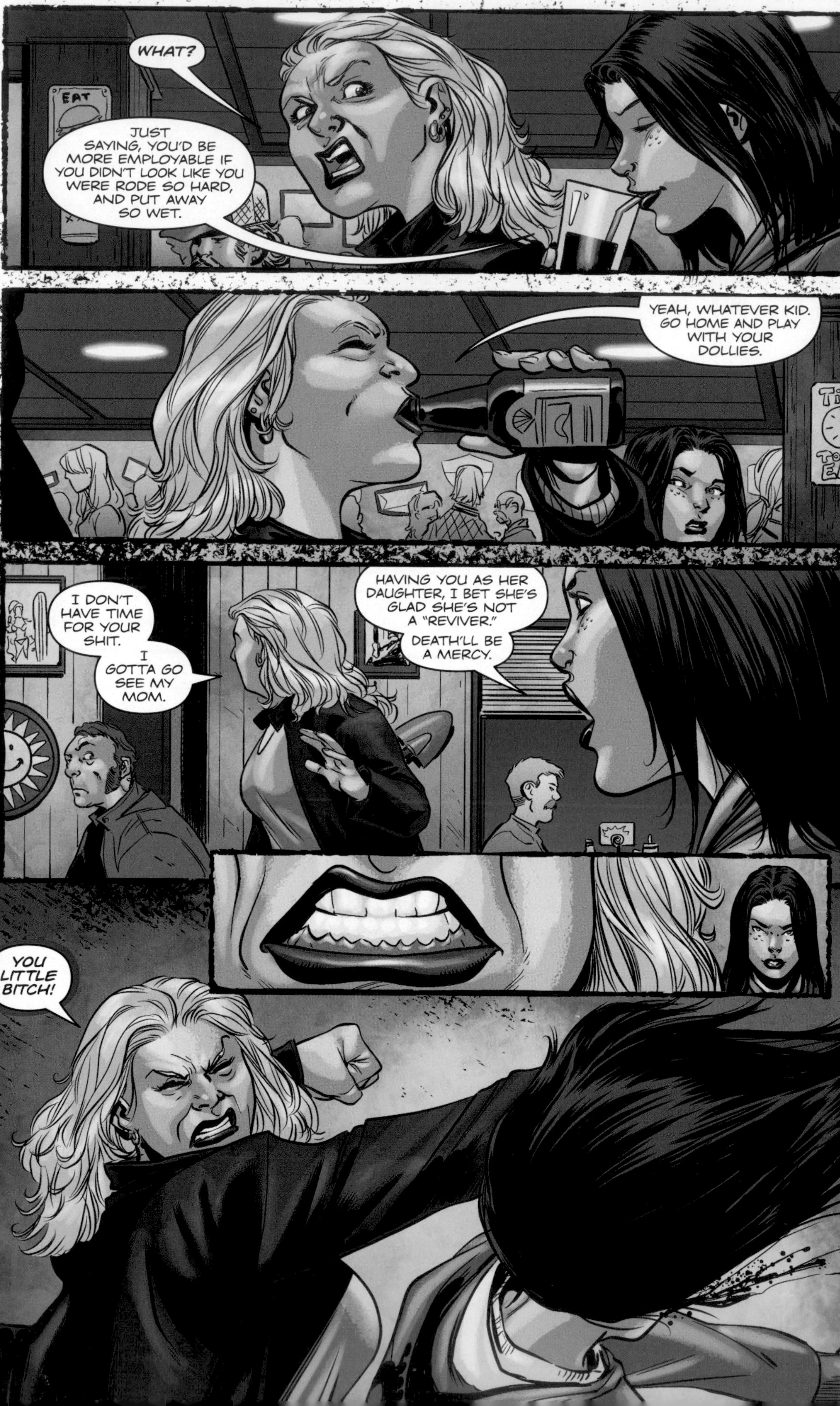
WHAT?
JUST SAYING, YOU'D BE MORE EMPLOYABLE IF YOU DIDN'T LOOK LIKE YOU WERE RODE SO HARD, AND PUT AWAY SO WET.
EAT
YEAH, WHATEVER KID. GO HOME AND PLAY WITH YOUR DOLLIES.
I DON'T HAVE TIME FOR YOUR SHIT.
I GOTTA GO SEE MY MOM.
HAVING YOU AS HER DAUGHTER, I BET SHE'S GLAD SHE'S NOT A "REVIVER."
DEATH'LL BE A MERCY.
YOU LITTLE BITCH!

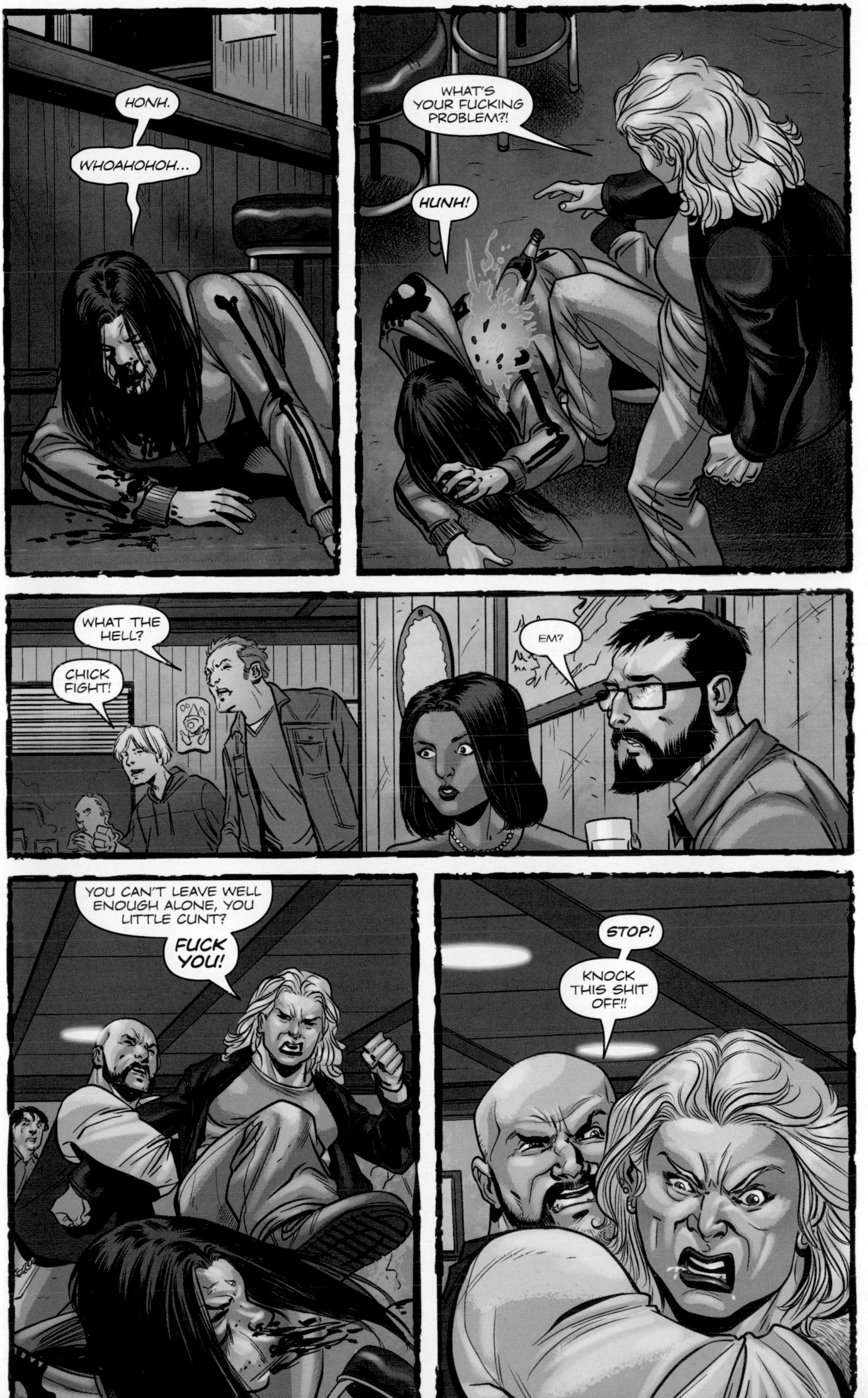
HONH.
WHOAHOHOH...
WHAT'S YOUR FUCKING PROBLEM?!
HUNH!
WHAT THE HELL?
CHICK FIGHT!
EM?
YOU CAN'T LEAVE WELL ENOUGH ALONE, YOU LITTLE CUNT?
FUCK YOU!
STOP!
KNOCK THIS SHIT OFF!!

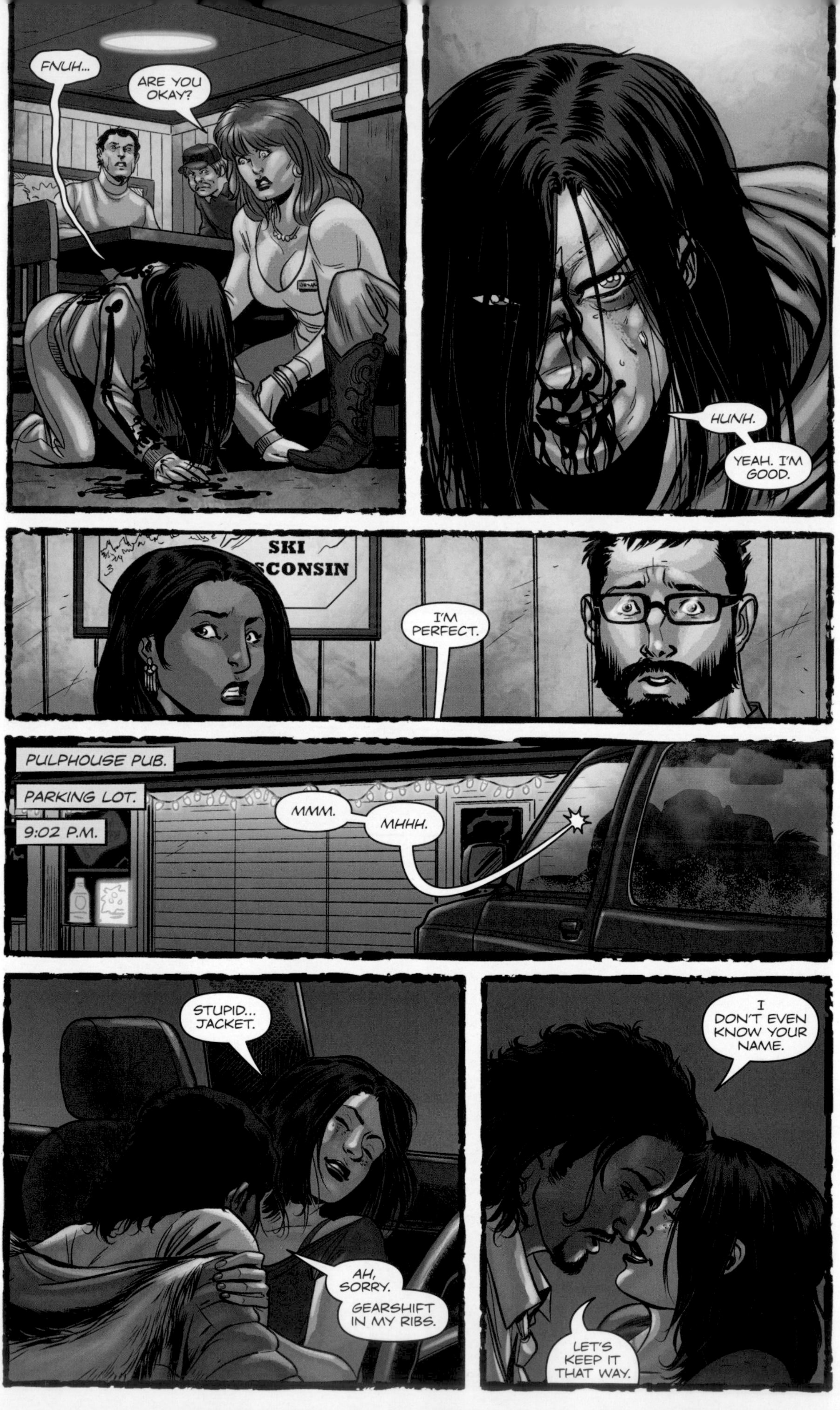
FNUH...
ARE YOU OKAY?
HUNH.
YEAH. I'M GOOD.
SKI
SCONSIN
I'M PERFECT.
PULPHOUSE PUB.
PARKING LOT.
9:02 P.M.
MMM.
MHHH.
STUPID... JACKET.
AH, SORRY.
GEARSHIFT IN MY RIBS.
I DON'T EVEN KNOW YOUR NAME.
LET'S KEEP IT THAT WAY.

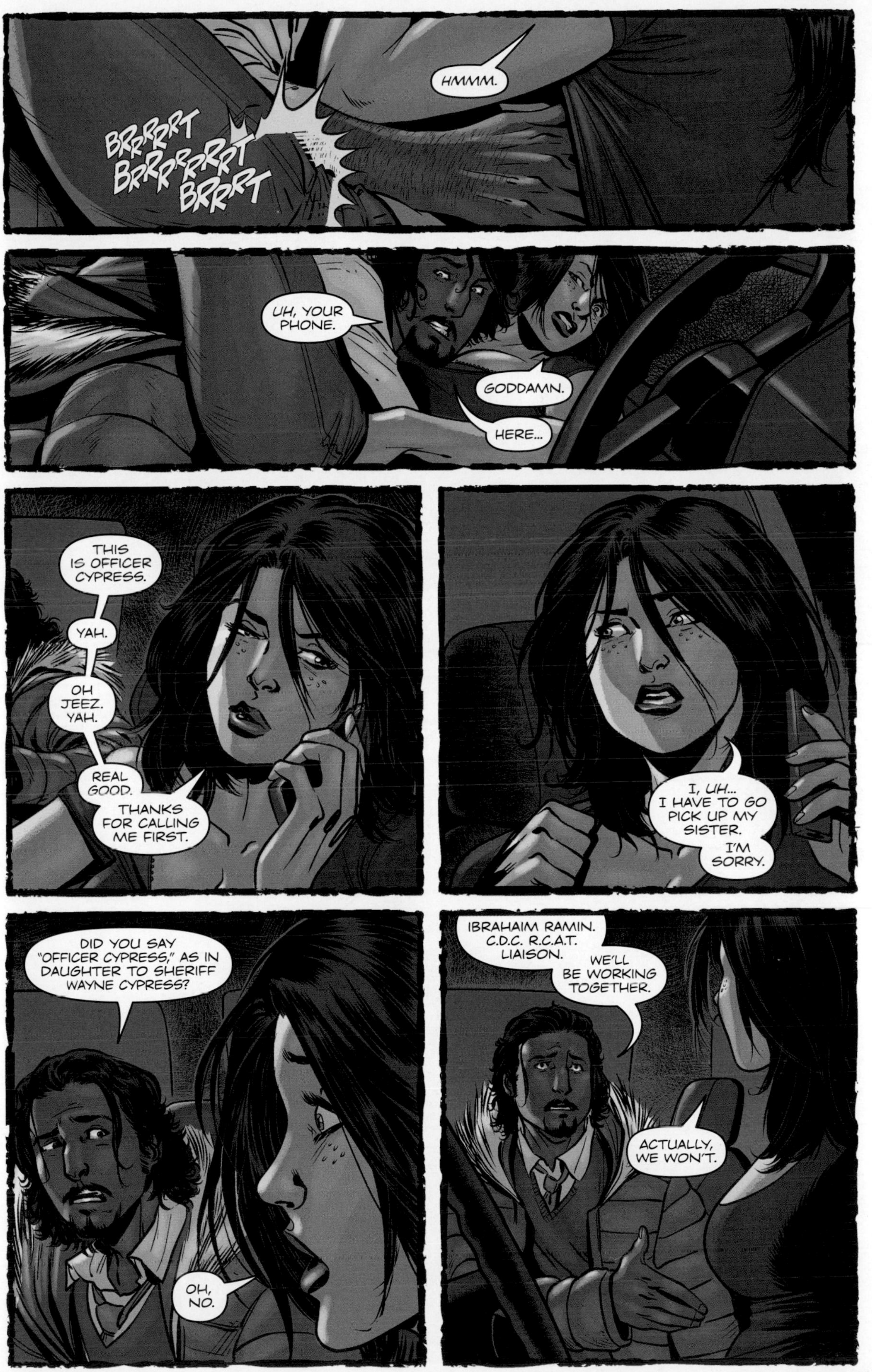
HMMM.
BRRRRRT BRRRRRRRT BRRRRT
UH, YOUR PHONE.
GODDAMN.
HERE...
THIS IS OFFICER CYPRESS.
YAH.
OH JEEZ. YAH.
REAL GOOD.
THANKS FOR CALLING ME FIRST.
I, UH... I HAVE TO GO PICK UP MY SISTER.
I'M SORRY.
DID YOU SAY "OFFICER CYPRESS," AS IN DAUGHTER TO SHERIFF WAYNE CYPRESS?
OH, NO.
IBRAHAIM RAMIN. C.D.C. R.C.A.T. LIAISON.
WE'LL BE WORKING TOGETHER.
ACTUALLY, WE WON'T.

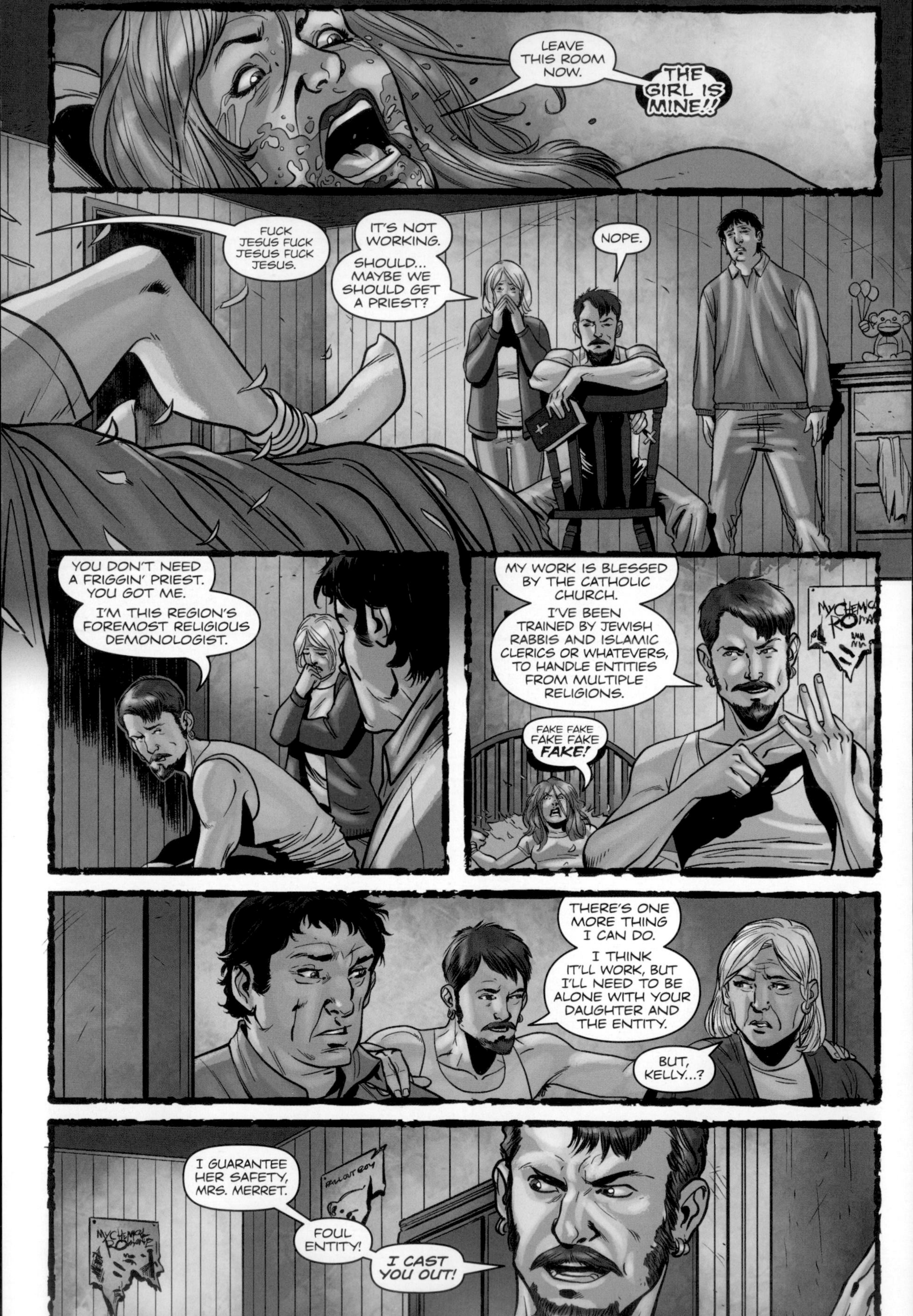
LEAVE THIS ROOM NOW.
THE GIRL IS MINE!!
FUCK JESUS FUCK JESUS FUCK JESUS.
IT'S NOT WORKING.
SHOULD... MAYBE WE SHOULD GET A PRIEST?
NOPE.
YOU DON'T NEED A FRIGGIN' PRIEST. YOU GOT ME.
I'M THIS REGION'S FOREMOST RELIGIOUS DEMONOLOGIST.
MY WORK IS BLESSED BY THE CATHOLIC CHURCH.
I'VE BEEN TRAINED BY JEWISH RABBIS AND ISLAMIC CLERICS OR WHATEVERS, TO HANDLE ENTITIES FROM MULTIPLE RELIGIONS.
FAKE FAKE FAKE FAKE FAKE!
THERE'S ONE MORE THING I CAN DO.
I THINK IT'LL WORK, BUT I'LL NEED TO BE ALONE WITH YOUR DAUGHTER AND THE ENTITY.
BUT, KELLY...?
I GUARANTEE HER SAFETY, MRS. MERRET.
FOUL ENTITY!
I CAST YOU OUT!

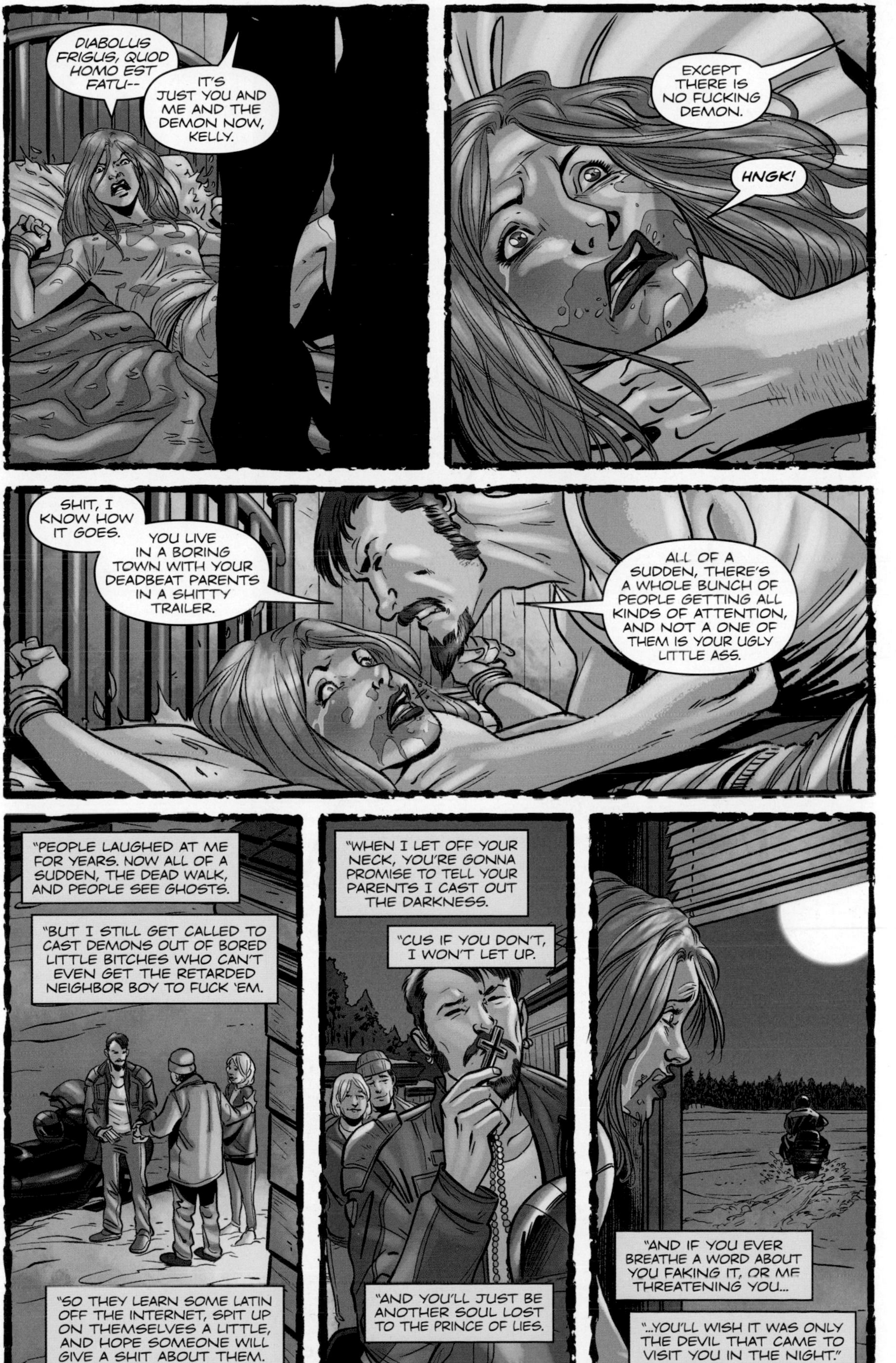

DIABOLUS FRIGUS, QUOD HOMO EST FATU--
IT'S JUST YOU AND ME AND THE DEMON NOW, KELLY.
EXCEPT THERE IS NO FUCKING DEMON.
HNGK!
SHIT, I KNOW HOW IT GOES.
YOU LIVE IN A BORING TOWN WITH YOUR DEADBEAT PARENTS IN A SHITTY TRAILER.
ALL OF A SUDDEN, THERE'S A WHOLE BUNCH OF PEOPLE GETTING ALL KINDS OF ATTENTION, AND NOT A ONE OF THEM IS YOUR UGLY LITTLE ASS.
"PEOPLE LAUGHED AT ME FOR YEARS. NOW ALL OF A SUDDEN, THE DEAD WALK, AND PEOPLE SEE GHOSTS.
"BUT I STILL GET CALLED TO CAST DEMONS OUT OF BORED LITTLE BITCHES WHO CAN'T EVEN GET THE RETARDED NEIGHBOR BOY TO FUCK 'EM.
"SO THEY LEARN SOME LATIN OFF THE INTERNET, SPIT UP ON THEMSELVES A LITTLE, AND HOPE SOMEONE WILL GIVE A SHIT ABOUT THEM.
"WHEN I LET OFF YOUR NECK, YOU'RE GONNA PROMISE TO TELL YOUR PARENTS I CAST OUT THE DARKNESS.
"CUS IF YOU DON'T, I WON'T LET UP.
"AND YOU'LL JUST BE ANOTHER SOUL LOST TO THE PRINCE OF LIES.
"AND IF YOU EVER BREATHE A WORD ABOUT YOU FAKING IT, OR ME THREATENING YOU...
"...YOU'LL WISH IT WAS ONLY THE DEVIL THAT CAME TO VISIT YOU IN THE NIGHT."

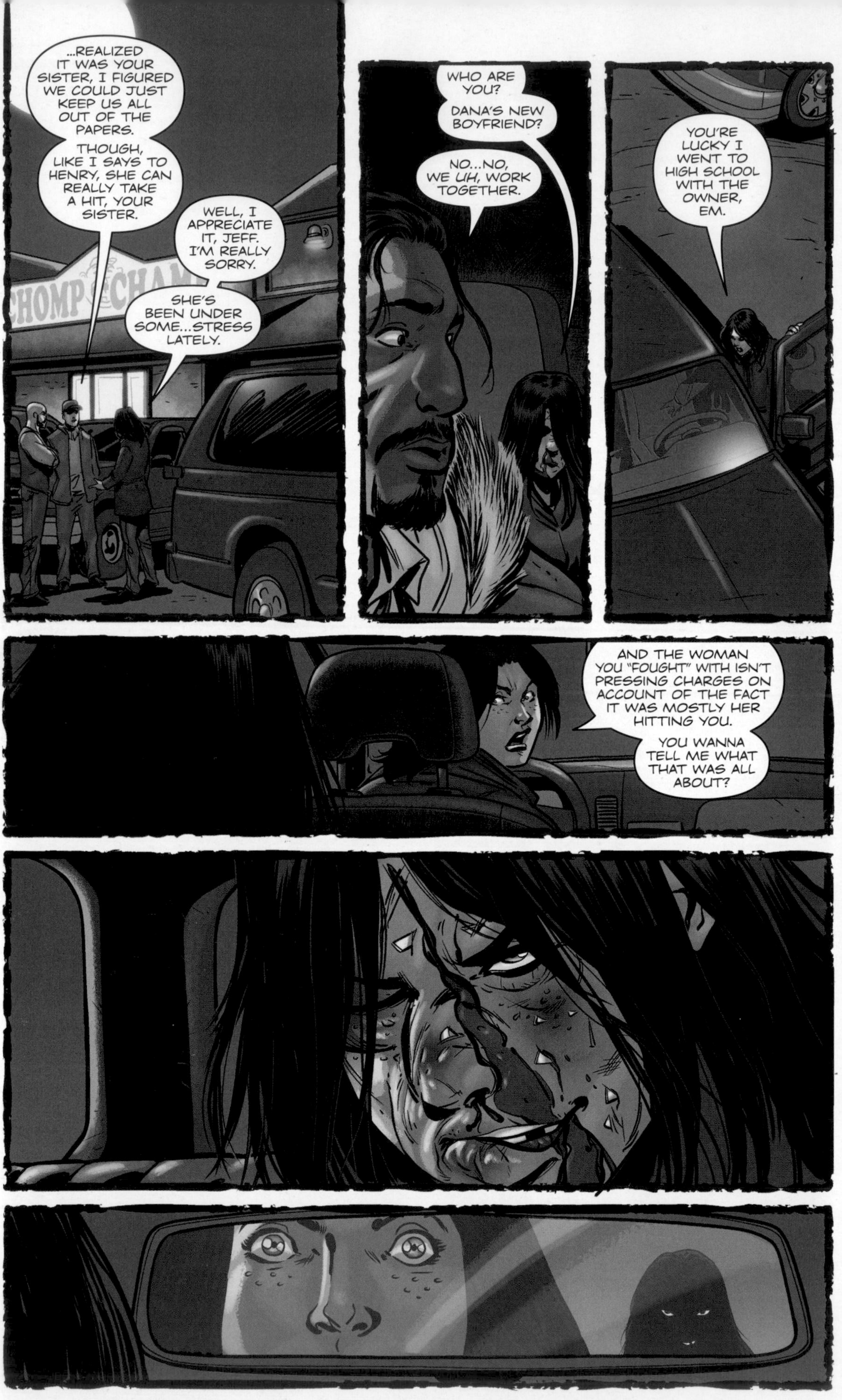
...REALIZED IT WAS YOUR SISTER, I FIGURED WE COULD JUST KEEP US ALL OUT OF THE PAPERS.
THOUGH, LIKE I SAYS TO HENRY, SHE CAN REALLY TAKE A HIT, YOUR SISTER.
WELL, I APPRECIATE IT, JEFF. I'M REALLY SORRY.
SHE'S BEEN UNDER SOME...STRESS LATELY.
CHOMP CHAMP
WHO ARE YOU?
DANA'S NEW BOYFRIEND?
NO...NO, WE UH, WORK TOGETHER.
YOU'RE LUCKY I WENT TO HIGH SCHOOL WITH THE OWNER, EM.
AND THE WOMAN YOU "FOUGHT" WITH ISN'T PRESSING CHARGES ON ACCOUNT OF THE FACT IT WAS MOSTLY HER HITTING YOU.
YOU WANNA TELL ME WHAT THAT WAS ALL ABOUT?

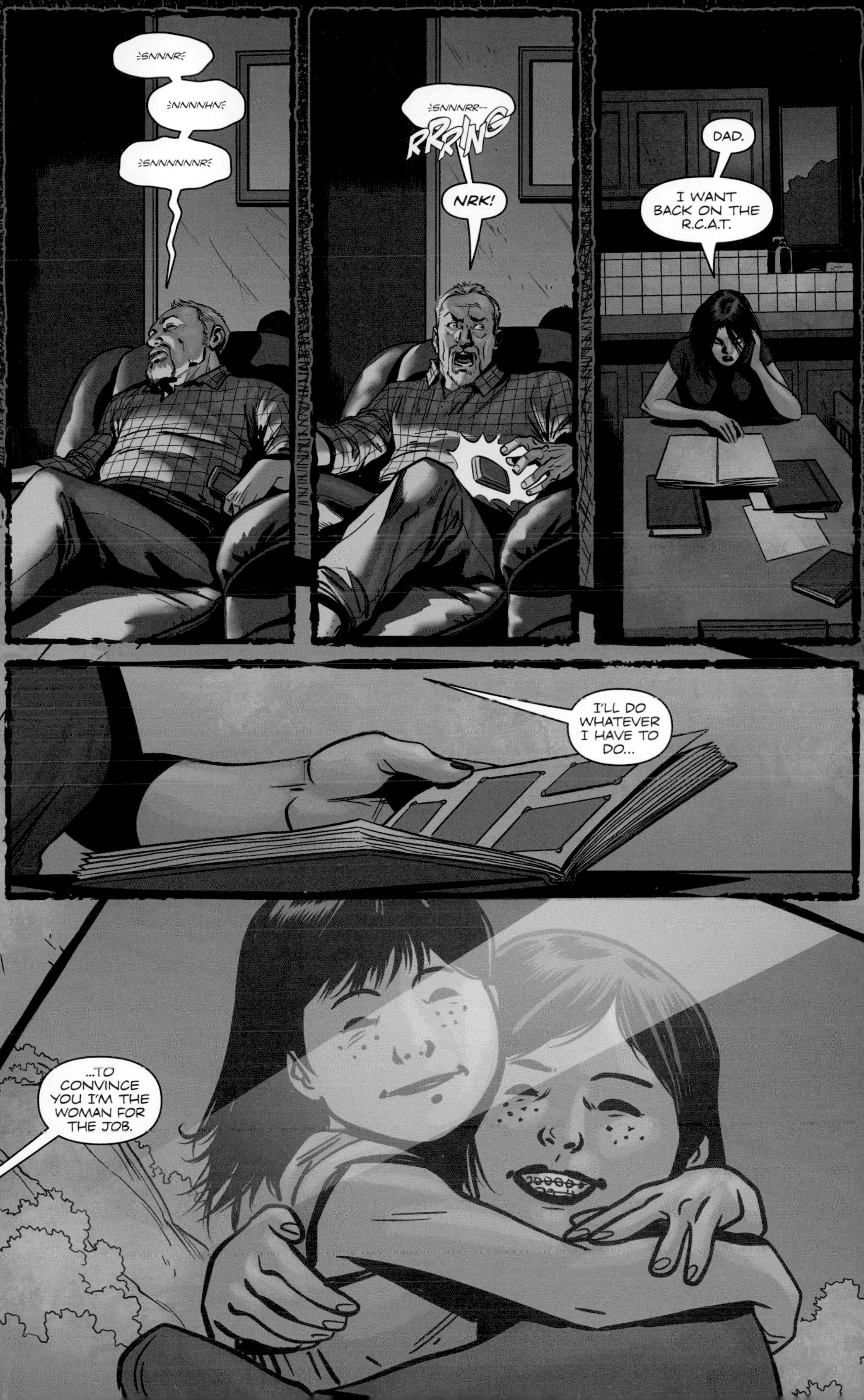
SNNNR
NNNNHN
SNNNNNNR
SNNNRR--
RRRING
NRK!
DAD.
I WANT BACK ON THE R.C.A.T.
I'LL DO WHATEVER I HAVE TO DO...
...TO CONVINCE YOU I'M THE WOMAN FOR THE JOB.

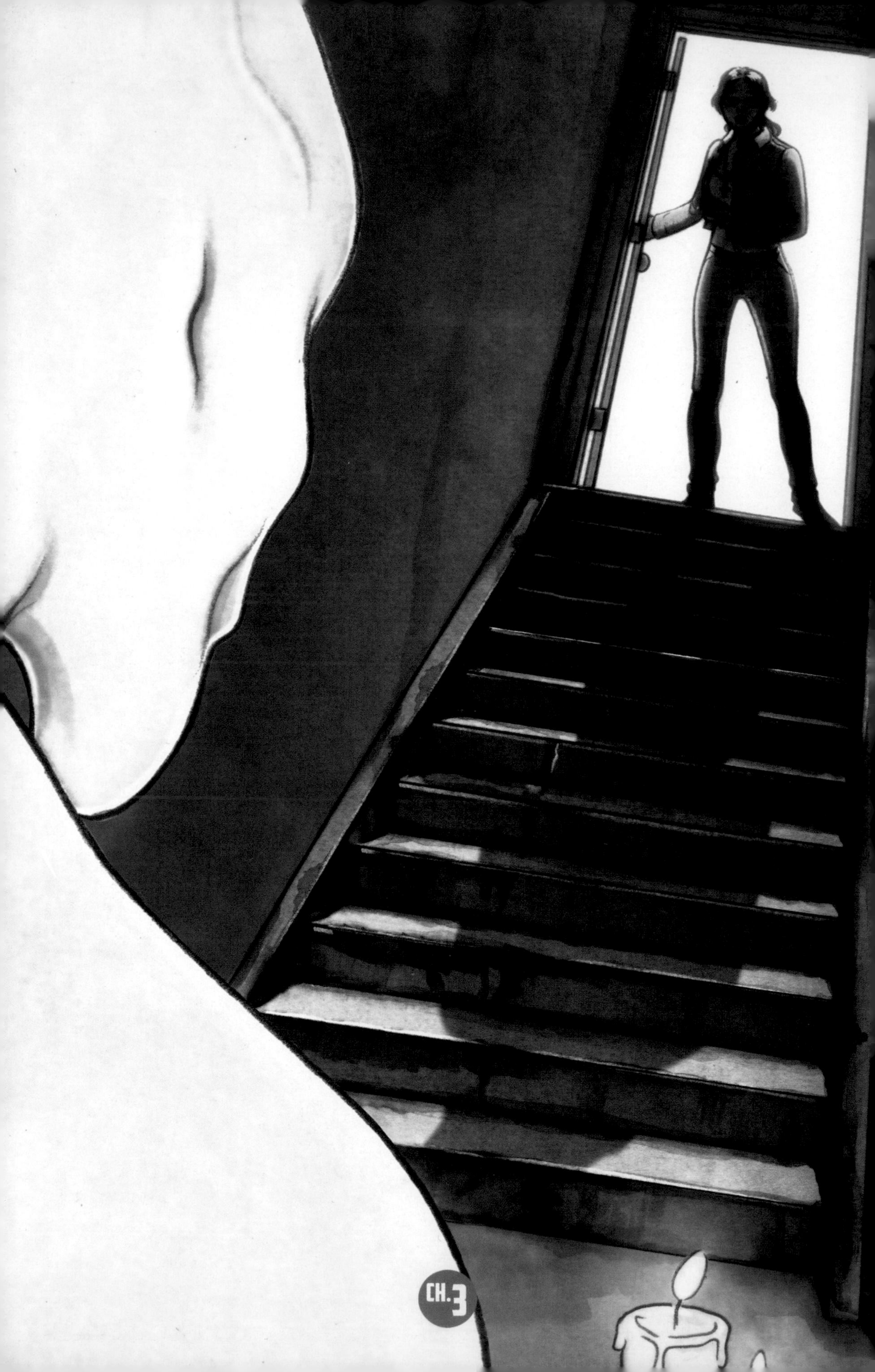
CH.3

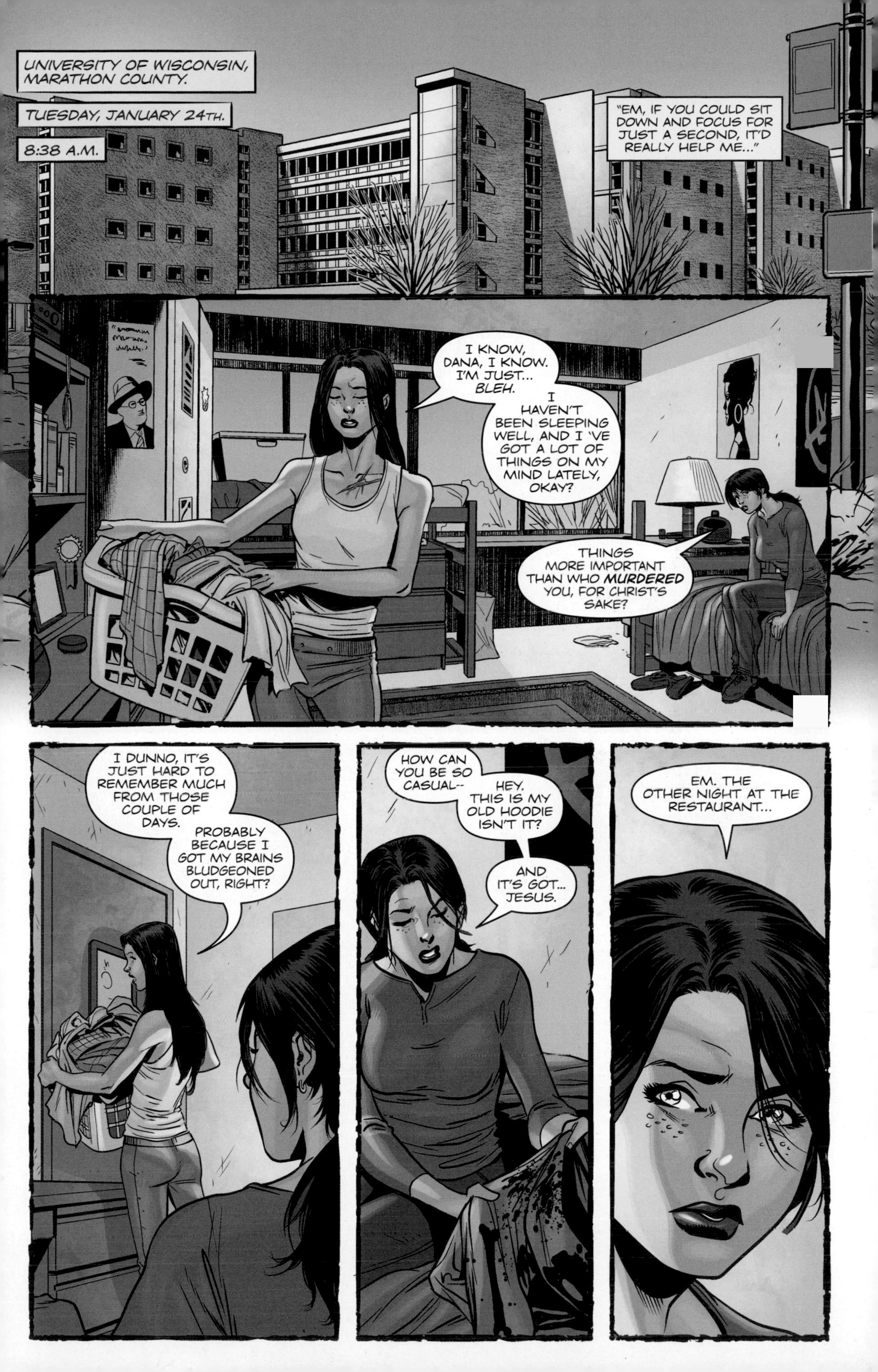
UNIVERSITY OF WISCONSIN, MARATHON COUNTY.
TUESDAY, JANUARY 24TH.
8:38 A.M.
"EM, IF YOU COULD SIT DOWN AND FOCUS FOR JUST A SECOND, IT'D REALLY HELP ME..."
I KNOW, DANA, I KNOW. I'M JUST... BLEH.
I HAVEN'T BEEN SLEEPING WELL, AND I 'VE GOT A LOT OF THINGS ON MY MIND LATELY, OKAY?
THINGS MORE IMPORTANT THAN WHO MURDERED YOU, FOR CHRIST'S SAKE?
I DUNNO, IT'S JUST HARD TO REMEMBER MUCH FROM THOSE COUPLE OF DAYS.
PROBABLY BECAUSE I GOT MY BRAINS BLUDGEONED OUT, RIGHT?
HOW CAN YOU BE SO CASUAL--
HEY. THIS IS MY OLD HOODIE ISN'T IT?
AND IT'S GOT... JESUS.
EM. THE OTHER NIGHT AT THE RESTAURANT...

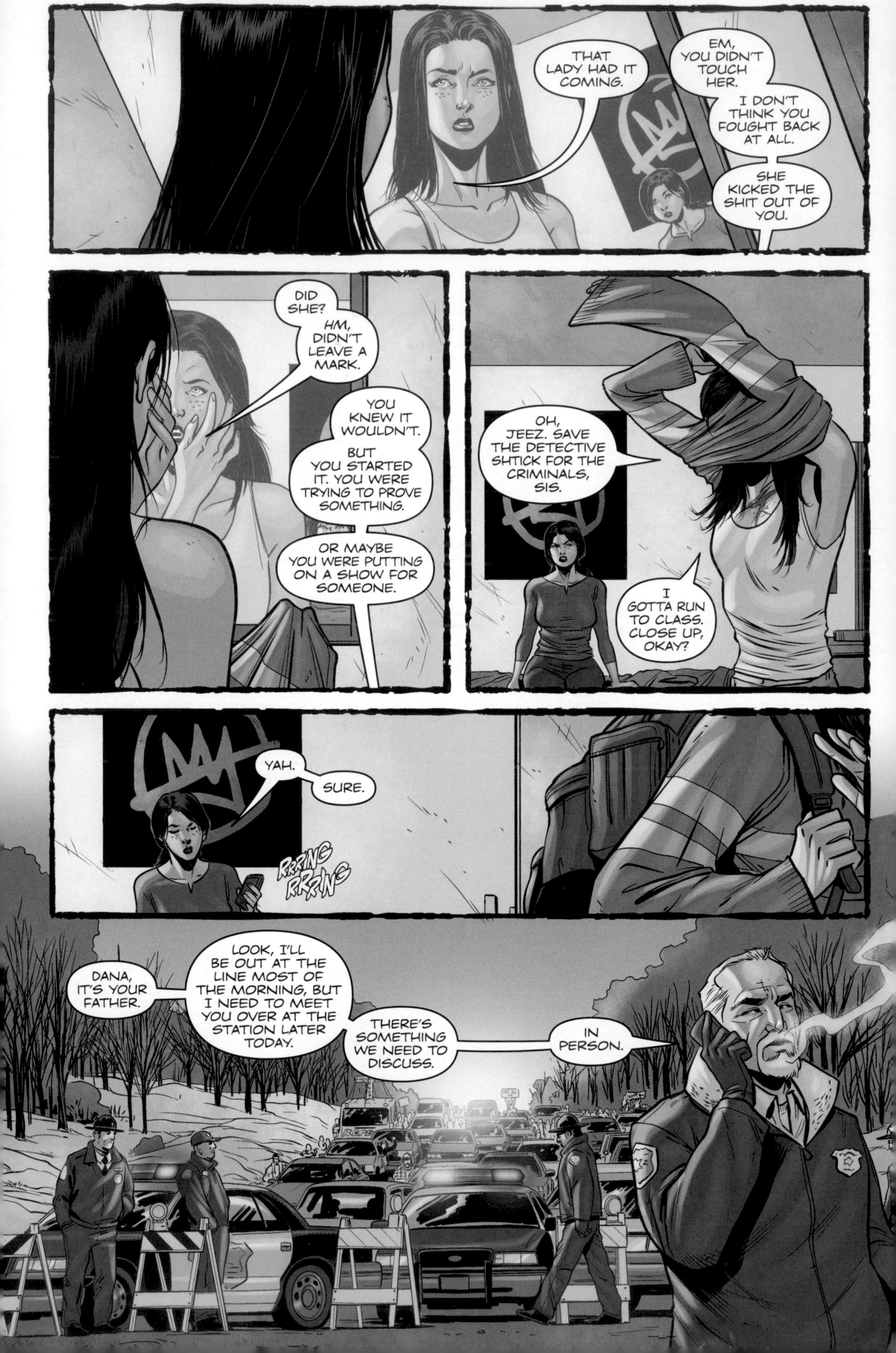
THAT LADY HAD IT COMING.
EM, YOU DIDN'T TOUCH HER.
I DON'T THINK YOU FOUGHT BACK AT ALL.
SHE KICKED THE SHIT OUT OF YOU.
DID SHE?
HM, DIDN'T LEAVE A MARK.
YOU KNEW IT WOULDN'T.
BUT YOU STARTED IT. YOU WERE TRYING TO PROVE SOMETHING.
OR MAYBE YOU WERE PUTTING ON A SHOW FOR SOMEONE.
OH, JEEZ. SAVE THE DETECTIVE SHTICK FOR THE CRIMINALS, SIS.
I GOTTA RUN TO CLASS. CLOSE UP, OKAY?
YAH.
SURE.
RRRING RRRING
DANA, IT'S YOUR FATHER.
LOOK, I'LL BE OUT AT THE LINE MOST OF THE MORNING, BUT I NEED TO MEET YOU OVER AT THE STATION LATER TODAY.
THERE'S SOMETHING WE NEED TO DISCUSS.
IN PERSON.

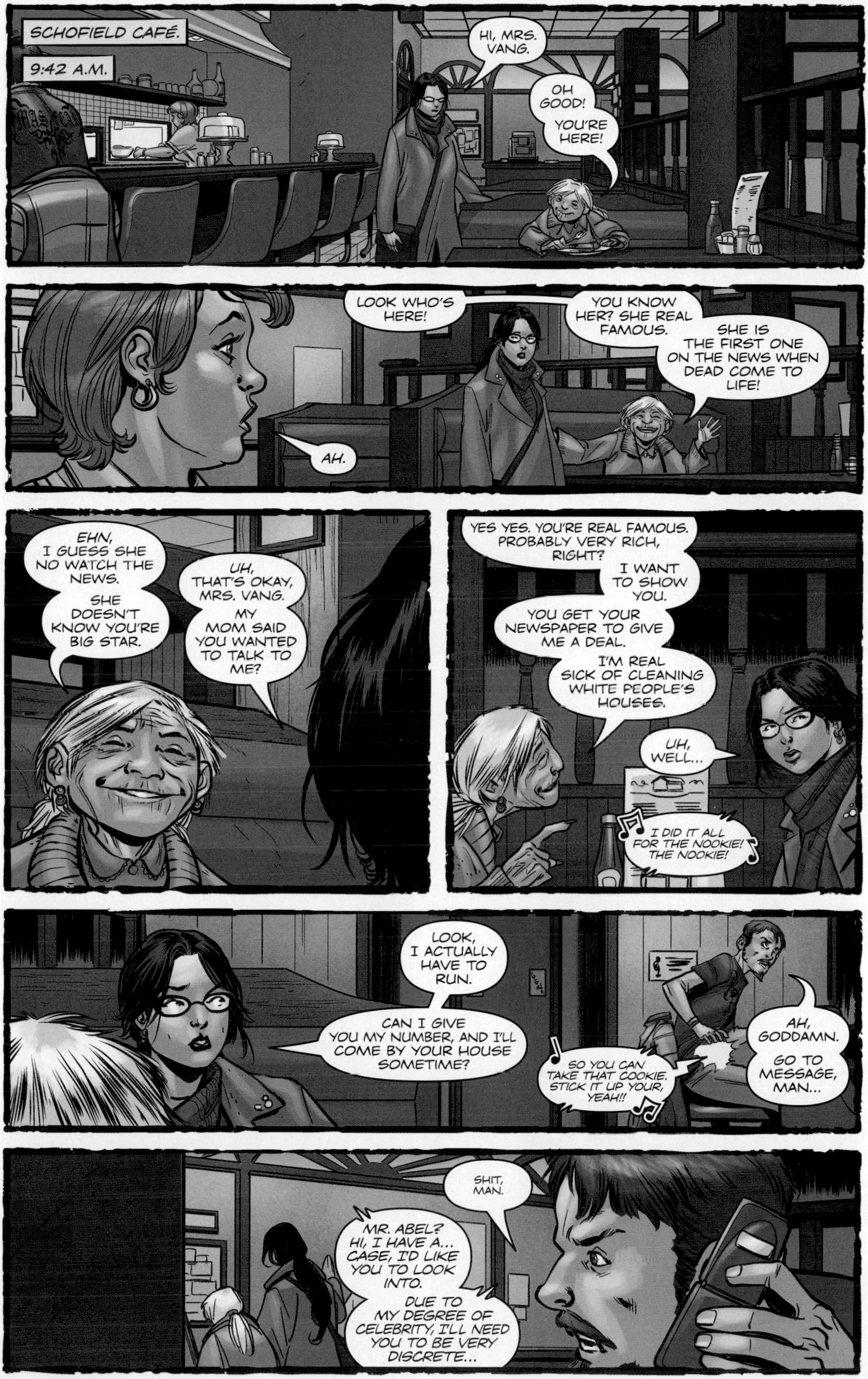
SCHOFIELD CAFÉ.
9:42 A.M.
HI, MRS. VANG.
OH GOOD! YOU'RE HERE!
LOOK WHO'S HERE!
YOU KNOW HER? SHE REAL FAMOUS.
SHE IS THE FIRST ONE ON THE NEWS WHEN DEAD COME TO LIFE!
AH.
EHN, I GUESS SHE NO WATCH THE NEWS.
SHE DOESN'T KNOW YOU'RE BIG STAR.
UH, THAT'S OKAY, MRS. VANG.
MY MOM SAID YOU WANTED TO TALK TO ME?
YES YES. YOU'RE REAL FAMOUS. PROBABLY VERY RICH, RIGHT?
I WANT TO SHOW YOU.
YOU GET YOUR NEWSPAPER TO GIVE ME A DEAL.
I'M REAL SICK OF CLEANING WHITE PEOPLE'S HOUSES.
UH, WELL...
I DID IT ALL FOR THE NOOKIE! THE NOOKIE!
LOOK, I ACTUALLY HAVE TO RUN.
CAN I GIVE YOU MY NUMBER, AND I'LL COME BY YOUR HOUSE SOMETIME?
SO YOU CAN TAKE THAT COOKIE. STICK IT UP YOUR, YEAH!!
AH, GODDAMN.
GO TO MESSAGE, MAN...
SHIT, MAN.
MR. ABEL? HI, I HAVE A... CASE, I'D LIKE YOU TO LOOK INTO.
DUE TO MY DEGREE OF CELEBRITY, I'LL NEED YOU TO BE VERY DISCRETE...

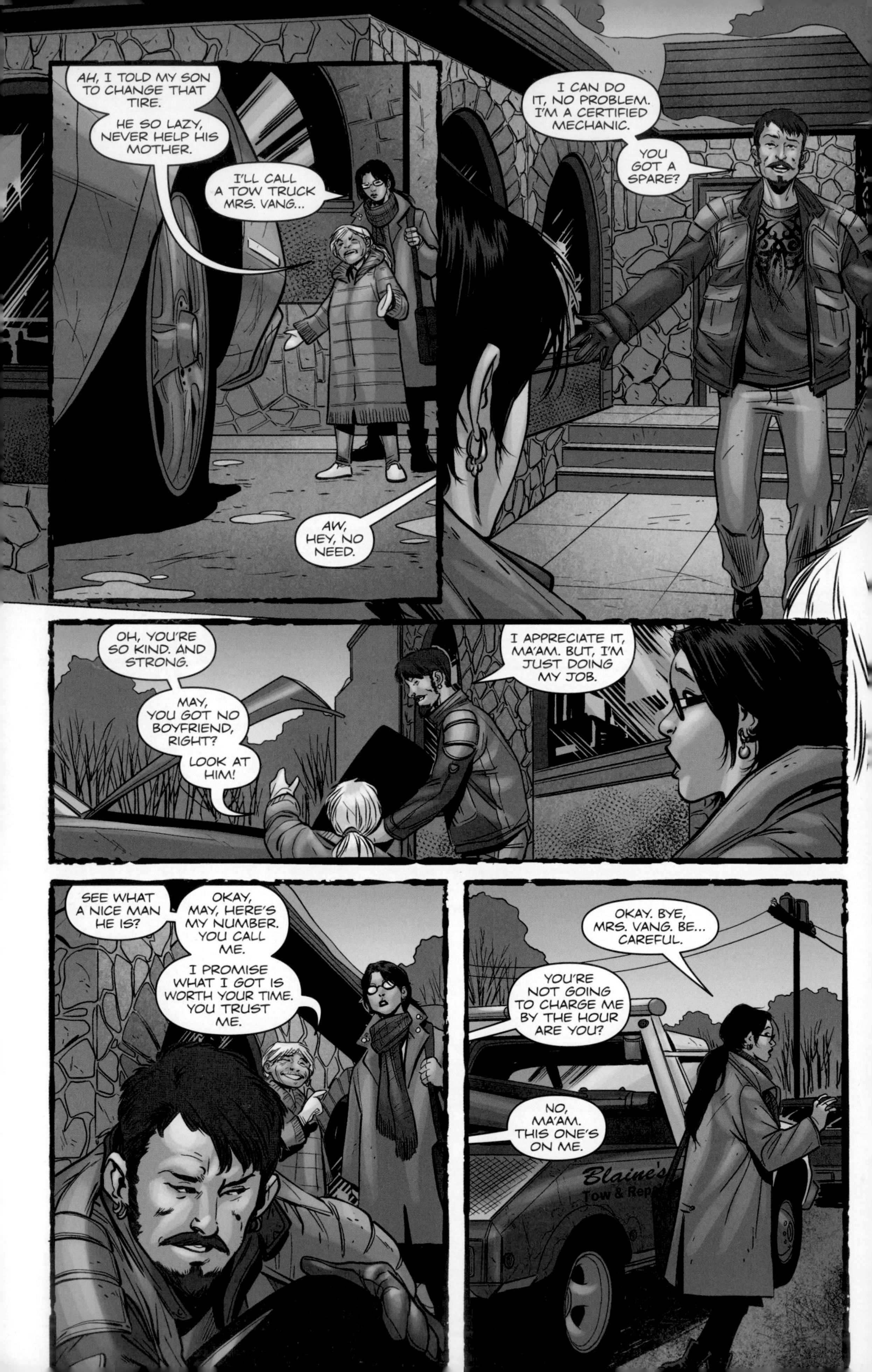
AH, I TOLD MY SON TO CHANGE THAT TIRE.
HE SO LAZY, NEVER HELP HIS MOTHER.
I'LL CALL A TOW TRUCK MRS. VANG...
AW, HEY, NO NEED.
I CAN DO IT, NO PROBLEM. I'M A CERTIFIED MECHANIC.
YOU GOT A SPARE?
OH, YOU'RE SO KIND. AND STRONG.
MAY, YOU GOT NO BOYFRIEND, RIGHT?
LOOK AT HIM!
I APPRECIATE IT, MA'AM. BUT, I'M JUST DOING MY JOB.
SEE WHAT A NICE MAN HE IS?
OKAY, MAY, HERE'S MY NUMBER. YOU CALL ME.
I PROMISE WHAT I GOT IS WORTH YOUR TIME. YOU TRUST ME.
OKAY. BYE, MRS. VANG. BE... CAREFUL.
YOU'RE NOT GOING TO CHARGE ME BY THE HOUR ARE YOU?
NO, MA'AM. THIS ONE'S ON ME.
Blaine's

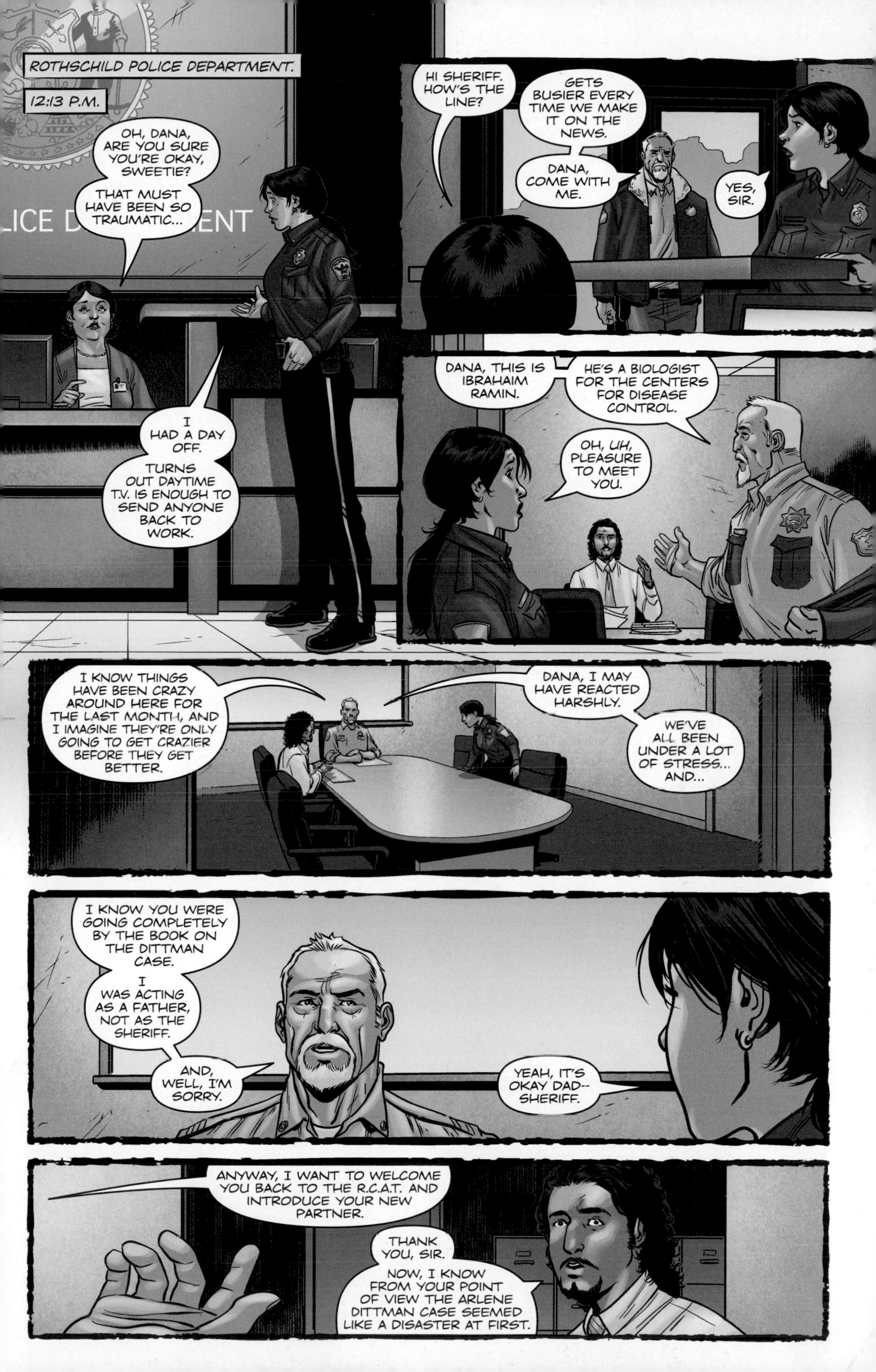
ROTHSCHILD POLICE DEPARTMENT.
12:13 P.M.
OH, DANA, ARE YOU SURE YOU'RE OKAY, SWEETIE?
THAT MUST HAVE BEEN SO TRAUMATIC...
LICE D ENT
I HAD A DAY OFF.
TURNS OUT DAYTIME T.V. IS ENOUGH TO SEND ANYONE BACK TO WORK.
HI SHERIFF. HOW'S THE LINE?
GETS BUSIER EVERY TIME WE MAKE IT ON THE NEWS.
DANA, COME WITH ME.
YES, SIR.
DANA, THIS IS IBRAHAIM RAMIN.
HE'S A BIOLOGIST FOR THE CENTERS FOR DISEASE CONTROL.
OH, UH, PLEASURE TO MEET YOU.
I KNOW THINGS HAVE BEEN CRAZY AROUND HERE FOR THE LAST MONTH, AND I IMAGINE THEY'RE ONLY GOING TO GET CRAZIER BEFORE THEY GET BETTER.
DANA, I MAY HAVE REACTED HARSHLY.
WE'VE ALL BEEN UNDER A LOT OF STRESS... AND...
I KNOW YOU WERE GOING COMPLETELY BY THE BOOK ON THE DITTMAN CASE.
I WAS ACTING AS A FATHER, NOT AS THE SHERIFF.
AND, WELL, I'M SORRY.
YEAH, IT'S OKAY DAD-- SHERIFF.
ANYWAY, I WANT TO WELCOME YOU BACK TO THE R.C.A.T. AND INTRODUCE YOUR NEW PARTNER.
THANK YOU, SIR.
NOW, I KNOW FROM YOUR POINT OF VIEW THE ARLENE DITTMAN CASE SEEMED LIKE A DISASTER AT FIRST.

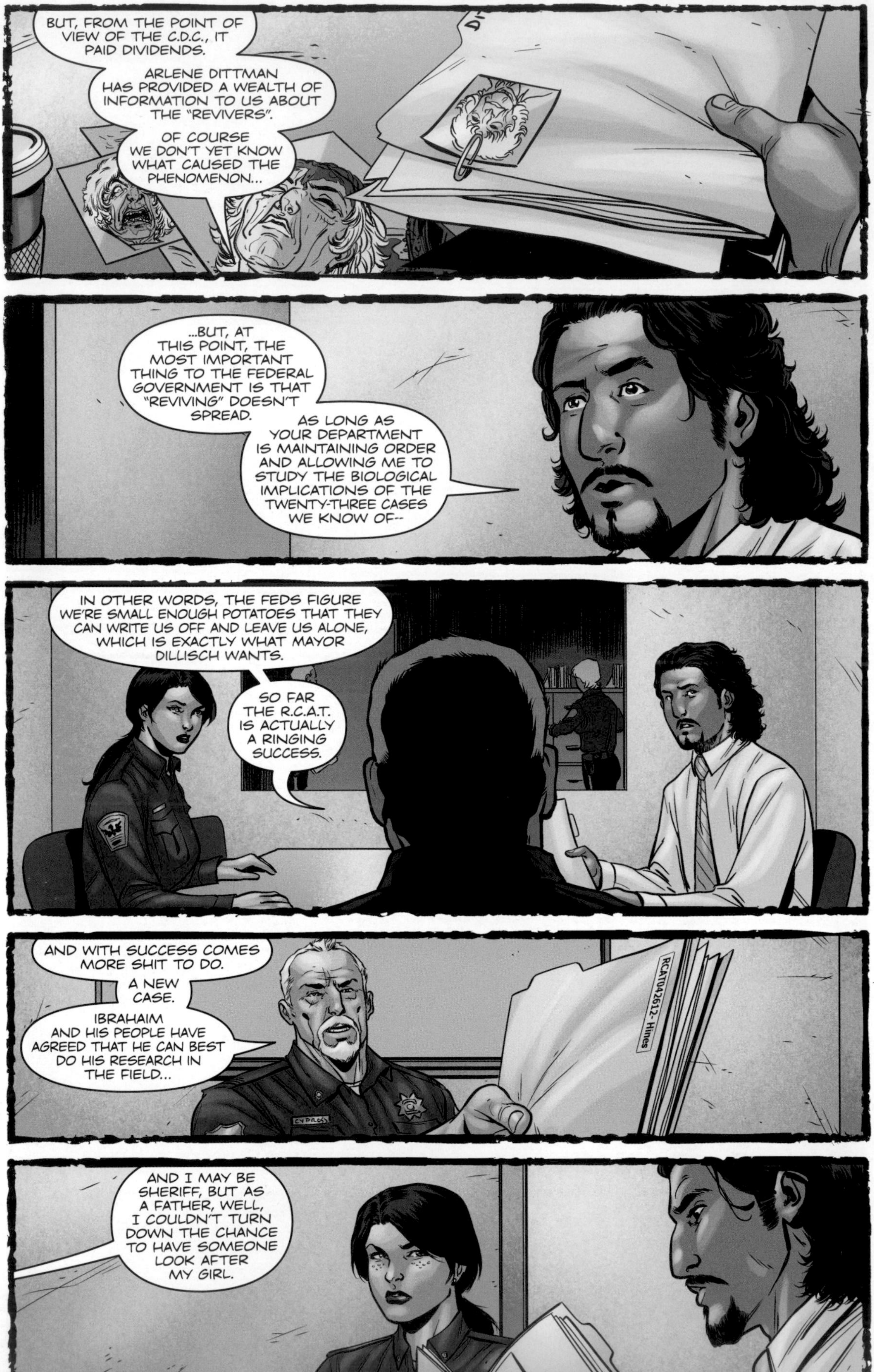
BUT, FROM THE POINT OF VIEW OF THE C.D.C., IT PAID DIVIDENDS.
ARLENE DITTMAN HAS PROVIDED A WEALTH OF INFORMATION TO US ABOUT THE "REVIVERS".
OF COURSE WE DON'T YET KNOW WHAT CAUSED THE PHENOMENON...
...BUT, AT THIS POINT, THE MOST IMPORTANT THING TO THE FEDERAL GOVERNMENT IS THAT "REVIVING" DOESN'T SPREAD.
AS LONG AS YOUR DEPARTMENT IS MAINTAINING ORDER AND ALLOWING ME TO STUDY THE BIOLOGICAL IMPLICATIONS OF THE TWENTY-THREE CASES WE KNOW OF--
IN OTHER WORDS, THE FEDS FIGURE WE'RE SMALL ENOUGH POTATOES THAT THEY CAN WRITE US OFF AND LEAVE US ALONE, WHICH IS EXACTLY WHAT MAYOR DILLISCH WANTS.
SO FAR THE R.C.A.T. IS ACTUALLY A RINGING SUCCESS.
AND WITH SUCCESS COMES MORE SHIT TO DO.
A NEW CASE.
IBRAHAIM AND HIS PEOPLE HAVE AGREED THAT HE CAN BEST DO HIS RESEARCH IN THE FIELD...
RCAT042612- Hines
AND I MAY BE SHERIFF, BUT AS A FATHER, WELL, I COULDN'T TURN DOWN THE CHANCE TO HAVE SOMEONE LOOK AFTER MY GIRL.

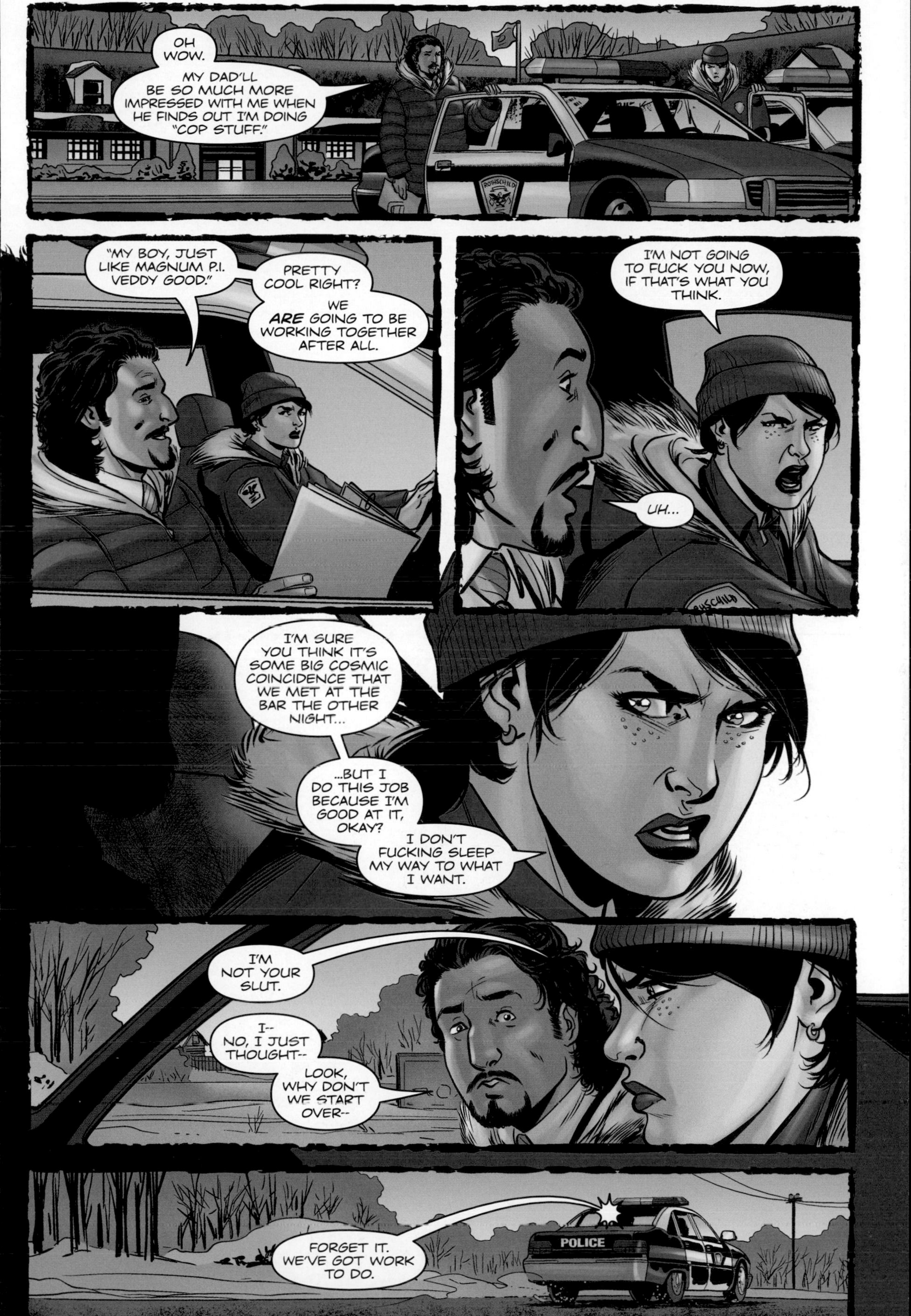

OH WOW.
MY DAD'LL BE SO MUCH MORE IMPRESSED WITH ME WHEN HE FINDS OUT I'M DOING "COP STUFF."
ROTHSCHILD
"MY BOY, JUST LIKE MAGNUM P.I. VEDDY GOOD."
PRETTY COOL RIGHT?
WE **ARE** GOING TO BE WORKING TOGETHER AFTER ALL.
I'M NOT GOING TO FUCK YOU NOW, IF THAT'S WHAT YOU THINK.
UH...
I'M SURE YOU THINK IT'S SOME BIG COSMIC COINCIDENCE THAT WE MET AT THE BAR THE OTHER NIGHT...
...BUT I DO THIS JOB BECAUSE I'M GOOD AT IT, OKAY?
I DON'T FUCKING SLEEP MY WAY TO WHAT I WANT.
I'M NOT YOUR SLUT.
I-- NO, I JUST THOUGHT--
LOOK, WHY DON'T WE START OVER--
POLICE
FORGET IT. WE'VE GOT WORK TO DO.

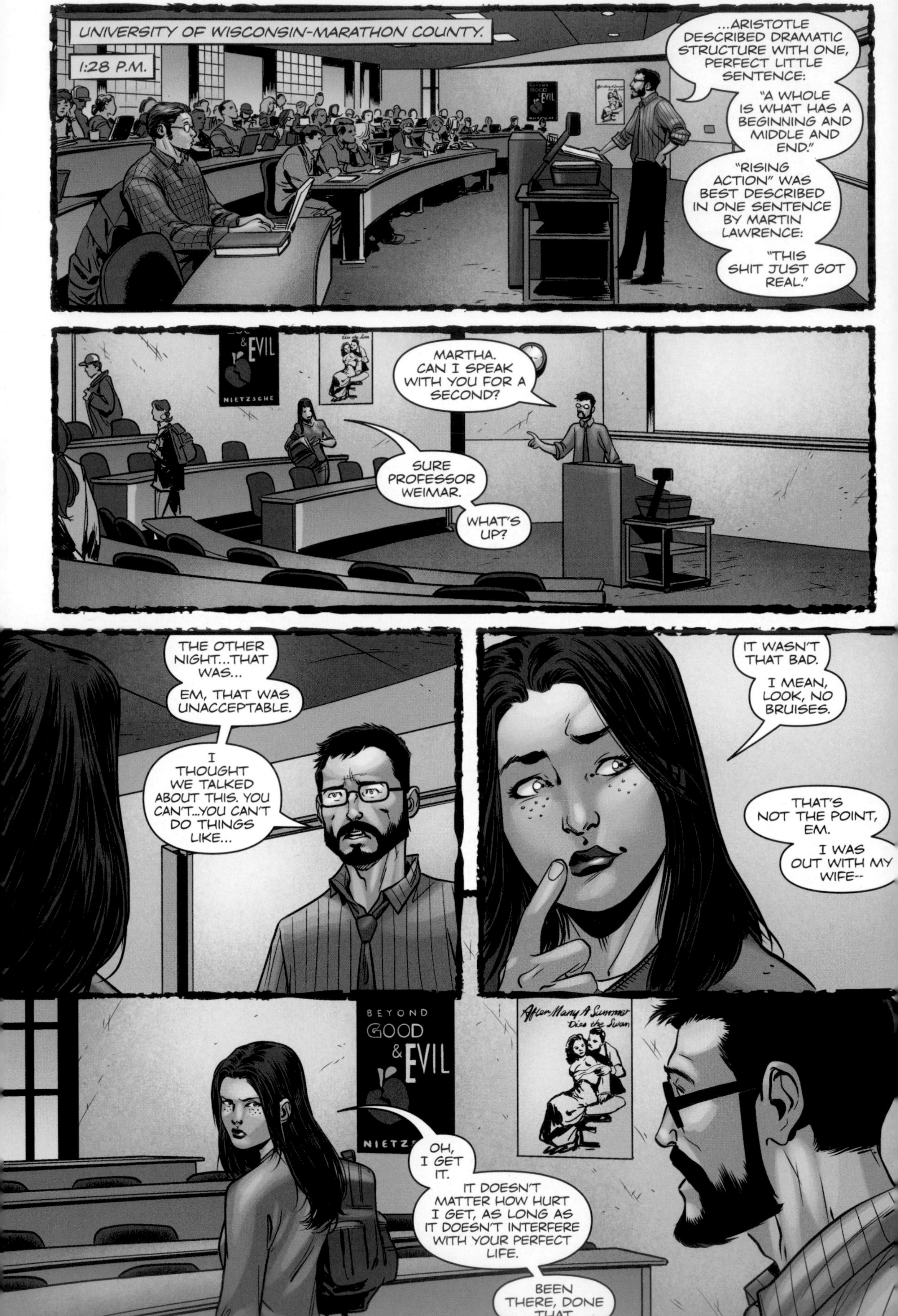
UNIVERSITY OF WISCONSIN-MARATHON COUNTY.
1:28 P.M.
...ARISTOTLE DESCRIBED DRAMATIC STRUCTURE WITH ONE, PERFECT LITTLE SENTENCE:
"A WHOLE IS WHAT HAS A BEGINNING AND MIDDLE AND END."
"RISING ACTION" WAS BEST DESCRIBED IN ONE SENTENCE BY MARTIN LAWRENCE:
"THIS SHIT JUST GOT REAL."
MARTHA. CAN I SPEAK WITH YOU FOR A SECOND?
SURE PROFESSOR WEIMAR.
WHAT'S UP?
THE OTHER NIGHT...THAT WAS...
EM, THAT WAS UNACCEPTABLE.
I THOUGHT WE TALKED ABOUT THIS. YOU CAN'T...YOU CAN'T DO THINGS LIKE...
IT WASN'T THAT BAD.
I MEAN, LOOK, NO BRUISES.
THAT'S NOT THE POINT, EM.
I WAS OUT WITH MY WIFE--
BEYOND GOOD & EVIL
NIETZS
After Many A Summer Dies the Swan
OH, I GET IT.
IT DOESN'T MATTER HOW HURT I GET, AS LONG AS IT DOESN'T INTERFERE WITH YOUR PERFECT LIFE.
BEEN THERE, DONE THAT.

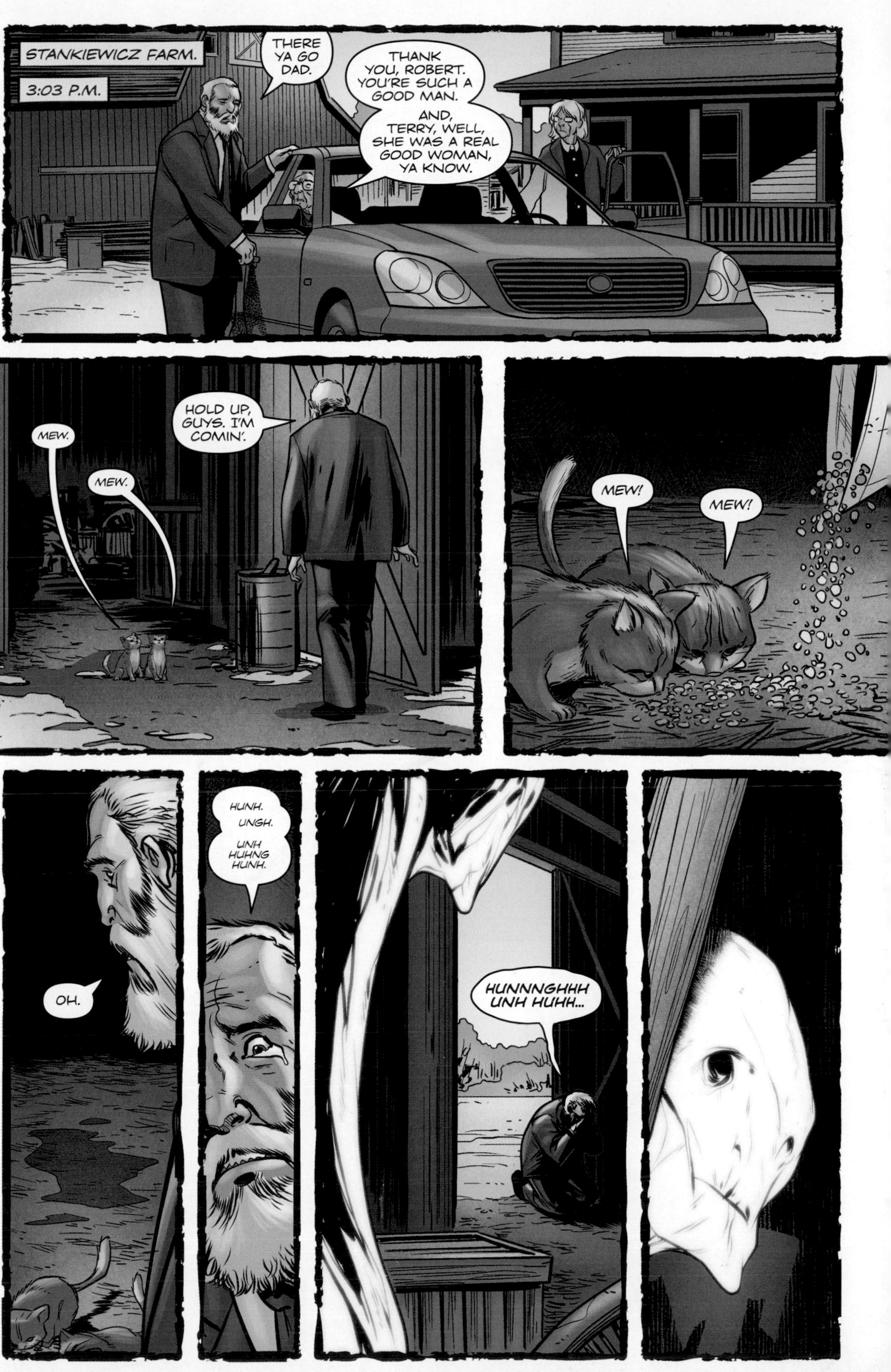
STANKIEWICZ FARM.
3:03 P.M.
THERE YA GO DAD.
THANK YOU, ROBERT. YOU'RE SUCH A GOOD MAN.
AND, TERRY, WELL, SHE WAS A REAL GOOD WOMAN, YA KNOW.
MEW.
MEW.
HOLD UP, GUYS. I'M COMIN'.
MEW!
MEW!
OH.
HUNH.
UNGH.
UNH HUHNG HUNH.
HUNNNGHHH UNH HUHH...

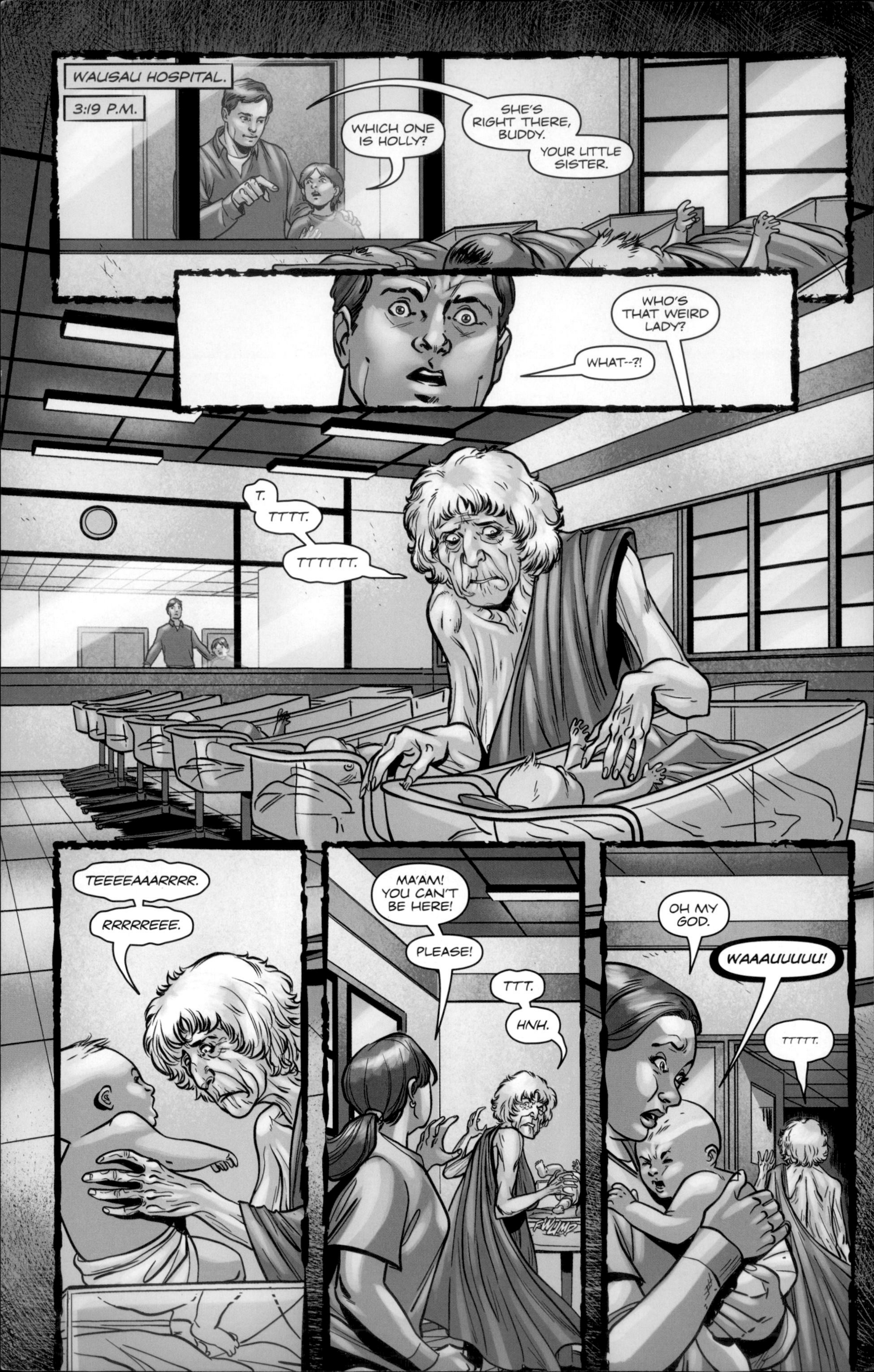
WAUSAU HOSPITAL.
3:19 P.M.
WHICH ONE IS HOLLY?
SHE'S RIGHT THERE, BUDDY.
YOUR LITTLE SISTER.
WHO'S THAT WEIRD LADY?
WHAT--?!
T.
TTTT.
TTTTTT.
TEEEEAAARRRR.
RRRRREEE.
MA'AM! YOU CAN'T BE HERE!
PLEASE!
TTT.
HNH.
FWUMP
OH MY GOD.
WAAAUUUUU!
TTTTT.

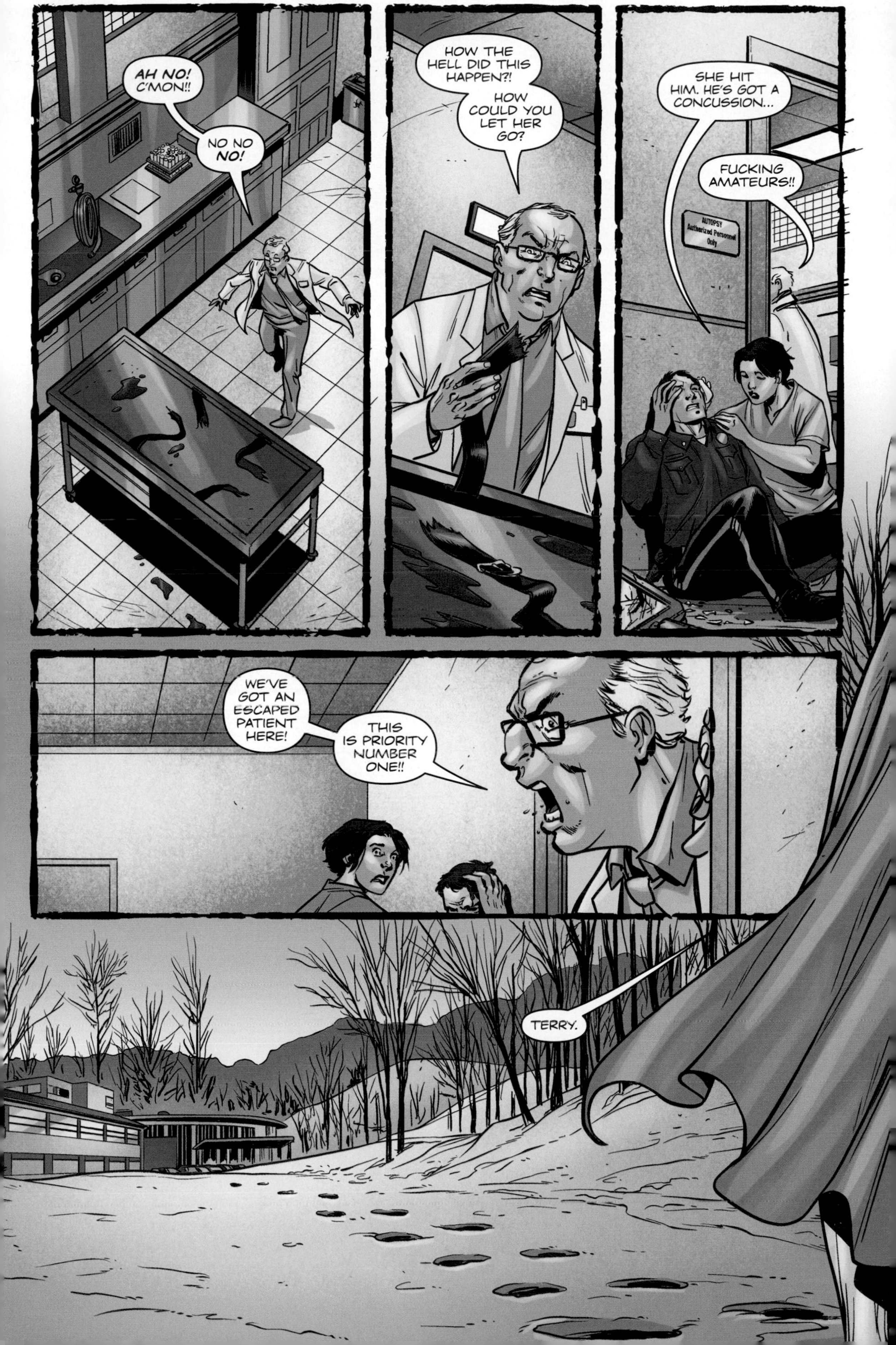
AH NO! C'MON!!
NO NO NO!
HOW THE HELL DID THIS HAPPEN?!
HOW COULD YOU LET HER GO?
SHE HIT HIM. HE'S GOT A CONCUSSION...
FUCKING AMATEURS!!
AUTOPSY Authorized Personnel Only
WE'VE GOT AN ESCAPED PATIENT HERE!
THIS IS PRIORITY NUMBER ONE!!
TERRY.

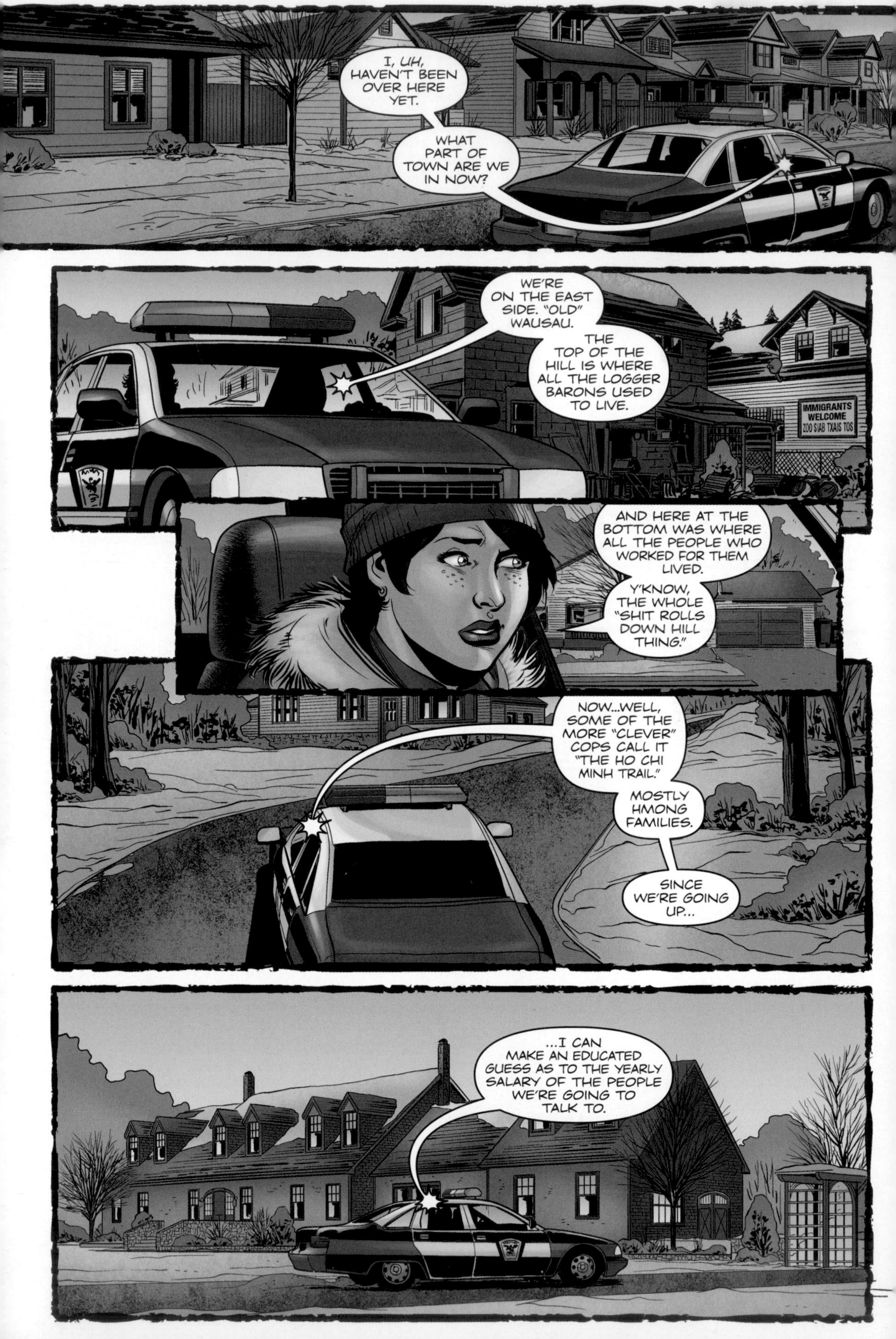
I, UH, HAVEN'T BEEN OVER HERE YET.
WHAT PART OF TOWN ARE WE IN NOW?
WE'RE ON THE EAST SIDE. "OLD" WAUSAU.
THE TOP OF THE HILL IS WHERE ALL THE LOGGER BARONS USED TO LIVE.
IMMIGRANTS WELCOME
ZOO SIAB TXAIS TOS
AND HERE AT THE BOTTOM WAS WHERE ALL THE PEOPLE WHO WORKED FOR THEM LIVED.
Y'KNOW, THE WHOLE "SHIT ROLLS DOWN HILL THING."
NOW...WELL, SOME OF THE MORE "CLEVER" COPS CALL IT "THE HO CHI MINH TRAIL."
MOSTLY HMONG FAMILIES.
SINCE WE'RE GOING UP...
...I CAN MAKE AN EDUCATED GUESS AS TO THE YEARLY SALARY OF THE PEOPLE WE'RE GOING TO TALK TO.

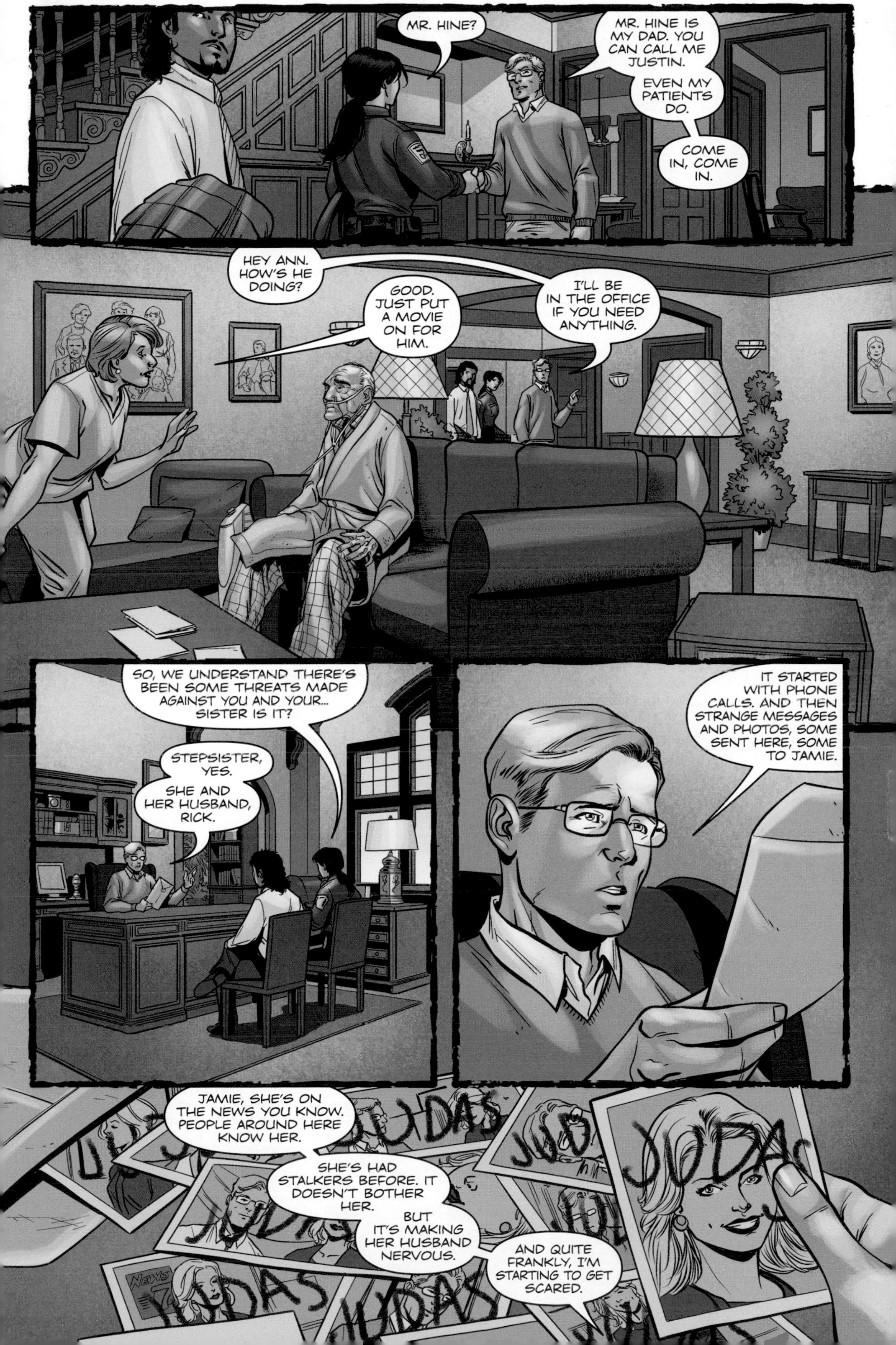
MR. HINE?
MR. HINE IS MY DAD. YOU CAN CALL ME JUSTIN.
EVEN MY PATIENTS DO.
COME IN, COME IN.
HEY ANN. HOW'S HE DOING?
GOOD. JUST PUT A MOVIE ON FOR HIM.
I'LL BE IN THE OFFICE IF YOU NEED ANYTHING.
SO, WE UNDERSTAND THERE'S BEEN SOME THREATS MADE AGAINST YOU AND YOUR... SISTER IS IT?
STEPSISTER, YES.
SHE AND HER HUSBAND, RICK.
IT STARTED WITH PHONE CALLS. AND THEN STRANGE MESSAGES AND PHOTOS, SOME SENT HERE, SOME TO JAMIE.
JAMIE, SHE'S ON THE NEWS YOU KNOW. PEOPLE AROUND HERE KNOW HER.
SHE'S HAD STALKERS BEFORE. IT DOESN'T BOTHER HER.
BUT IT'S MAKING HER HUSBAND NERVOUS.
AND QUITE FRANKLY, I'M STARTING TO GET SCARED.
JUDAS
JUDAS
JUDAS

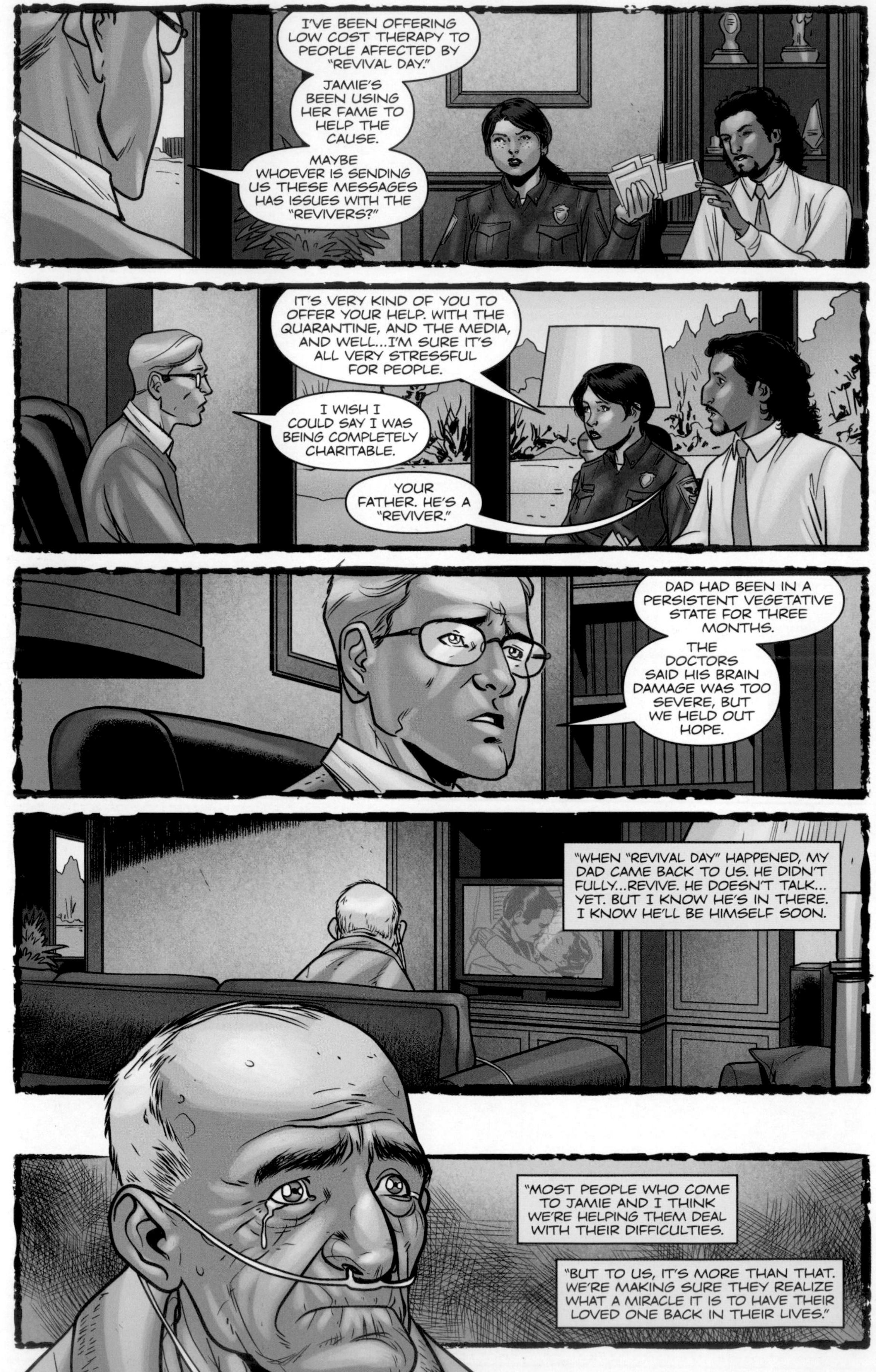
I'VE BEEN OFFERING LOW COST THERAPY TO PEOPLE AFFECTED BY "REVIVAL DAY."
JAMIE'S BEEN USING HER FAME TO HELP THE CAUSE.
MAYBE WHOEVER IS SENDING US THESE MESSAGES HAS ISSUES WITH THE "REVIVERS?"
IT'S VERY KIND OF YOU TO OFFER YOUR HELP. WITH THE QUARANTINE, AND THE MEDIA, AND WELL...I'M SURE IT'S ALL VERY STRESSFUL FOR PEOPLE.
I WISH I COULD SAY I WAS BEING COMPLETELY CHARITABLE.
YOUR FATHER. HE'S A "REVIVER."
DAD HAD BEEN IN A PERSISTENT VEGETATIVE STATE FOR THREE MONTHS.
THE DOCTORS SAID HIS BRAIN DAMAGE WAS TOO SEVERE, BUT WE HELD OUT HOPE.
"WHEN "REVIVAL DAY" HAPPENED, MY DAD CAME BACK TO US. HE DIDN'T FULLY...REVIVE. HE DOESN'T TALK... YET. BUT I KNOW HE'S IN THERE. I KNOW HE'LL BE HIMSELF SOON.
"MOST PEOPLE WHO COME TO JAMIE AND I THINK WE'RE HELPING THEM DEAL WITH THEIR DIFFICULTIES.
"BUT TO US, IT'S MORE THAN THAT. WE'RE MAKING SURE THEY REALIZE WHAT A MIRACLE IT IS TO HAVE THEIR LOVED ONE BACK IN THEIR LIVES."

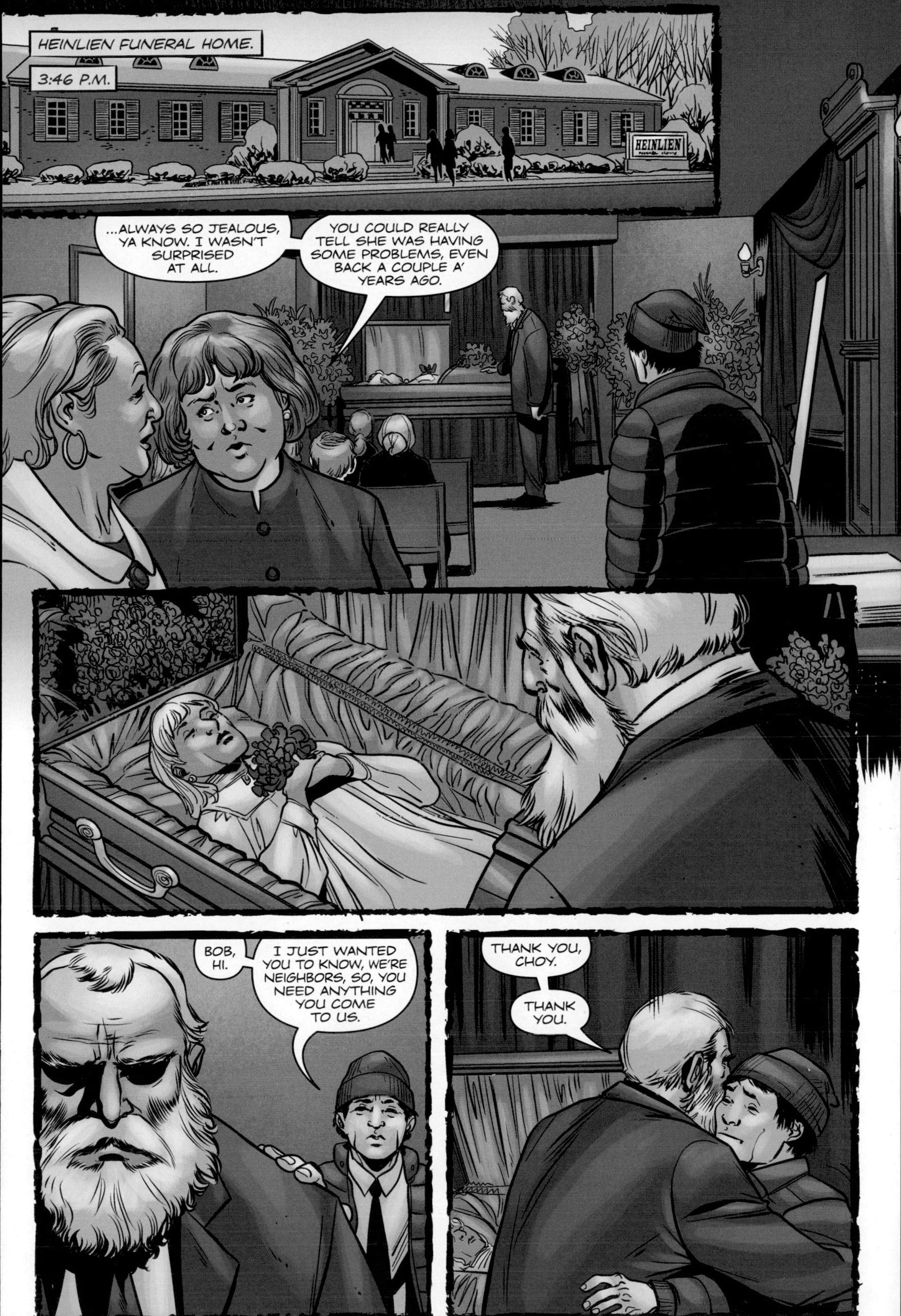
HEINLIEN FUNERAL HOME.
3:46 P.M.
HEINLIEN
...ALWAYS SO JEALOUS, YA KNOW. I WASN'T SURPRISED AT ALL.
YOU COULD REALLY TELL SHE WAS HAVING SOME PROBLEMS, EVEN BACK A COUPLE A' YEARS AGO.
BOB, HI.
I JUST WANTED YOU TO KNOW, WE'RE NEIGHBORS, SO, YOU NEED ANYTHING YOU COME TO US.
THANK YOU, CHOY.
THANK YOU.

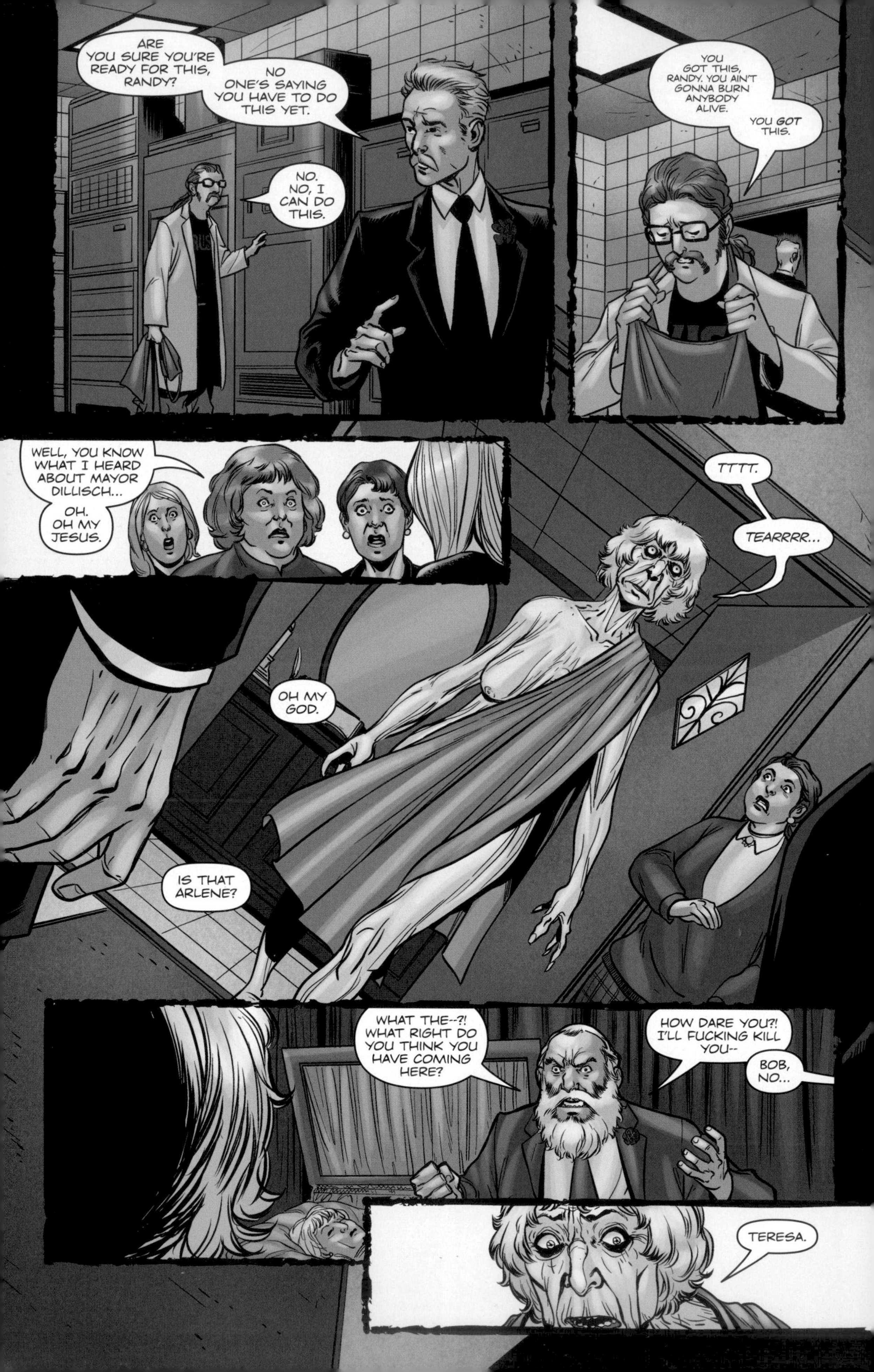
ARE YOU SURE YOU'RE READY FOR THIS, RANDY?
NO ONE'S SAYING YOU HAVE TO DO THIS YET.
NO. NO, I CAN DO THIS.
YOU GOT THIS, RANDY. YOU AIN'T GONNA BURN ANYBODY ALIVE.
YOU GOT THIS.
WELL, YOU KNOW WHAT I HEARD ABOUT MAYOR DILLISCH...
OH. OH MY JESUS.
TTTT.
TEARRRR...
OH MY GOD.
IS THAT ARLENE?
WHAT THE--?! WHAT RIGHT DO YOU THINK YOU HAVE COMING HERE?
HOW DARE YOU?! I'LL FUCKING KILL YOU--
BOB, NO...
TERESA.

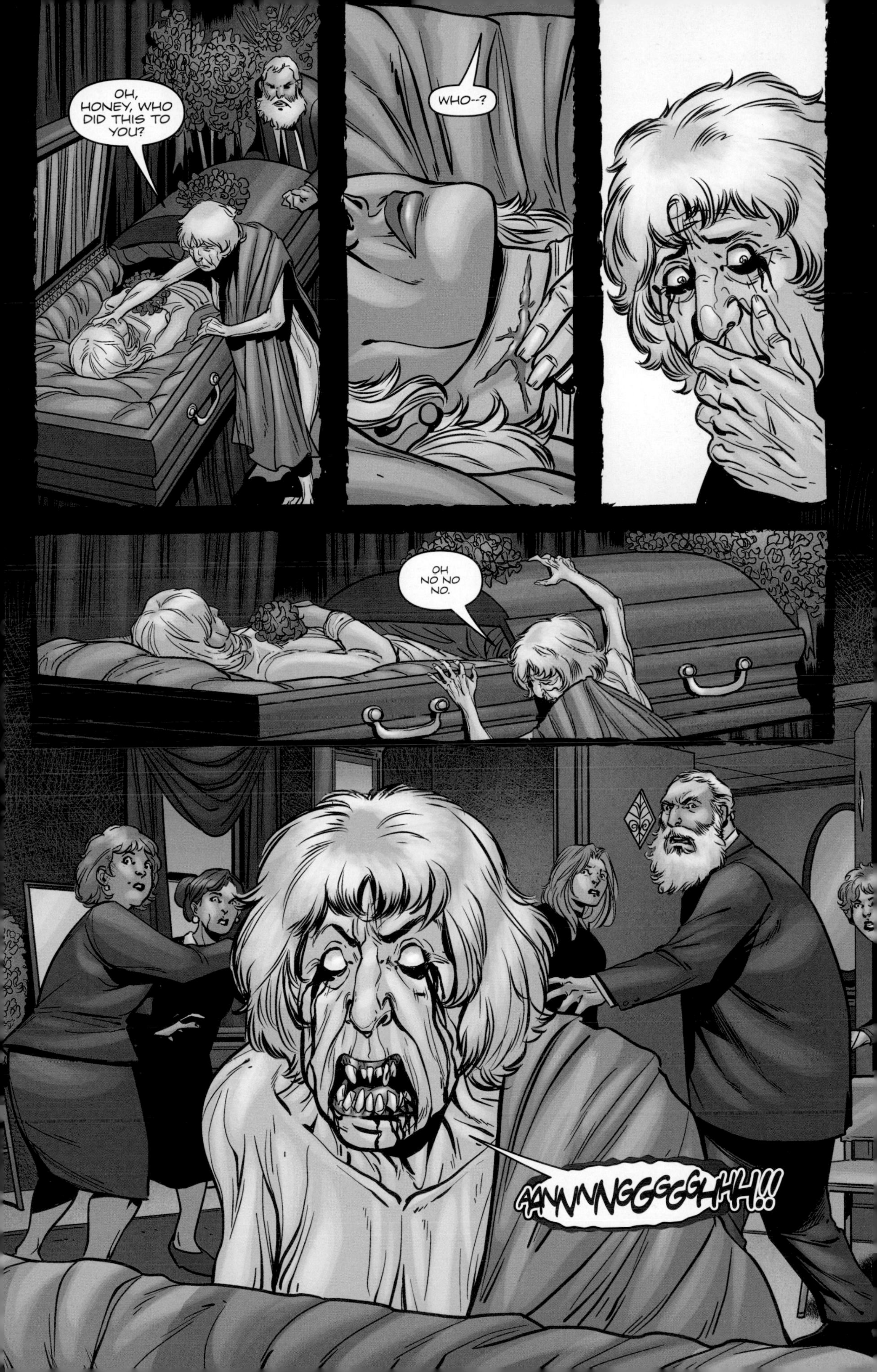
OH, HONEY, WHO DID THIS TO YOU?
WHO--?
OH NO NO NO.
AANNNNGGGGGHHH!!

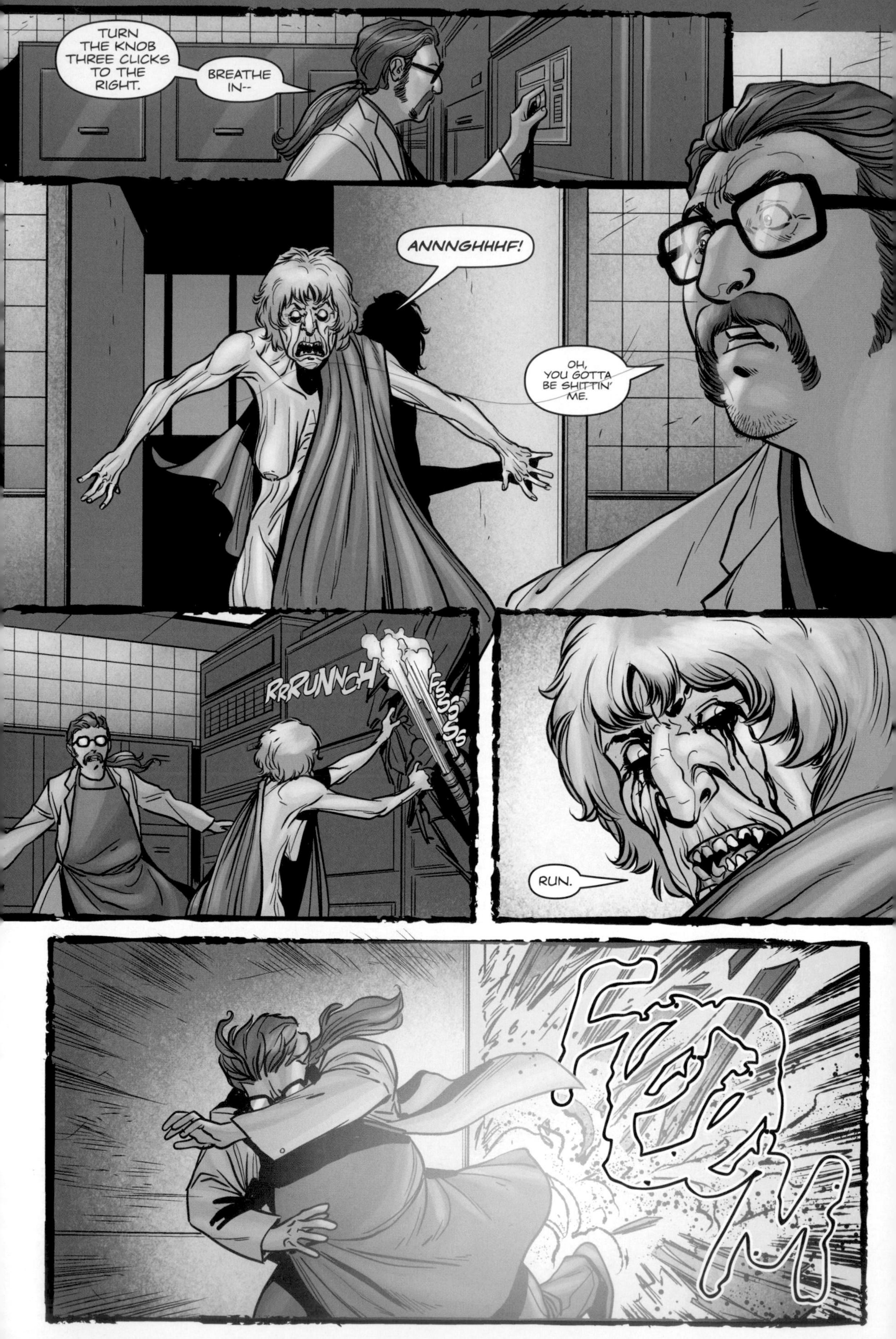
TURN THE KNOB THREE CLICKS TO THE RIGHT.
BREATHE IN--
ANNNGHHHF!
OH, YOU GOTTA BE SHITTIN' ME.
RRRUNNCH
RUN.

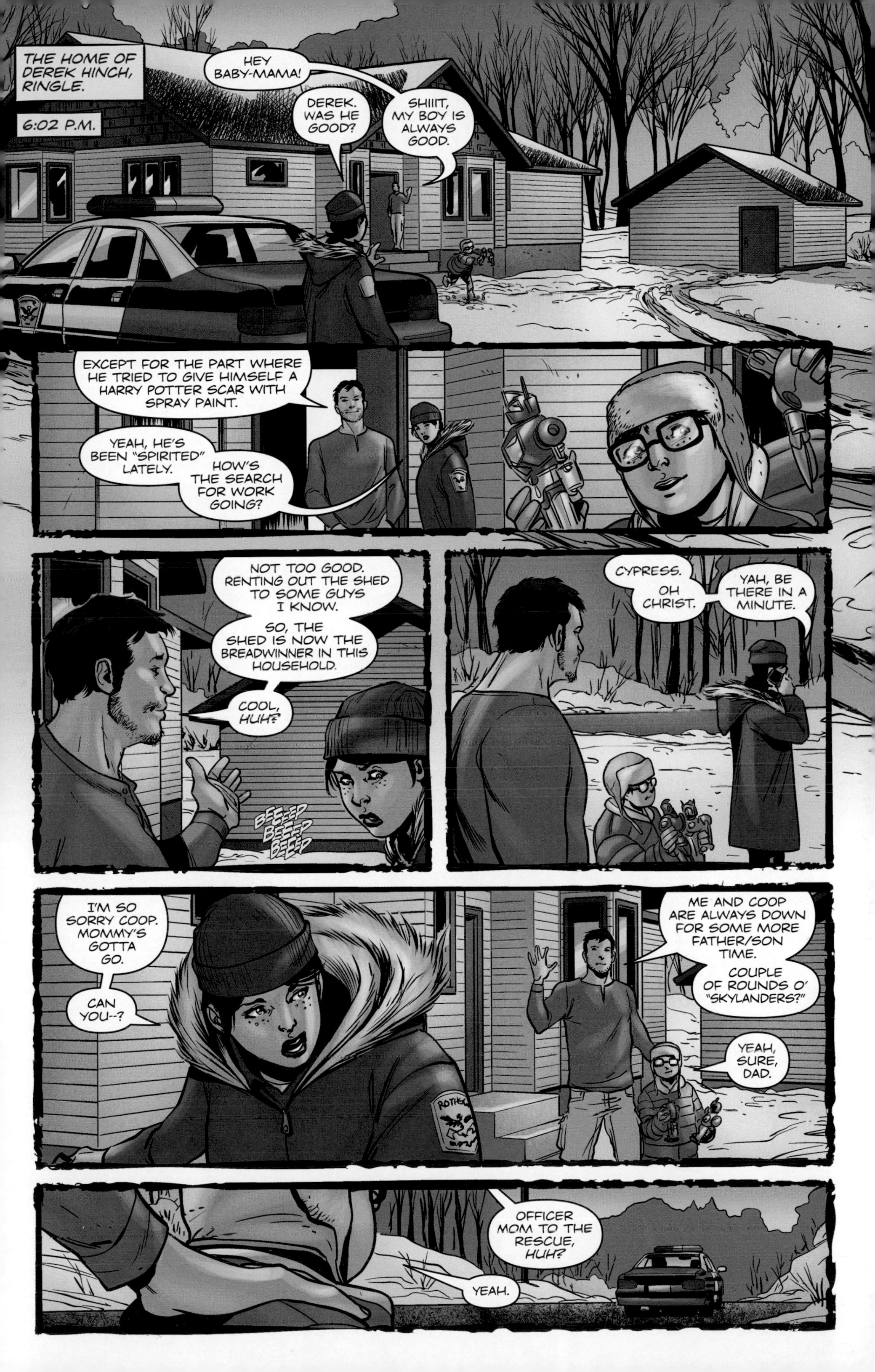

THE HOME OF DEREK HINCH, RINGLE.
6:02 P.M.
HEY BABY-MAMA!
DEREK. WAS HE GOOD?
SHIIIT, MY BOY IS ALWAYS GOOD.
EXCEPT FOR THE PART WHERE HE TRIED TO GIVE HIMSELF A HARRY POTTER SCAR WITH SPRAY PAINT.
YEAH, HE'S BEEN "SPIRITED" LATELY.
HOW'S THE SEARCH FOR WORK GOING?
NOT TOO GOOD. RENTING OUT THE SHED TO SOME GUYS I KNOW.
SO, THE SHED IS NOW THE BREADWINNER IN THIS HOUSEHOLD.
COOL, HUH?
BEEEP BEEEP BEEEP
CYPRESS.
OH CHRIST.
YAH, BE THERE IN A MINUTE.
I'M SO SORRY COOP. MOMMY'S GOTTA GO.
CAN YOU--?
ME AND COOP ARE ALWAYS DOWN FOR SOME MORE FATHER/SON TIME.
COUPLE OF ROUNDS O' "SKYLANDERS?"
YEAH, SURE, DAD.
OFFICER MOM TO THE RESCUE, HUH?
YEAH.

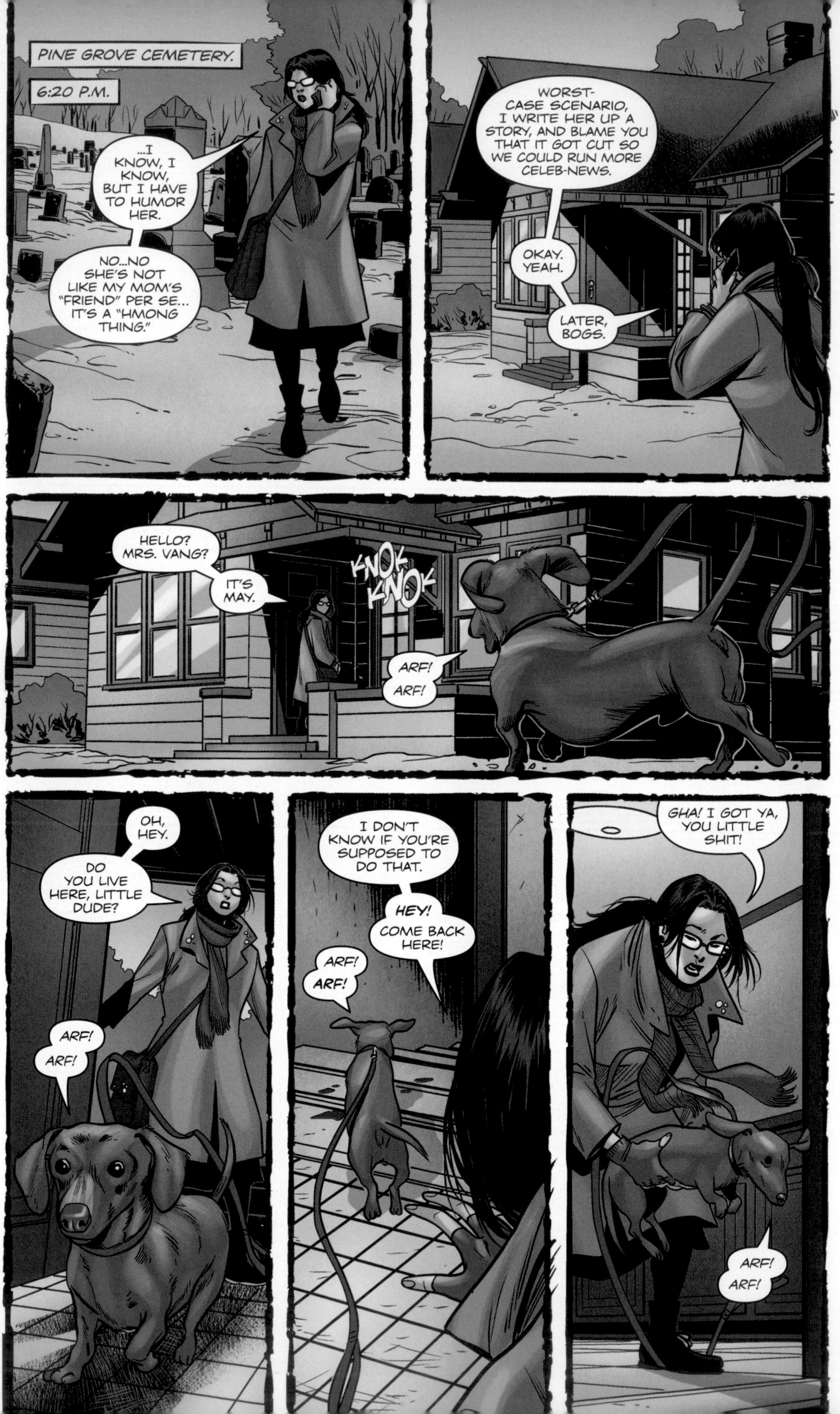
PINE GROVE CEMETERY.
6:20 P.M.
...I KNOW, I KNOW, BUT I HAVE TO HUMOR HER.
NO...NO SHE'S NOT LIKE MY MOM'S "FRIEND" PER SE... IT'S A "HMONG THING."
WORST-CASE SCENARIO, I WRITE HER UP A STORY, AND BLAME YOU THAT IT GOT CUT SO WE COULD RUN MORE CELEB-NEWS.
OKAY. YEAH.
LATER, BOGS.
HELLO? MRS. VANG?
IT'S MAY.
KNOK KNOK
ARF! ARF!
OH, HEY.
DO YOU LIVE HERE, LITTLE DUDE?
ARF! ARF!
I DON'T KNOW IF YOU'RE SUPPOSED TO DO THAT.
HEY! COME BACK HERE!
ARF! ARF!
GHA! I GOT YA, YOU LITTLE SHIT!
ARF! ARF!

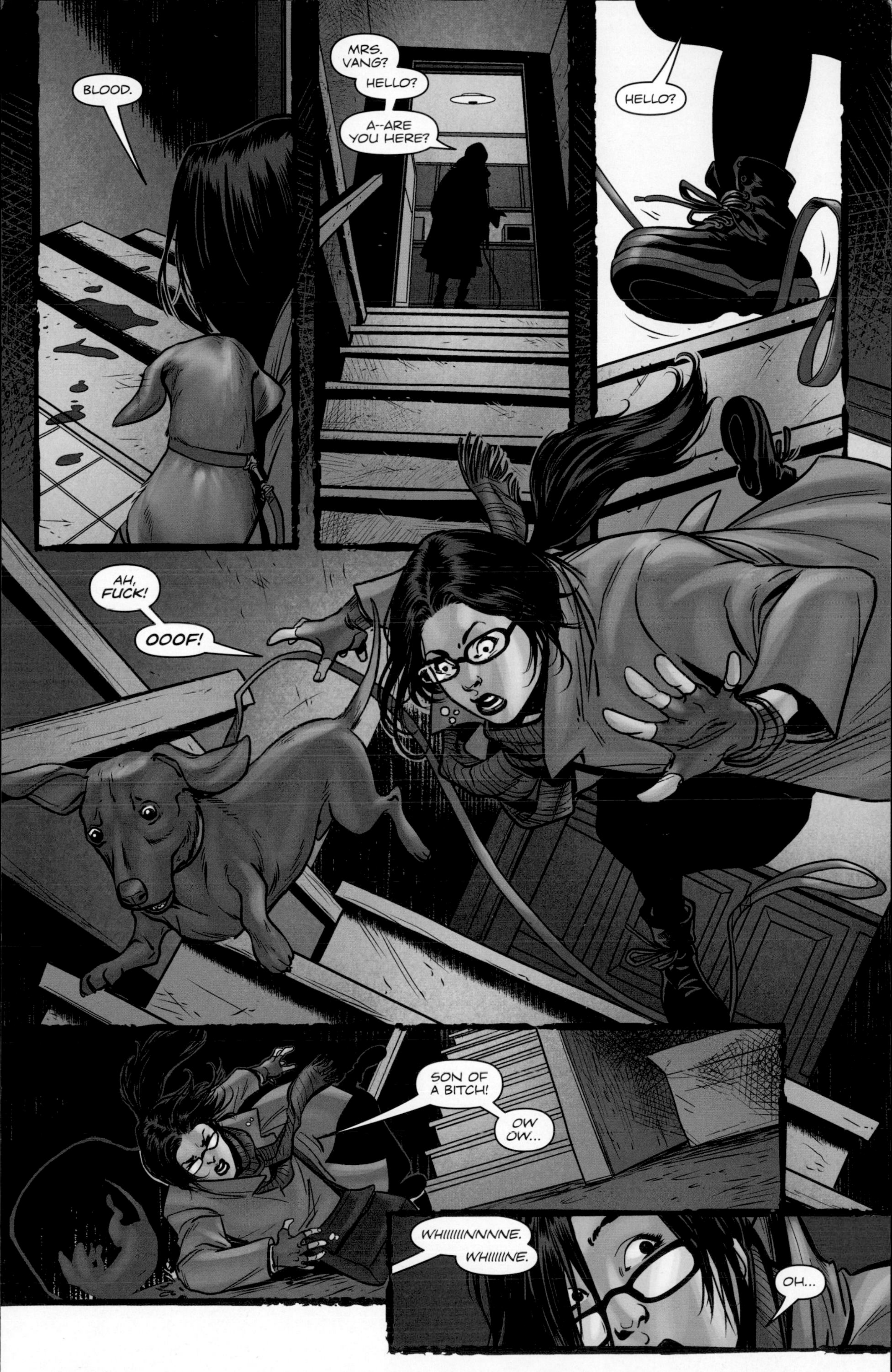
BLOOD.
MRS. VANG?
HELLO?
A--ARE YOU HERE?
HELLO?
AH, FUCK!
OOOF!
SON OF A BITCH!
OW OW...
WHIIIIIINNNNE.
WHIIIIINE.
OH...

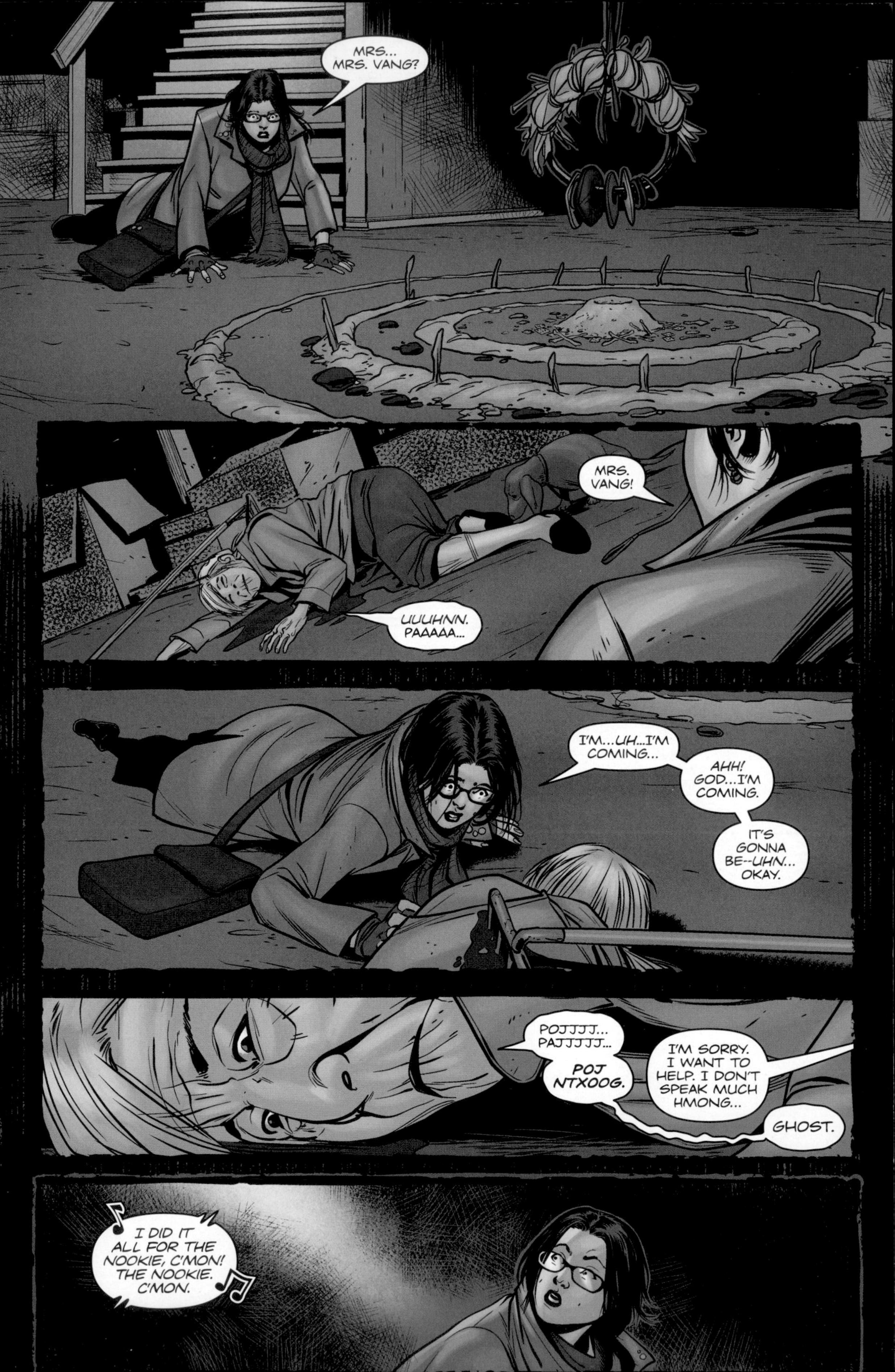
MRS... MRS. VANG?
MRS. VANG!
UUUHNN. PAAAAA...
I'M...UH...I'M COMING...
AHH! GOD...I'M COMING.
IT'S GONNA BE--UHN... OKAY.
POJJJJ... PAJJJJJ... POJ NTXOOG.
I'M SORRY. I WANT TO HELP. I DON'T SPEAK MUCH HMONG...
GHOST.
I DID IT ALL FOR THE NOOKIE, C'MON! THE NOOKIE. C'MON.

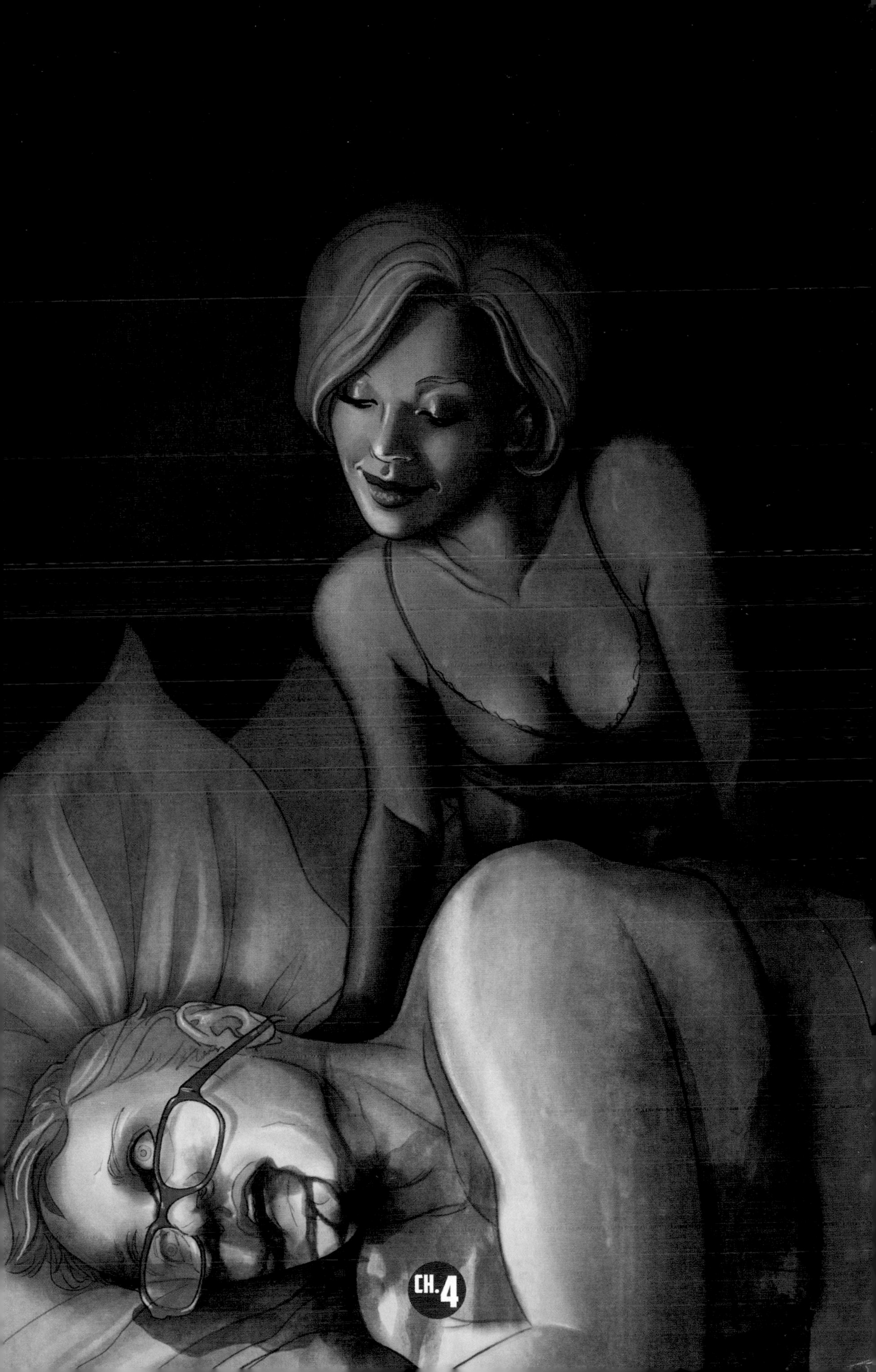
CH. 4

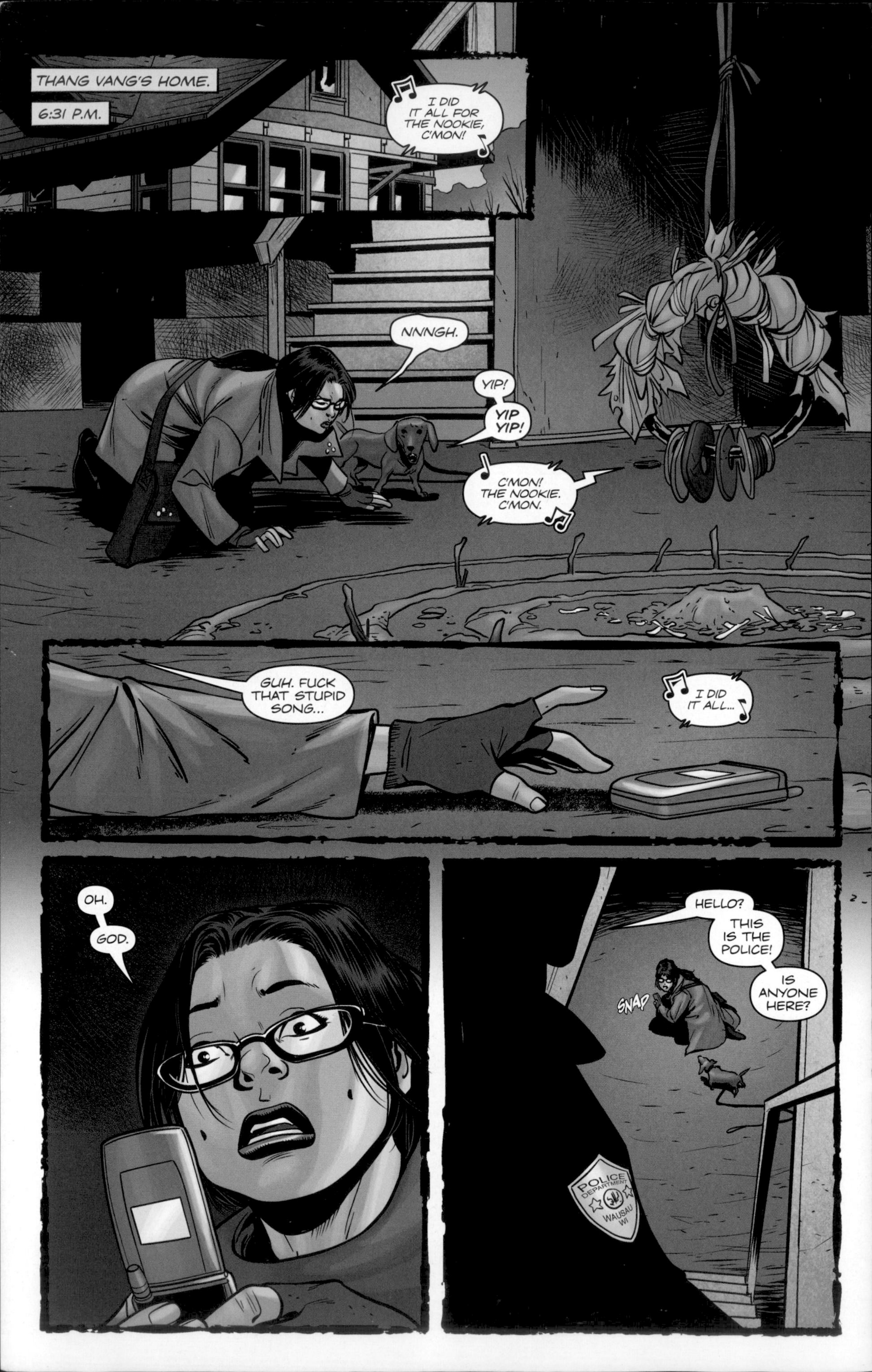
THANG VANG'S HOME.
6:31 P.M.
I DID IT ALL FOR THE NOOKIE, C'MON!
NNNGH.
YIP!
YIP YIP!
C'MON! THE NOOKIE. C'MON.
GUH. FUCK THAT STUPID SONG...
I DID IT ALL...
OH.
GOD.
HELLO?
THIS IS THE POLICE!
IS ANYONE HERE?
SNAP
POLICE DEPARTMENT WAUSAU WI

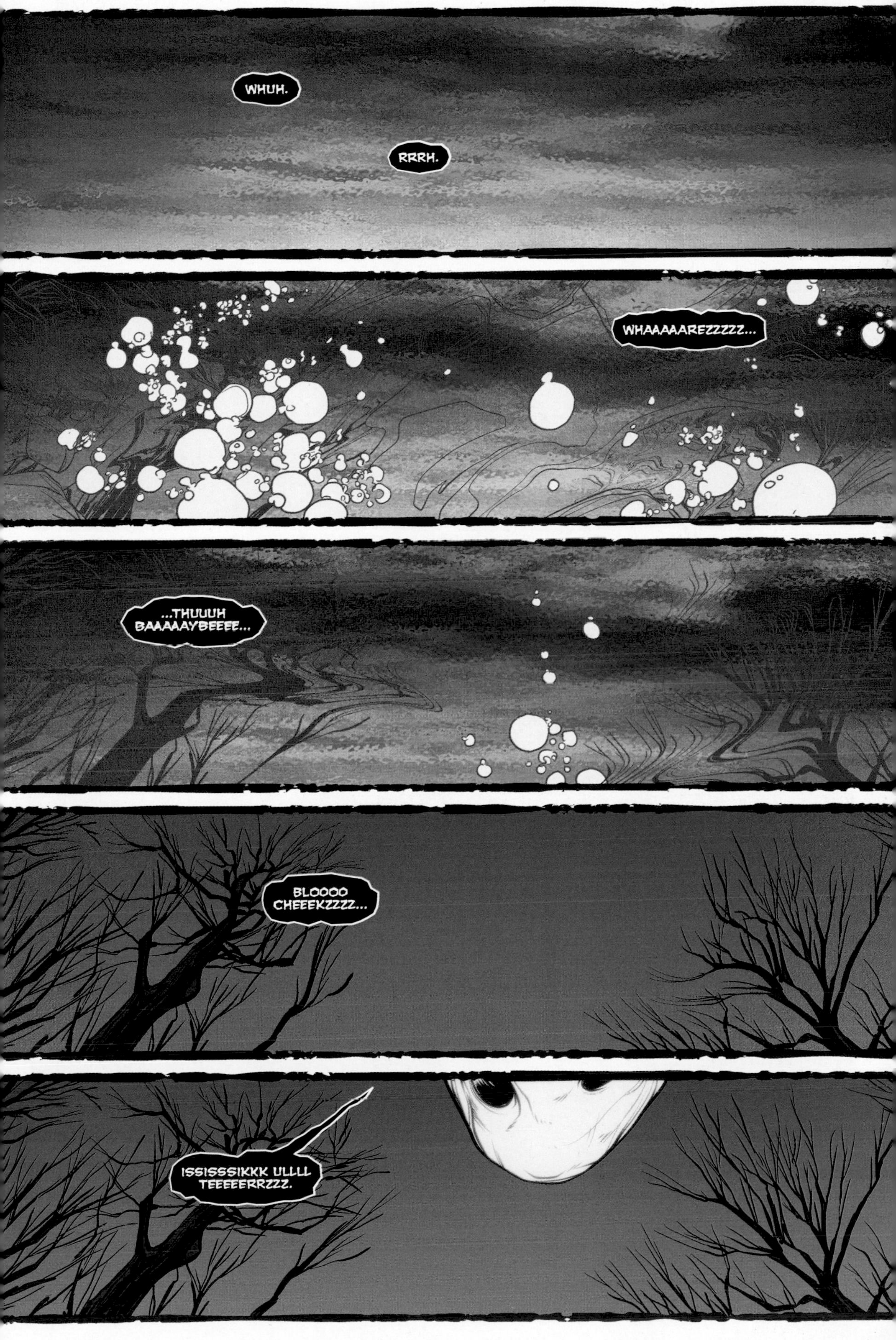
WHUH.
RRRH.
WHAAAAAREZZZZZ...
...THUUUH BAAAAAYBEEEE...
BLOOOO CHEEEKZZZZ...
ISSISSSIKKK ULLLL TEEEEERRZZZ.

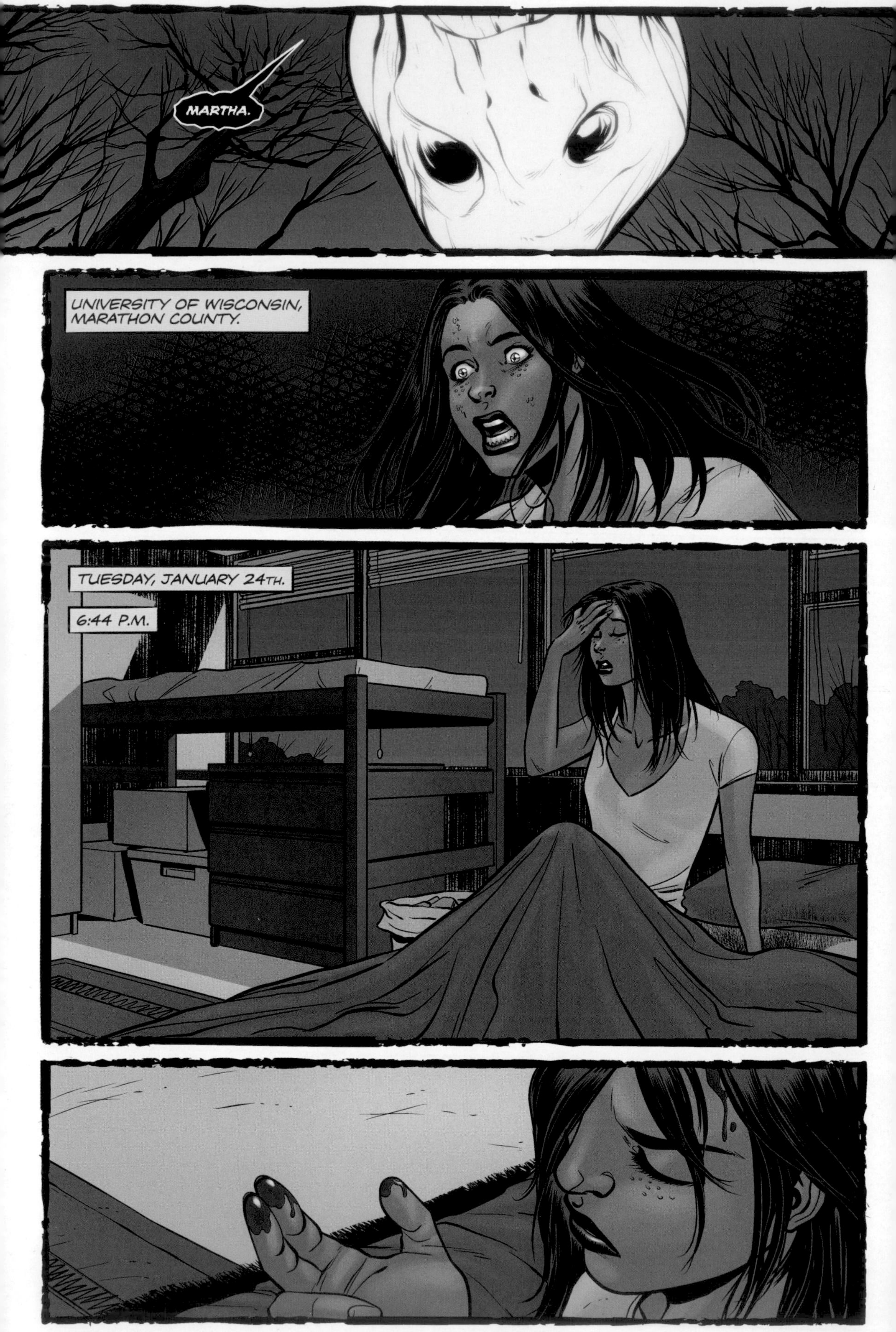
MARTHA.
UNIVERSITY OF WISCONSIN, MARATHON COUNTY.
TUESDAY, JANUARY 24TH.
6:44 P.M.

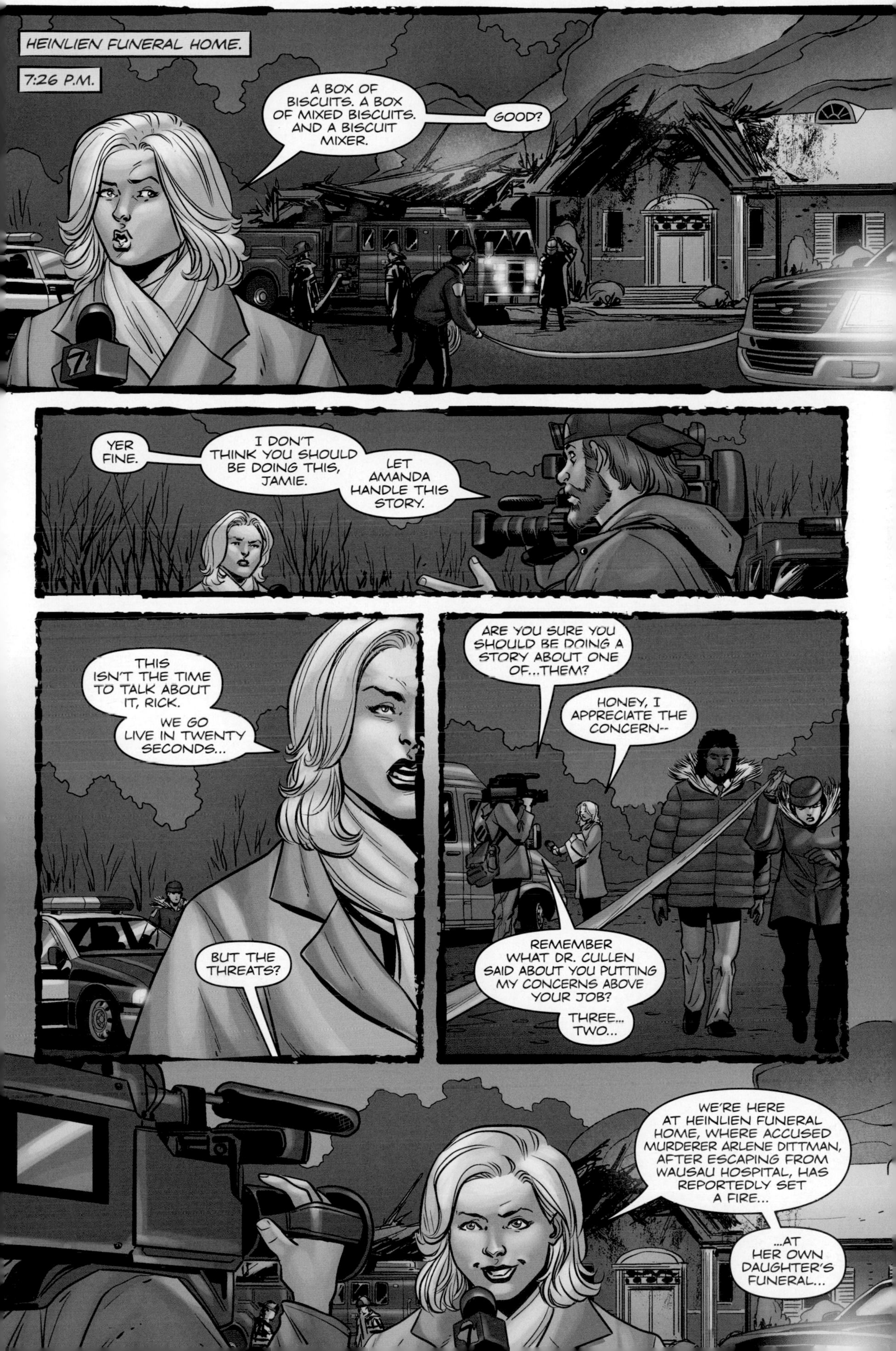
HEINLIEN FUNERAL HOME.
7:26 P.M.
A BOX OF BISCUITS. A BOX OF MIXED BISCUITS. AND A BISCUIT MIXER.
GOOD?
YER FINE.
I DON'T THINK YOU SHOULD BE DOING THIS, JAMIE.
LET AMANDA HANDLE THIS STORY.
THIS ISN'T THE TIME TO TALK ABOUT IT, RICK.
WE GO LIVE IN TWENTY SECONDS...
BUT THE THREATS?
ARE YOU SURE YOU SHOULD BE DOING A STORY ABOUT ONE OF...THEM?
HONEY, I APPRECIATE THE CONCERN--
REMEMBER WHAT DR. CULLEN SAID ABOUT YOU PUTTING MY CONCERNS ABOVE YOUR JOB?
THREE... TWO...
WE'RE HERE AT HEINLIEN FUNERAL HOME, WHERE ACCUSED MURDERER ARLENE DITTMAN, AFTER ESCAPING FROM WAUSAU HOSPITAL, HAS REPORTEDLY SET A FIRE...
...AT HER OWN DAUGHTER'S FUNERAL...

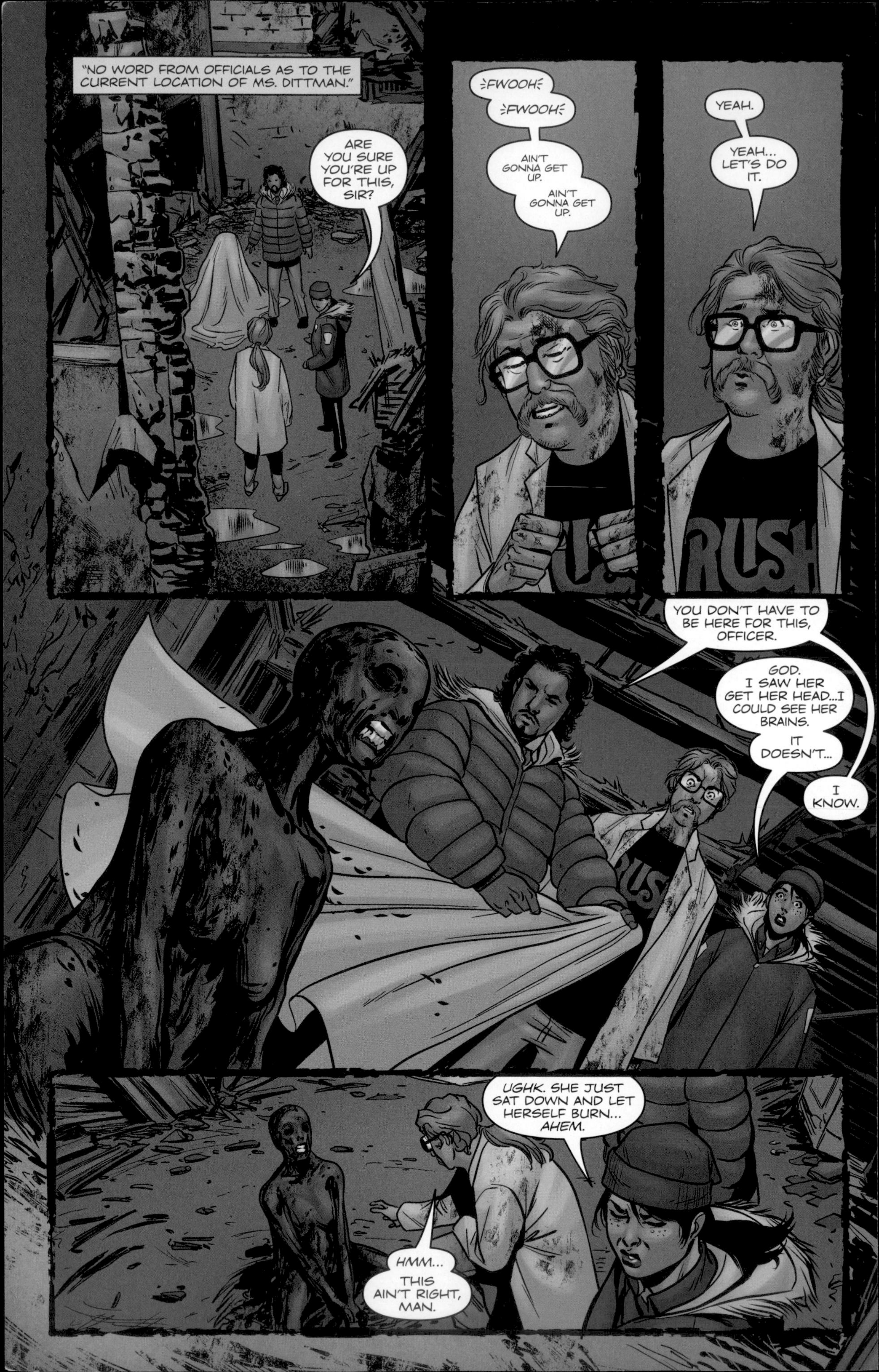
"NO WORD FROM OFFICIALS AS TO THE CURRENT LOCATION OF MS. DITTMAN."
ARE YOU SURE YOU'RE UP FOR THIS, SIR?
FWOOH
FWOOH
AIN'T GONNA GET UP.
AIN'T GONNA GET UP.
YEAH.
YEAH... LET'S DO IT.
RUSH
YOU DON'T HAVE TO BE HERE FOR THIS, OFFICER.
GOD. I SAW HER GET HER HEAD...I COULD SEE HER BRAINS.
IT DOESN'T...
I KNOW.
UGHK. SHE JUST SAT DOWN AND LET HERSELF BURN... AHEM.
HMM... THIS AIN'T RIGHT, MAN.

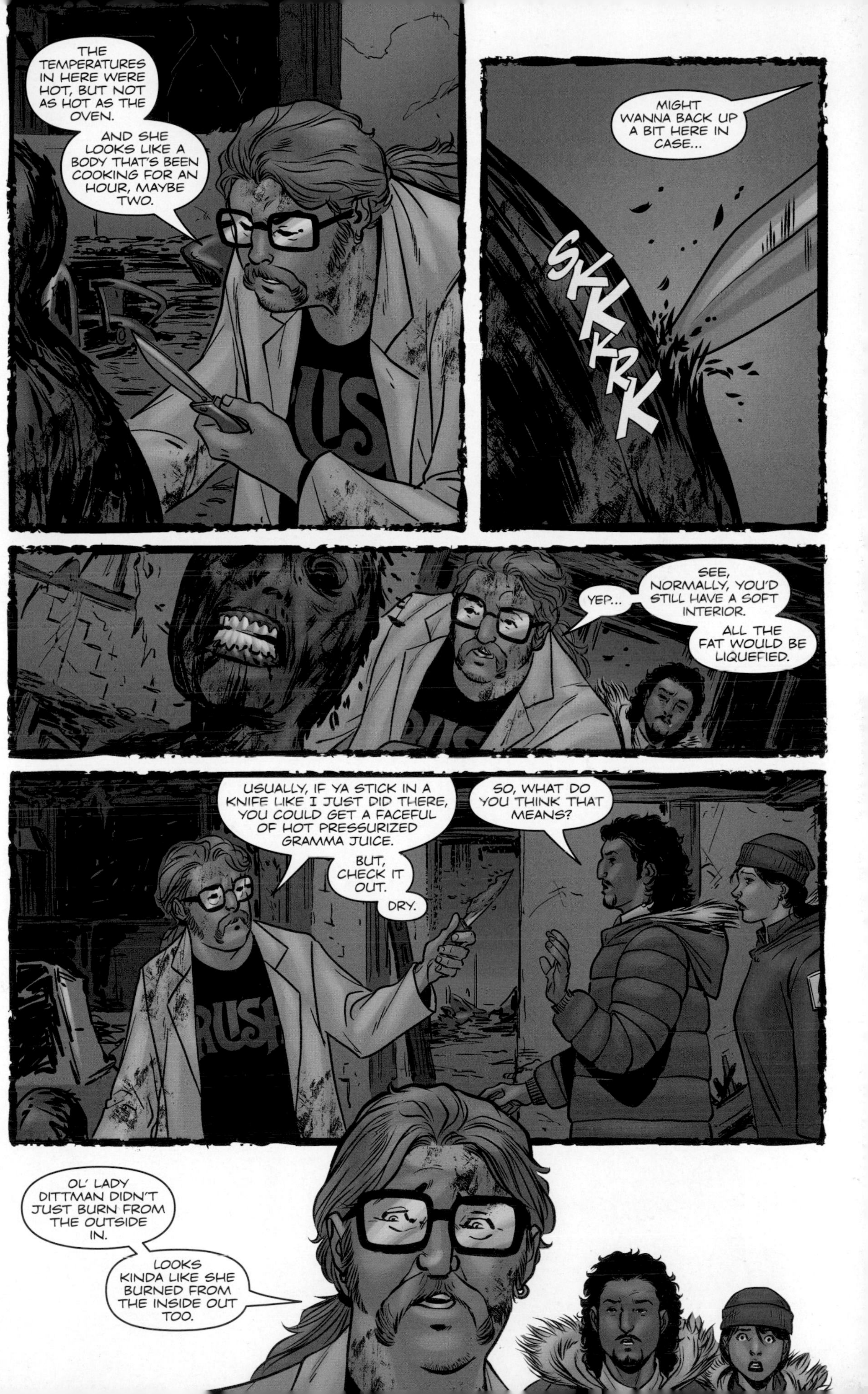
THE TEMPERATURES IN HERE WERE HOT, BUT NOT AS HOT AS THE OVEN.
AND SHE LOOKS LIKE A BODY THAT'S BEEN COOKING FOR AN HOUR, MAYBE TWO.
MIGHT WANNA BACK UP A BIT HERE IN CASE...
SKKKRK
YEP...
SEE, NORMALLY, YOU'D STILL HAVE A SOFT INTERIOR.
ALL THE FAT WOULD BE LIQUEFIED.
USUALLY, IF YA STICK IN A KNIFE LIKE I JUST DID THERE, YOU COULD GET A FACEFUL OF HOT PRESSURIZED GRAMMA JUICE.
BUT, CHECK IT OUT.
DRY.
SO, WHAT DO YOU THINK THAT MEANS?
OL' LADY DITTMAN DIDN'T JUST BURN FROM THE OUTSIDE IN.
LOOKS KINDA LIKE SHE BURNED FROM THE INSIDE OUT TOO.

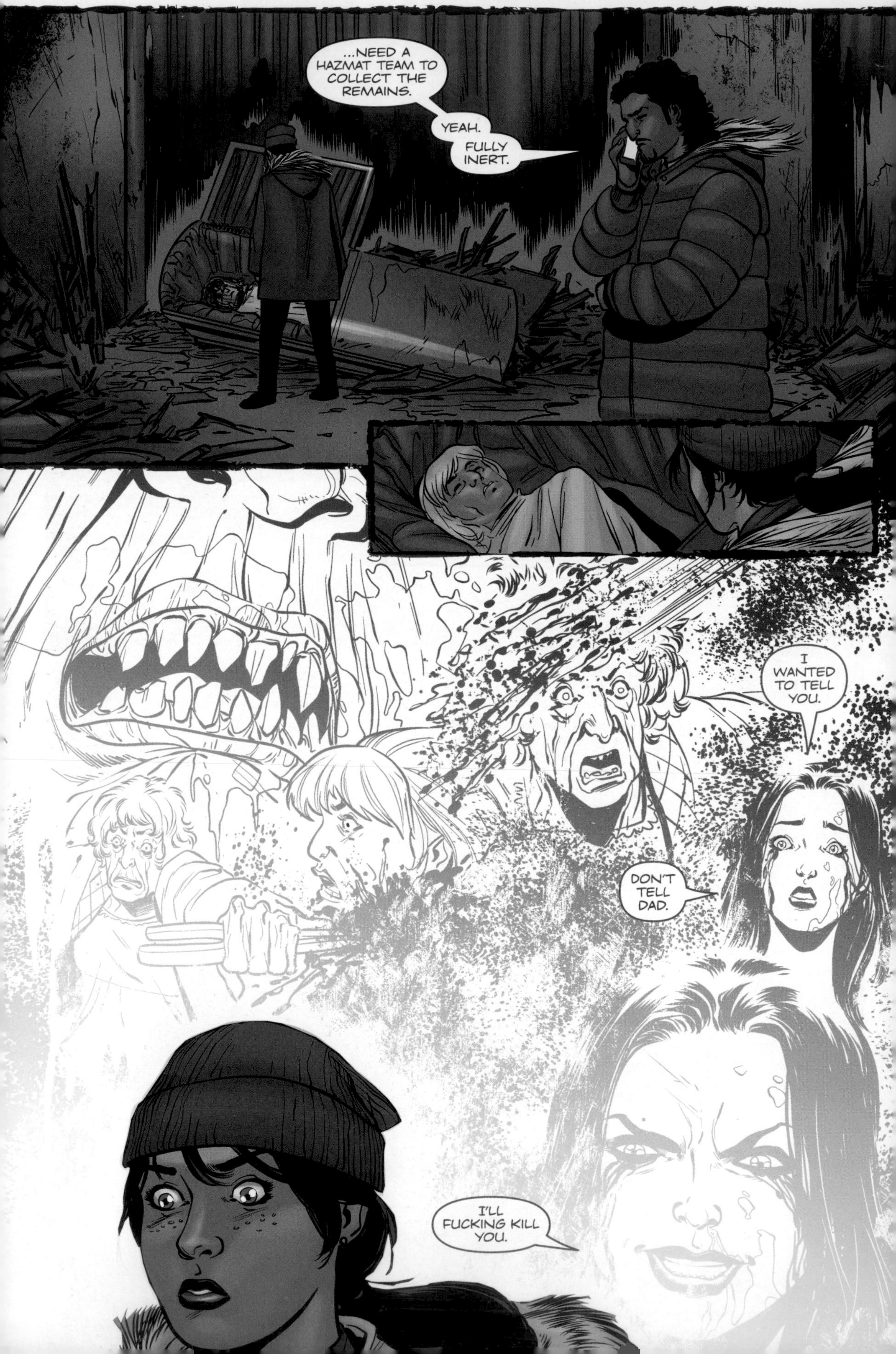
...NEED A HAZMAT TEAM TO COLLECT THE REMAINS.
YEAH.
FULLY INERT.
I WANTED TO TELL YOU.
DON'T TELL DAD.
I'LL FUCKING KILL YOU.

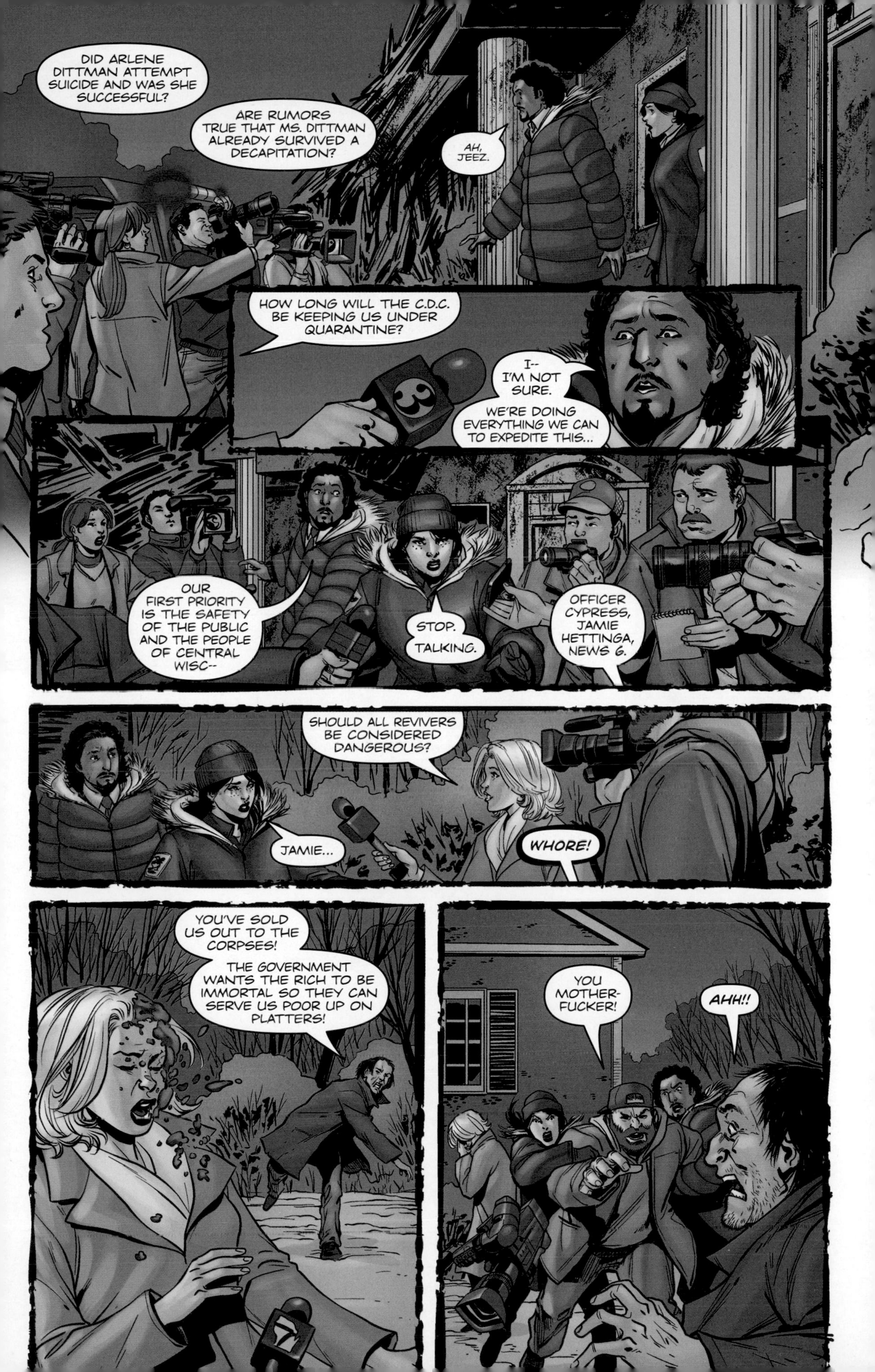
DID ARLENE DITTMAN ATTEMPT SUICIDE AND WAS SHE SUCCESSFUL?
ARE RUMORS TRUE THAT MS. DITTMAN ALREADY SURVIVED A DECAPITATION?
AH, JEEZ.
HOW LONG WILL THE C.D.C. BE KEEPING US UNDER QUARANTINE?
I-- I'M NOT SURE.
WE'RE DOING EVERYTHING WE CAN TO EXPEDITE THIS...
OUR FIRST PRIORITY IS THE SAFETY OF THE PUBLIC AND THE PEOPLE OF CENTRAL WISC--
STOP.
TALKING.
OFFICER CYPRESS, JAMIE HETTINGA, NEWS 6.
SHOULD ALL REVIVERS BE CONSIDERED DANGEROUS?
JAMIE...
WHORE!
YOU'VE SOLD US OUT TO THE CORPSES!
THE GOVERNMENT WANTS THE RICH TO BE IMMORTAL SO THEY CAN SERVE US POOR UP ON PLATTERS!
YOU MOTHER-FUCKER!
AHH!!

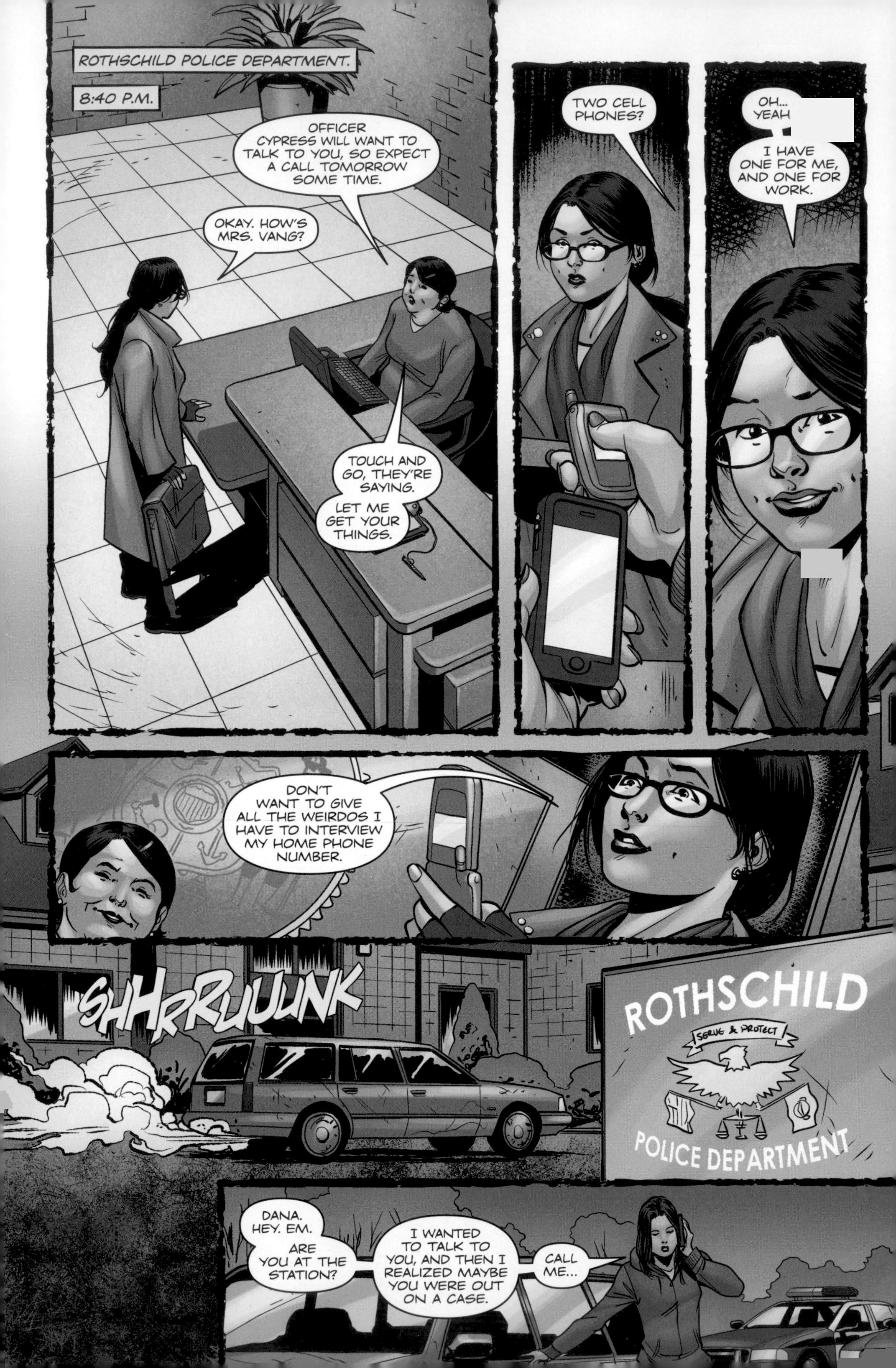
ROTHSCHILD POLICE DEPARTMENT.
8:40 P.M.
OFFICER CYPRESS WILL WANT TO TALK TO YOU, SO EXPECT A CALL TOMORROW SOME TIME.
OKAY. HOW'S MRS. VANG?
TOUCH AND GO, THEY'RE SAYING.
LET ME GET YOUR THINGS.
TWO CELL PHONES?
OH... YEAH
I HAVE ONE FOR ME, AND ONE FOR WORK.
DON'T WANT TO GIVE ALL THE WEIRDOS I HAVE TO INTERVIEW MY HOME PHONE NUMBER.
SHHRRUUUNK
ROTHSCHILD
SERVE & PROTECT
POLICE DEPARTMENT
DANA. HEY. EM.
ARE YOU AT THE STATION?
I WANTED TO TALK TO YOU, AND THEN I REALIZED MAYBE YOU WERE OUT ON A CASE.
CALL ME...

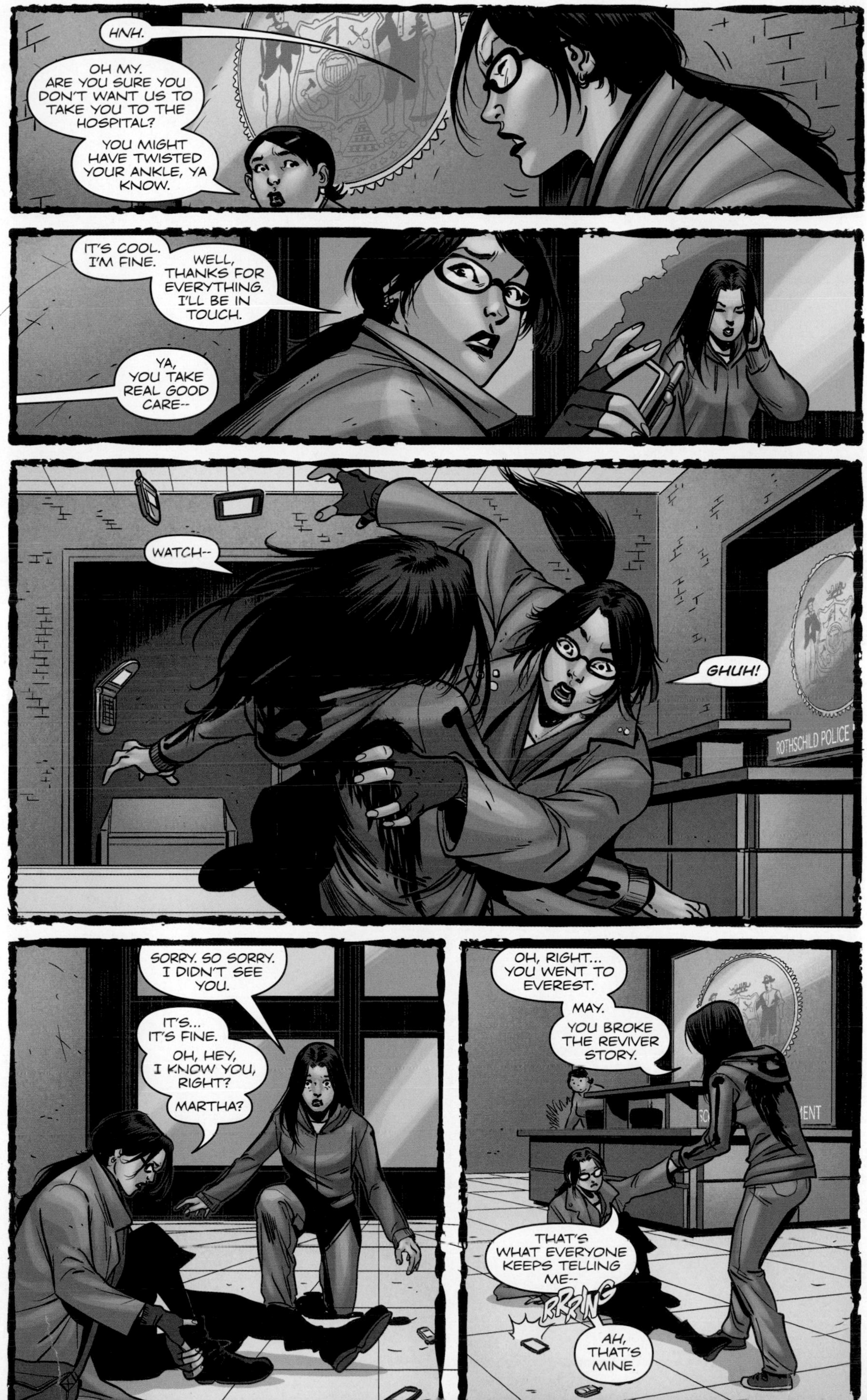
HNH.
OH MY. ARE YOU SURE YOU DON'T WANT US TO TAKE YOU TO THE HOSPITAL?
YOU MIGHT HAVE TWISTED YOUR ANKLE, YA KNOW.
IT'S COOL. I'M FINE.
WELL, THANKS FOR EVERYTHING. I'LL BE IN TOUCH.
YA, YOU TAKE REAL GOOD CARE--
WATCH--
GHUH!
ROTHSCHILD POLICE
SORRY. SO SORRY. I DIDN'T SEE YOU.
IT'S... IT'S FINE.
OH, HEY, I KNOW YOU, RIGHT?
MARTHA?
OH, RIGHT... YOU WENT TO EVEREST.
MAY.
YOU BROKE THE REVIVER STORY.
THAT'S WHAT EVERYONE KEEPS TELLING ME--
RRRING
AH, THAT'S MINE.

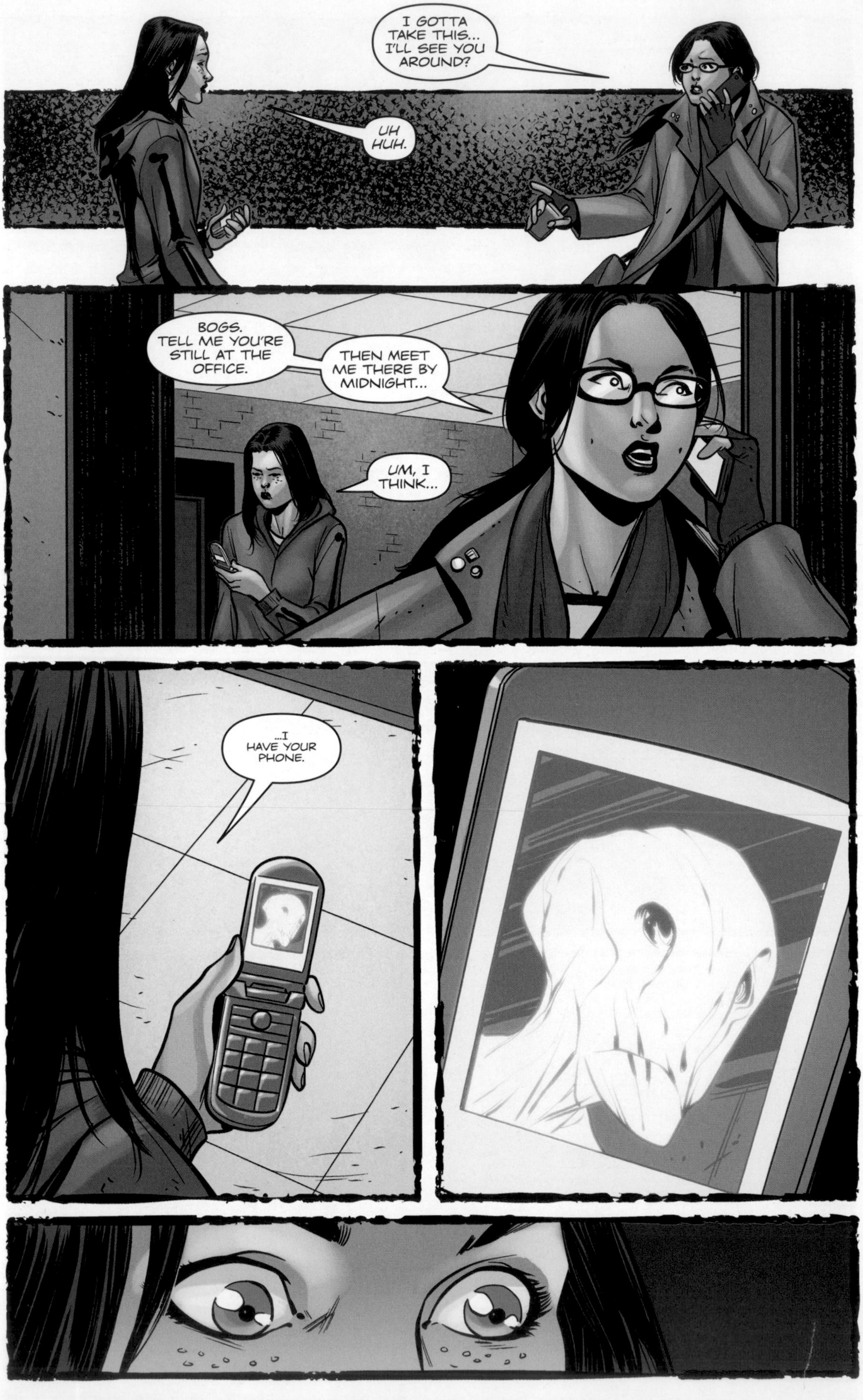
I GOTTA TAKE THIS... I'LL SEE YOU AROUND?
UH HUH.
BOGS. TELL ME YOU'RE STILL AT THE OFFICE.
THEN MEET ME THERE BY MIDNIGHT...
UM, I THINK...
...I HAVE YOUR PHONE.

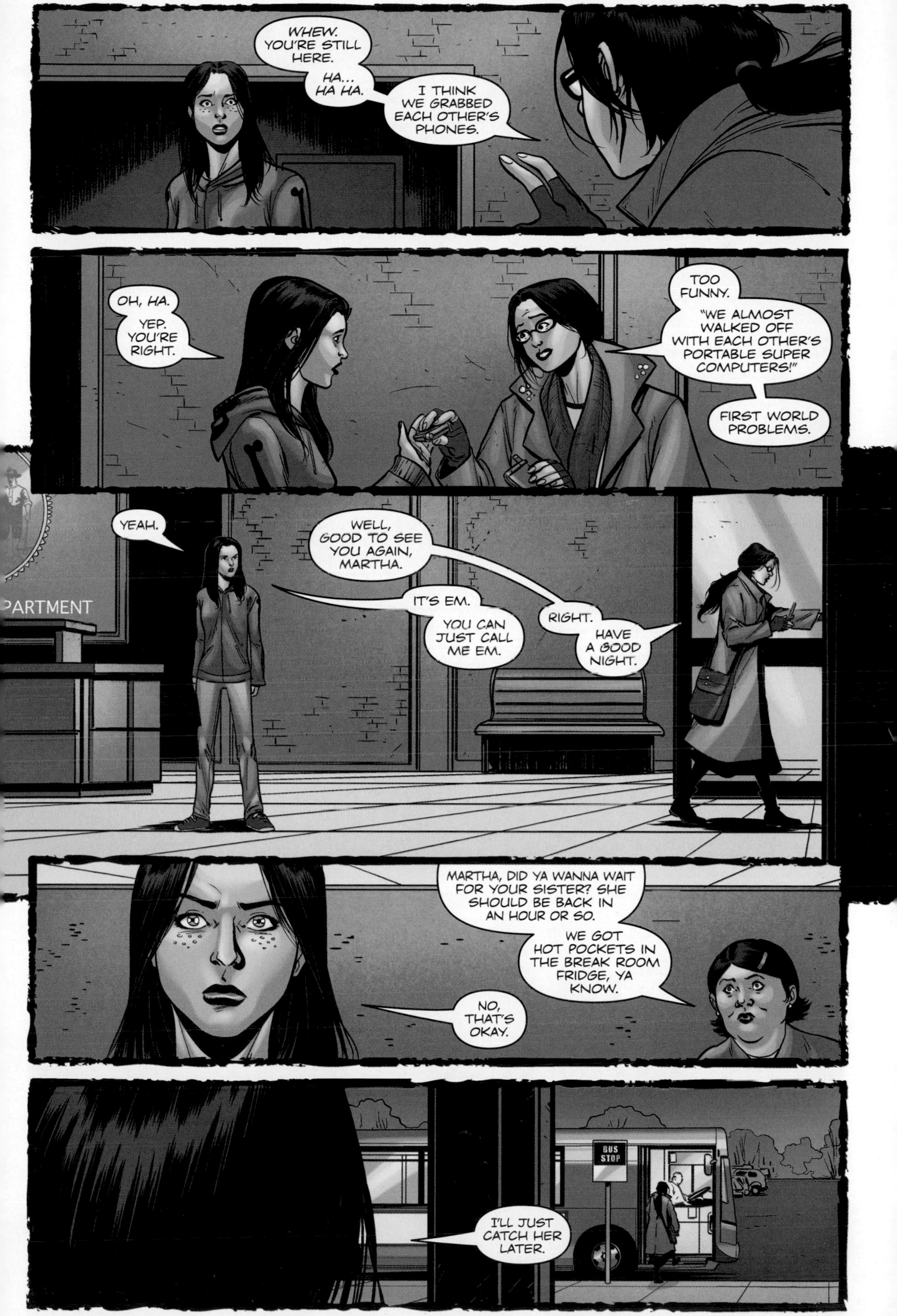
WHEW. YOU'RE STILL HERE.
HA... HA HA.
I THINK WE GRABBED EACH OTHER'S PHONES.
OH, HA.
YEP. YOU'RE RIGHT.
TOO FUNNY.
"WE ALMOST WALKED OFF WITH EACH OTHER'S PORTABLE SUPER COMPUTERS!"
FIRST WORLD PROBLEMS.
PARTMENT
YEAH.
WELL, GOOD TO SEE YOU AGAIN, MARTHA.
IT'S EM.
YOU CAN JUST CALL ME EM.
RIGHT.
HAVE A GOOD NIGHT.
MARTHA, DID YA WANNA WAIT FOR YOUR SISTER? SHE SHOULD BE BACK IN AN HOUR OR SO.
WE GOT HOT POCKETS IN THE BREAK ROOM FRIDGE, YA KNOW.
NO, THAT'S OKAY.
BUS STOP
I'LL JUST CATCH HER LATER.

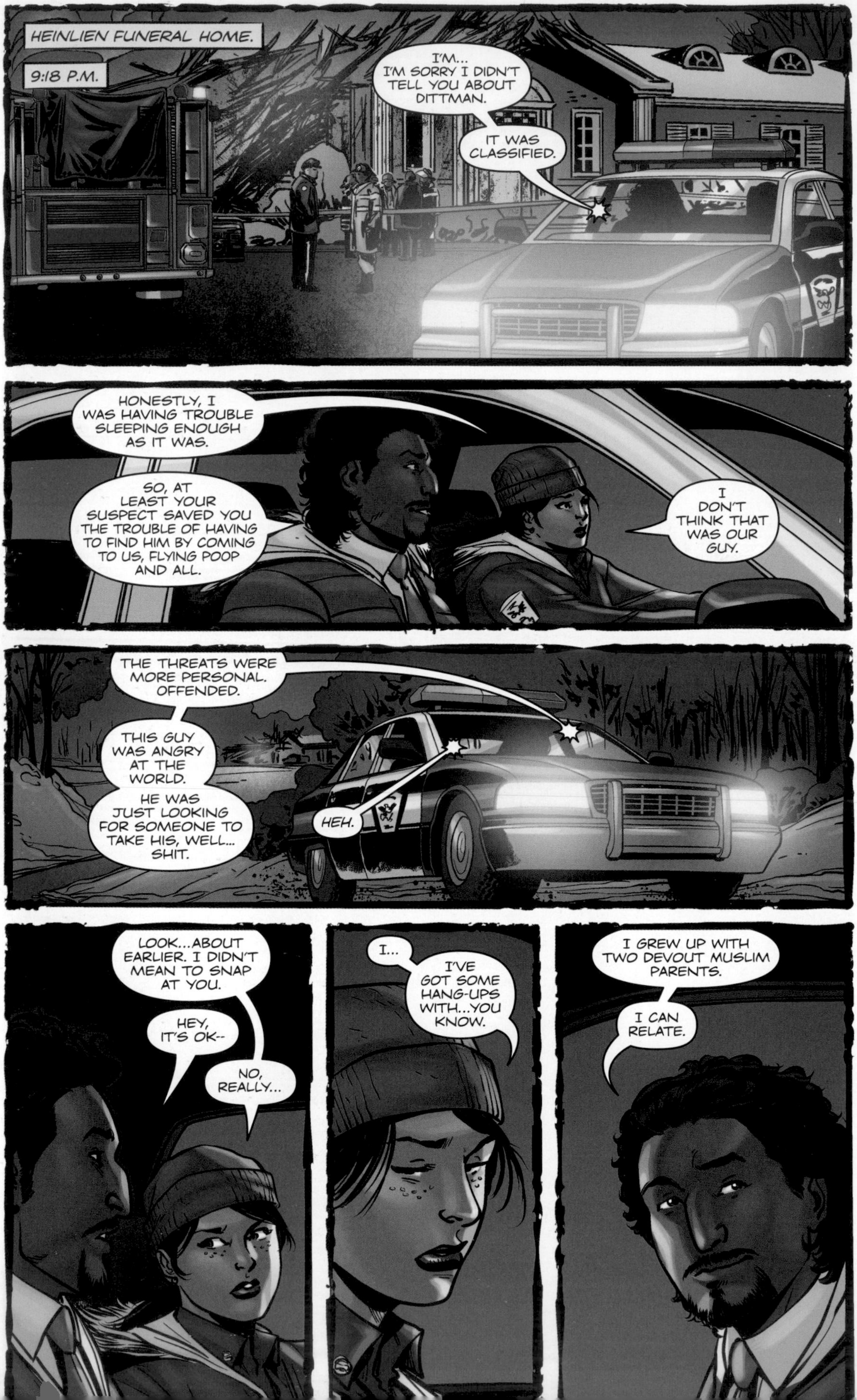
HEINLIEN FUNERAL HOME.
9:18 P.M.
I'M... I'M SORRY I DIDN'T TELL YOU ABOUT DITTMAN.
IT WAS CLASSIFIED.
HONESTLY, I WAS HAVING TROUBLE SLEEPING ENOUGH AS IT WAS.
SO, AT LEAST YOUR SUSPECT SAVED YOU THE TROUBLE OF HAVING TO FIND HIM BY COMING TO US, FLYING POOP AND ALL.
I DON'T THINK THAT WAS OUR GUY.
THE THREATS WERE MORE PERSONAL. OFFENDED.
THIS GUY WAS ANGRY AT THE WORLD.
HE WAS JUST LOOKING FOR SOMEONE TO TAKE HIS, WELL... SHIT.
HEH.
LOOK...ABOUT EARLIER. I DIDN'T MEAN TO SNAP AT YOU.
HEY, IT'S OK--
NO, REALLY...
I...
I'VE GOT SOME HANG-UPS WITH...YOU KNOW.
I GREW UP WITH TWO DEVOUT MUSLIM PARENTS.
I CAN RELATE.

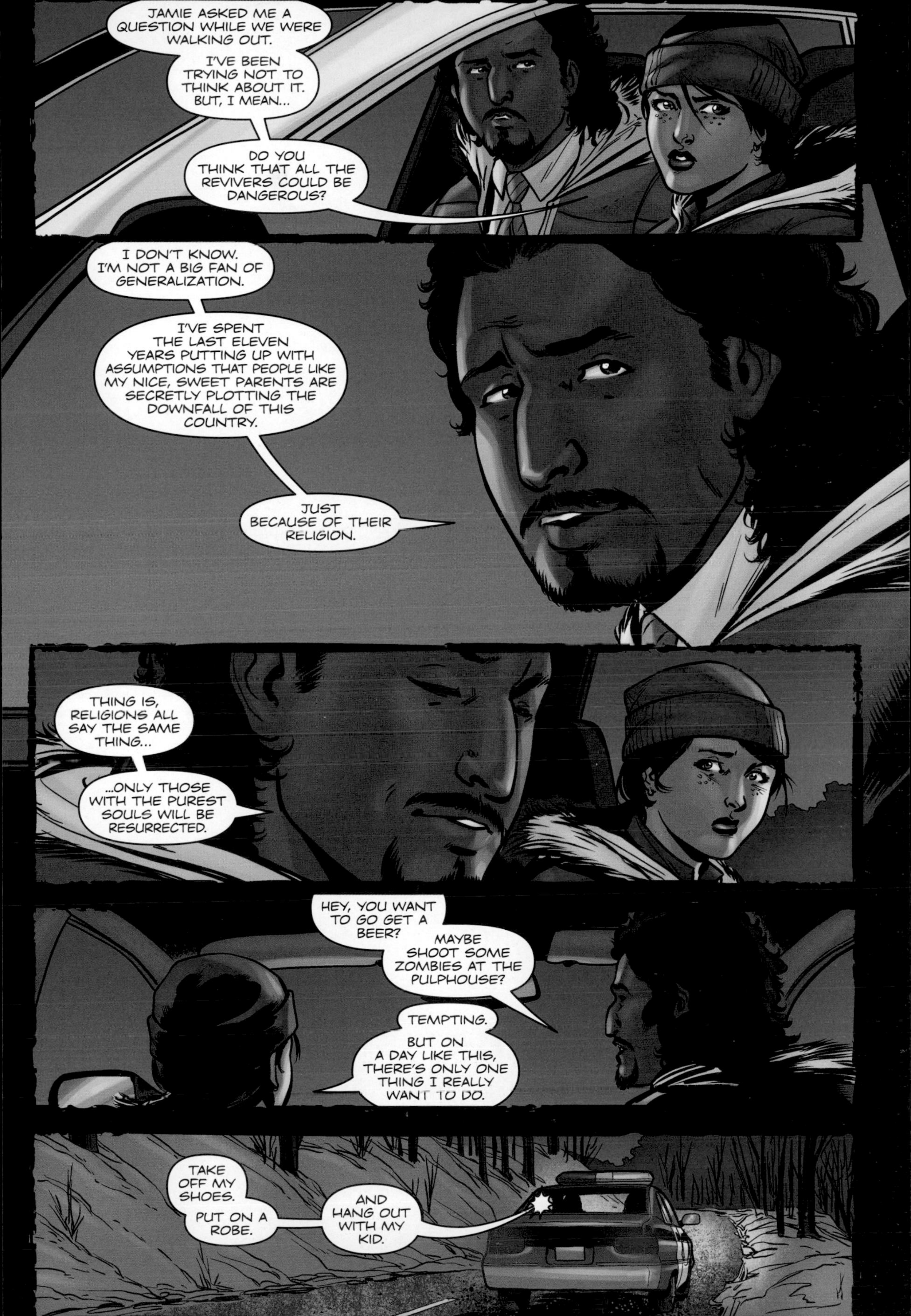
JAMIE ASKED ME A QUESTION WHILE WE WERE WALKING OUT.
I'VE BEEN TRYING NOT TO THINK ABOUT IT. BUT, I MEAN...
DO YOU THINK THAT ALL THE REVIVERS COULD BE DANGEROUS?
I DON'T KNOW. I'M NOT A BIG FAN OF GENERALIZATION.
I'VE SPENT THE LAST ELEVEN YEARS PUTTING UP WITH ASSUMPTIONS THAT PEOPLE LIKE MY NICE, SWEET PARENTS ARE SECRETLY PLOTTING THE DOWNFALL OF THIS COUNTRY.
JUST BECAUSE OF THEIR RELIGION.
THING IS, RELIGIONS ALL SAY THE SAME THING...
...ONLY THOSE WITH THE PUREST SOULS WILL BE RESURRECTED.
HEY, YOU WANT TO GO GET A BEER?
MAYBE SHOOT SOME ZOMBIES AT THE PULPHOUSE?
TEMPTING.
BUT ON A DAY LIKE THIS, THERE'S ONLY ONE THING I REALLY WANT TO DO.
TAKE OFF MY SHOES.
PUT ON A ROBE.
AND HANG OUT WITH MY KID.

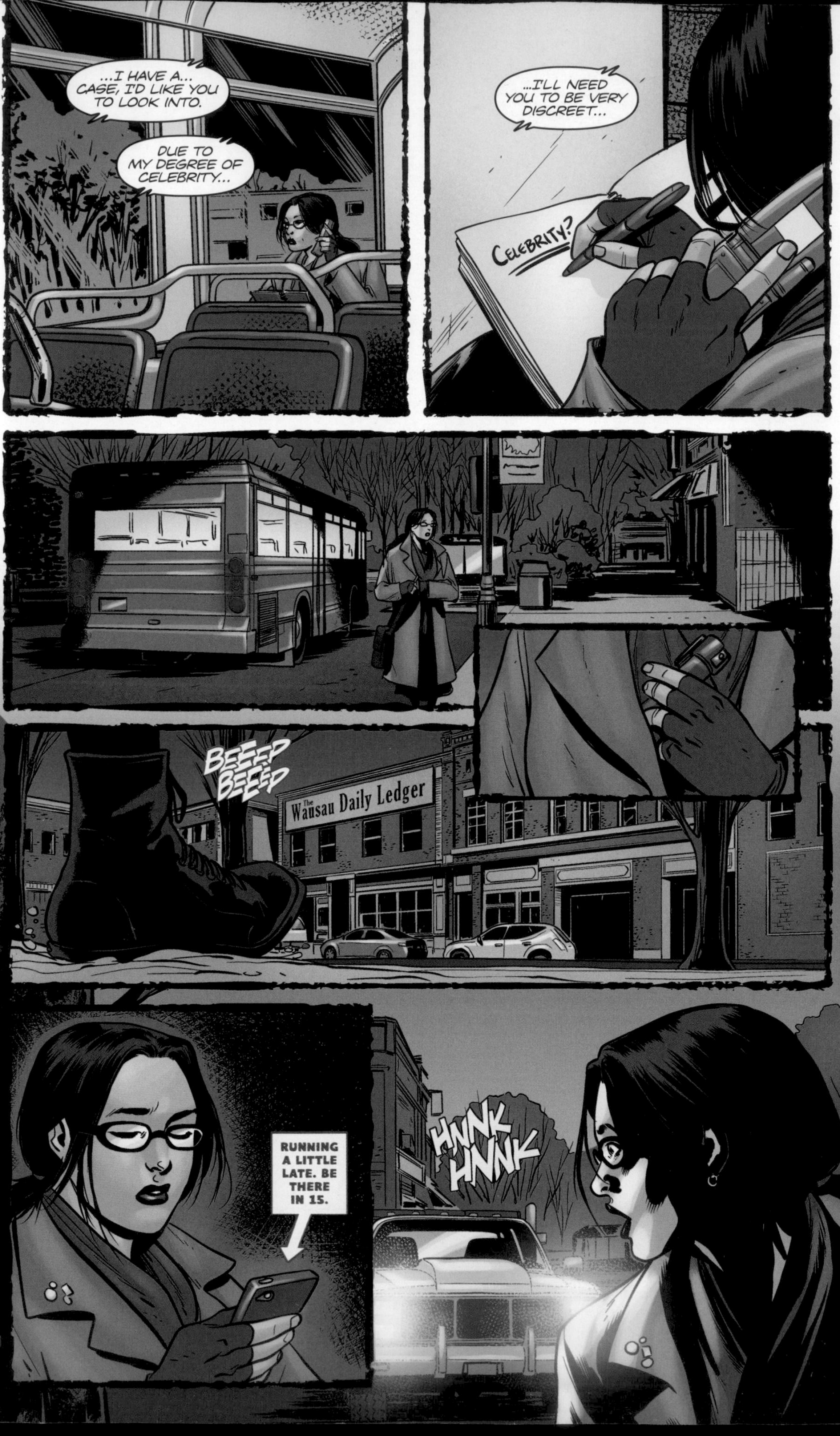
...I HAVE A... CASE, I'D LIKE YOU TO LOOK INTO.
DUE TO MY DEGREE OF CELEBRITY...
...I'LL NEED YOU TO BE VERY DISCREET...
CELEBRITY?
BEEEP BEEEP
The Wausau Daily Ledger
RUNNING A LITTLE LATE. BE THERE IN 15.
HNNK HNNK

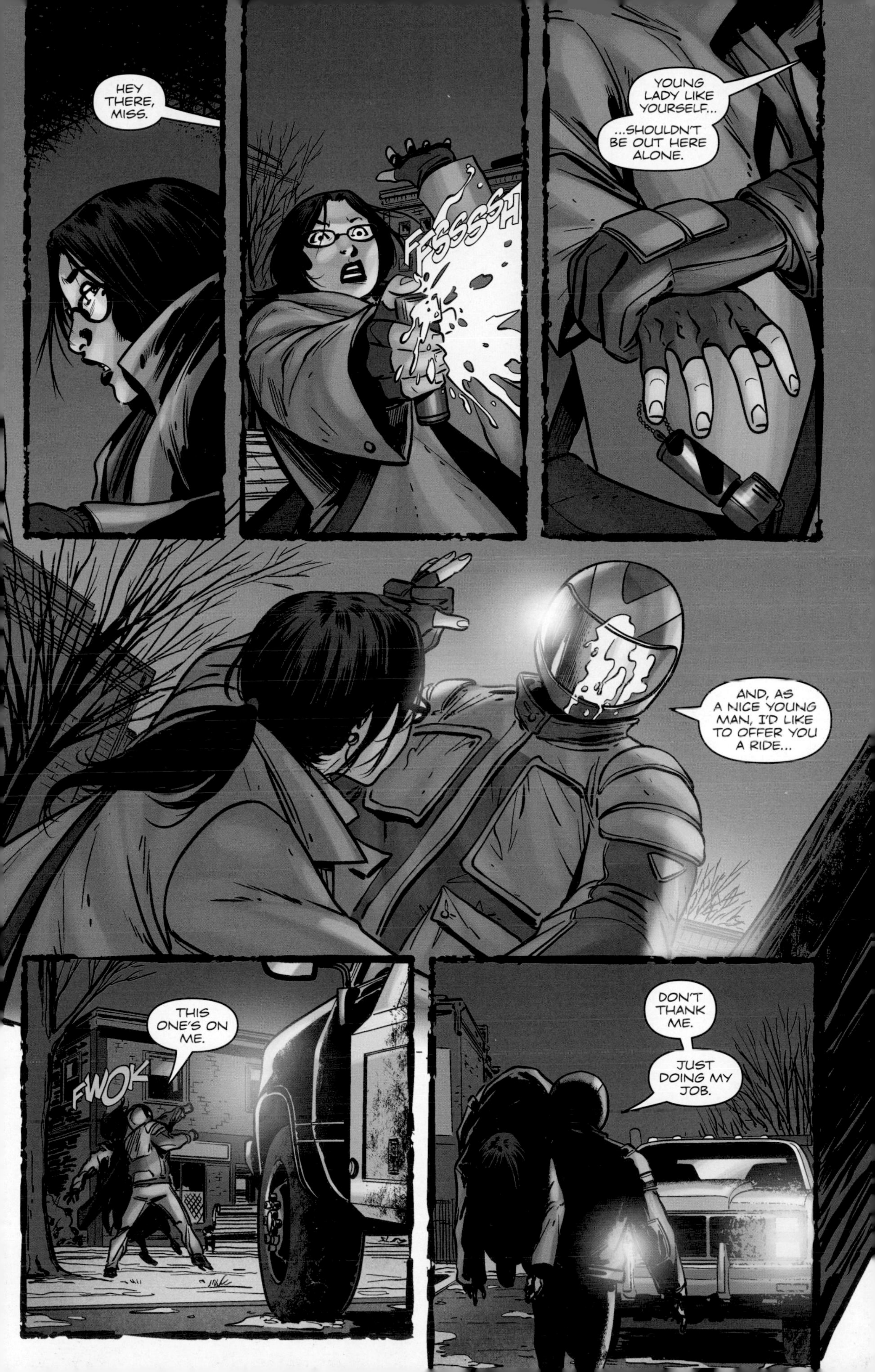
HEY THERE, MISS.
FFSSSSH
YOUNG LADY LIKE YOURSELF...
...SHOULDN'T BE OUT HERE ALONE.
AND, AS A NICE YOUNG MAN, I'D LIKE TO OFFER YOU A RIDE...
THIS ONE'S ON ME.
FWOK
DON'T THANK ME.
JUST DOING MY JOB.

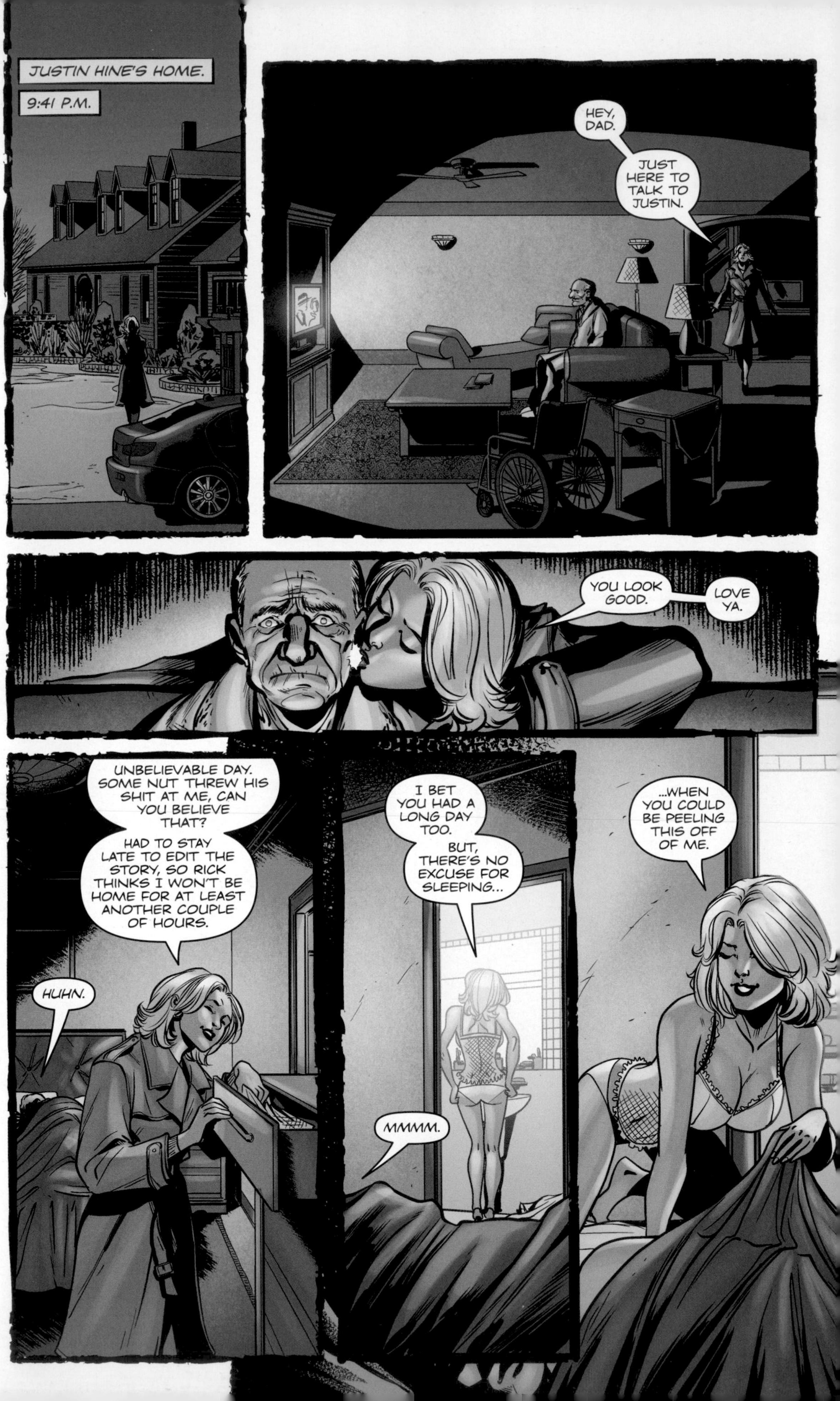
JUSTIN HINE'S HOME.
9:41 P.M.
HEY, DAD.
JUST HERE TO TALK TO JUSTIN.
YOU LOOK GOOD.
LOVE YA.
UNBELIEVABLE DAY. SOME NUT THREW HIS SHIT AT ME, CAN YOU BELIEVE THAT?
HAD TO STAY LATE TO EDIT THE STORY, SO RICK THINKS I WON'T BE HOME FOR AT LEAST ANOTHER COUPLE OF HOURS.
HUHN.
I BET YOU HAD A LONG DAY TOO.
BUT, THERE'S NO EXCUSE FOR SLEEPING...
MMMM.
...WHEN YOU COULD BE PEELING THIS OFF OF ME.

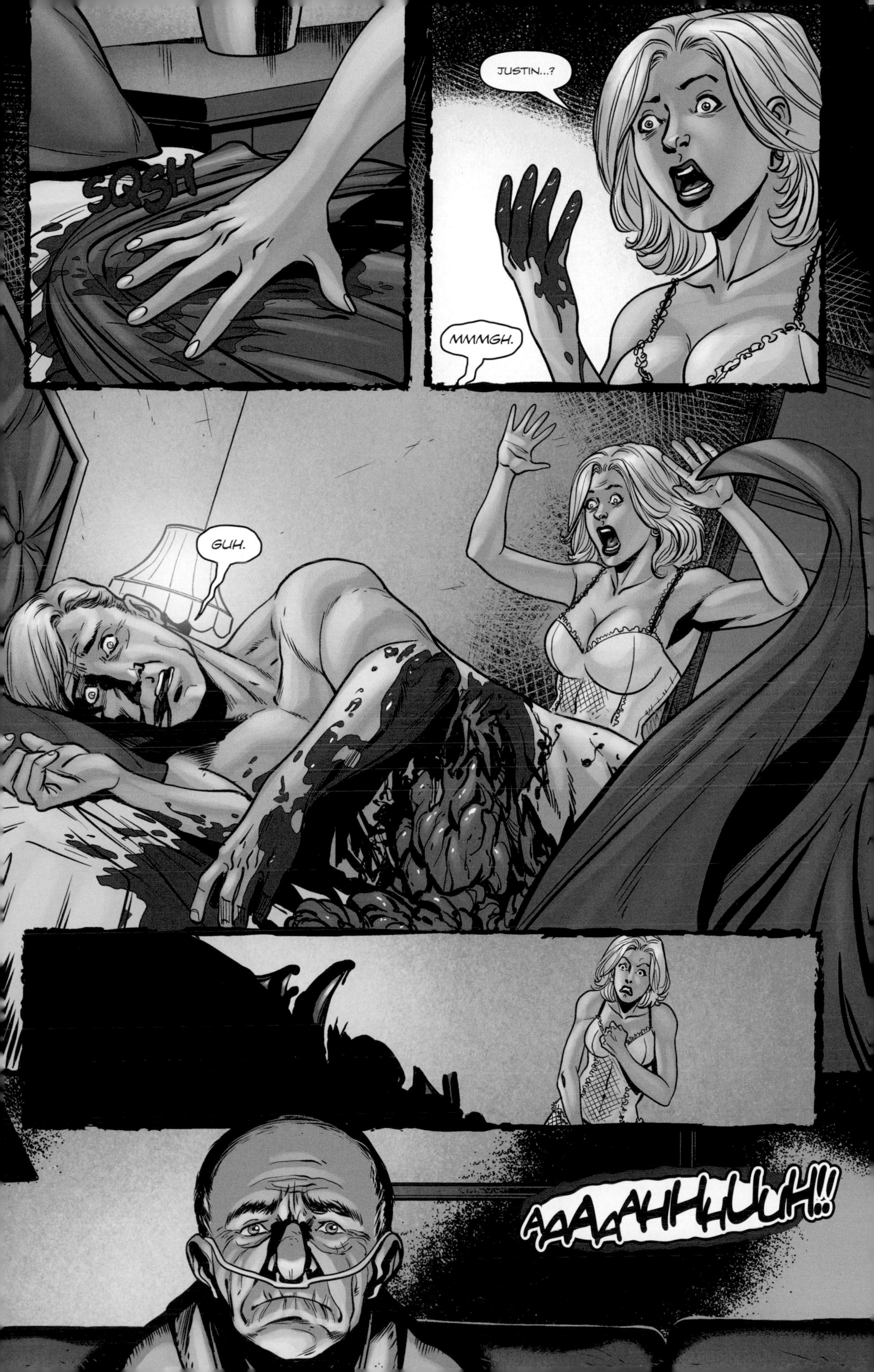
SQSH
JUSTIN...?
MMMGH.
GUH.
AAAAAHHHUUUH!!

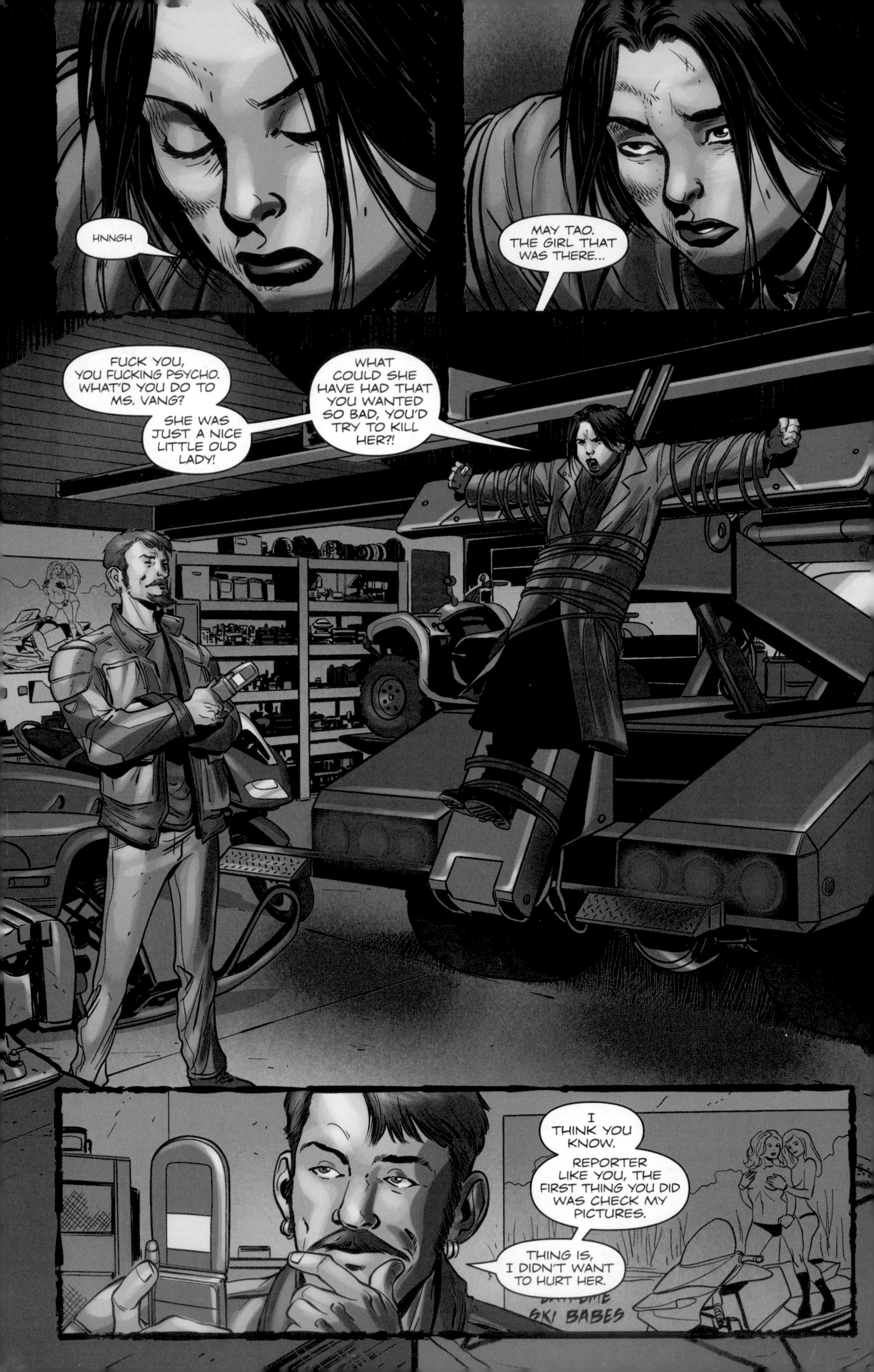
HNNGH
MAY TAO. THE GIRL THAT WAS THERE...
FUCK YOU, YOU FUCKING PSYCHO. WHAT'D YOU DO TO MS. VANG?
SHE WAS JUST A NICE LITTLE OLD LADY!
WHAT COULD SHE HAVE HAD THAT YOU WANTED SO BAD, YOU'D TRY TO KILL HER?!
I THINK YOU KNOW.
REPORTER LIKE YOU, THE FIRST THING YOU DID WAS CHECK MY PICTURES.
THING IS, I DIDN'T WANT TO HURT HER.
SKI BABES

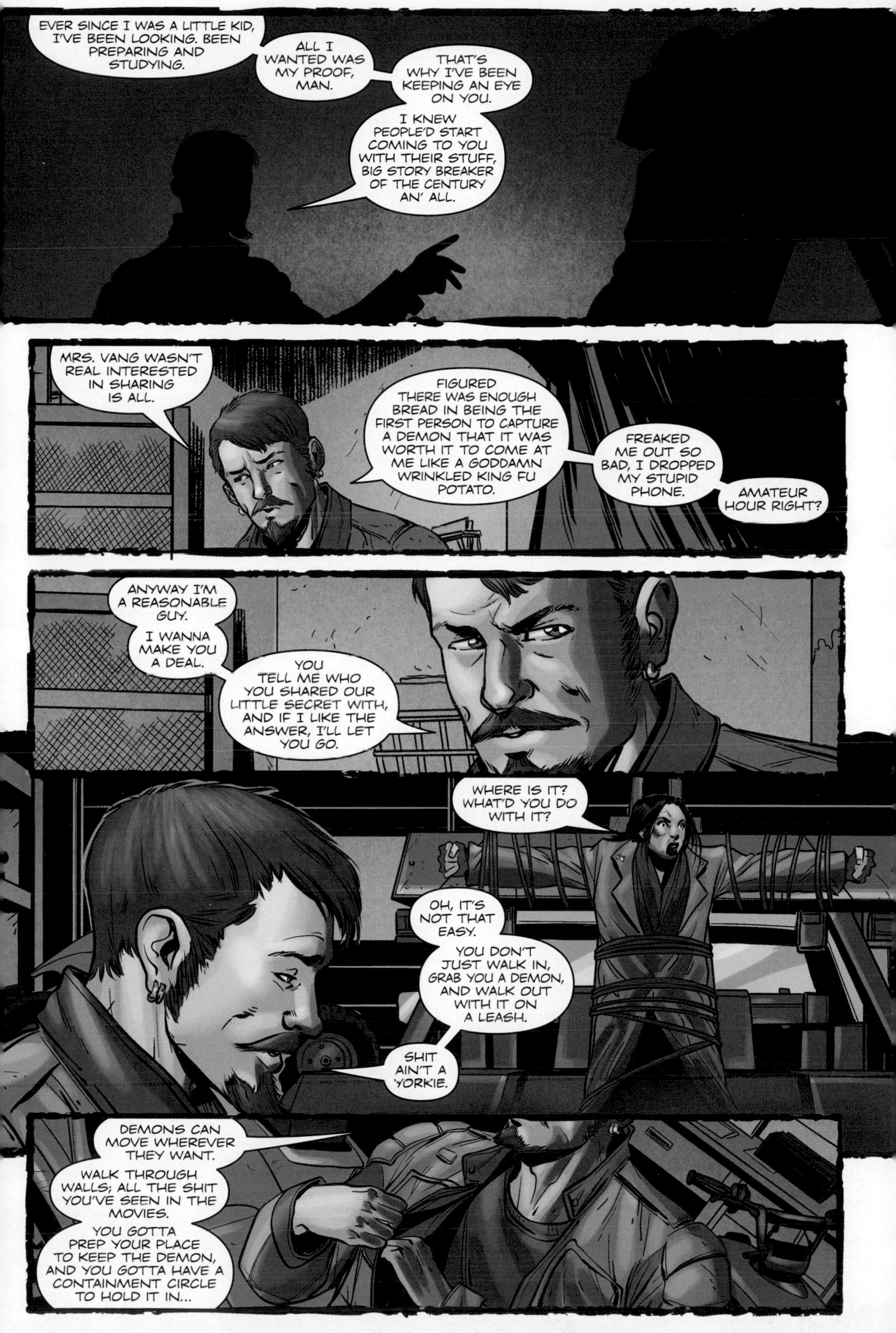
EVER SINCE I WAS A LITTLE KID, I'VE BEEN LOOKING. BEEN PREPARING AND STUDYING.
ALL I WANTED WAS MY PROOF, MAN.
THAT'S WHY I'VE BEEN KEEPING AN EYE ON YOU.
I KNEW PEOPLE'D START COMING TO YOU WITH THEIR STUFF, BIG STORY BREAKER OF THE CENTURY AN' ALL.
MRS. VANG WASN'T REAL INTERESTED IN SHARING IS ALL.
FIGURED THERE WAS ENOUGH BREAD IN BEING THE FIRST PERSON TO CAPTURE A DEMON THAT IT WAS WORTH IT TO COME AT ME LIKE A GODDAMN WRINKLED KING FU POTATO.
FREAKED ME OUT SO BAD, I DROPPED MY STUPID PHONE.
AMATEUR HOUR RIGHT?
ANYWAY I'M A REASONABLE GUY.
I WANNA MAKE YOU A DEAL.
YOU TELL ME WHO YOU SHARED OUR LITTLE SECRET WITH, AND IF I LIKE THE ANSWER, I'LL LET YOU GO.
WHERE IS IT? WHAT'D YOU DO WITH IT?
OH, IT'S NOT THAT EASY.
YOU DON'T JUST WALK IN, GRAB YOU A DEMON, AND WALK OUT WITH IT ON A LEASH.
SHIT AIN'T A YORKIE.
DEMONS CAN MOVE WHEREVER THEY WANT.
WALK THROUGH WALLS; ALL THE SHIT YOU'VE SEEN IN THE MOVIES.
YOU GOTTA PREP YOUR PLACE TO KEEP THE DEMON, AND YOU GOTTA HAVE A CONTAINMENT CIRCLE TO HOLD IT IN...

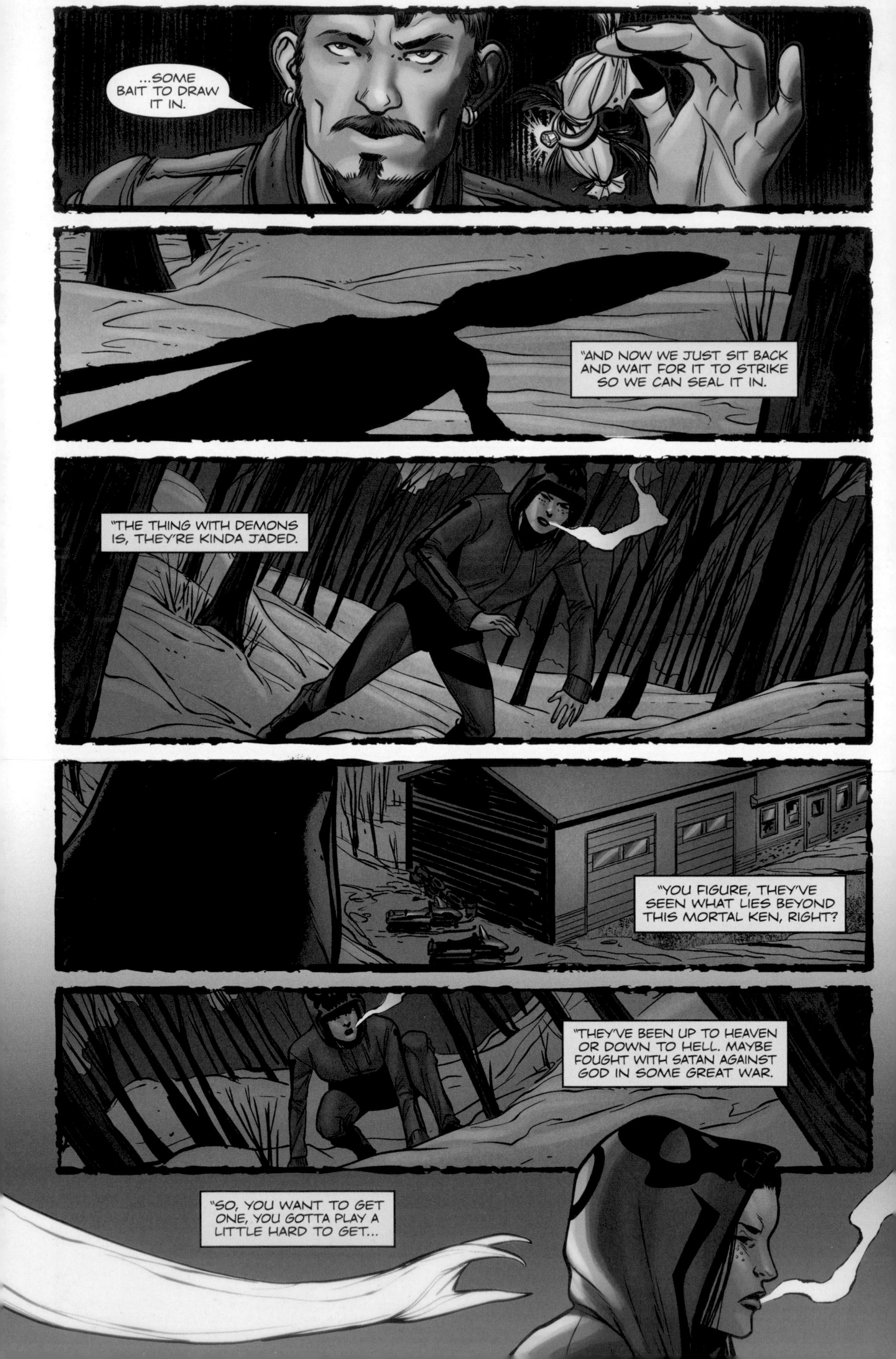
...SOME BAIT TO DRAW IT IN.
"AND NOW WE JUST SIT BACK AND WAIT FOR IT TO STRIKE SO WE CAN SEAL IT IN.
"THE THING WITH DEMONS IS, THEY'RE KINDA JADED.
"YOU FIGURE, THEY'VE SEEN WHAT LIES BEYOND THIS MORTAL KEN, RIGHT?
"THEY'VE BEEN UP TO HEAVEN OR DOWN TO HELL. MAYBE FOUGHT WITH SATAN AGAINST GOD IN SOME GREAT WAR.
"SO, YOU WANT TO GET ONE, YOU GOTTA PLAY A LITTLE HARD TO GET...

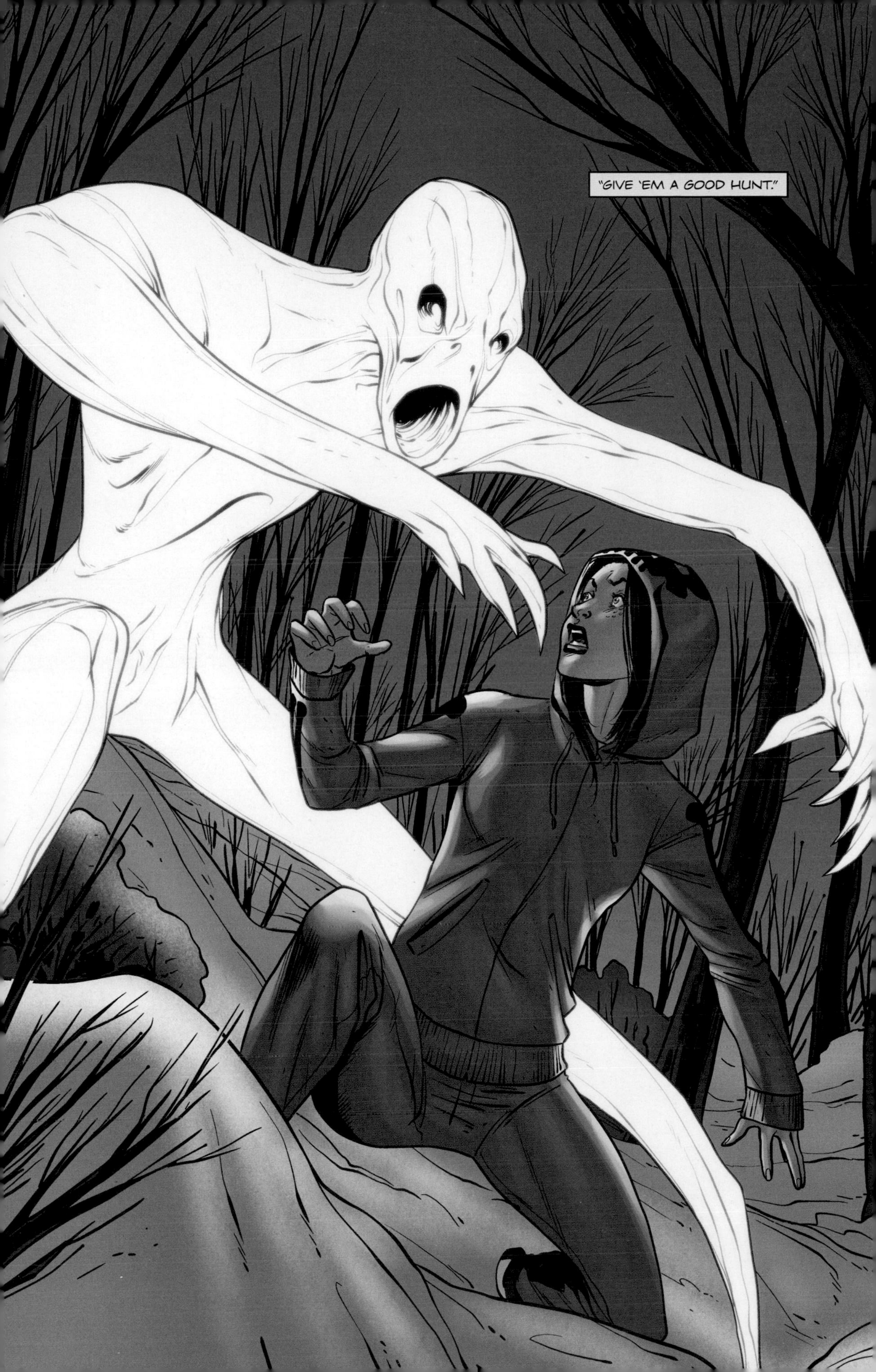
"GIVE 'EM A GOOD HUNT."

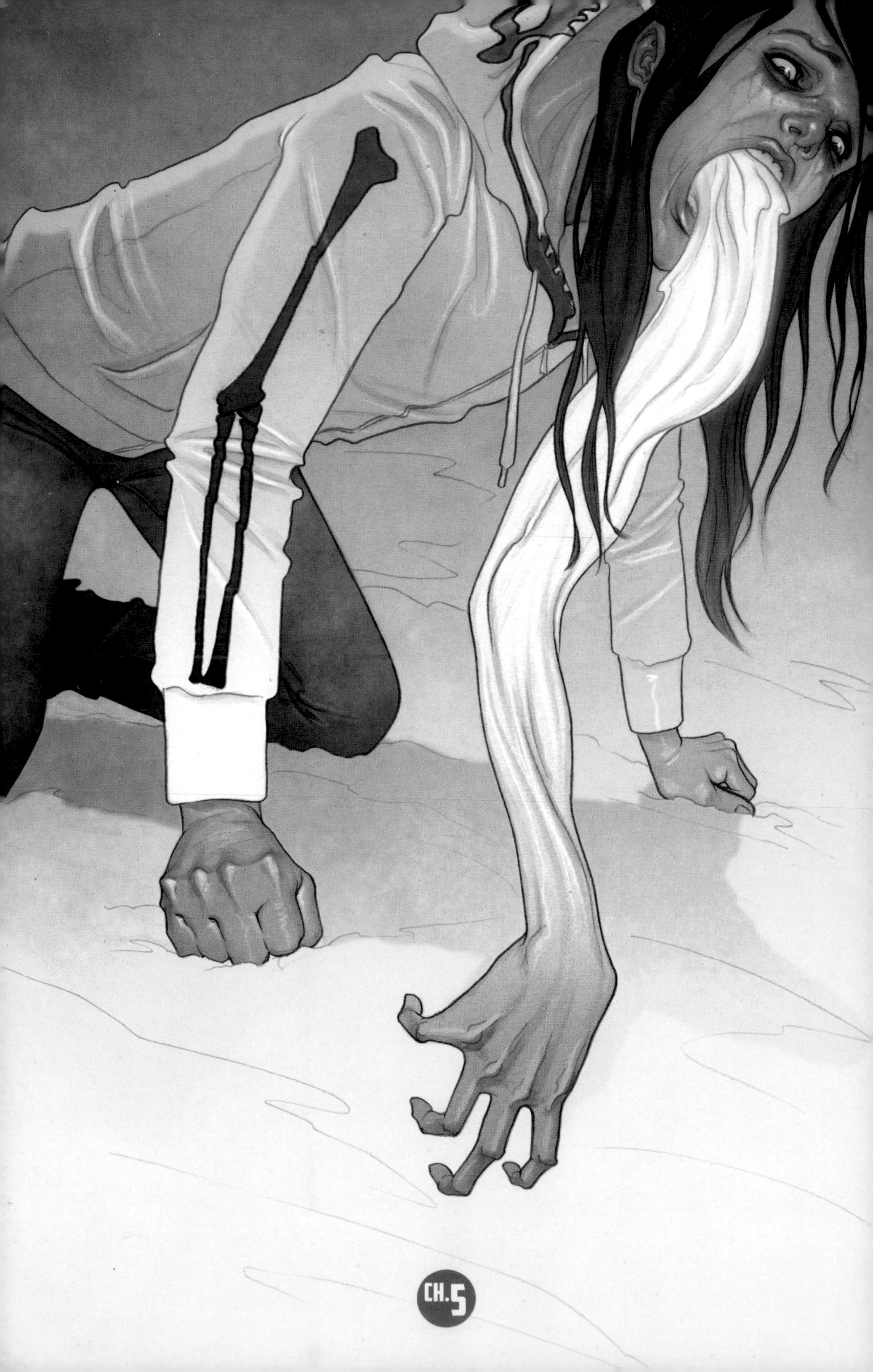
CH.5

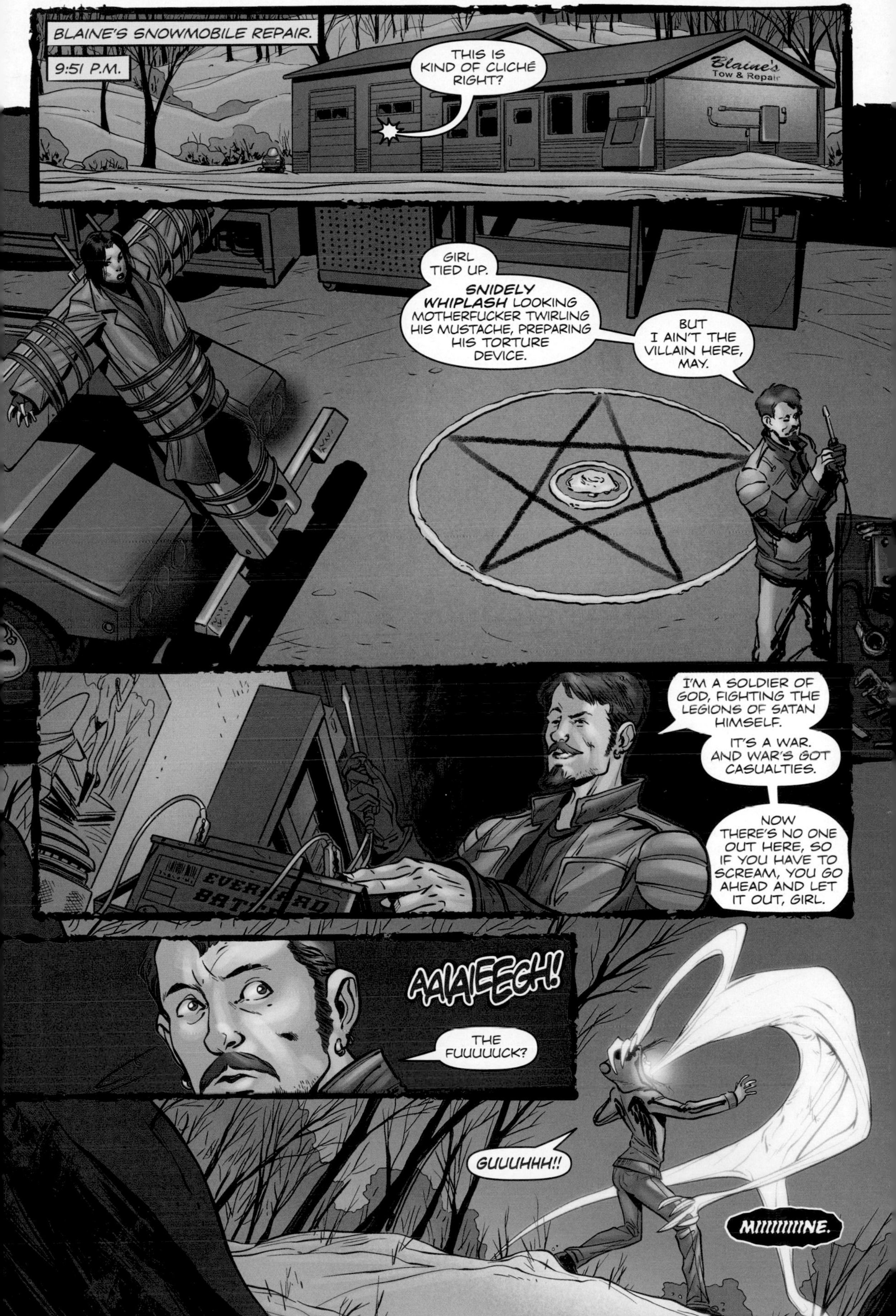
BLAINE'S SNOWMOBILE REPAIR.
9:51 P.M.
Blaine's Tow & Repair
THIS IS KIND OF CLICHÉ RIGHT?
GIRL TIED UP.
SNIDELY WHIPLASH LOOKING MOTHERFUCKER TWIRLING HIS MUSTACHE, PREPARING HIS TORTURE DEVICE.
BUT I AIN'T THE VILLAIN HERE, MAY.
I'M A SOLDIER OF GOD, FIGHTING THE LEGIONS OF SATAN HIMSELF.
IT'S A WAR. AND WAR'S GOT CASUALTIES.
NOW THERE'S NO ONE OUT HERE, SO IF YOU HAVE TO SCREAM, YOU GO AHEAD AND LET IT OUT, GIRL.
AAIAIEEGH!
THE FUUUUUCK?
GUUUHHH!!
MIIIIIIIINE.

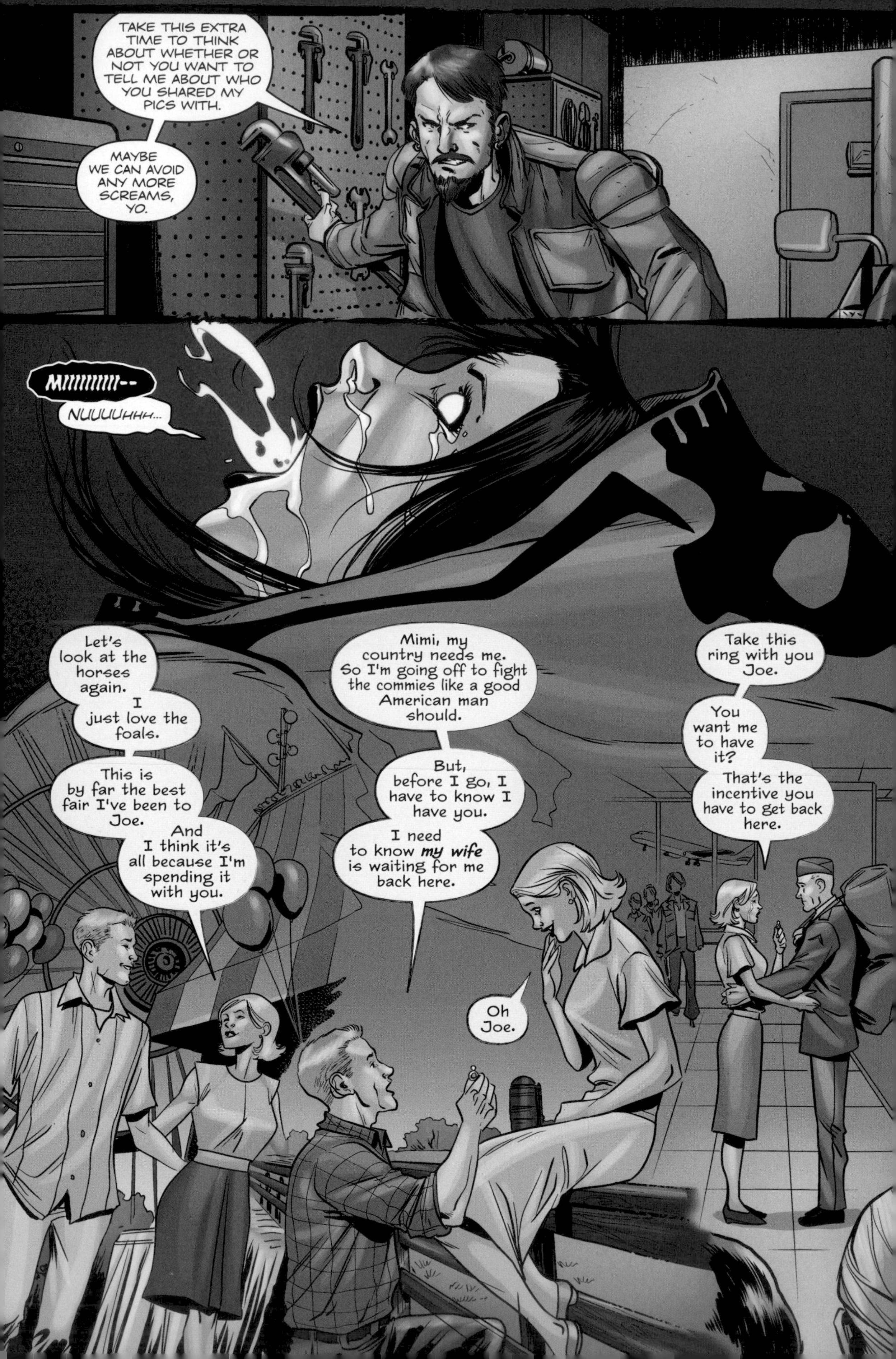
TAKE THIS EXTRA TIME TO THINK ABOUT WHETHER OR NOT YOU WANT TO TELL ME ABOUT WHO YOU SHARED MY PICS WITH.
MAYBE WE CAN AVOID ANY MORE SCREAMS, YO.
MIIIIIIIII--
NUUUUHHH...
Let's look at the horses again.
I just love the foals.
This is by far the best fair I've been to Joe.
And I think it's all because I'm spending it with you.
Mimi, my country needs me. So I'm going off to fight the commies like a good American man should.
But, before I go, I have to know I have you.
I need to know *my wife* is waiting for me back here.
Oh Joe.
Take this ring with you Joe.
You want me to have it?
That's the incentive you have to get back here.

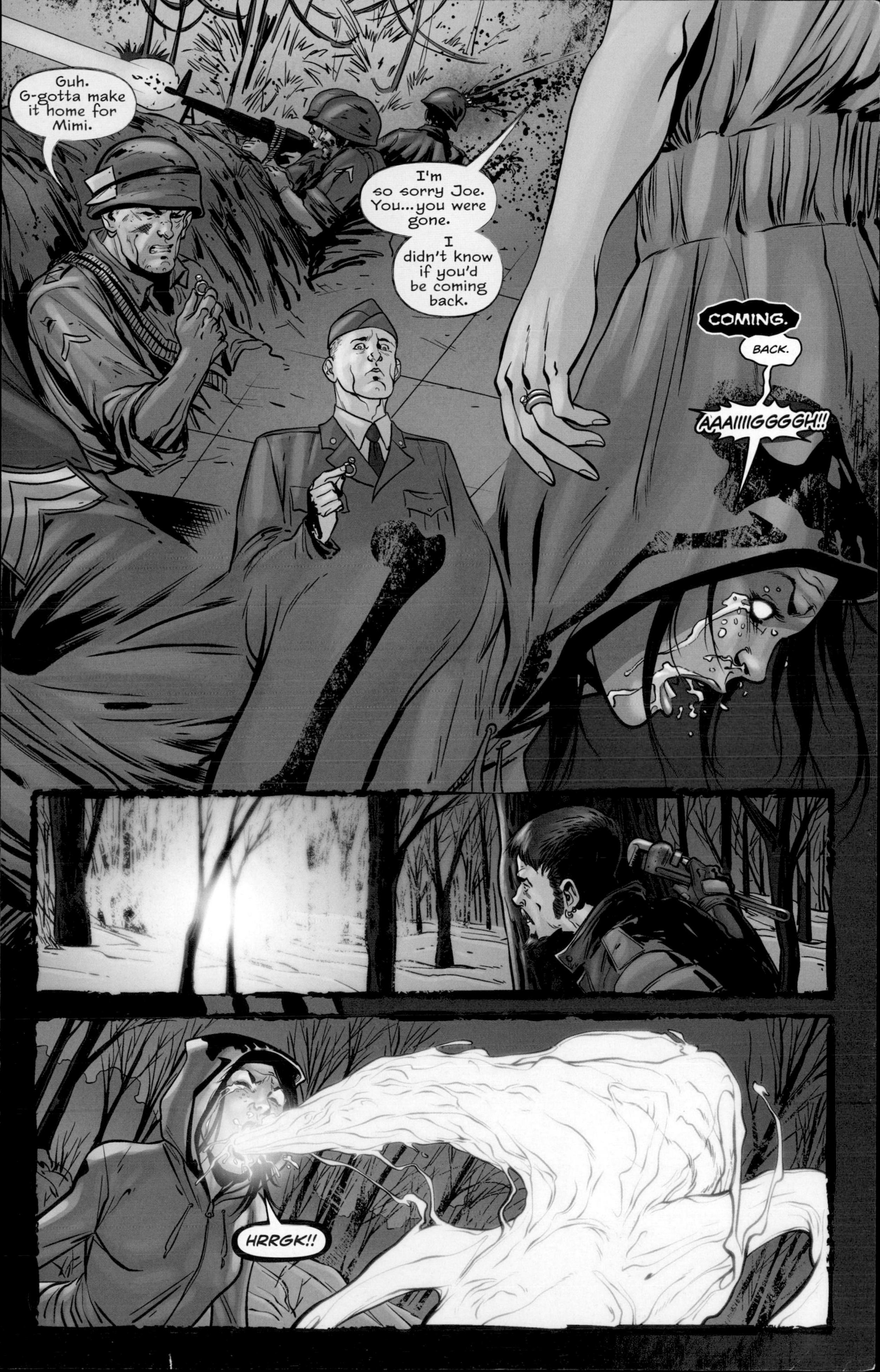
Guh. G-gotta make it home for Mimi.
I'm so sorry Joe. You...you were gone.
I didn't know if you'd be coming back.
COMING.
BACK.
AAAIIIIGGGGH!!
HRRGK!!

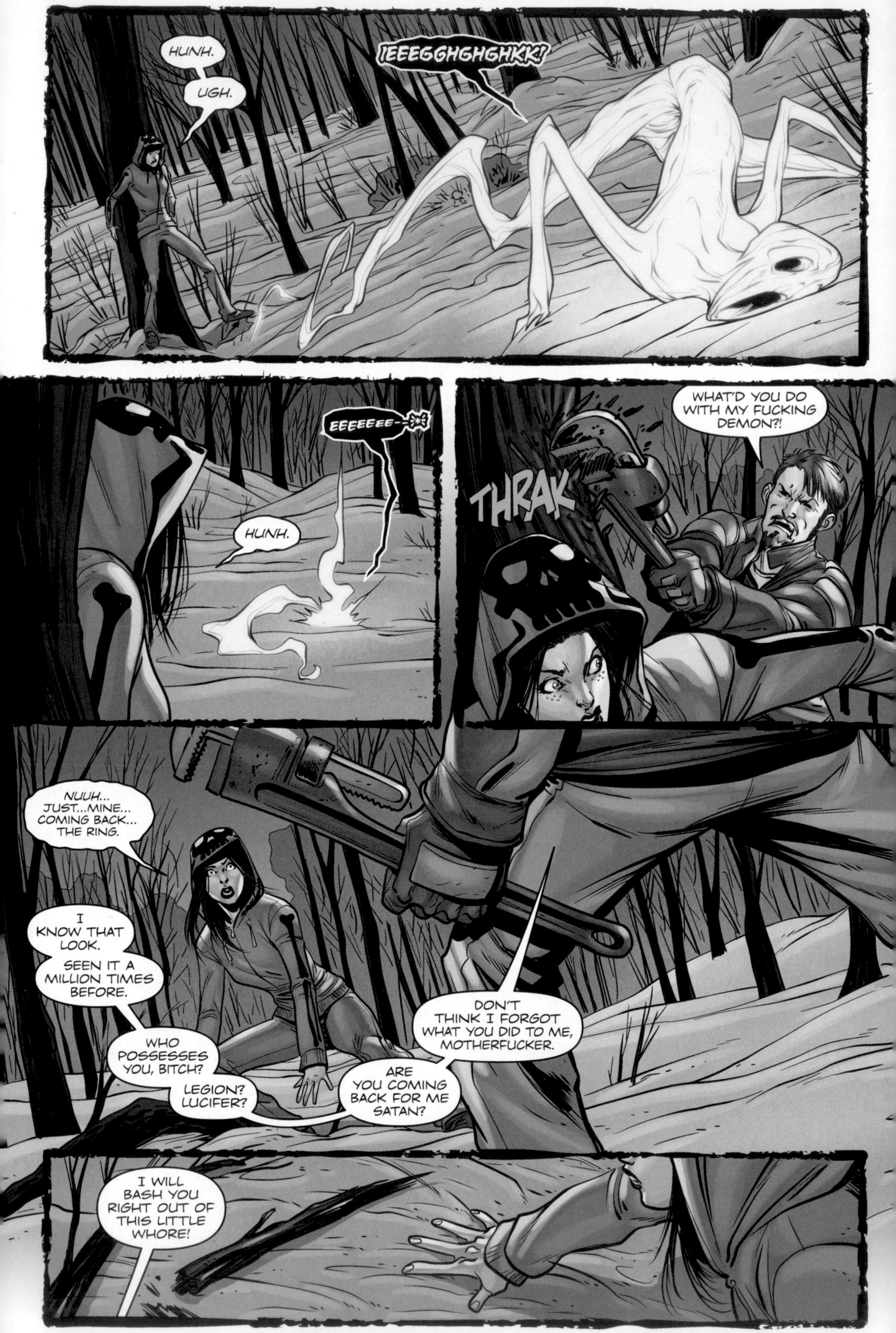
HUNH.
UGH.
IEEEGGHGHGHKK!
EEEEEEE
HUNH.
WHAT'D YOU DO WITH MY FUCKING DEMON?!
THRAK
NUUH... JUST...MINE... COMING BACK... THE RING.
I KNOW THAT LOOK.
SEEN IT A MILLION TIMES BEFORE.
WHO POSSESSES YOU, BITCH?
LEGION? LUCIFER?
ARE YOU COMING BACK FOR ME SATAN?
DON'T THINK I FORGOT WHAT YOU DID TO ME, MOTHERFUCKER.
I WILL BASH YOU RIGHT OUT OF THIS LITTLE WHORE!

GRAND AVENUE INN.
IBRAHAIM RAMIN'S APARTMENT.
9:54 P.M.

BEEEEP
BEEEEP
BEEEEP

RAMIN.

HEY ABE. IT'S AMI. HOW ARE YOU?

I'M GOOD, AMI.

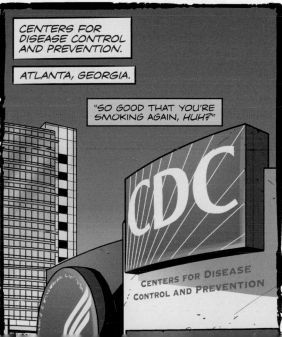

CENTERS FOR DISEASE CONTROL AND PREVENTION.

ATLANTA, GEORGIA.

"SO GOOD THAT YOU'RE SMOKING AGAIN, HUH?"

CDC

CENTERS FOR DISEASE
CONTROL AND PREVENTION

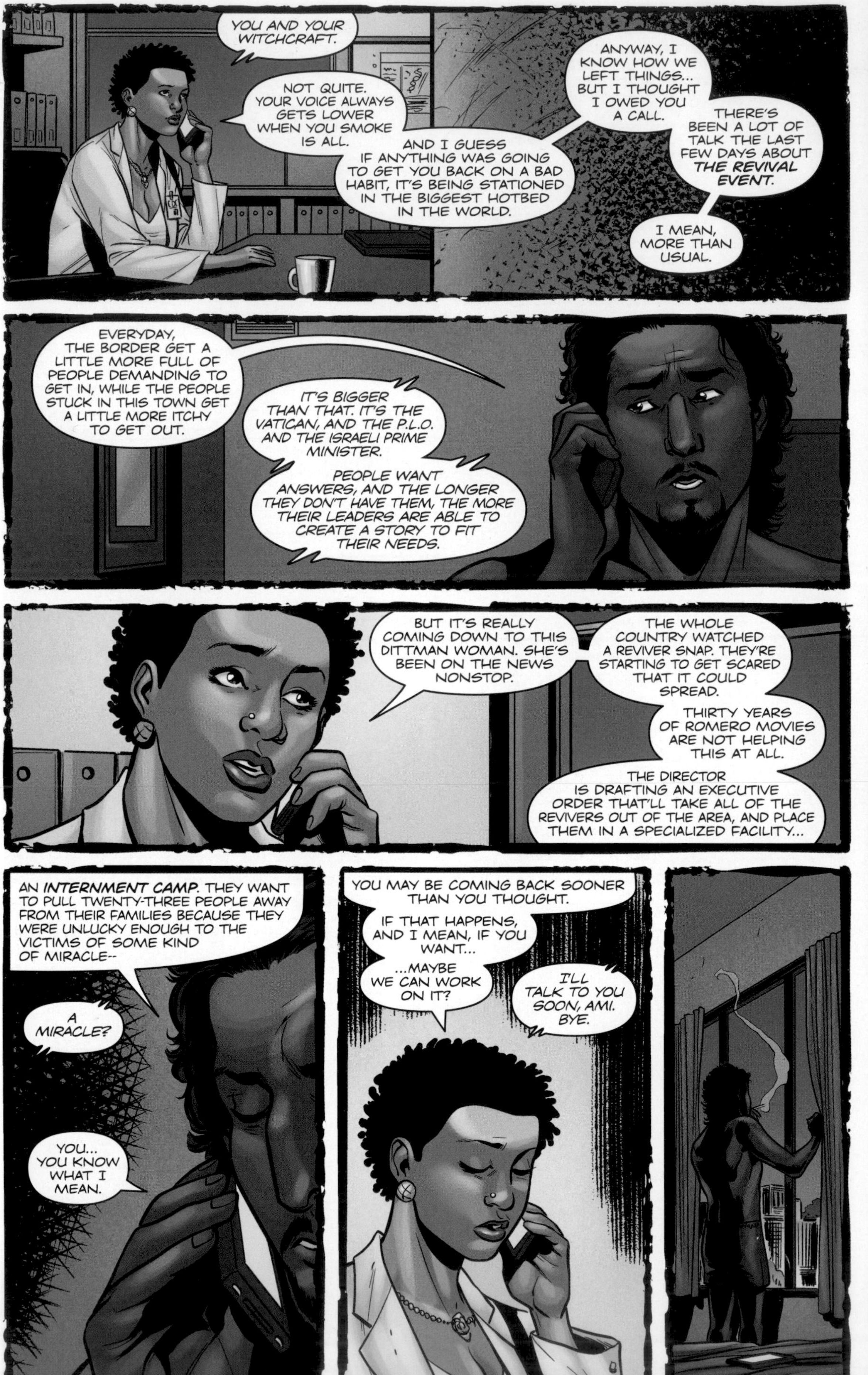
YOU AND YOUR WITCHCRAFT.
NOT QUITE. YOUR VOICE ALWAYS GETS LOWER WHEN YOU SMOKE IS ALL.
AND I GUESS IF ANYTHING WAS GOING TO GET YOU BACK ON A BAD HABIT, IT'S BEING STATIONED IN THE BIGGEST HOTBED IN THE WORLD.
ANYWAY, I KNOW HOW WE LEFT THINGS... BUT I THOUGHT I OWED YOU A CALL.
THERE'S BEEN A LOT OF TALK THE LAST FEW DAYS ABOUT *THE REVIVAL EVENT*.
I MEAN, MORE THAN USUAL.
EVERYDAY, THE BORDER GET A LITTLE MORE FULL OF PEOPLE DEMANDING TO GET IN, WHILE THE PEOPLE STUCK IN THIS TOWN GET A LITTLE MORE ITCHY TO GET OUT.
IT'S BIGGER THAN THAT. IT'S THE VATICAN, AND THE P.L.O. AND THE ISRAELI PRIME MINISTER.
PEOPLE WANT ANSWERS, AND THE LONGER THEY DON'T HAVE THEM, THE MORE THEIR LEADERS ARE ABLE TO CREATE A STORY TO FIT THEIR NEEDS.
BUT IT'S REALLY COMING DOWN TO THIS DITTMAN WOMAN. SHE'S BEEN ON THE NEWS NONSTOP.
THE WHOLE COUNTRY WATCHED A REVIVER SNAP. THEY'RE STARTING TO GET SCARED THAT IT COULD SPREAD.
THIRTY YEARS OF ROMERO MOVIES ARE NOT HELPING THIS AT ALL.
THE DIRECTOR IS DRAFTING AN EXECUTIVE ORDER THAT'LL TAKE ALL OF THE REVIVERS OUT OF THE AREA, AND PLACE THEM IN A SPECIALIZED FACILITY...
AN *INTERNMENT CAMP*. THEY WANT TO PULL TWENTY-THREE PEOPLE AWAY FROM THEIR FAMILIES BECAUSE THEY WERE UNLUCKY ENOUGH TO THE VICTIMS OF SOME KIND OF MIRACLE--
A MIRACLE?
YOU... YOU KNOW WHAT I MEAN.
YOU MAY BE COMING BACK SOONER THAN YOU THOUGHT.
IF THAT HAPPENS, AND I MEAN, IF YOU WANT...
...MAYBE WE CAN WORK ON IT?
I'LL TALK TO YOU SOON, AMI. BYE.

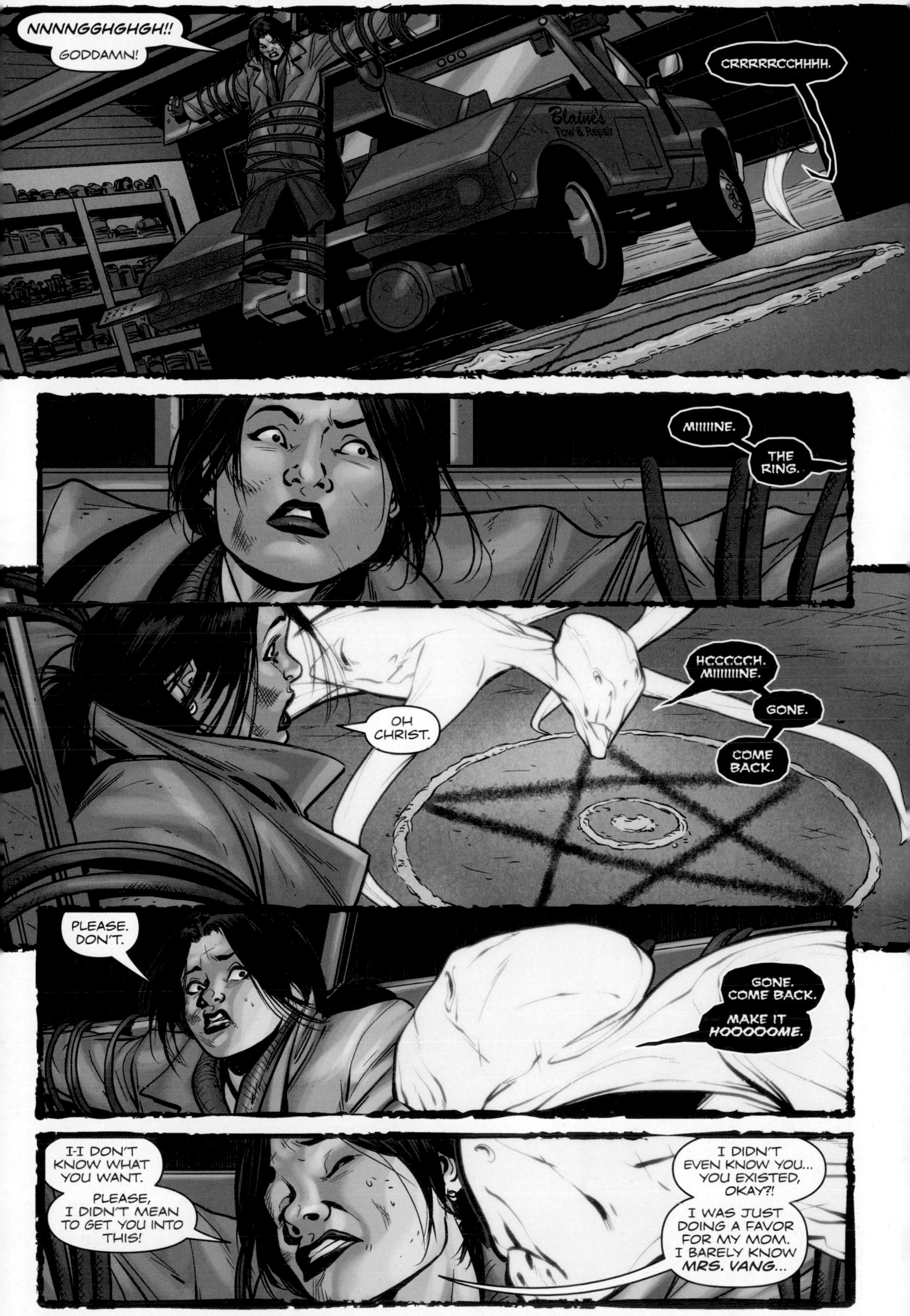
NNNNGGHGHGH!!
GODDAMN!
Blaine's Tow & Repair
CRRRRRCCHHHH.
MIIIIINE.
THE RING.
OH CHRIST.
HCCCCCH. MIIIIIINE.
GONE.
COME BACK.
PLEASE. DON'T.
GONE. COME BACK.
MAKE IT HOOOOOME.
I-I DON'T KNOW WHAT YOU WANT.
PLEASE, I DIDN'T MEAN TO GET YOU INTO THIS!
I DIDN'T EVEN KNOW YOU... YOU EXISTED, OKAY?!
I WAS JUST DOING A FAVOR FOR MY MOM. I BARELY KNOW MRS. VANG...

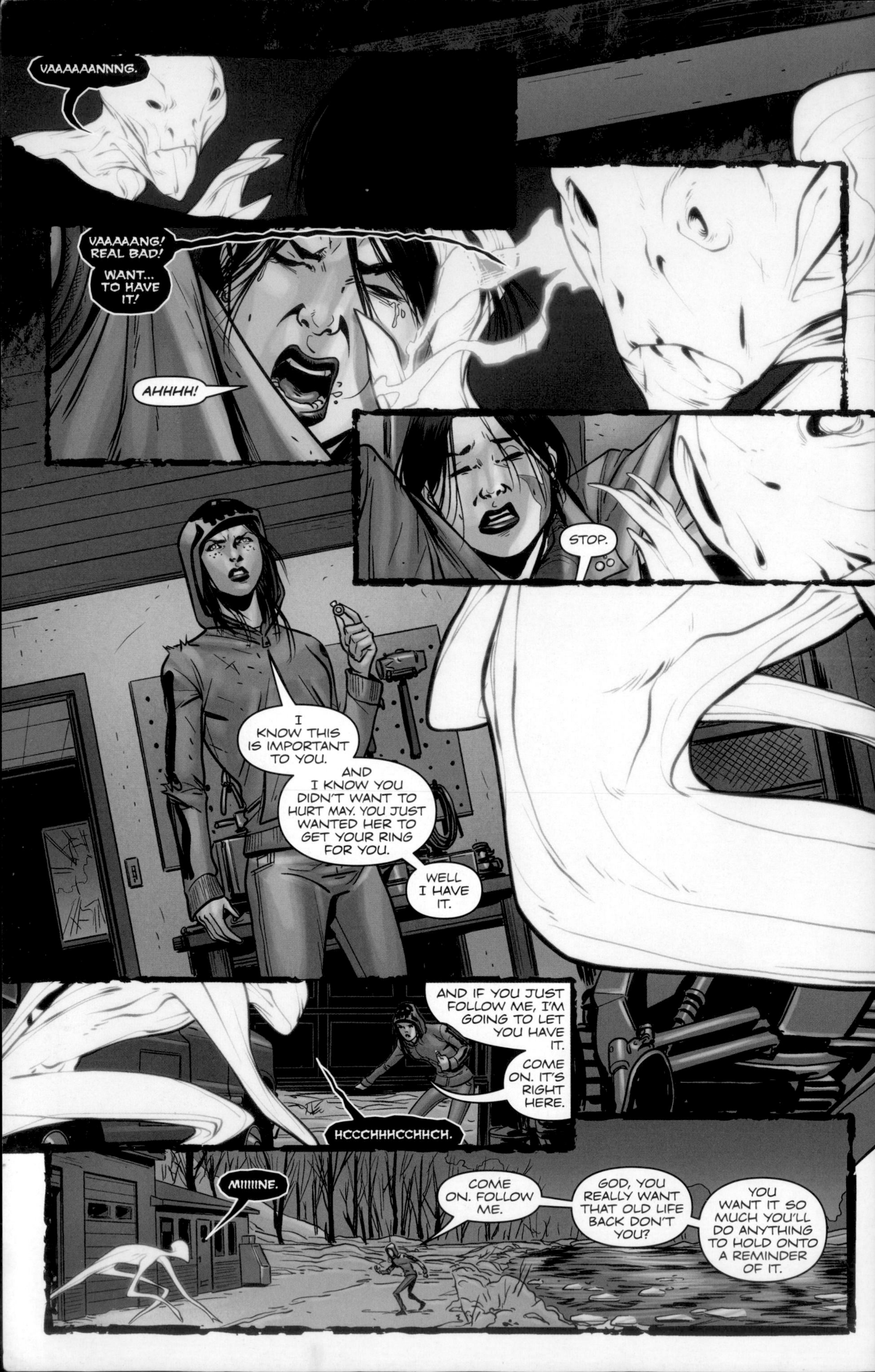
VAAAAAANNNG.
VAAAAANG! REAL BAD!
WANT... TO HAVE IT!
AHHHH!
STOP.
I KNOW THIS IS IMPORTANT TO YOU.
AND I KNOW YOU DIDN'T WANT TO HURT MAY. YOU JUST WANTED HER TO GET YOUR RING FOR YOU.
WELL I HAVE IT.
AND IF YOU JUST FOLLOW ME, I'M GOING TO LET YOU HAVE IT.
COME ON. IT'S RIGHT HERE.
HCCCHHHCCHHCH.
MIIIIINE.
COME ON. FOLLOW ME.
GOD, YOU REALLY WANT THAT OLD LIFE BACK DON'T YOU?
YOU WANT IT SO MUCH YOU'LL DO ANYTHING TO HOLD ONTO A REMINDER OF IT.

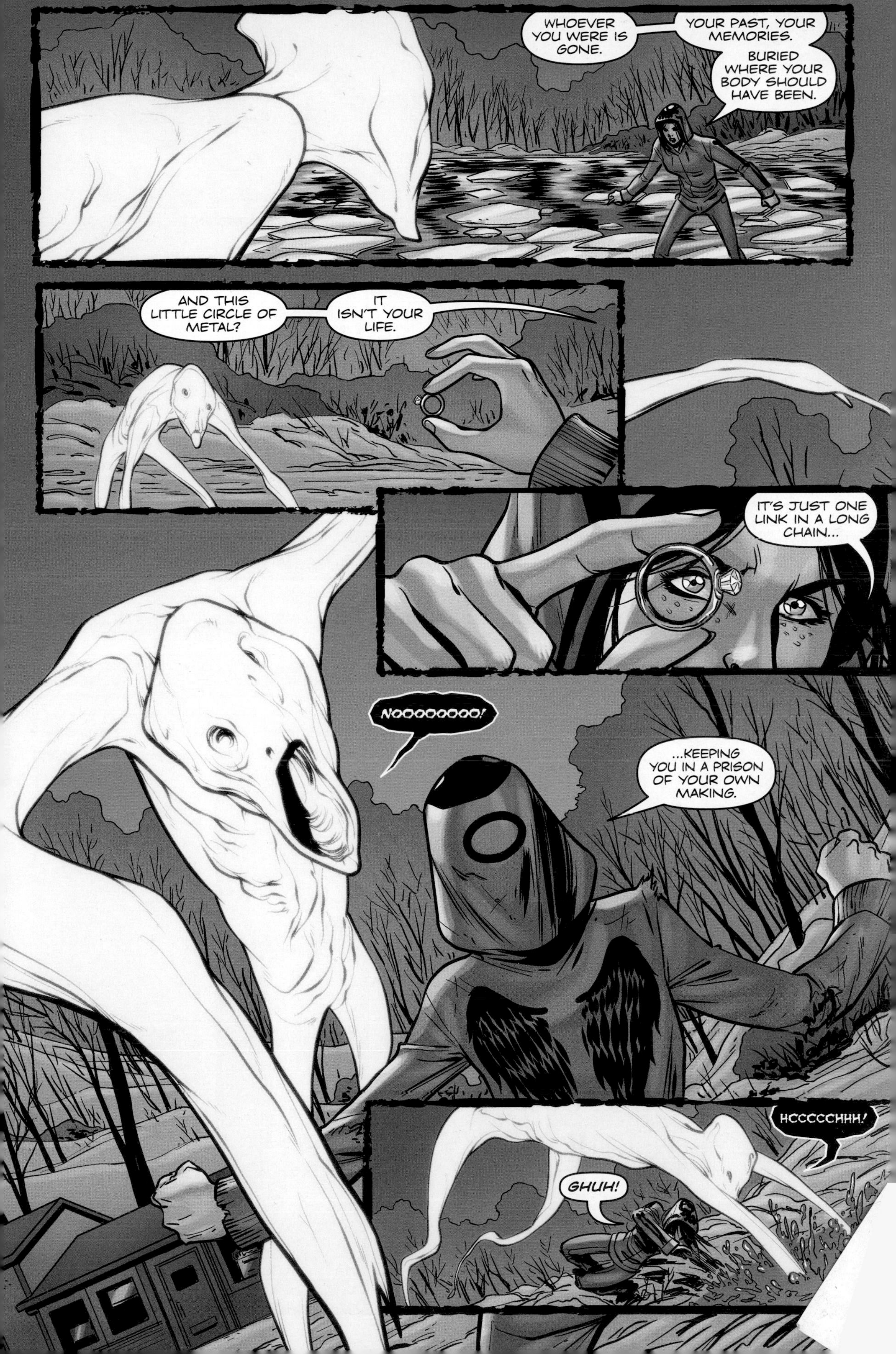
WHOEVER YOU WERE IS GONE.
YOUR PAST, YOUR MEMORIES.
BURIED WHERE YOUR BODY SHOULD HAVE BEEN.
AND THIS LITTLE CIRCLE OF METAL?
IT ISN'T YOUR LIFE.
IT'S JUST ONE LINK IN A LONG CHAIN...
NOOOOOOOO!
...KEEPING YOU IN A PRISON OF YOUR OWN MAKING.
HCCCCCHHH!
GHUH!

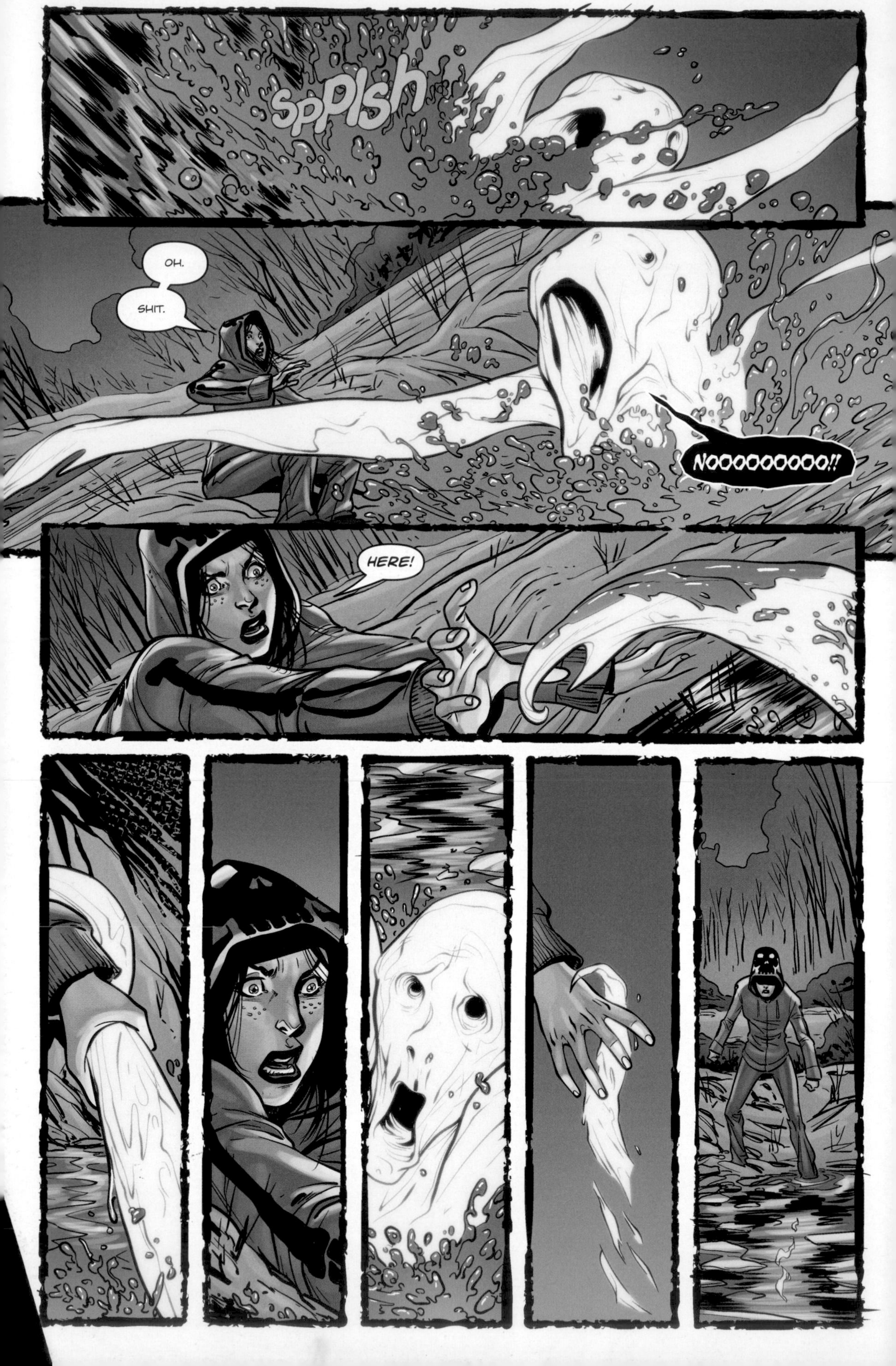
SPPLSH
OH.
SHIT.
NOOOOOOOOO!!
HERE!

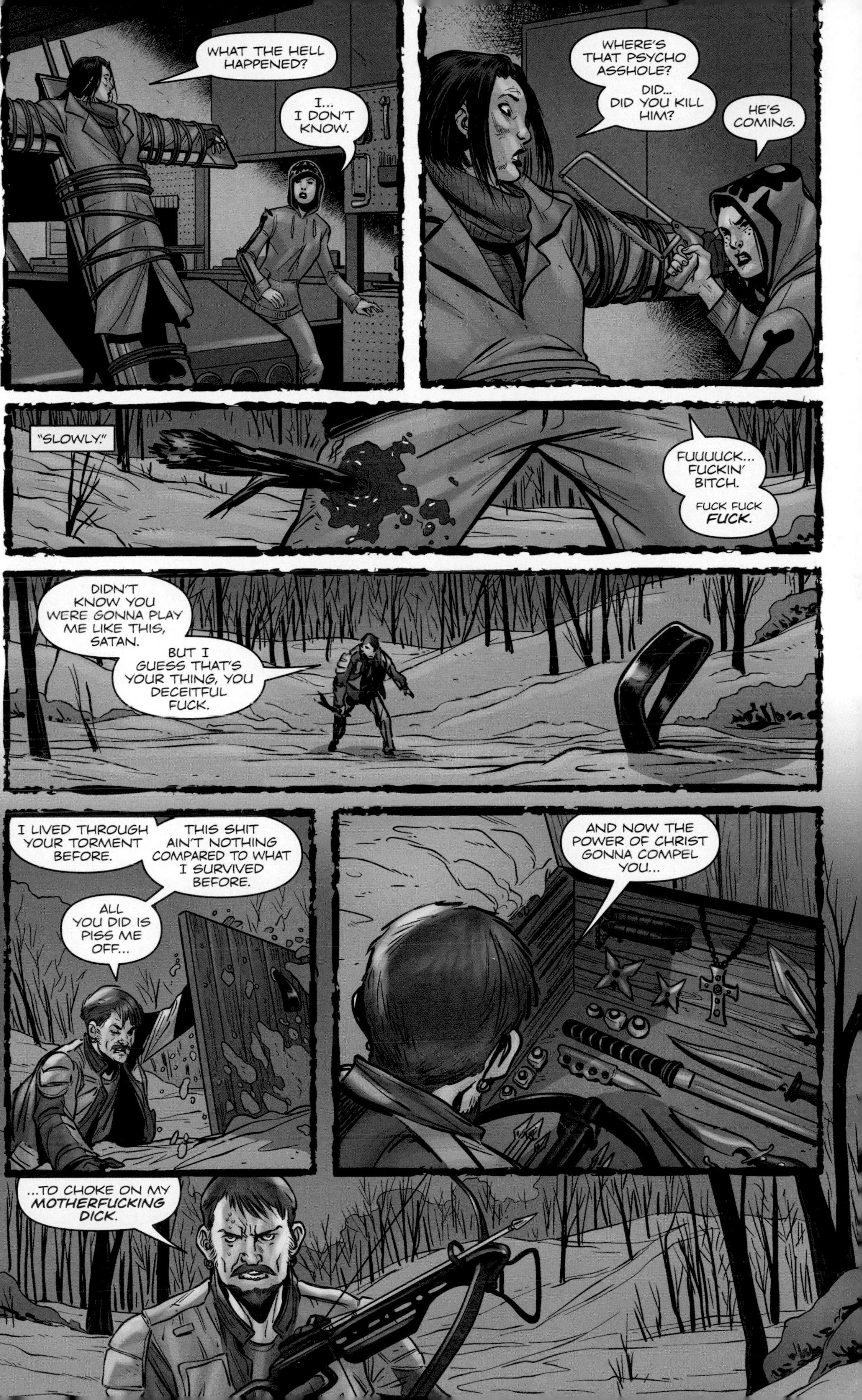
WHAT THE HELL HAPPENED?
I... I DON'T KNOW.
WHERE'S THAT PSYCHO ASSHOLE?
DID... DID YOU KILL HIM?
HE'S COMING.
"SLOWLY."
FUUUUCK... FUCKIN' BITCH.
FUCK FUCK **FUCK**.
DIDN'T KNOW YOU WERE GONNA PLAY ME LIKE THIS, SATAN.
BUT I GUESS THAT'S YOUR THING, YOU DECEITFUL FUCK.
I LIVED THROUGH YOUR TORMENT BEFORE.
THIS SHIT AIN'T NOTHING COMPARED TO WHAT I SURVIVED BEFORE.
ALL YOU DID IS PISS ME OFF...
AND NOW THE POWER OF CHRIST GONNA COMPEL YOU...
...TO CHOKE ON MY ***MOTHERFUCKING DICK***.

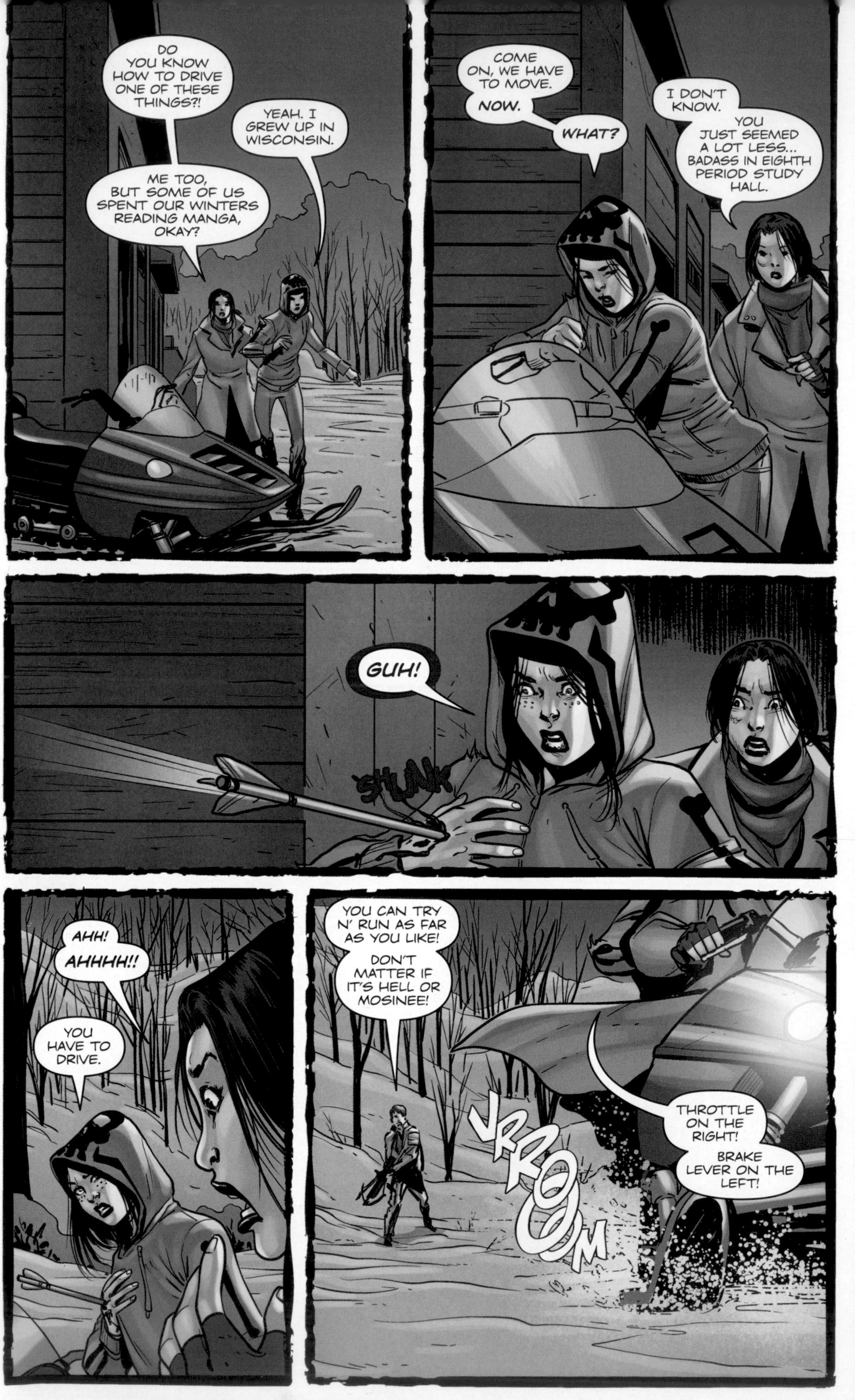

DO YOU KNOW HOW TO DRIVE ONE OF THESE THINGS?!
YEAH. I GREW UP IN WISCONSIN.
ME TOO, BUT SOME OF US SPENT OUR WINTERS READING MANGA, OKAY?
COME ON, WE HAVE TO MOVE.
NOW.
WHAT?
I DON'T KNOW.
YOU JUST SEEMED A LOT LESS... BADASS IN EIGHTH PERIOD STUDY HALL.
GUH!
SHUNK
AHH!
AHHHH!!
YOU HAVE TO DRIVE.
YOU CAN TRY N' RUN AS FAR AS YOU LIKE!
DON'T MATTER IF IT'S HELL OR MOSINEE!
VRROOOM
THROTTLE ON THE RIGHT!
BRAKE LEVER ON THE LEFT!

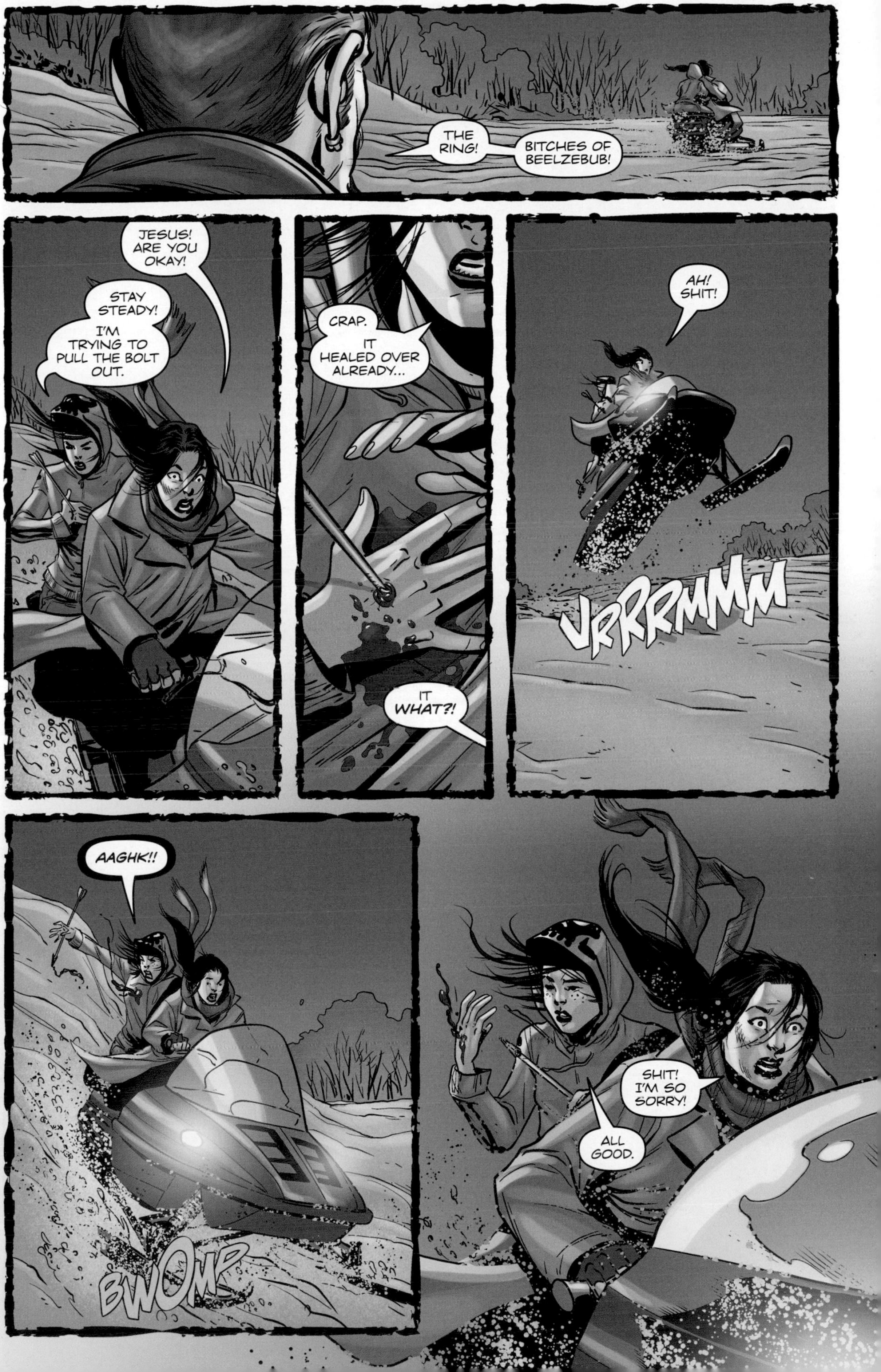
THE RING!
BITCHES OF BEELZEBUB!
JESUS! ARE YOU OKAY!
STAY STEADY!
I'M TRYING TO PULL THE BOLT OUT.
CRAP.
IT HEALED OVER ALREADY...
IT WHAT?!
AH! SHIT!
VRRRMMM
AAGHK!!
BWOMP
SHIT! I'M SO SORRY!
ALL GOOD.

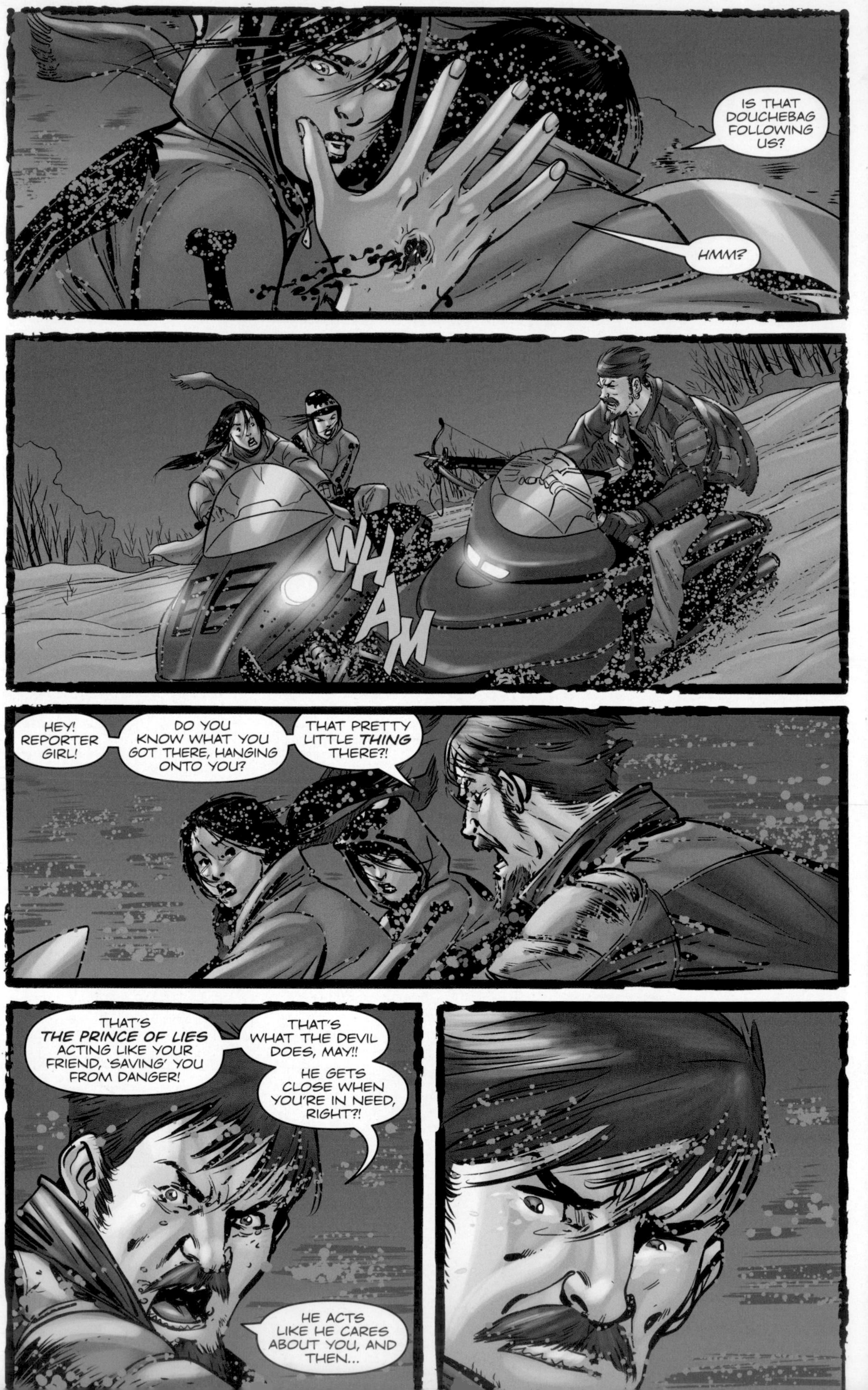
IS THAT DOUCHEBAG FOLLOWING US?
HMM?
WHAM
HEY! REPORTER GIRL!
DO YOU KNOW WHAT YOU GOT THERE, HANGING ONTO YOU?
THAT PRETTY LITTLE *THING* THERE?!
THAT'S ***THE PRINCE OF LIES*** ACTING LIKE YOUR FRIEND, 'SAVING' YOU FROM DANGER!
THAT'S WHAT THE DEVIL DOES, MAY!!
HE GETS CLOSE WHEN YOU'RE IN NEED, RIGHT?!
HE ACTS LIKE HE CARES ABOUT YOU, AND THEN...

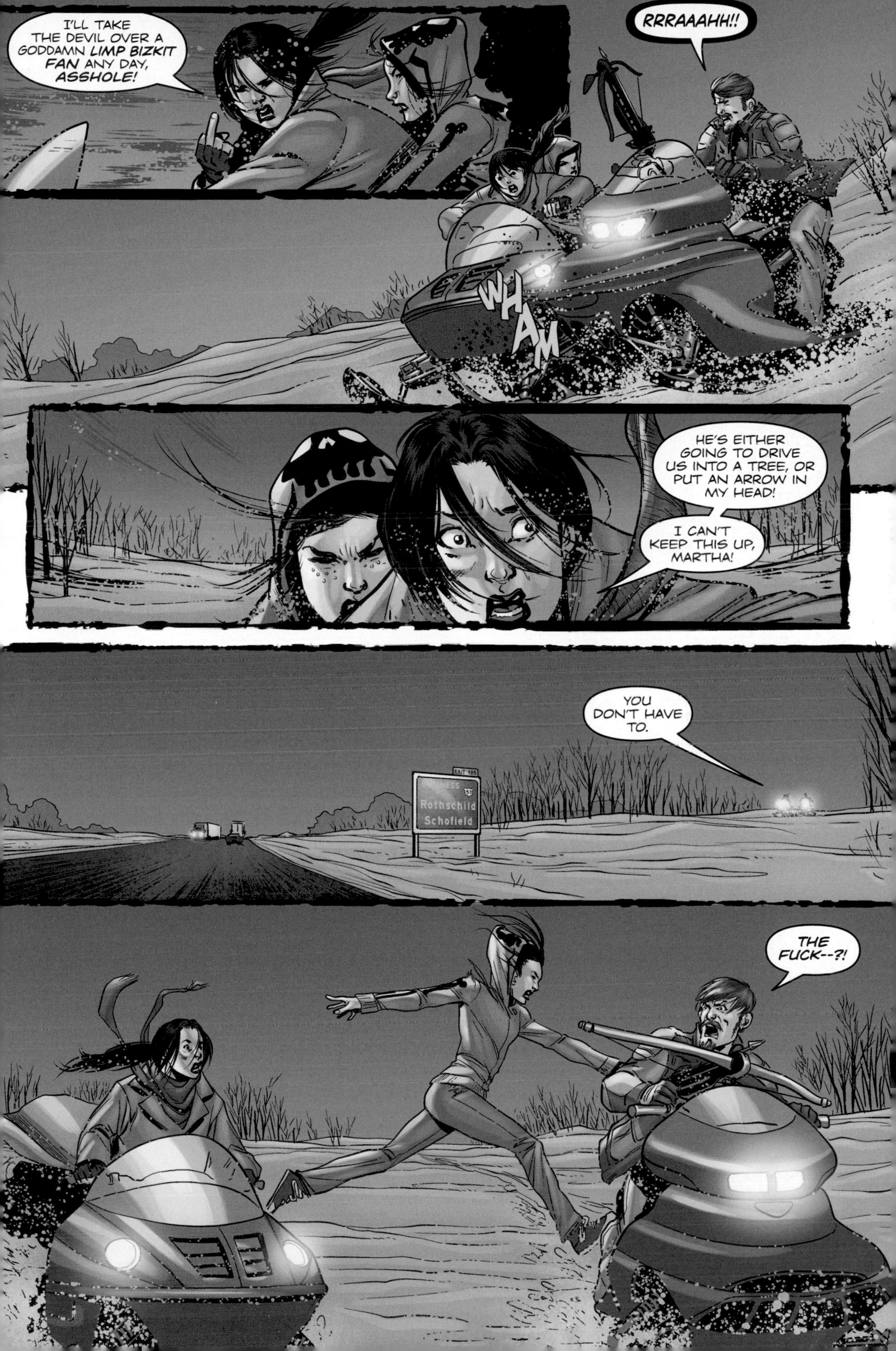
I'LL TAKE THE DEVIL OVER A GODDAMN LIMP BIZKIT FAN ANY DAY, ASSHOLE!
RRRAAAHH!!
WHAM
HE'S EITHER GOING TO DRIVE US INTO A TREE, OR PUT AN ARROW IN MY HEAD!
I CAN'T KEEP THIS UP, MARTHA!
EXIT 185
BUSINESS
Rothschild
Schofield
YOU DON'T HAVE TO.
THE FUCK--?!

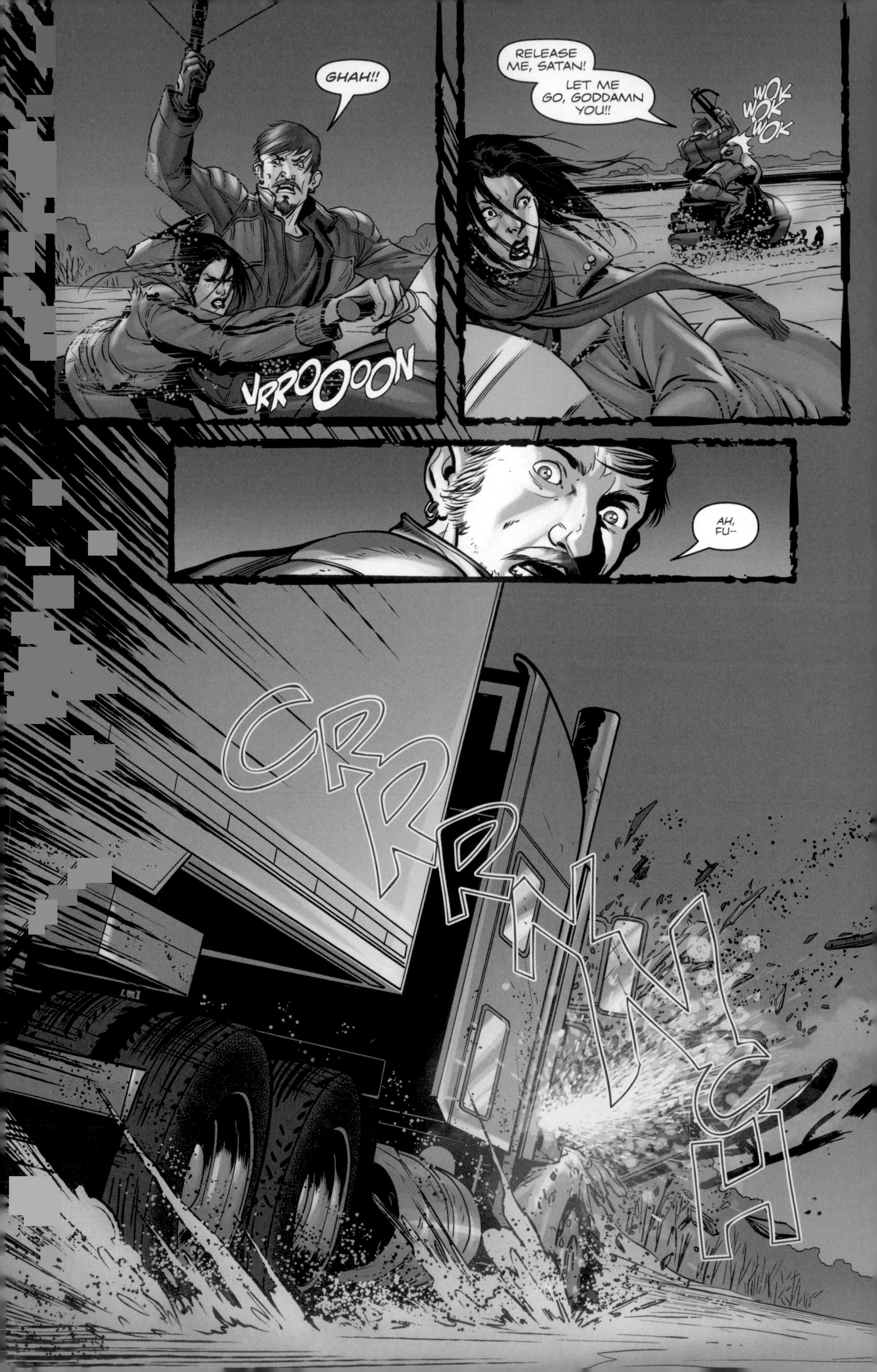
GHAH!!
VRROOOOON
RELEASE ME, SATAN!
LET ME GO, GODDAMN YOU!!
WOK WOK WOK
AH, FU--
CRRNNNCH

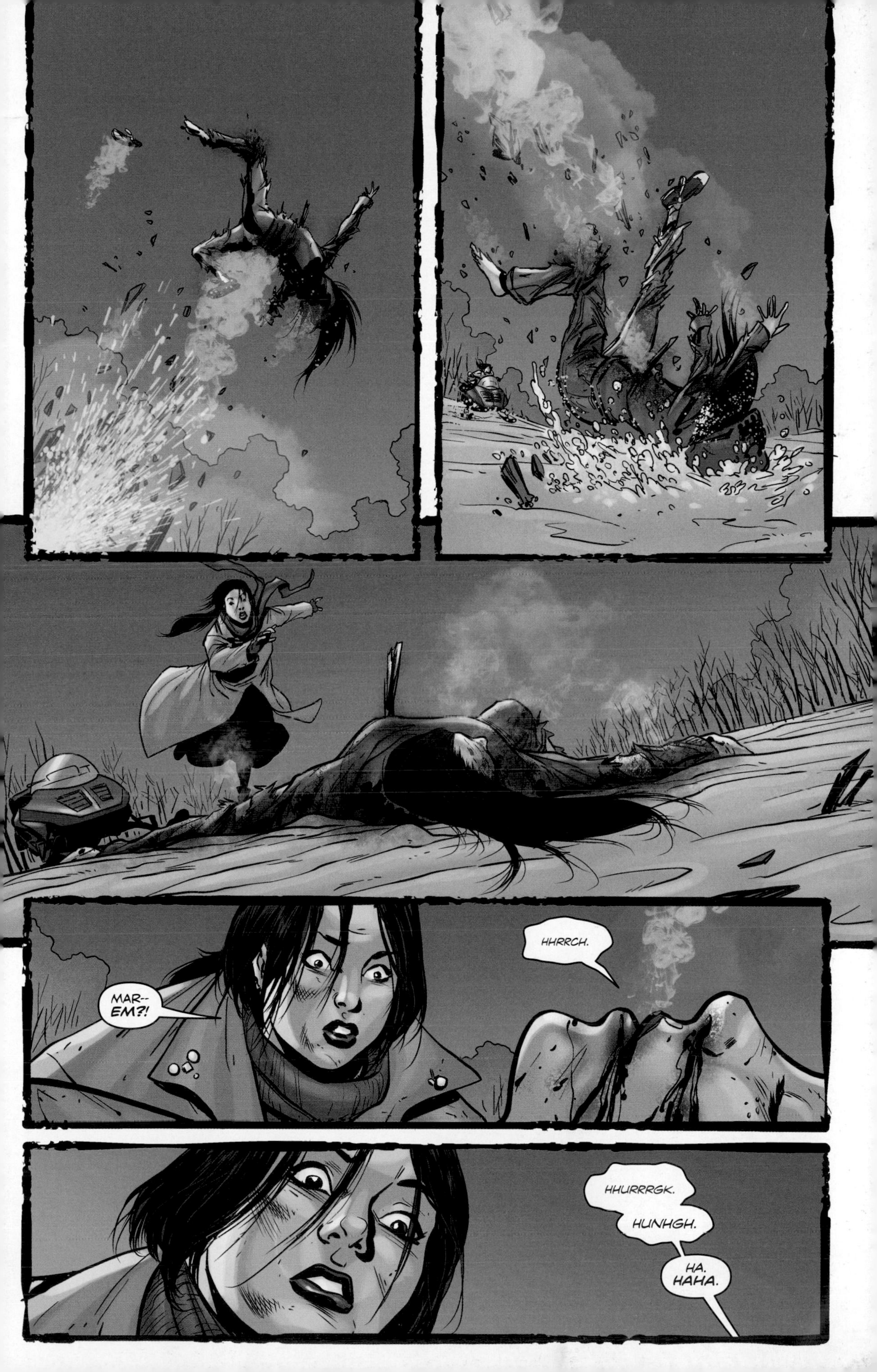
HHRRCH.
MAR--
EM?!
HHURRRGK.
HUNHGH.
HA.
HAHA.

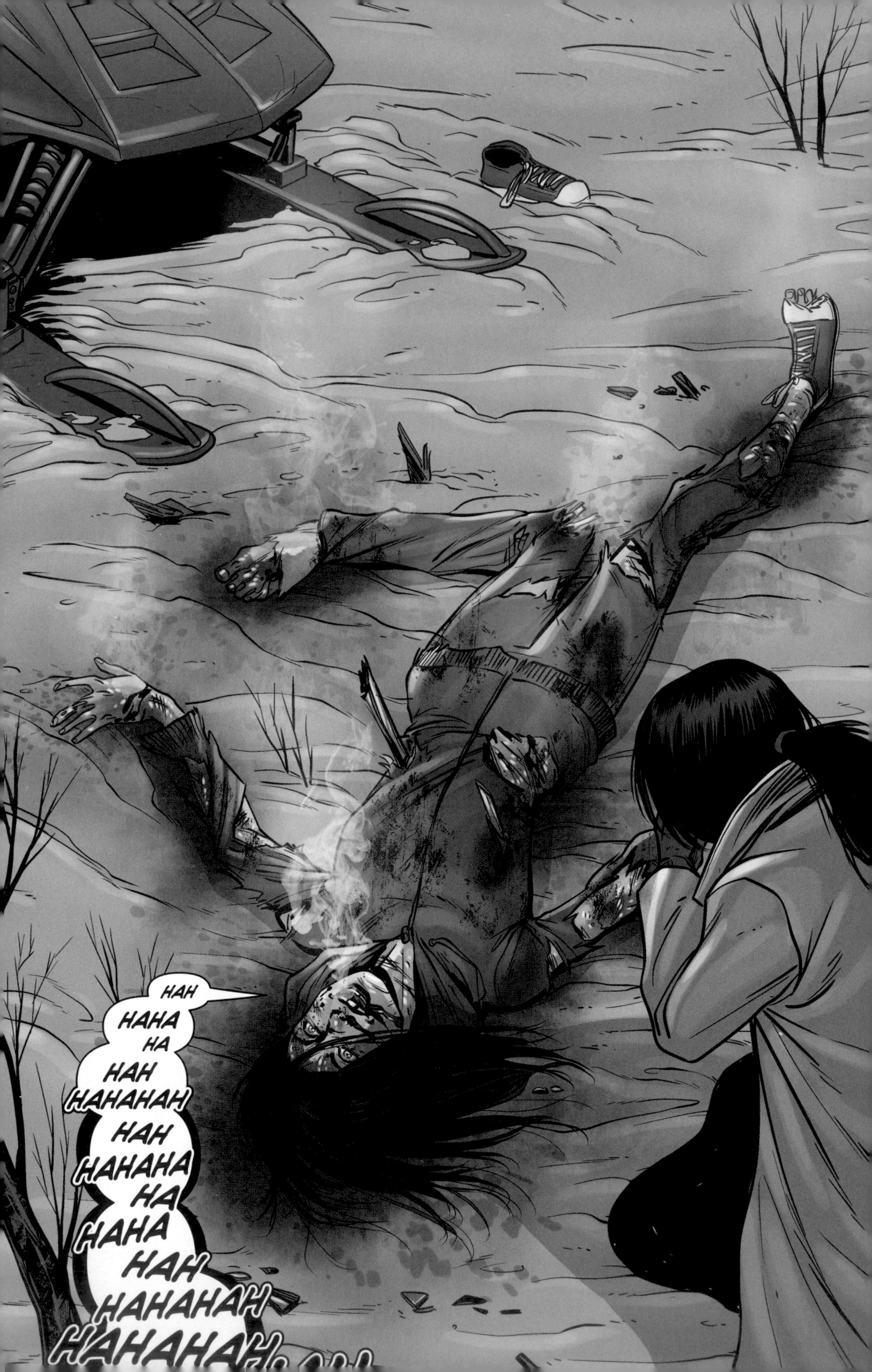
HAH
HAHA
HA
HAH
HAHAHAH
HAH
HAHAHA
HA
HAHA
HAH
HAHAHAH
HAHAHAH

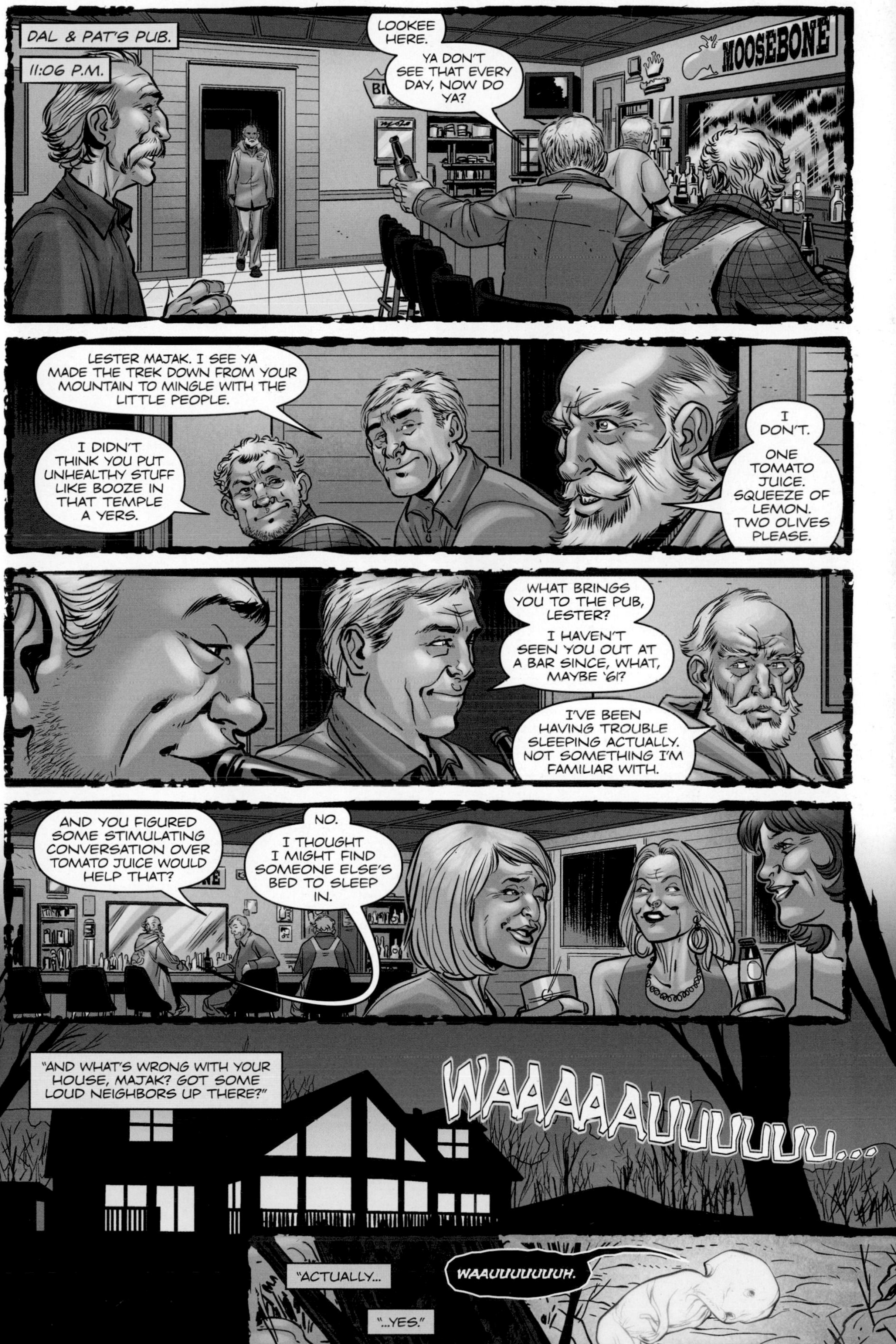
DAL & PAT'S PUB.
11:06 P.M.
LOOKEE HERE.
YA DON'T SEE THAT EVERY DAY, NOW DO YA?
MOOSEBONE
LESTER MAJAK. I SEE YA MADE THE TREK DOWN FROM YOUR MOUNTAIN TO MINGLE WITH THE LITTLE PEOPLE.
I DIDN'T THINK YOU PUT UNHEALTHY STUFF LIKE BOOZE IN THAT TEMPLE A YERS.
I DON'T.
ONE TOMATO JUICE. SQUEEZE OF LEMON. TWO OLIVES PLEASE.
WHAT BRINGS YOU TO THE PUB, LESTER?
I HAVEN'T SEEN YOU OUT AT A BAR SINCE, WHAT, MAYBE '61?
I'VE BEEN HAVING TROUBLE SLEEPING ACTUALLY. NOT SOMETHING I'M FAMILIAR WITH.
AND YOU FIGURED SOME STIMULATING CONVERSATION OVER TOMATO JUICE WOULD HELP THAT?
NO.
I THOUGHT I MIGHT FIND SOMEONE ELSE'S BED TO SLEEP IN.
"AND WHAT'S WRONG WITH YOUR HOUSE, MAJAK? GOT SOME LOUD NEIGHBORS UP THERE?"
WAAAAAUUUUUU...
"ACTUALLY...
WAAUUUUUUUH.
"...YES."

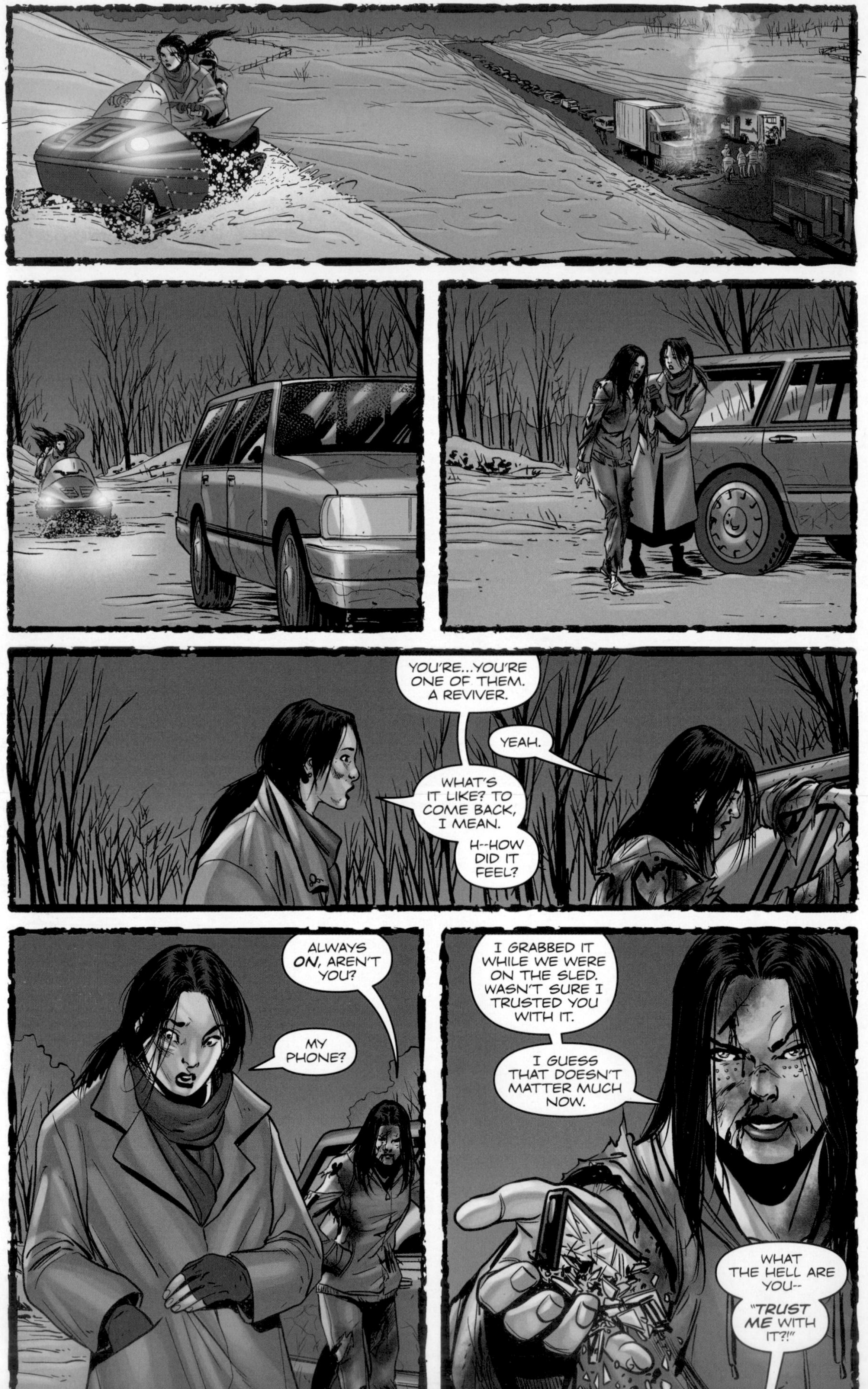

YOU'RE...YOU'RE ONE OF THEM. A REVIVER.
YEAH.
WHAT'S IT LIKE? TO COME BACK, I MEAN.
H--HOW DID IT FEEL?
ALWAYS ON, AREN'T YOU?
MY PHONE?
I GRABBED IT WHILE WE WERE ON THE SLED. WASN'T SURE I TRUSTED YOU WITH IT.
I GUESS THAT DOESN'T MATTER MUCH NOW.
WHAT THE HELL ARE YOU--
"TRUST ME WITH IT?!"

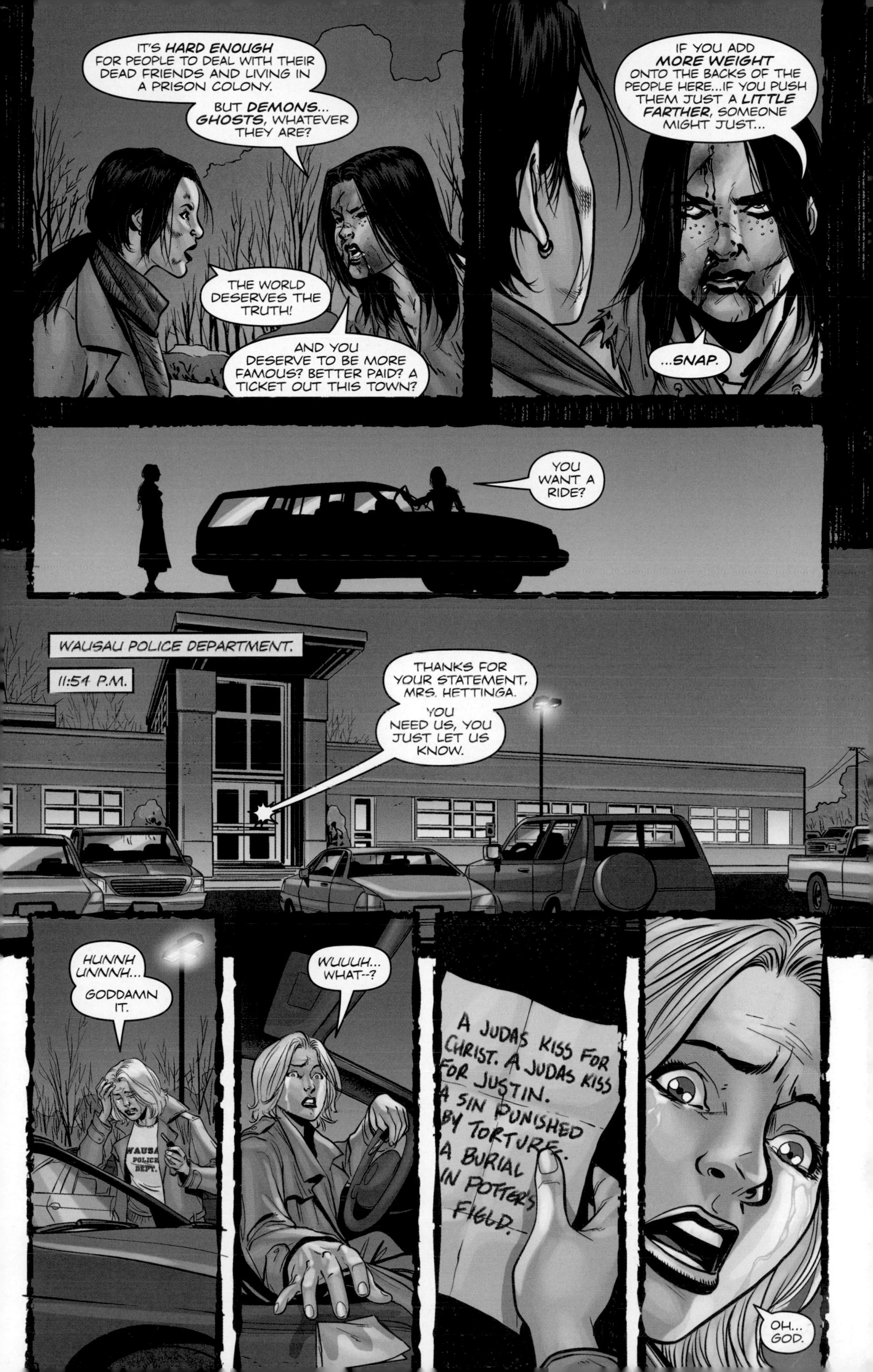
IT'S HARD ENOUGH FOR PEOPLE TO DEAL WITH THEIR DEAD FRIENDS AND LIVING IN A PRISON COLONY.
BUT DEMONS... GHOSTS, WHATEVER THEY ARE?
THE WORLD DESERVES THE TRUTH!
AND YOU DESERVE TO BE MORE FAMOUS? BETTER PAID? A TICKET OUT THIS TOWN?
IF YOU ADD MORE WEIGHT ONTO THE BACKS OF THE PEOPLE HERE...IF YOU PUSH THEM JUST A LITTLE FARTHER, SOMEONE MIGHT JUST...
...SNAP.
YOU WANT A RIDE?
WAUSAU POLICE DEPARTMENT.
11:54 P.M.
THANKS FOR YOUR STATEMENT, MRS. HETTINGA.
YOU NEED US, YOU JUST LET US KNOW.
HUNNH UNNNH...
GODDAMN IT.
WAUSAU POLICE DEPT.
WUUUH... WHAT--?
A JUDAS KISS FOR CHRIST. A JUDAS KISS FOR JUSTIN. A SIN PUNISHED BY TORTURE. A BURIAL IN POTTER'S FIELD.
OH... GOD.

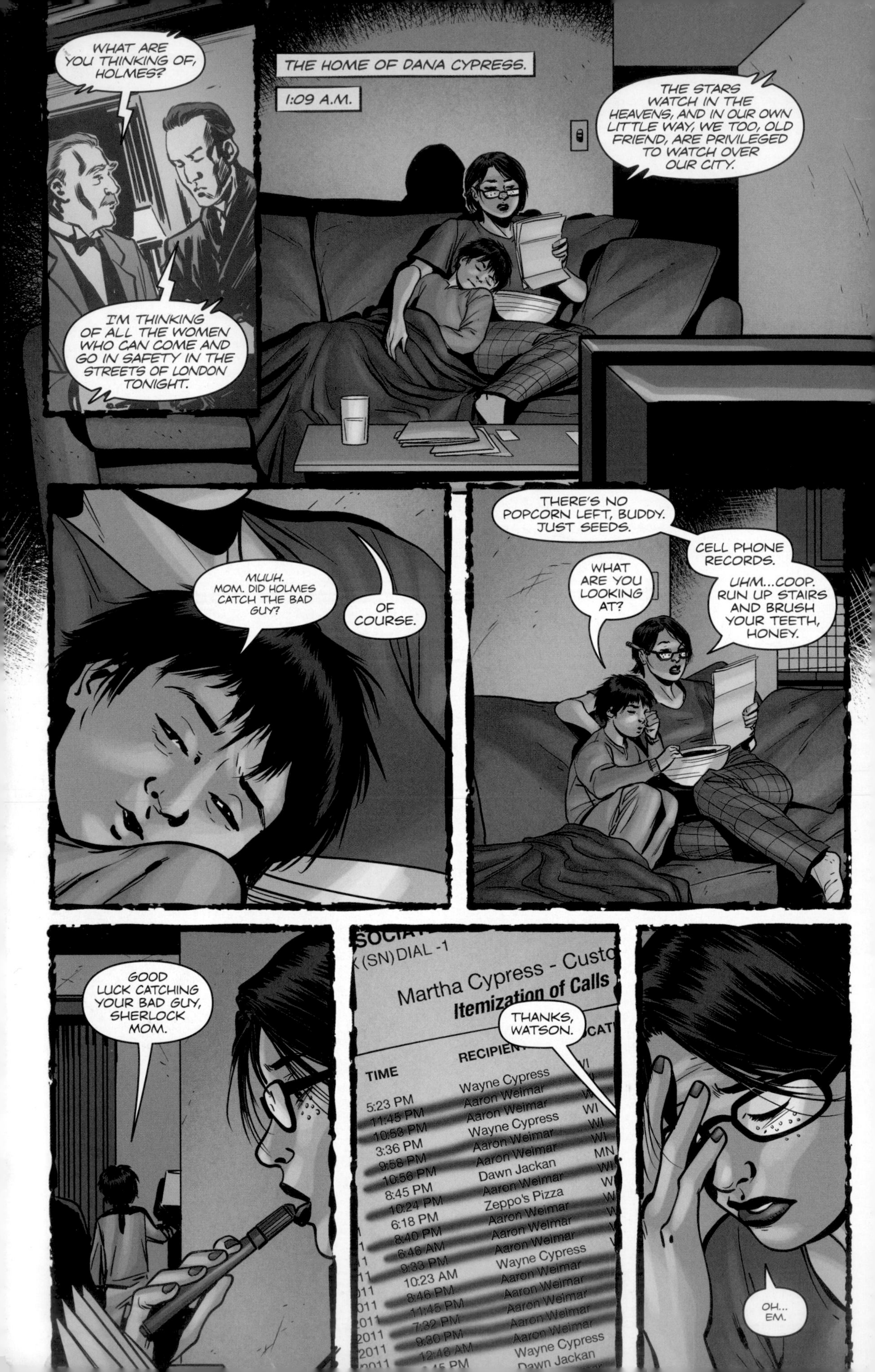

WHAT ARE YOU THINKING OF, HOLMES?
I'M THINKING OF ALL THE WOMEN WHO CAN COME AND GO IN SAFETY IN THE STREETS OF LONDON TONIGHT.
THE HOME OF DANA CYPRESS.
1:09 A.M.
THE STARS WATCH IN THE HEAVENS, AND IN OUR OWN LITTLE WAY, WE TOO, OLD FRIEND, ARE PRIVILEGED TO WATCH OVER OUR CITY.
MUUH. MOM. DID HOLMES CATCH THE BAD GUY?
OF COURSE.
THERE'S NO POPCORN LEFT, BUDDY. JUST SEEDS.
WHAT ARE YOU LOOKING AT?
CELL PHONE RECORDS.
UHM...COOP. RUN UP STAIRS AND BRUSH YOUR TEETH, HONEY.
GOOD LUCK CATCHING YOUR BAD GUY, SHERLOCK MOM.
Martha Cypress - Custo
Itemization of Calls
TIME
RECIPIEN
5:23 PM Wayne Cypress
11:45 PM Aaron Weimar
10:53 PM Aaron Weimar
3:36 PM Wayne Cypress
9:58 PM Aaron Weimar
10:56 PM Aaron Weimar
8:45 PM Dawn Jackan
10:24 PM Aaron Weimar
6:18 PM Zeppo's Pizza
8:40 PM Aaron Weimar
6:46 AM Aaron Weimar
9:33 PM Aaron Weimar
10:23 AM Wayne Cypress
8:46 PM Aaron Weimar
11:45 PM Aaron Weimar
7:32 PM Aaron Weimar
9:30 PM Aaron Weimar
12:46 AM Aaron Weimar
Wayne Cypress
Dawn Jackan
THANKS, WATSON.
OH... EM.

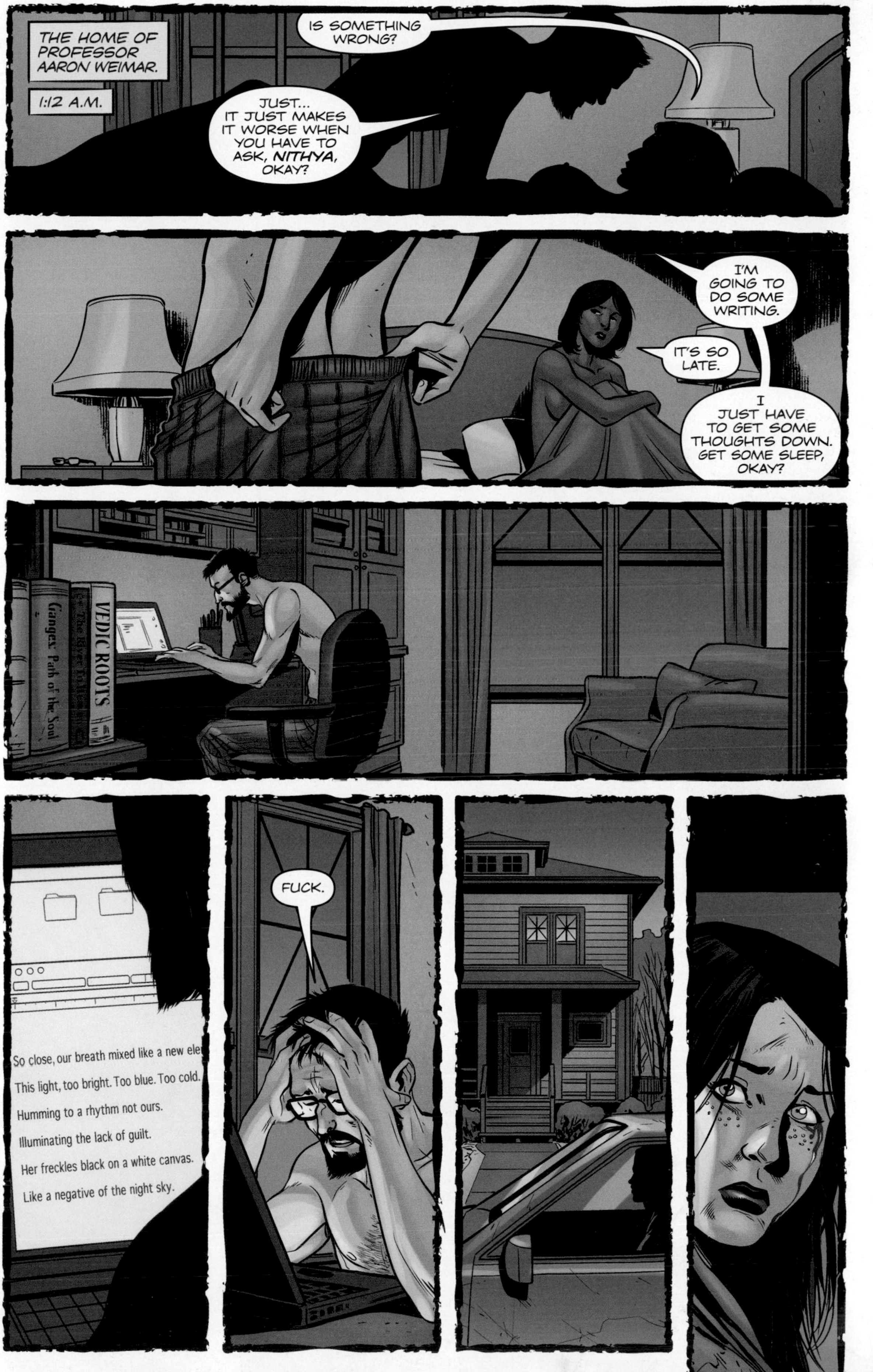
THE HOME OF PROFESSOR AARON WEIMAR.
1:12 A.M.
IS SOMETHING WRONG?
JUST... IT JUST MAKES IT WORSE WHEN YOU HAVE TO ASK, NITHYA, OKAY?
I'M GOING TO DO SOME WRITING.
IT'S SO LATE.
I JUST HAVE TO GET SOME THOUGHTS DOWN. GET SOME SLEEP, OKAY?
VEDIC ROOTS
Ganges: Path of the Soul
So close, our breath mixed like a new ele
This light, too bright. Too blue. Too cold.
Humming to a rhythm not ours.
Illuminating the lack of guilt.
Her freckles black on a white canvas.
Like a negative of the night sky.
FUCK.

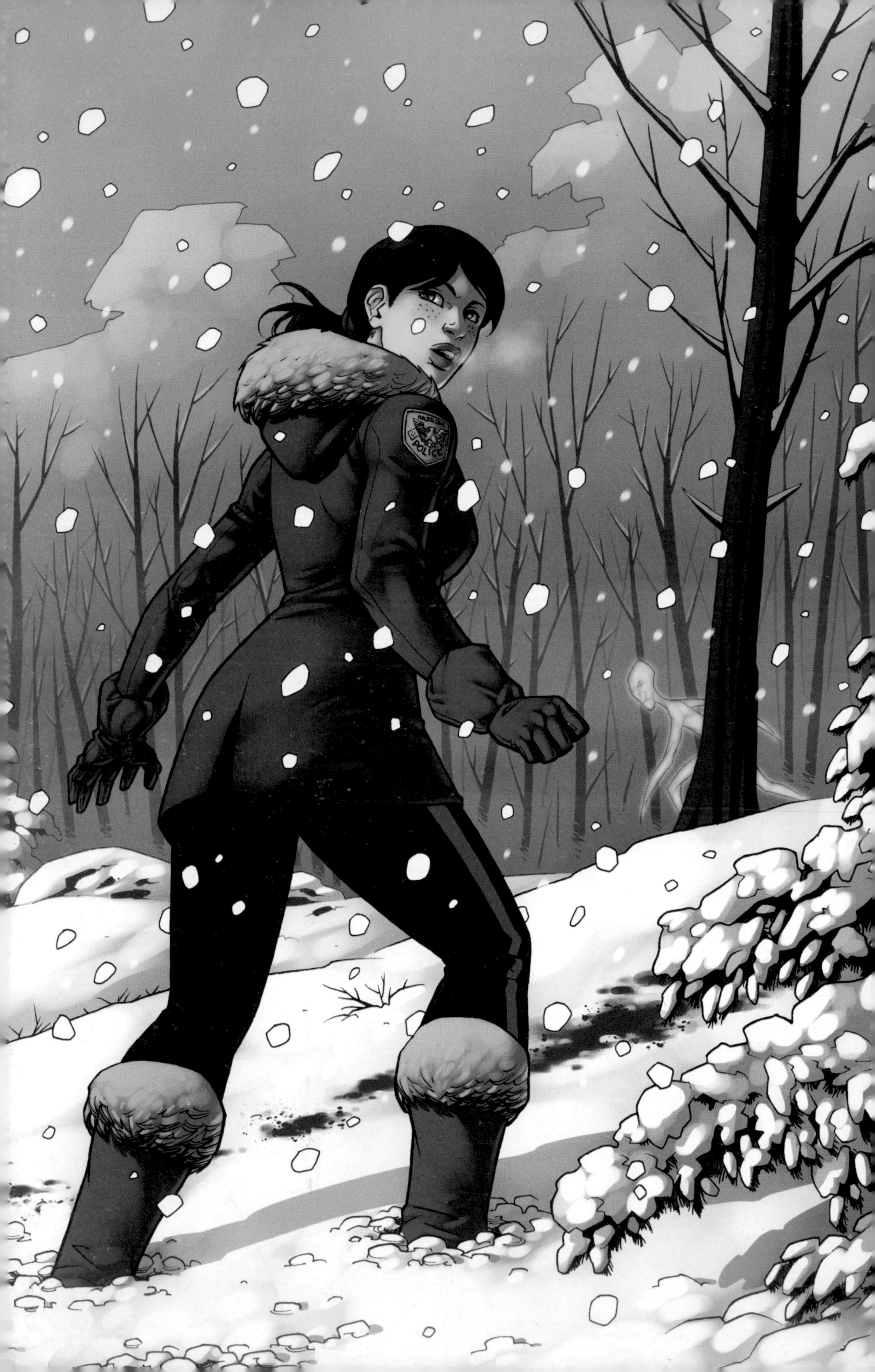
POLICE

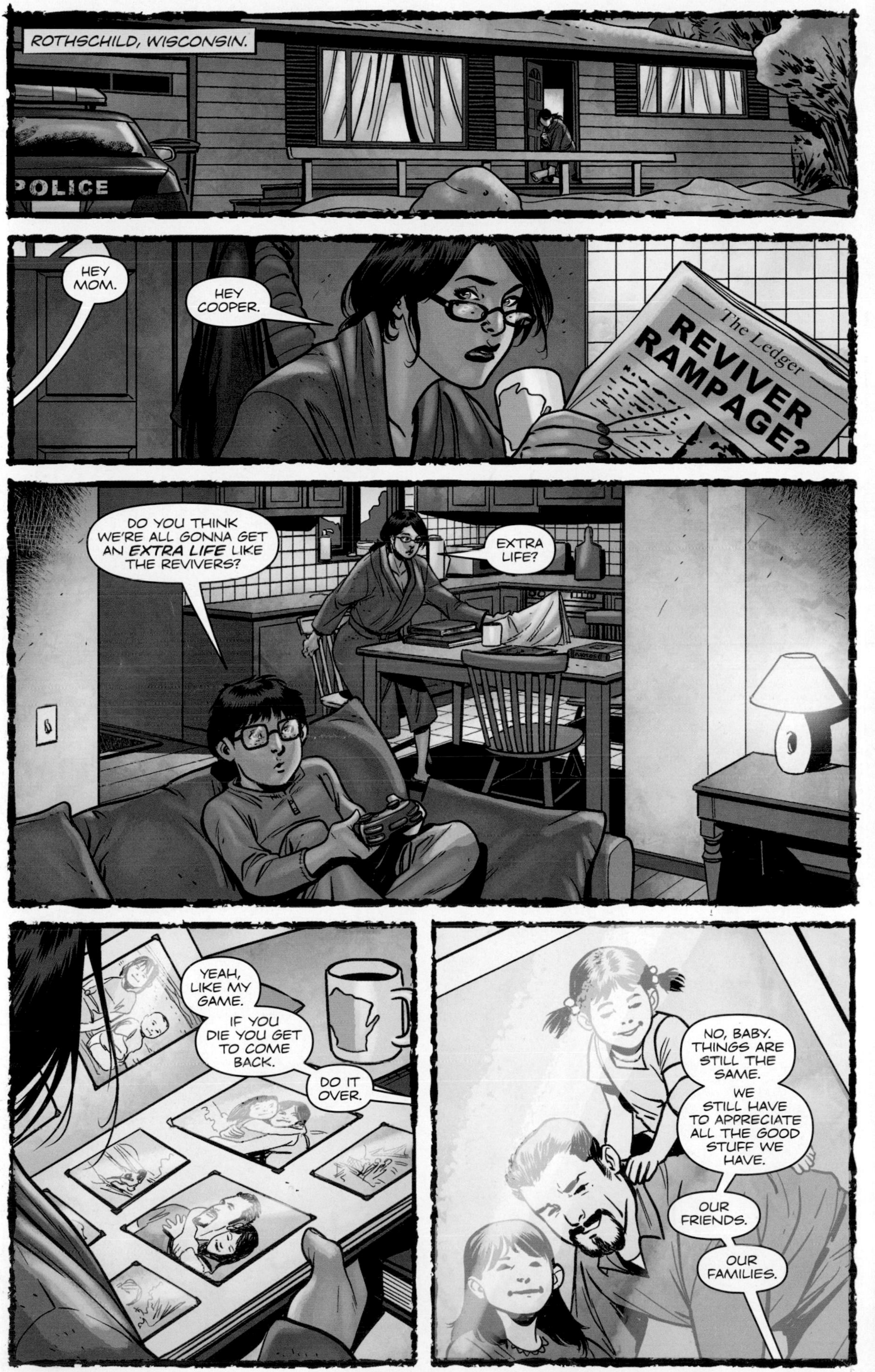
ROTHSCHILD, WISCONSIN.
POLICE
HEY MOM.
HEY COOPER.
The Ledger
REVIVER RAMPAGE?
DO YOU THINK WE'RE ALL GONNA GET AN *EXTRA LIFE* LIKE THE REVIVERS?
EXTRA LIFE?
YEAH, LIKE MY GAME.
IF YOU DIE YOU GET TO COME BACK.
DO IT OVER.
NO, BABY. THINGS ARE STILL THE SAME.
WE STILL HAVE TO APPRECIATE ALL THE GOOD STUFF WE HAVE.
OUR FRIENDS.
OUR FAMILIES.

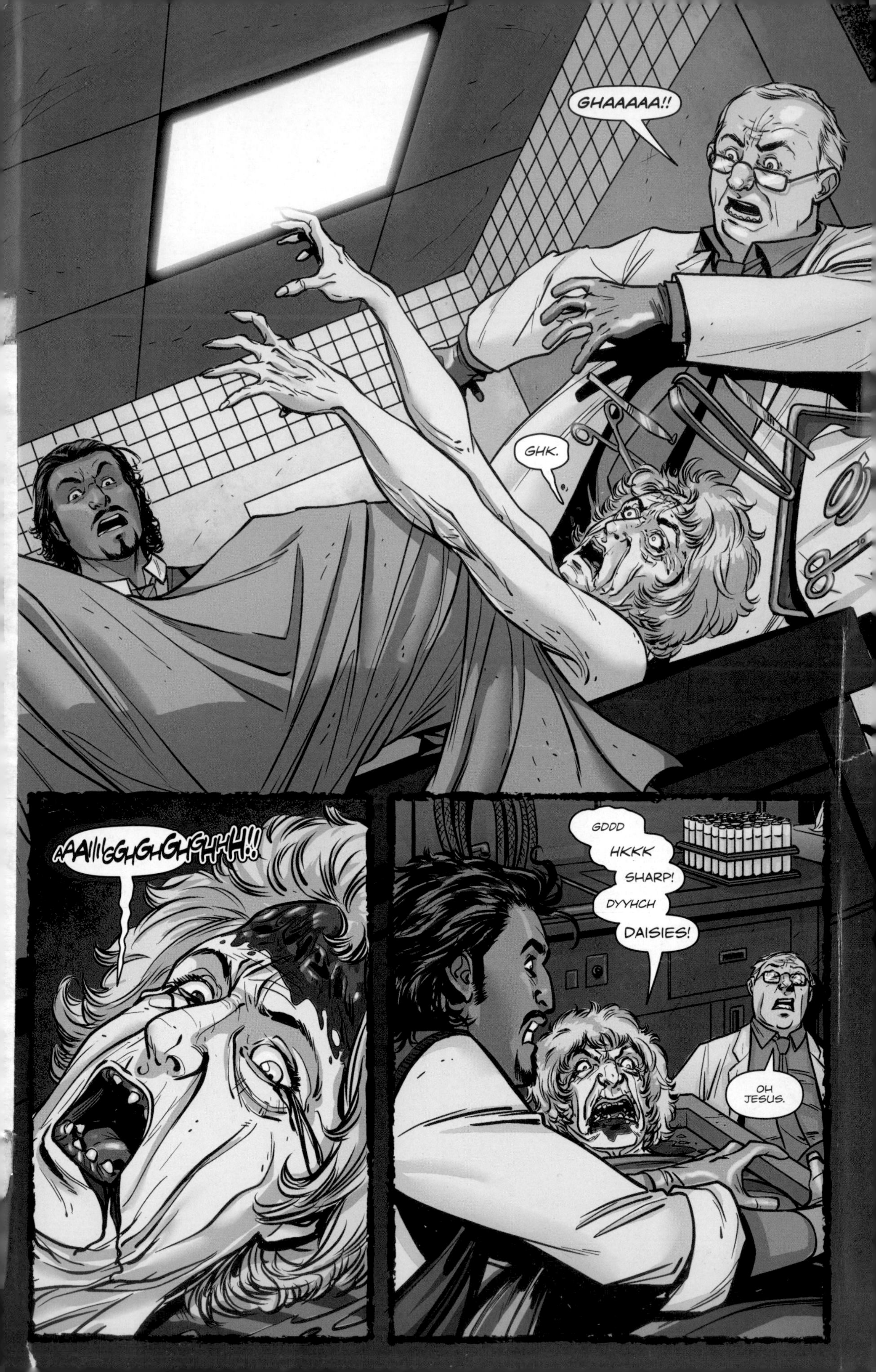
GHAAAAA!!
GHK.
AAAIIIGGHGHGHGHHH!!
GDDD
HKKK
SHARP!
DYYHCH
DAISIES!
OH JESUS.

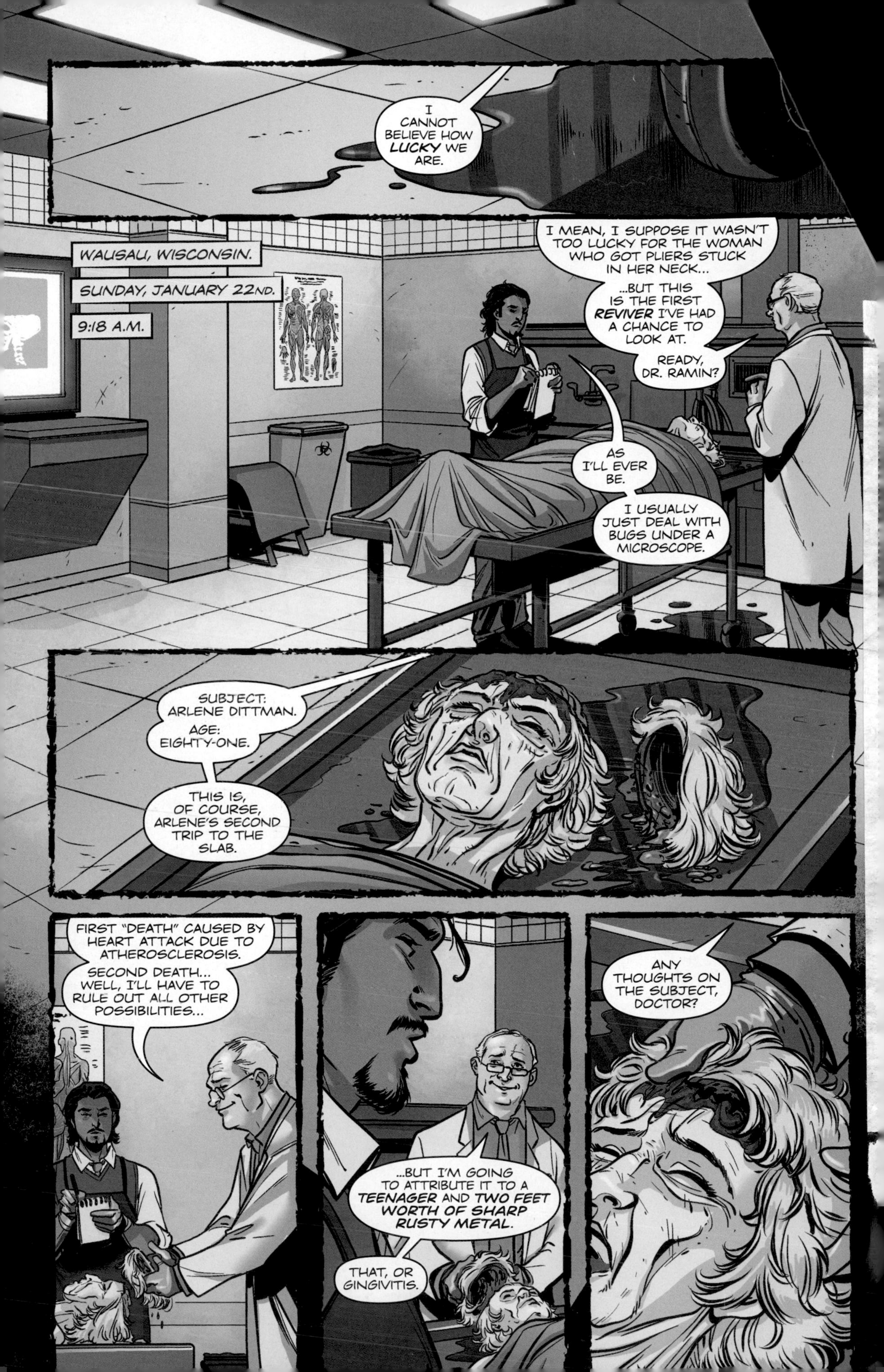
I CANNOT BELIEVE HOW LUCKY WE ARE.
WAUSAU, WISCONSIN.
SUNDAY, JANUARY 22ND.
9:18 A.M.
I MEAN, I SUPPOSE IT WASN'T TOO LUCKY FOR THE WOMAN WHO GOT PLIERS STUCK IN HER NECK...
...BUT THIS IS THE FIRST REVIVER I'VE HAD A CHANCE TO LOOK AT.
READY, DR. RAMIN?
AS I'LL EVER BE.
I USUALLY JUST DEAL WITH BUGS UNDER A MICROSCOPE.
SUBJECT: ARLENE DITTMAN.
AGE: EIGHTY-ONE.
THIS IS, OF COURSE, ARLENE'S SECOND TRIP TO THE SLAB.
FIRST "DEATH" CAUSED BY HEART ATTACK DUE TO ATHEROSCLEROSIS.
SECOND DEATH... WELL, I'LL HAVE TO RULE OUT ALL OTHER POSSIBILITIES...
...BUT I'M GOING TO ATTRIBUTE IT TO A TEENAGER AND TWO FEET WORTH OF SHARP RUSTY METAL.
THAT, OR GINGIVITIS.
ANY THOUGHTS ON THE SUBJECT, DOCTOR?

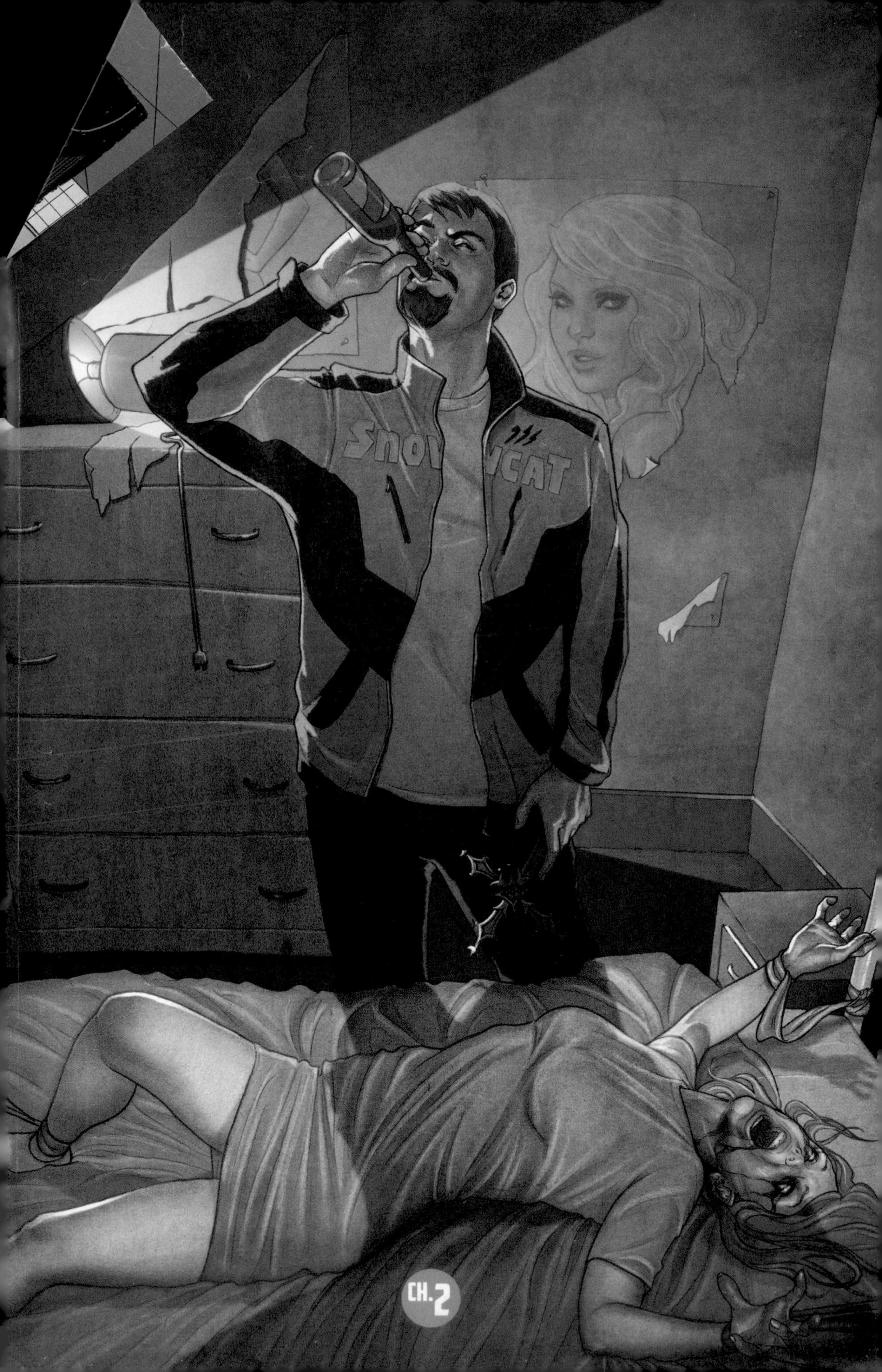
CH. 2